What *Love* Means
to You People

NANCYKAY SHAPIRO

What *Love* Means to You People

THOMAS DUNNE BOOKS
St. Martin's Press
New York

THOMAS DUNNE BOOKS.
An imprint of St. Martin's Press.

Design by Kathryn Parise
ISBN 0-312-34789-8
ISBN 13-978-0-312-34789-5

For Rory Metcalf

ACKNOWLEDGMENTS

Many people were helpful and generous to me during the years of writing this novel.

I'd like to thank the Ragdale Foundation, where parts of this were first drafted; Regina McBride, whose writing workshops helped me develop the characters; as well as my writers' group: Lydia Cortes, Jay Klokker, Jennifer Wortham, Hope Brennan, Rory Metcalf, and Jason Price.

Thanks also to Jennifer Shortall, Alex Jeffers, Kristen Chancey, as well as to my agent, Anna Stein, and my editor, Anne Merrow.

Finally, thanks to New York City, which provides continuous inspiration and interest.

Part One

1

Jim Glaser still did what needed to be done, every day.

Forty-five minutes on the Lifecycle first thing in the morning, followed by another half hour dropping sweat on the Cybex machines. Surrounded by mirrors, but not looking at anyone, least of all himself. Unabridged books on tape helped, but he missed whole passages while his mind wandered and didn't bother to rewind. All he did anymore was read, but so fast that novels blurred into one another and he didn't pause to question the muddle of stories he'd melded together from separate books. Zak got into all of them in the end, spoiling every love scene and topping every tragedy.

Still, he was functioning well these days, arriving at the agency a little before ten, alert from the gym. When your name was one of those on the door, you could do what you liked about punctuality—an attitude he'd disdained a couple of years ago. Still, the important thing was showing up, and show up he did—able to smile, to joke, to conceal his newborn boredom with what they did here. True, he gave not, as in the old days, 110 percent, but on a consistent basis a good seventy-five. He also avoided client contact whenever he could. That kind of sustained effort to be "on" was more than he cared to muster anymore.

His two partners thought he was a brave trooper because he'd unfailingly come in through his darkness, even in the worst days of the first year, when the antidepressant didn't help and he'd sometimes had to ask Robin to hold his calls because he could not speak without falling into sobs.

So, he still worked, still worked out. Still got lost in the lives of fictional people. Still volunteered, two evenings a week, with the abandoned babies at Bellevue. Went to the occasional cocktail party, industry function, art gallery opening, mingling and chatting, bubble-encased. Still went shopping, browsing through his fog for the book or moisturizer or shirt that would penetrate the veil of indifference for a little while.

But there were so many things he just didn't do anymore. Didn't call his friends—the handful that were left. Didn't make any new ones. Didn't go to plays, concerts, movies. Made no more dinner parties or drives up to Dutchess County on the weekends. Rented no porn videos. Eyed no men on the street.

But today, because Samantha's father was dying in Florida, Jim went to a shoot. GARB, a British clothing chain that was marching over the globe, was very high-profile, extra-super special high maintenance. They insisted on a partner overseeing everything in person and acted as though they were selling the cure for cancer. Up until now, Jim had steered clear of fashion clients. This was Samantha's baby.

But he owed Samantha, so here he was, stepping into the frenetic activity in the photographer's studio, a loft near the Flatiron Building. Techno boomed from five-foot speakers, clothes were strewn everywhere, the chirping of the models mingling with the dictatorial or coaxing voices of the stylists, photographer, clients. No one sat still. To Jim's eye, the clothes were hideous—skimpy tops and tight skirts shown on disturbingly attenuated fifteen-year-olds.

Finally, his resentment of the controlled chaos around him was too much. Jim sat down away from the others and opened his briefcase. He kept a dog-eared paperback of *Middlemarch* there because it was easy to open it at any page, anytime, and be transported.

"I've read that."

A voice over his shoulder. Jim turned. The photographer's assistant, one of those East Village children, all piercings and tats and—was it? yes—gray eyeliner. He'd read a book.

"Have you," Jim said.

"Yeah, I just finished it the other night. Coincidence." Perching on the back of the sofa where Jim was sitting, he dipped a finger down to touch the book's cover, the way a woman in a rowboat trails her hand in the water.

"And what did you like about it?"

"Is there anything *not* to like about it?"

Jim raised an eyebrow.

"Well . . . one thing I liked. Where she talks about how if we were aware of everything going on with the people around us, it would be like hearing grass grow and the heartbeats of squirrels. That just really struck me."

Now Jim turned in his seat for a better look at the boy. Largish eyes of a radiant gray more arresting than mere cheap blue. Pink, bowed mouth. Rippled nose with a slender ring in one nostril. Cheekbones and a clean jaw. Short bleached hair in trailing bangs, pointy sideburns. Silver rings climbing one earlobe, small smaller smallest. An appealing athletic body, too, in white chinos and a tank shirt. Quite nice, despite the trivializing modifications.

Glancing around at the denizens of the loft, the boy cocked his head. "Imagine hearing the heartbeats of *these* squirrels!"

"I would prefer not to."

The boy rolled his eyes. "Oh, the humanity!"

"Yes. Very good!" Jim laughed.

The answering smile, full of recognition and—could it be?—gratitude, was ravishing. In the next moment Jim felt silly, as if he'd caught himself glancing into a teenybopper magazine and lingering over the fresh young faces there.

"No one around here reads—" The boy's head whipped around.

"Yeah, all right!" he called to Tony, the photographer, who was shouting his name. "Duty calls." He brushed a finger against the book cover in good-bye.

For a few moments Jim sat, idly watching the boy. He had an economical way of moving around the people and equipment, he smiled often, he was an attractive kid. Got up to look a lot more superficial than he might be.

The next day Jim was back there again—watching prancing idiots take pictures of schmattas, waiting on a client who kept calling but didn't show up. For the last year he'd meant to tell his partners he wanted out. But he'd put that off day by day, convinced that, without the office to go to, he was capable of passing days without going out, without speaking to anyone.

"You look like you could use this."

It was Book Boy. Once again dressed entirely in white, and wielding not coffee, but a tall glass of milk.

This was so unexpected that Jim didn't protest; he drank, looking up over the glass rim at the kid, who stayed beside him, ready to take back the empty.

Jim wasn't sure he was being flirted with—yet what else was this about? Simple human kindness at the GARB shoot? It wasn't what you looked for, was it?

The boy said, "Better?" He smiled that affecting smile. There was seemingly no agenda in it; it was just a smile. *He thinks I'm straight, the little dope. So what, I might as well be. Neuter is what I am now.* He handed the glass back, the boy was called away again, and that was that.

The whole encounter, or maybe it was just the milk, did calm him down. He felt ready again to make the effort; he mixed, chatted, encouraged, doing all the things he'd once been naturally good at. The client called two or three more times, not apologizing, still wanting him to wait there. The photographer was shorthanded; the boy—Seth, as his name was called every minute or two—never stopped moving. He made the models giggle, he took Tony's abuse, which was only half-playful, with grace.

Later, Jim tried the bathroom door and found it locked. He needed five minutes away from them all. Just five minutes to hyperventilate, maybe lean out the window and scream, or talk to Zak, one of their frequent little conversations where he had to supply both sides of the dialogue.

The door opened and he was face-to-face with Seth. Jim forgot to avoid the eyes. Seth paused for a split second, surprise lighting up those unusual grays. Then he brushed past and it was the mouth that stayed with Jim; moist, pink, pliant as a rubber band, it went *zing!* into his imagination. Unzipping at the toilet, he was half-hard. How long since that had happened? He knew, but it would be mortifying to voice the number. He splashed his face and arms with cold water.

After that, he looked up from his Filofax at Seth from time to time to remind himself that he was nothing, and that nothing had changed. The kid wasn't his type anyway. Practically a baby. He squinted to read the title of the novel that stuck out of his waistband. *The Good Soldier.* Well, he knew what to read, anyway.

By lunchtime, the client was still absent. Jim went to the front of the loft, leaned on the window, and looked down into the street.

Seth appeared at his elbow. In a whisper, he said, "You'll get soot all over that nice white shirt."

Jim stepped back, brushed at his sleeve, shrugged. Again he glanced at the boy. Each time he saw more. Creamy, poreless skin, pale as a courtesan's, stretched over unpretentious but cultivated muscle. On the upper arm, a Celtic knot tattoo, the kind you saw on half the young people in Manhattan, but in baby colors: azure and pink. And on the back of the opposite shoulder, positioned to take advantage of the cut of his guinea T-shirt, a sheaf of gladioli in black and gray lines that seemed to shimmer just above the surface of his skin, subtle and fine. Again, that mixture of the clichéd and the unexpected.

Returning his gaze to the street, he saw, instead, the boy's reflection in the glass. His down-turned eyes, the ripple in the bridge of his nose. That mouth. The only word for that mouth was *pretty*.

At their backs, the music suddenly died, leaving the loft in a bubble of silence that felt heavy as lead, and then someone rolled through the FM stations. The gabble of music and voices startled him; for a moment, in the ease of standing near this boy, he'd forgotten his shattered life.

Seth said, "I'm supposed to find out what you want for lunch."

Jim didn't take his eyes off the street. "You."

Suddenly his heart was going hard, heat rose up through him, he was like one of those speeded-up botany films, the bloom opening. "I mean," he said, turning his head slowly to look at Seth, whose eyes and mouth had gone shiny with confusion, "I'd like to take you to lunch."

The boy nodded, looking a little stupid, but his manner brought Jim forward. Surprised at himself, at this movement within.

Seth said, "I . . . I don't . . . I mean, I can't usually get out at lunchtime."

"Then come to dinner with me. That would be better anyway. Come tonight."

Still there was that uncertainty, the gray eyes darting up to take soundings. This was charming, unexpected in the boy, interesting. "Let me get this right. You're asking me for a date?"

"We can talk about *Middlemarch*." It was fun to watch him figuring it out, and gratifying—almost embarrassing—to see his pleasure in the discovery.

"Yes! I'd love—I'd like—I mean, I think I'm free for dinner later." A blush rose up his neck, spread across his face. "What should I get you for lunch right now, though?" He held up his pencil and pad, ready.

But Jim glanced at his watch. "Never mind lunch. I've got to get

back to the office. I'll meet you at eight." He named the place, a bar in Chelsea, and walked away. No sense dragging this out, and as for the clients, let them scream all they wanted, he would not wait for them another moment.

As he emerged from the elevator into the building lobby, Seth came flying out of the stairwell, skidding to a dramatic stop and thrusting something at him.

"You forgot this."

His suit jacket. Seth licked his lips as he held it out, and then he blushed again, magnificently. Jim wanted to take his shoulders in his hands and kiss him, but instead he just took the jacket and shrugged into it. "Thanks."

Seth's smile was wavery, raw. "Later, then."

"Right," Jim said. "I'll see you later."

Nothing like this had happened to him in months and months and months—marking more than two years since he'd lost Zak, and the large chunks of himself that had slid away with him.

Locked in the bathroom, Seth McKenna replayed that last exchange, giving him the jacket and the licking of his lips, because he got parched when he was nervous. Then going all red, because maybe Jim Glaser would take the licking as a tacky come-on.

He drank water out of his cupped hands, splashed his face, and then inspected himself in the mirror. Beads of water clung to his darkened eyelashes and rolled down his cheeks. His ears felt hot. He turned his face back and forth, tugged at his nose ring, pulled his lips back over his teeth, rolled his eyes, wondering how he appeared to Jim. He was in a tizzy, a real one, and it had come when and where he least expected it.

That first day of the shoot, Seth had checked out the clients and agency people, as he checked out everybody. Most of the time there would be at least a couple of queers with whom he could share what

Tony called "the secret homo handshake." To Seth the whole lot of them formed a sophisticated, po-mo circus: dressed in clothes that were a heightened parody of what regular people wore, concentrating hard, grinning through their routines, faces turned toward the lights. And like actual jaded circus people, nobody was watching anyone else's act. He didn't like them—they were obscurely frightening in their hipness, as though they knew things and wielded powers Seth couldn't even formulate for himself.

But the head honcho—Jim—wasn't like that. He was distinctly Seth's type—massive and sleepy-faced, a little like Robert Mitchum. Being near him made Seth feel agreeably elastic and tingly. But his excellent dark suit, white shirt, precisely knotted silk tie, placed Jim Glaser out of Seth's reach, in the sphere of serious, connected, well-to-do people. As far as he could determine, the man was straight. He wore a wedding band. He was also ancient: forty if he was anything at all.

Gradually, Seth noticed how all the circus clowns went to him in order to take off their rubber noses and relax for a few minutes. He had, despite the power suit, a benign magnetism. Even the wide-eyed models approached him finally, like baby llamas at a petting zoo. Jim Glaser never raised his voice. He had a courteous, contained, weary manner. He dealt with people, whether they were the skittish, nervy GARB clients or Tony's wispiest bell-bottomed gofer, with a kindness and gentle expectancy that was almost courtly. He didn't flatter the models, nor did he snap his fingers at them or call them "you." In between the social moments, Seth saw him close his eyes or stare into space in a way that suggested more going on in his head than the stresses of business. Seth liked Jim Glaser's face. It was heavy without being fat, the lips and nose and brow were voluptuous. The intelligent eyes, slightly bulging, were half-lidded over so you couldn't tell right away what color they were. His curly brown hair wanted to grow down over his forehead. He was in charge, yet even in his solidity, he looked as though he was waiting, without hope, for someone to come

to his aid. The appearance of that battered copy of *Middlemarch* gave Seth courage to make his own approach.

A little cologne had clung to the collar of Glaser's jacket; putting his hands to his nose, Seth could smell it still. Despite their conversation, it was still hard to credit him as queer, but Seth had been in Manhattan long enough to know that he knew barely anything about the varieties of people he might encounter; he was still capable of being wrong, being astonished. Seth thought himself, in a purely abstract way, good enough for damn near anybody. He'd never, since coming to the city, had much trouble getting what he wanted in bars or on the street. Yet here he was, flushed, nervous, feeling so *lucky*.

Then he remembered that yesterday, Tony had taken Polaroids of everybody, just fooling around while the models pecked at their lunch. Seth rooted around on the big worktable strewn with contact sheets, odd bits of film, mail, work orders, stained Chinese menus, and found Jim's snapshot.

Yesterday—hell, this morning, or an hour ago, he'd never have seen this picture. Not been thrilled to find it in the pile and be able to hold it in the curve of his palm. Aw, *fuck*.

"Where's the lunch?" Tony materialized before him, clapped his hands. "C'mon, let's unpack it, let's go."

"Uh . . ." Seth tore his eyes away from the little image. The colloquy with Jim Glaser at the window seemed like hours ago. "I haven't gone to get it yet, I was—"

"You—*Jesus*, Seth!" Tony slammed his hands down on the table. "Get going! We should've been *finished* with it by now!"

2

Not knowing what Jim would be wearing or where they'd go, Seth decided to change, and rushed to get ready at home. At the door of his tenement on Stanton near Clinton, he buzzed his own apartment, hoping to get no answer. He was in no mood for his roommate, Charlie, who would hover, asking questions and making obnoxious assumptions.

Charlie's infrequent appearances left the floor knee-deep in tissue paper and shopping bags bearing the names of locked-door boutiques on Madison Avenue. He left his things around, some with the price tags still attached, other things the price of which Seth did not care to guess: gold rings and bracelets and Rolex watches, silk briefs by the dozen. Tiny cell phones, notebook computers, leather goods that smelled like insouciance. Treasures came and went. Charlie came and went, referring to the men he juggled by their initials, as in, *SV wants to take me down to Key West next week*, or *RB paid a cute little spic to piss in my mouth last night*. Seth had stopped even feigning interest in these details and also pretended not to notice the loot. It was bad enough to be struggling to make the rent on this tiny bug-infested hovel without being called to witness Charlie's idea of the high life.

Just that morning, Charlie had come in at five, turned all the lights on, and stripped off his clothes to invoke Seth's sympathy for a huge purpling bruise on the back of his thigh.

"Look what DL did to me. And I didn't even deserve it!" He pouted.

"You're going to get your throat cut one of these days!" Seth said. "I don't know how you face yourself in the mirror long enough to fucking shave!"

"God, you're a priss. You're hot-looking, Seth, but that attitude's *not* going to get you anywhere. Besides, I'm having the time of my life." He showed his blank, beautiful grin. Everybody said he looked like Tom Cruise.

The ridiculous part was that Charlie had come out of nowhere. Seth had inherited the coveted rent-stabilized lease from a buddy who was a link on a long chain of Hampshire College friends and their older siblings who'd passed through it in the last fifteen years, making the apartment not exactly affordable, but at least possible. The two classmates he'd shared it with had moved out at different times, recruiting others, not fellow alumni, to take their places; in this way, Charlie had come upon him. Seth winced to think he'd actually had a fling with the guy: four nights of bedded bliss when he moved in, followed by months of this torture. Being in possession of the lease at least gave him dibs on the sole bedroom, a chamber seven by nine feet, shut off by a picturesque but inadequate pair of glass doors that wouldn't latch. Charlie just barged in as he pleased. He had what they called the kitchen, the only other room in the tiny apartment besides the bathroom, which contained only a toilet. The actual bath was in the kitchen, along with the sink, and Charlie's futon, doubling as a sofa. There had been a third roommate, too, but Charlie had dismissed him and absorbed the cost.

Seth said, "Oh, come on. You despise all these men and they despise you, or soon will. Where's the fun in that? And get your dick out of my face." He rolled over, pulling the blanket up over his head. "I've told you already I don't want to know where you go or what— and *who*—you do, and I mean it. Why do you stay in this hellhole? Why don't you get one of these guys to give you an apartment?"

"All in good time. Besides, I don't *stay* here," Charlie said, flipping through Seth's mail. "I pass through here. It's convenient to have a place to drop in where no one can find me. It's time-out."

"Hey! Leave those things alone."

Charlie threw his hands up. "I don't know why you care. I pay my share, don't I? And it's way more than your share, I strongly suspect—it was never even thirds. I'm probably paying four-fifths of the goddamn rent by now. But hell, I view that as my contribution to the arts."

He paid, it was true, usually in crumpled large-denomination bills left lying on the floor near the sink, or in checks written to Cash on the accounts of men with addresses uptown. It was the one thing he could be relied on for, even if he only did it so as to have something else to throw back in Seth's face.

"And," Charlie pointed out, "I'm hardly ever here."

"Yeah," Seth said, shoving him aside to bolt himself into the toilet, "but when you are, you leave such a *stink!*"

He wasn't there now. The only evidence of Charlie's recent presence was a crumpled tube of bronzer left on the kitchen sink. Seth ran a bath, praying for enough hot water to fill the tub.

He had a white linen suit, yellowed at the knees and elbows but imbued with the curious dignity of the aged, which he'd found in a secondhand shop in his college town. The label said *Higginbotham—Bombay;* he liked to imagine the suit had seen the final days of the raj. It was a little too large, but he liked the way it hung on him. With it he wore only a new white ribbed tank undershirt, and tucked a gold silk handkerchief Hannah had given him into the breast pocket.

Before dressing he shaved, although it was scarcely necessary, and wondered whether to forgo the eyeliner. He wore it partly to *épater les bourgeois* and partly because without it he thought his eyes looked as if they'd been sketched in, then partially erased. He'd been wearing it long enough that the stark appearance of his pale lids seemed odd. Maybe he'd leave it off—a man like Jim wouldn't want to be seen with someone who wore a nose ring—but then, Jim had *asked* to see him, mascara, piercings, and all. So he went ahead with it, mouth opened, tongue curled up a little, just the way he'd seen the girls in his dorm do it, countless times.

First, he decided he'd hang back a quarter hour, so as not to seem eager. But that might give Jim the idea that he wanted to make a big entrance for reasons of vanity. Instead he hurried to get to the bar first.

As it was, at the door he bumped into Jim, whose big hand curled around his elbow to steady him.

He gave Seth a good-natured once-over. "Still in white!"

"It's my thing, I guess."

For the first time he wondered if maybe Jim would think he looked absurd in his treasured suit; he wore chinos, a crisp white shirt beneath a dark linen jacket. Seth's eyes riveted greedily on the dark hair that showed in his open collar.

"It's good to have a thing," he said, sounding as shy as Seth felt. Then he peered through the glass door into the bar. "Y'know . . . could you wait to have a drink when we sit down to eat? It looks awfully noisy in there."

"Whatever you want." Seth thought of those movies where the lovers meet for the first time, and then one of them just touches the other, says, "Let's go," and then the scene cuts to them in bed. Could they do that now? Who cared about drinks or eating?

They rode downtown in a cab. Seth was glad Jim didn't try to make small talk. It was enough just to try to breathe normally.

At the restaurant bar, Seth asked for beer, while Jim had a martini. It was good to hold the sweating Sam Adams bottle in his hand, the cold cut through his floaty feeling. Jim was talking, but he couldn't really hear him over the music. Somehow this didn't seem that important, it was enough to watch his mouth move. He was nervous and content; he smiled, and this seemed to be the right thing to do, because Jim suddenly smiled, too, a wide smile full of welcome and relief. He laid his hand gently, electrically, on Seth's knee, and slowly leaned toward him so his mouth was close to Seth's ear.

"You've got this . . . well, *remarkable* smile. I hope you know what I mean."

Back in college Cleon used to tell him, *You smile just like a happy, dopey little kid. When you suck cock I can just imagine what you must've looked like when you were little, getting around a big ole ice-cream cone.*

Jim sat back. "You're blushing again." With a laugh, he said, "My God. Look at you. Like—what's that line in 'Sweet Jane'? 'Children are the only ones who blush'?"

His face scorching, Seth said, "I'm not a child."

"Obviously. How old are you?"

"Twen—" Seth hesitated; older guys, so said Charlie, always wanted you young, but he wasn't getting that vibe from Jim. In fact, the opposite, so he added a bit. "Twenty-six."

"Twenty-*six*?"

No. That wouldn't work. He retrenched to the truth. "Three. I just turned twenty-three."

Jim pursed his lips, but he couldn't hear the whistle over the noise of the bar.

"What's the matter?" Seth said. "You're twice my age?"

"Whoa! Not quite."

"Well, whatever. So what?"

Just then the hostess came up to take them to their table. The dining room was dark; tiny lights flickered at each table. She led them to a banquette in a corner.

While they ate, Jim asked questions. Seth told him about how he worked for Tony three or four days a week while studying painting at Cooper Union. How wonderful Cooper Union was, and how wonderful that it was *free*, and how, when he'd spent all his money on rent and art supplies, he went to gallery openings to get something to eat. Jim's sympathetic expression made it easy to talk; he said rather more than he meant to about Tony's nasty streak and his boredom with the job. Then, under the influence of the freely flowing wine and more of

Jim's questions, he told all about the painters he liked, from that first wondrous exposure in tenth grade to a projected slide of Eakins's *Max Schmidt in a Single Skull*. Every time he paused, wondering if he was rattling on too much, Jim asked another question that started him up again. Finally he asked, "So, what about your own paintings? Are you any good?"

Seth wondered if there wasn't something mocking in Jim's smile.

"I don't know. I hope I will be. Some days I am."

All the time Seth was eating without tasting, but the wine threaded heat through his veins, made his head bob and body throb. Thinking ahead to the actuality of being skin to skin with Jim, wanting to drop to his knees for him. Imagining the solemnity with which Jim might lift his ankles to his shoulders, before—All the while he was only dimly aware of the stupid smile on his face, the hot flush of his neck and face.

"So," Jim said next, "I hear a little twang in your voice—you're from the Midwest. Whereabouts?"

Here was the line of questioning Seth dreaded. It yanked the various parts of him down from the ceiling and up from the gutter, slapping them together all wrong. He began to suspect he'd had way too much to drink. "Nebraska."

"Nebraska!" Jim laughed. People in the East always laughed at the mention of Nebraska. When in fact the place wasn't, in Seth's experience, the least bit funny. "That's one of those states I have never thought much about. The capital of Nebraska is Omaha."

"Lincoln, actually."

"Is that where you grew up? Lincoln?"

"Uh, yeah." This untruth escaped his lips before he made a conscious decision about it, but as soon as it was out, he felt a curious hope float up inside him. He could say—couldn't he?—what he liked. What would be in his favor. Fenced in by the table and Jim's big body, he felt himself moving on some kind of conveyor belt, carrying him—where? More wine.

"And your parents—what do they do?"

"Well . . . they teach at the university, actually."

Jim displayed no surprise at this. And after all, why not? It was plausible, Jim would never check it. He could set himself up in the other's mind as nestled securely into the educated middle class, right where he'd always most yearned to be. Because he was certain that a man like Jim, a sophisticated New Yorker who thought of Nebraska with a grin, would never take him seriously if he admitted to Drinkwater, to Ma with her bruises, Roy with the resentful glint always in his eye, the shabby gas station-café, the tiny house with its leaky roof and sagging porch.

"What do they teach?"

"English, both of them."

"Ah, so your interest in books?"

"Oh, all my life. Our whole house, filled—" He took a deep breath. He knew that house from treasure-filled attic to vast cellars; had invented it as a child, peopled it with that wonderful made-up mother and father whose son he ought to have been, and shared it only with his sister Cassie, who, like him, understood the uses and exigencies of the imagination.

Jim shifted, buttering a piece of bread. Seth hoped this meant they were going to talk about something else. Like when they were going to get into bed and what they'd do there.

"And were you happy, growing up in Lincoln, Nebraska?" There seemed to be some change in the acoustics of the noisy room, or else of Seth's ears, because his voice seemed farther away now. Jim should have asked, if he'd wanted his question to make any sense at all, something like, *Weren't you happy, sometimes for entire afternoons, when your grandmother was still alive, letting you help in her garden? Climbing trees with your sister, or hiding with her in the graveyard, when you understood each other completely, or it seemed so anyway, those were good times, even with Roy's shadow hanging over the close of every afternoon, weren't they? In books, of course, taking your mind beyond anything*

Roy could understand or penetrate, and that was happy, wasn't it, in a way? So, in short, it wouldn't be entirely accurate, would it, to say you were unhappy *every minute*, growing up there in Nebraska?

He shrugged. "Sure."

He could have said, *I didn't know what real happiness was until the first time I got hold of a paintbrush and found out what my hand and eye and mind were made for.* But this would have sounded pretentious. Seth always suspected, anyway, that his fervor about painting and drawing, as about books and art and sex and friendships, made him seem childish. So many of the people he met in his art-school classes were cool, jaded toward their own talents, however grand or meager, and toward the passing carnival of Manhattan life. So few of them seemed eager for, or worried about, finding someone particular to love and look after, although they certainly plotted and schemed enough about their places on the social pyramid and getting laid. Their artistic concerns often seemed to be more about ambition for fame than anything else, so that Seth wondered if he was ridiculously naïve in his desire merely to paint well. Often he felt he was swimming against the stream, even as the people around him left him lonely and bemused. He loved New York, loved his comely, decorated body, his freedom that was still such a magical thing. He took the deprivations of his life without fuss; hard work and the occasional missed meal didn't frighten him the way it did some of his classmates. He could feel superior to these peers who, with their suburban senses of entitlement, seemed to be half-asleep. Even his fear, always twisting at the back of his mind, was finer-tuned than any they could lay claim to.

"When did you know you were gay?"

"Sort of, always."

"Was it hard for you to accept? I always hear that young people these days have a much easier time of it, but I wonder if that can really be true."

Oh, man. "What do you want me to say, that I got beat up all the time and my life was miserable?"

"Well, was it? Were you? That's not so unusual, unfortunately."

"No, of course not." How easily these words slipped out, and the conveyor belt went along, taking him away from them and all their consequences. Saying these things made his heart beat hard, but he kept his blushes down.

"I was athletic. I lettered in track." Remembering how the jocks who taunted him in the locker room would titter from the sidelines when he was getting into his starting stance, his ass in the air, still made his stomach clench. "I didn't come out until I left home. But my parents were cool about it. They encouraged me to go East to college, they thought I'd fit in better."

"Your parents were *cool* about it? When did they know?"

"Well," Seth said, telling it the way he wished it had been, "they figured me out pretty early. They always used to say I was *a sensitive boy*. They weren't *total* provincials. But they never said anything about it until I did first."

"Lucky you. So I guess you go back often, to visit them?"

"No. I don't go back there at all." True. Then the conveyor conveyed him to: "I mean—they're not around anymore. They . . . they died." He felt himself gliding past a scene he'd often wished for: the pickup, twisted around a tree, in flames, completely over and out, and Roy the same way facedown in the road. He didn't picture his mother, but she was there, too, because Seth never could figure what would become of her widowed again, so better to give her a quick end. Never knowing what hit her. Which would make a change from her usual routine with Roy. He'd had this fantasy so often, but he couldn't say it out loud, so he grasped for something else. "What happened was—our house burned down. While I was away at my first year of college. We had one of those big old wooden Victorians, a real beauty. But there was a gas explosion in the night, it went up like a pile of cardboard—"

Seth wasn't prepared for the immediate impact of his words. Jim's hands clenched the table edge, his face darkened. "What an awful, awful thing. Christ, I'm sorry. Your parents, both at the same time . . .

it's terrible. And then on top of it, your childhood home, all your family things, your memories. . . ."

Already Seth regretted the story, but it was too late to go back on it, not if he hoped to keep the evening going. He'd only meant to dispose neatly of the family issue, so he wouldn't have to refer to them anymore, but now he saw he'd done far more than merely put them aside; he should've said something less dramatic. Still, Jim's distress just made him more attractive.

"Hard, yeah, of course it was hard." As he said the words, his throat tightened; he really felt the loss of that imaginary family. "I don't have anyone else—apart from my sister. . . . So after the funerals I went back to college, but for a couple of months I couldn't really do much of anything, or—" After the episode with the booze and pills at the end of his first semester, his despair was bottomless. He'd stopped going to class, stayed in bed, reading and smoking, brooding endlessly about how tenuous were his links to life, while outside it snowed and snowed. The only thing that kept him from trying suicide a second time was dread at the idea of failing at it again. Then one day, for no apparent reason, he woke feeling well. That summer he'd scrambled to finish up his incompletes and hang on to his scholarship. The two things, the real suicide attempt and the made-up family tragedy, dovetailed perfectly in his head.

"What about your sister?"

"She, um . . ." He wouldn't say *she* was dead, he was superstitious about that because even now, he loved her. "Cassie was staying at a girlfriend's the night of the fire. . . . She's still in Lincoln."

Jim's belief in his account made Seth half-believe it himself. After all, with great and deliberate care, he'd remade his body and his persona. All that was mortifying to recall could be reinvented.

"Do you see much of her? Is she still in college?"

"No. No to both questions. The thing is . . . she got in with the wrong people, and she never did go to college. We kind of had a falling out over that, and . . . we've been out of touch."

"That's too bad," Jim said. "When you're all each other have left. Don't you miss her?"

The question caught him by surprise. He'd gotten into the habit of avoiding thoughts about Cassie. She belonged to Drinkwater, to the self he'd discarded. "Yeah. We used to be close. But . . . I went away, and she kind of changed, I changed . . . our lives are really different. There's nothing I can do about it."

"So you're alone in the world," Jim said. He shifted in his seat, became distant, attention trained inward.

Seth excused himself and fled to the men's room. He pissed and pressed wet paper towels to his burning forehead and cheeks. The evening had gotten away from him somehow. He wished he hadn't lied, or at least not that way. Couldn't he have said, *I'm not close to my folks? They're not in my life anymore.* So simple, but it hadn't occurred to him when Jim was looking at him so closely and he'd been all flushed with wine and desire. Seth let the cold water run over his wrists. *I'm a fuckup, that's all, I get excited and my brains go out the window.*

They strolled uptown, the cool air restoring his confidence. Jim made chit-chat. At the corner of Houston Street and Broadway, he stopped.

The sidewalks were crowded, a line stretched outside the Angelika movie house, cars pouring into the intersection with ceaseless movement. A perfect night. Seth was all lit up inside and ready to fall into Jim's arms, to be borne away and fucked for hours.

"Listen," Jim said. "I, ah . . . I live close by, and I think I'm going to just go—I mean, I'm ready to call it a night."

Huh?

Jim said, "Do you need a cab?"

"No. No, I don't take cabs." Seth flashed back on the restaurant, the check that Jim barely glanced at. He'd slipped a silvery card into the folder and laid it back on the table. A man who could obviously have damn near anything he wanted, but had decided to pass on him. Seth stepped back, felt himself beginning a long recessional. "Thanks for dinner, anyway."

"Yes, I enjoyed it. Thank *you*," Jim said. Seth didn't look up into his face, just kept moving backward, counting his steps. Another ten and he'd turn his back on Jim and begin to run. But he was stopped before he could turn. Jim there, bulking up close.

"Seth, I'd like to see you again. I'll call—no, wait, I hate that, don't you?"

"What?"

"That 'I'll call' shit. What are you doing on Sunday afternoon?"

"Nothing. I mean, whatever you want." He felt as though his lungs had floated up in his chest and he was only breathing lightly across them like a breeze across a shallow pool of water. The headlights of the cars and the colored traffic lights and the people moving around them just made an abstract pattern around Jim's face.

"What shall we do? Have you seen the new Cindy Shermans?"

He indicated that he'd like to see them. He wished he could open his mouth all the way up and suck air in that way.

"I'll meet you at Metro Pictures at two on Sunday. Well, good night. Be careful—you're a little tipsy."

Seth thought that this was a new twist on exchanging phone numbers as a blow-off. By the time he reached his door, his eyes were burning, his hands were fists. He sat on the edge of his bed and rocked himself, shivering although it was a warm evening. Jim Glaser, whom he felt suddenly unable to live without, could very well do without *him*.

Often he found himself imagining that one day soon he'd round the corner of Stanton Street and find nothing there that he knew, no lock to fit his key. In dreams he wandered a New York with nowhere to sit down, no phone numbers to call, no faces to coalesce from the passing crowd into a smile of recognition. He'd awaken and start counting on his fingers the number of people he knew, convinced that most of them wouldn't notice if he disappeared.

Seth pulled the phone toward him and punched in Hannah's number. By the sixth ring he knew he'd get the machine, and hung up. He ran through the mental list of his art-school pals; he wasn't in the habit of calling any of them.

He thought of his sister, whose angry silence resonated even in his noisy New York life.

He told Jim that she'd fallen in with the wrong people. Who were in fact just his mother and Roy, who'd done everything short of locking her up to stymie her escape.

But he blamed her for not trying harder. After all, she was just as smart as he was. Perhaps her fault was that she blended in too easily. Cassie wasn't a problem student like him, to be dealt with at last by Mr. Lucas Hecklin, the M-to-Z guidance counselor at Flanagan County High.

That day in the early fall of his sophomore year, he'd sat, cloaked in attitude, for a long time in Hecklin's tiny office, staring at the toes of his work boots, while on the other side of the desk the old man stared at him.

He hoped that if he sat still enough, this scene would just pop like bubble gum and leave him standing out by the bleachers, where he could smoke a much-needed cigarette. No matter what Hecklin said, they couldn't prove he'd had anything to do with the big blaze at Frawley's. Just because he'd set a few minor fires around the school grounds during his free periods—just for the hell of it, what was the big deal, nothing got really burned. It let him forget himself a little, building those fires, he liked feeding them with snippets of wood, like passing treats to a playful puppy. It was better to do that than to get wasted or fool with guns, wasn't it? Even so, he didn't care much one way or the other whether he was punished or not. He was enduring this, sunk down into himself, the way he endured everything. There

would be bad times with Roy, and not a lot of good times with anyone else, either way.

And then an impossible thing happened. Mr. Hecklin opened the
middle drawer of his desk with a shriek of metal, took out a crumpled
pack of smokes confiscated from some kid in the bathroom, the
matchbook still neatly folded between the cellophane and the pack.
He shook out a cigarette, lit it, and handed it to Seth across the desk.

"Go ahead, smoke it. And while you do, I want you to listen to me."

He hesitated, but there was something so unexpected about Mr.
Hecklin's face, his eyes behind the black rims of his glasses, that he
took the cigarette and felt he was doing the man a favor.

"I want you out of here, McKenna. I'm not talking about ex-
pelling you. I want you out of Flanagan County—out of Nebraska—
out in the right way.

"You're a smart kid. Not a genius, but I know about all the reading
you do. You've got a finer mind than just about anyone else in your
class, if you'd *apply* it to something. If you behave yourself and study, I
promise you—I *promise* you—I'll see you get a scholarship to a good
college, out of state. Afterward you won't have to come back here ever
again. Just cut out all this crap you've been pulling for the next two
years and work like you've never worked before, and you'll be free."

Seth dragged his fingers through his hair and stared at Mr. Hecklin through the greasy hanks.

Finally he said, "Why? Why would you do that for me?"

The man sighed, the buttons on his shirt straining. He had never
seen an adult with quite that expression on his face before; it made
him nervous.

"Because," Mr. Hecklin said, "you just don't belong here. You
know where you belong? You belong in New York . . . or San Fran-
cisco. I know what your problem is." He leaned forward, his eyes mag-
nified behind the thick lenses. "And I just don't want you to end up
like me."

The cigarette fell from Seth's parted lips, rolled off his thigh, and landed on the floor; he thought if he bent over to grab it, he'd pass out. Seth squeezed his hands together and tried to convince himself that he hadn't heard Mr. Hecklin right. *I know what your problem is.* Oh, God, no.

The man was suddenly on his feet. "Pick up that cigarette before you set yourself on fire. You're not going to play with matches anymore, you hear me? And try washing your hair once in a while. I'll keep my promise if you study hard and quit being such a little jerk. Make your grades, play a sport, get an extracurricular activity, it doesn't matter what. You are going to shape up. Stand up straight, boy!"

And to his own amazement, Seth *did* shape up.

A couple of weeks before he left to take up his scholarship at Hampshire College, Seth was invited to attend Mr. Hecklin's retirement party. It turned out that he lived in a hamlet some miles beyond Flanagan, with his mother, in just the sort of cramped wooden box Seth himself had grown up in. The mother, a heavily made-up plump little woman, had a good-timey smile, and seemed, although she was over eighty, younger than her son. She treated Mr. Hecklin with a cheerful disregard, as though he was an impediment to, rather than the cause of, her party. Seth took photographs of the guests and from Massachusetts sent a set to him; Mr. Hecklin responded with a letter, and a correspondence began. At first, Seth was as reticent as with his sister, but when the old man dropped hints about how he hoped college was all Seth had hoped for, he responded frankly. Hecklin assured him that the letters, once pored over, met the flame of the kitchen gas ring. Seth wondered if old Mrs. Hecklin tried to read her son's mail.

That last summer at home, he and Cassie barely spoke. The last time he saw her was the morning he set out for Massachusetts. They spent the night before sitting up in his room, pretending to play cards, eyeing the clock. Outside the patched window screens, the night was soft. In the room, pressure built up into heat and thunder:

Cassie began to cry. When he took her in his arms, she tried to stop her wails against his shoulder. He thought he knew what she was afraid of: Roy, unalloyed, unabsorbed. The café, which took so many of her hours and returned nothing. Her own solitude.

She pretended to be comforted by his rocking and whispering, pulled herself together, and blew her nose. Before dawn, with Roy and Mary asleep in the stubborn conviction that he'd never dare to disobey them, they hitchhiked to the truck stop on the interstate—a place he'd gone to cruise, but never before with his sister, never to catch a Greyhound bus. They stood in the little shelter, his single duffel bag at his feet, watching the sky lighten from dark to pink, the stars disappear one by one, and finally the lights of the coach swing into view. She hugged him so tight he thought he'd have to wrench himself away before the driver shut the door in his face; but at the last, he'd felt her hand on his back, giving him a firm shove up the steps. He kept his eyes on her as long as he could, while the bus turned in the big parking lot.

Pushing the silent phone away, Seth thought about going out again, maybe to find someone for the rest of the night.

Except that tricking didn't ease this loneliness, it only replaced one unease with another. Men his age were competitors more than anything else; he was always wary, no matter how affable the other guy was. It was hard to let go, to capitulate. Afterward he always wanted to sleep alone.

He yanked off his clothes and ran a bath. Soaked for a long while, flicking through skin mags he didn't bother to try to keep dry. When the hot water had done its work, drawing the tension out of his limbs to center in his groin, he jerked off, arching his body up at the crucial moment to crest the water so he shot up into the air. To his amazement, one drop of cum hit the bare dangling lightbulb with a sizzling snap.

3

Back home, Jim felt he'd made a nick-of-time escape.

This Seth character was too young, too pierced, too eccentrically costumed, to think of as dating material; it was clear that the boy had expected nothing but a one-night stand. Why had he even asked him to dinner? Well, to be honest with himself, Jim thought, it was to assuage the baldness of his desire just to have him. All evening, while he'd made conversation, he'd thought of almost nothing but taking Seth home and fucking him, with force and few words. Desire, dormant for so long he'd thought never to feel it again, seized him with its vivid, specific crudeness. While Seth talked, he'd sat there with a hard-on stirring in his trousers, imagined feeding it to the boy, pinching his nipples, biting the hard slope of his belly, digging his fingers up his ass. He'd ring all the changes of that fresh young body for one night, get this odd attraction out of his system, and afterward slip back into the comfortable nullity he hadn't wanted to breach before.

Until they'd gotten to Seth's family, and the whole timbre of their give and take, which until then had all been pointed in one direction, shifted. It was like picking up a book to find that the volume did not match the dust jacket. Seth's was a sultry porn cover, but the opening paragraphs were something altogether else. The boy understood what it was to have the props of your life pulled out from under you. A mental image came to him, probably wildly inaccurate but compelling, of a turreted house burning unchecked on the horizon of a vast Wyeth prairie, gray grass waving against a dark sky.

That inner glimpse bollixed up all his simple lust, made him curious and sympathetic. Except that he was sure he couldn't afford to be curious and sympathetic with anyone new—least of all a kid like that. Jim didn't like to do things that ended up seeming unkind, and it was clear, parting from him, that he'd burst the kid's balloon. Which was flattering to his vanity, and therefore made him feel even more like a heel. But not so much more that he didn't resolve to call the next day and break the date.

At least he'd given the kid a good supper and not made him perform for it; the way Seth talked, he subsisted on ramen noodles and squares of cheese scrounged at openings. It wasn't much, but it was a little something.

The next day Jim looked through the notes he'd jotted in his Filofax during the shoot. But he'd forgotten after all to ask for Seth's number and didn't even know his last name. So, thinking how lousy it felt to be stood up in a public place, Jim went to the gallery.

Seth's grin concealed none of his surprise when Jim walked in. It was touching, how he made no attempt to play it cool, to hold himself back. Jim found that smile just as stirring as it was the other day, and he had no defense prepared against it.

Around them, half a dozen huge color photographs of threatening masks and mannequins loomed. Jim glanced around at them. "Did you look at these already?"

"Yeah, but I can look at them again."

"No, I was thinking . . . could we go get some coffee? Or would you like a drink?"

Seth shrugged. "Sure."

"Because there's something I think I'd better say to you before . . . well, before anything else."

"Okay. Sure." Seth nodded, the pretty smile gone; his shoulders slumped. There was that emotionalism again, unconcealed, that made Jim feel flattered and apprehensive and aroused.

In the bar, Seth sat facing him at a little table, fidgeting with his pack of cigarettes, waiting. Jim saw that he was too self-conscious in his presence to smoke without permission, so he nodded to him, and watched with what relief he went through the ritual of lighting up. But he didn't know how to begin what he wanted to say or if he even wanted to say it anymore. Was he trying to get rid of this boy or bring him closer? And was talking about Zak the way to do either of those things? But not to mention him seemed furtive.

He took a deep breath. "Look," he said, affecting a nonchalance that made his stomach clench, "there's no reason why you should give a shit about this, but I just want to put it out there, otherwise it'll bother me. Friday was the first time I've dated at all since my lover died. That was over two years ago now, but—"

Seth nodded, a student ready to learn.

He stopped. "I don't know why I brought it up." He tried to laugh. "Stupid. Forget it. Doesn't matter."

"But why not?"

"Because we don't even know each other."

"But—oh. You've changed your mind—I thought, since you showed up after all. . . ."

He's already making me feel responsible for him, Jim thought, seeing the raw disappointment in his face. "I . . . no. It's just that . . . it's been a long time that I've been . . . shut down."

"Shut down, yeah," Seth murmured, and in that Jim heard paragraphs of meaning.

"Since he's been gone, I haven't had to deal at all with anyone else's expectations. And . . . you're very young."

"I'm older than I seem. Inside, I mean."

"Look," Jim said, suddenly impatient, "there's almost *twenty years* between us, that's not trivial, and we're very different sorts of men, and—it's perfectly natural, at your age, to be out there, having the best time you can have with as many people as you can have it with—I've done that myself. This is a tiresome conversation to have, but I don't want to give you the wrong impression. I wasn't thinking clearly when I asked you to have dinner with me, and the other night you seemed to have expectations that—no, no," he said, seeing Seth shrink, "I don't mean to embarrass you, it's wonderfully flattering to be wanted, especially by someone like you, you're . . . lovely . . . but I've had time to think since, and I—"

"Here's what I hear you saying," Seth broke in. His eyes were very bright and he spoke with an angry distinction. "I hear you saying you're not up for tricking, and to you I *am* a trick, I'm just a *kid* with a ring through my nose. Did I get that right?"

Jim would have preferred not to hear it spelled out so blatantly, but he gave one churlish nod.

"All right, but listen," Seth said. "I have this roommate, Charlie. He's always got at least two or three rich older guys in thrall. They buy him stuff, take him places, and throw money at him, and he takes it all and then mocks them behind their backs and steals from them. It's disgusting."

Jim wondered where this was going. Seth was looking into his drink as he talked, not checking Jim for reactions.

"When I first met him, he brought me along a couple of times to parties given by his—benefactors. Now I'm as curious and horny as the next guy, but there was stuff going on there—they wanted me to do stuff that—disgusted me. Just the way I got *looked at*—it took me days to wash off." Seth glanced up. "I don't want to be that kind of boy, I don't want to be *taken* for that kind of boy."

Jim was speechless. From the beginning Seth had indicated a willingness to leap into his arms, but suddenly this.

"I don't think there's any question of that between us," Jim said, trying to keep it light.

"Well, anyway," Seth mumbled, a deep flush spreading across his cheeks and down his neck. "I only give it away for free. I want that understood."

Jim started to laugh, but caught himself. This aggressive decency touched him. Theirs was not a conversation he'd ever imagined two men could have in New York in the nineties. He kept his gaze fixed on his beer, and Seth stared at the tabletop.

"Look," Seth said quietly, "this is embarrassing as hell, and I'm going to wish I'd kept my mouth shut, but . . . when I first saw you, at the shoot, I had such a feeling about you . . . I'd never felt it before about anyone. Especially in a place like that. That you were really hot and really gentle at the same time. It's always either one or the other with guys, but you—I wanted to find out what you were about."

Jim sat back, amazed. *Really hot and really gentle.* This was the best thing, the most unexpected thing, anyone had said to him in years.

"Anyway," Seth added, the blush fading to leave him pale and uneasy, "there's no point to this, really, is there? You've got a whole life established, so, of course, I'm not the kind of serious boyfriend you're going to want anyway, when you're ready to want one again, because frankly I *am* a—a—kid with a ring through his nose. You thought the other day you wanted to get me into bed, and then you changed your mind, and that's all it ever was for you. So even though I—oh, shit. I should shut up now. Obviously this isn't going anywhere."

The room seemed darker, objects farther away. "I am . . . honored . . . by your attraction to me, and your frankness. . . . I can't pretend I'm not moved." Jim paused, feeling his way. "But we're both very anxious about . . . the disparities between us, and . . . it's for a good reason, I'm sure. We shouldn't start something that we're each uncomfortable with." He began to get up. In a moment he could be on the street and walking home, shaking his head over another miscalculation in his human arithmetic.

But Seth put a hand out to stop him. "No, don't go. I can stand it—if you can."

After they'd been to a half-dozen galleries, they went for coffee. Seth showed him a much-folded map of Manhattan, partially marked with a yellow highlighter.

"I got this before I graduated from college. I decided it would be cool to go down every street. The ones I've done already are yellow. I take photographs from certain vantage points. And I try to photograph at least one person on each block, if I can. Sometimes I make sketches, too, or pick up things that I find. I use the material in my paintings."

Jim looked at the map. "Doesn't this get dangerous? Do you go dressed all in white like that? Are you going to walk every block in Harlem, in Morningside Heights?"

"Well, I pick my times. Sunday mornings early are good for dubious places—it's usually quiet. I do have different clothes I wear sometimes, dark stuff, sunglasses."

"Have you ever gotten into trouble?" Jim's head filled with terrible scenes; he imagined Seth being pulled apart by thugs as if he were made of taffy.

"Not really. I had a couple of close calls. One time I was walking on Avenue D and a bunch of guys surrounded me, fell into step with me. One of them said, 'Hey, man, how you doin'?' with that wheedling voice, you know, trouble. So for some reason, I said, 'Not too good.' And he said 'Yeah, whazzup?' And I said, 'Well, my mom just died.' And he said, 'Aw man, that's too bad,' and the next thing I knew, they'd peeled off and disappeared."

"Lucky for you."

"Yeah, lucky for me." Seth lit a cigarette with studied nonchalance. "I try not to be afraid of too much."

"Do you have to try very hard or is it easy for you?"

"What kind of question is that?"

"It's a question. We're having a conversation."

"No, you're implying something."

Jim raised an eyebrow. "I am?"

"Tell me what *you're* afraid of!" Seth challenged. "I can't imagine you being afraid of anything, really."

"Now that's foolish. What kind of a monster do you think I am?"

"A monster? No! But you, you're too—" Seth sketched something in the air with his hands that Jim took to mean he was too big and strong to have any core of vulnerability.

"Stop that. What you're saying is idiotic."

Seth leapt up. "This is stupid. Let's go."

Following him out to the avenue, regretting his outburst, Jim said, "Already we're lost in illusions about each other. On our second date." He shook his head. "Oh, the humanity."

But Seth smiled. "Our second date."

Seth obviously liked the sound of it.

They began to walk, Seth shambling along the curb, balancing sometimes on the edge, eyes down, as if he was prospecting the gutter for lost treasure. When they again reached the corner of Houston and Broadway, Jim realized with a little frisson that he still wasn't ready to let the boy know where he lived. The whole afternoon had been a shock to him, and now he was beginning again to compose ways to let Seth down easy. After all, it was absurd, what the boy had said to him before, entirely premature, and frankly, kind of weird. *I only give it away for free.* How would that sound if recounted, for example, to his friends Clyde and Billy? *A sure sign of a swindler, trying to lull you before he gulls you*, that's what Clyde would say.

All right then.

But still. This time they were standing on the north side, Jim's side. *Christ, maybe I should just bring him home. Draw the shades on Zak, deep-six the deep thoughts, and get laid. Stop pretending I'm not human, that twenty-three-year-old ass is going to throw itself at me twice.* He could see the bulge of Seth's cock in his chinos, even as the kid was backing away.

"Okay," Seth said. "Thanks for today. Those Shermans were intense."

"Yeah."

"Okay," Seth repeated, taking a couple of small recessional steps. "G'night."

"Wait. I don't have your phone number."

"I'm in the book. My name is McKenna. McKenna on Stanton Street."

"Yes, but you don't have my—"

Seth was half-turned, keeping an eye on the Walk/Don't Walk sign. "That's all right. You'll call me. So long, Jim. G'night." The light had changed, and he was already trotting across, away.

When he reached the island that divided the eastbound lane from the westbound, Jim shouted at him, "But what if I don't!"

Seth reared around, his body loose and fluid as a colt's, and suddenly he was laughing, he was running back, sprinting across as the cars began coming toward him, knocking him back against the plate-glass storefront, and even then he kept coming, mouth against his, right out there on the street grinding and kissing and laughing at the same time, and then he sprang away, a white blur, dashing back into traffic, and Jim heard him sing out, "You'll call me! I know you will!"

Jim knew exactly when he'd last had sex. It had been a perfunctory Sunday morning lay, not at all what he or Zak would have wanted had they known it was going to be the last time. But it was their last time. Zak was gone.

Except that he really wasn't gone, because two years was nothing. Nothing softened, nothing receded, in only two years. Two years didn't negate the possibility that Jim could come home from work and find him in the kitchen trimming vegetables in his shirtsleeves. Two years! Jim only had to close his eyes in order to *smell* him! Two years was just the very tip of the *beginning* of Not Anymore.

But now Jim was walking home along Broadway with the warm impress of Seth's kiss on his mouth. He felt as if he'd awakened in a freezing room, groping all about himself but unable to find the comforter anywhere. Shivering, alone, he let himself into the loft and turned on all the lights.

4

After parting from Jim, Seth walked around for hours, exultant, going in and out of bars, seeing the effect of his excitement mirrored in the attentive glances of other men. He drank a beer here, danced for a while there, but spoke to no one and went home clutching his anticipation to himself like a bouquet.

All week Seth phoned his answering machine every chance he got, spent as much time at home as he could, waiting for the call. Unable to concentrate on his painting, he sleepwalked through classes, hastening home to huddle in bed with his sketchbook, waiting, fantasizing. His sleep was even more broken than usual, punctuated by vivid, violent dreams. He began his monthly letter to Mr. Hecklin half a dozen times, wanting to put his emotions on paper, but it was impossible to write the psychedelic gusts of his Jim fantasies or to omit them. He even tried to write to his sister, but that remained just as undoable as ever. Although he'd just finished it, he began to reread *Middlemarch*.

He had the Polaroid of Jim that Tony had taken, and even though his distracted half-frown wasn't notably sexy, he stared at it while he jerked off, and he jerked off more than usual, almost as often, it felt like, as he checked the machine.

No call came that week, or the following week. *You don't want him anyway*, Seth told himself. *He won't have even heard of any of the bands you like. He probably listens to cast albums and goes to the opera. And he's going to be old really soon*. But his sketchbook was filling with drawings of Jim, based on that one Polaroid and his memory of the man's air of weary benevolence, his powerful, laconic presence. On the Friday night almost two weeks after he'd last seen Jim, he went to the studio at Cooper Union, where he had three paintings under way. But the light seemed murky, his hand trembled. After throwing everything back into his locker, he drifted in a loop around the Village.

As he passed a corner restaurant whose facade was thrown open to the warm evening, three men seated at a table that was almost out on the sidewalk were laughing out loud. Seth didn't know what made him glance at them, a middle-aged trio with wineglasses in front of them and ties half-unknotted. But their laughter, so raucous, arrested him, and in the way that one's own name swims up from a page of undifferentiated text, he realized that one of them was Jim.

He stopped dead. The streetscape flattened out into a plane of spangled colors in the periphery of his vision, and as his head pounded in time with his heart, he stared. The men's merriment was subsiding; one of them topped up the wineglasses, and Jim, still smiling, put his hand through his hair. Seth felt the movement of those fingers as though they were touching him. Someone bumped into him from behind, but Seth didn't shift, heard nothing, was just his two hungry eyes.

Then one of the men noticed him, and returned Seth's stare, idly at first and then appraisingly, curious.

A moment later, Jim and the other man, who had been talking together, turned to the third, who was eyeing Seth now with a little sneer, as the fox regarded the grapes, and then they were all looking at him. Seth's gaze caught Jim's and Jim's mouth opened.

Slowly, not detaching his gaze from Jim's face, Seth pulled away, turned the corner. Jim's head turned with him, and over his friend's shoulder he looked at Seth with an expression that was almost angry, and then almost wistful, and it might have been almost something else, but by then he'd advanced too far, even walking backward, to see Jim anymore.

It was past midnight, and he was drowsing in bed over the last fifty pages of *Middlemarch*, when the phone rang.

"How did you know where I was going to be? Why did you stand there staring like that?"

Hearing Jim's voice, a rage tore through him like fire racing up a rope—*now* he was calling, *now* because he was paranoid! But then the rope fell to ashes, and he couldn't find the anger anymore.

"I was just walking around. I didn't know you were going to be there. How could I have known?"

A silence after this, which he chose to hear as apologetic.

"Well, how are you?"

Seth couldn't bring himself to answer. Jim didn't care, not really, because if he did, he'd have called before this. He'd only felt this way once before, that another person could change the shape of everything just by existing. Cleon Nash, his one serious boyfriend in college, had done it, but that felt like nothing but a poor underpainting for this, where the color was going on in deep impasto strokes.

"Seth? You still there?"

"I'm here."

"You looked . . . coming out of the dark . . . all in white, your pale shoulders . . . like an apparition."

"Did I?" he whispered, suddenly wishing this soft nonconversation could go on all night.

"You've been all right, since . . . I saw you last?"

"Were those friends I saw you with? They weren't clients. You looked like you were having too much fun for them to be clients." Although he hadn't been conscious of looking at them at the time, Seth saw them now, two oddly similar-looking men, rather colorless, and older than Jim. Not the sort of companions Jim would've had in his imagination.

"Yes, Clyde and Billy, old friends. My oldest friends now. Who are left."

Seth wanted to ask if they'd said anything about him or if Jim had explained to them who he was. Breathing was difficult. Bewildered, he put his hand on his thrumming chest.

A suspicious edge came into Jim's tone. "Why are you gasping like that? You're not—"

He sat up and coughed to make his heart go right. "No, I'm not doing anything."

Another pause, which he filled up with imaginings: Where was Jim right now? Sprawled on a sofa with the muted TV flickering nearby? Or naked in bed with the phone cradled on his shoulder?

Jim said, "I'd like to see you."

Although he knew he should be haughty, because Jim had jerked him around, he felt ready to fly to him at once. With his eyes closed and the receiver pressed against his cheek he imagined himself in Jim's arms, smooching, undressing. "When?"

"Meet me in the morning for breakfast."

Seth wanted to say, *If I come over now, I'll still be there for breakfast*, but somehow he knew Jim would receive that with a silence less humble than the last one.

Italian pop music played in the café, sun poured relentlessly through the plate glass. Their flirtatious waiter, dressed in bacon-and-egg-patterned pajamas, set glasses of fresh orange juice in front of them. Jim was crisp and friendly. Seth feared, as he watched him tuck into his omelet, that he'd only asked him here to confirm to himself once and for all that there was nothing doing.

"Tell me," Seth said, "about your lover—the one who's dead."

The fork slipped from Jim's hand, bounced on the edge of the table, and disappeared. Seth handed over his own; he couldn't summon his appetite.

"Why do you want to know about Zak?"

"You started to tell me about him the last time. So you must have wanted to."

He frowned. "But why should you want to hear about him?"

"Because it's important to you. I'm interested."

Jim sat back and pushed his plate away. A sadness moved over him that made it impossible to sit still.

He got up, put some money on the table, and headed for the door. Seth hastened to catch up.

"I'm sorry, I—wait!"

"Walk with me."

They passed the restaurant suppliers on the Bowery, Chinatown, the municipal buildings, and the Financial District. They didn't speak, but once or twice, just at the moments when he was aware of the boy's restiveness, Jim touched his arm, just a quick squeeze of the elbow. It kept him quiet. Jim knew he couldn't bear to hear him chatter, but neither could he have stood it if he peeled off and left him.

They ended up in Battery Park, at the place where the ferries load up for the trip to the Statue of Liberty. Jim dropped onto a bench facing the slip. Crowds of people eddied around in the sun. *The whole happy heedless heterosexual world,* Jim thought, glancing around at the children with balloons bobbing over their heads, the tourists talking their polyglot, cameras poised. Snapshot heaven.

And at Seth, who stood out here as he did everywhere, in his white clothes, facing him on the bench with his legs tucked up. Gracefully muscled arm bent, head resting on his palm. Waiting with that open don't-hurt-me face. Seth prompted, "Tell me how you met."

Does he imagine, this boy, that just because he looks like that, he can get me to do anything he wants? Is that what this is about? Maybe he thought he was doing him a favor, that he'd find this therapeutic.

But even as he asked himself these questions, he began talking. "How we met. Simple. Zak's family moved in next door to our family the summer before we started second grade. Our mothers became best friends. So really, he was always there in my life."

"Always there," Seth echoed, his eyes widening.

"When he d-d-died—we were in the midst of remaking our lives. Plans we'd been working toward for five years were coming together. Zak had already left the bank, took early retirement, and I was beginning to transition away from the agency, too. We had a big house up in Dutchess County, we were doing a lot of work on it with the idea that we would . . ." Saying these things made him self-conscious, as if he was opening his wallet and flashing the contents.

Seth put his cigarette out on the wooden bench slat and leaned forward attentively.

"That we would . . ." Jim paused. From the corner of his eye he counted up the silver rings ascending Seth's ear rim. Fuck it. He'd gone this far. "Would mostly raise the kids there. We were awaiting the birth of a baby that we'd arranged to adopt. He was born six days into Zak's death"—that's how he thought of it, as an ongoing condition—"but I was too broken up to go through with the adoption."

He stared at the ferry chugging toward the slip, its bow crowded with parents and children, wondering, as he always did and always mocked himself for doing, whether Max was among them, living a different life than they'd planned for him, with a different name. He'd been adopted, Jim knew, by another Manhattan couple. He might pass him any day on the street in his mother's arms.

When he glanced up, Jim just had time to notice, before Seth turned his head away, that the boy's eyes were bright with moisture. Jesus, what was he trying to prove by this show of welling up? Seth blinked and rubbed his eyes, murmuring something about the painful brightness of the sun off the water. There was a delicacy to his expression, and his silence.

"Of course, I realize there's something a little ridiculous about the grief of anyone who's so well-off as I am. That's partly why I try to keep it to myself. Also, people find it so tiresome."

"I'm so sorry."

"Yes, I'm sure you . . . I mean, thank you."

He still dreamed about the country house, about Zak in its leaf-shaded rooms, simple little dreams about the things they'd done there, painting, putting up bookshelves. In the dreams he heard bird-song through the open windows, heard the children playing nearby, but always woke up before he saw their faces. Nothing went wrong in these dreams, nothing ominous darkened them. And that was the horror of them. All of that sweet normality had been sucked out of his waking life.

Fran from the adoption agency still called him from time to time. He always thanked her politely. He wanted a son or daughter, very much, almost as much as he wanted Zak to be alive again. But the two things were equally removed from possibility.

Seth called him back to himself. "Tell me how you got together with him, how it went from being best pals to being *a thing*."

He was lovely, unconscious of himself with the sun striking off his bits of silver. *Ah, I should have let myself go . . . if I was paunchy and slack now, this kid would never have looked at me. Which is what I want. Isn't it? Zak, tell me, isn't it? It's you I'm being true to.*

Seth smiled. "Go on please. I'm listening."

"In college, every time a holiday rolled around, Zak turned up in Manhattan with a different girlfriend. He wasn't a beauty, but he had immense charm and a way of collecting people. These women he dated were terrific, brainy and gorgeous. Meanwhile, I took girls out sometimes and wondered why I wasn't connecting with them. I used to have these elaborate sexy dreams about guys in my classes, I'd come and wake up and feel disgusted with myself.

"Then we'd finished college. I was doing graduate work at Columbia, I had an apartment up there. Zak moved in with me, which is what we'd always planned, and started on Wall Street. I was finally seeing a girl whom I thought I might ask to marry me. I spent a lot of time with her trying to convince myself I wanted to be spending a lot of time with her.

"I didn't propose and didn't propose, and then one day, to my tremendous relief, Lois told me she'd been getting serious with somebody else behind my back. By then I had a big box of *Drummer* magazines stashed under my bed, and the pages were *all* stuck together. Around this time, Zak's endless supply of beautiful girlfriends dried up. He started bringing guys home. I'd get up in the night to piss and there'd be some naked man in the bathroom ahead of me. Now if you can believe it, I actually went on for a while *not* admitting to myself what this meant. Zak never explicitly said anything about it. And I didn't ask him. It was the original 'don't ask, don't tell' policy.

"Then, we went home to Long Island for Thanksgiving—our mothers made Thanksgiving every year, taking turns whose house it would be at. There we are at the table, his parents, my parents—we must have been twenty people that year—and Zak taps his knife against his glass, and stands up, and he's wearing this beatific smile, looking around from face to face to face—he *loved* everybody there— he opens his mouth and says, 'I want you all to know I'm gay.'"

Seth whistled. "Holy shit! What happened then?"

"Pandemonium ensued. It was a ridiculous thing for Zak to do, it was mean, really, and he wasn't a mean person. I guess he wanted to get it over with all at once. And to make matters worse, when nobody rushed to embrace him, when he saw that they were just going to go on with their hand-wringing and protests, Zak got up from the table and stalked out. Of course, I went after him. I remember pausing on the lawn and looking in the window where the families were still at the table with their mouths and hands going, all these people we loved. I remember thinking, 'This is what happens when you're one of *those*, everybody's inside in the warmth and the light, and you're out here shivering in the dark.'"

Seth's sigh took him by surprise. *I thought you were the one whose folks were so cool with it.* He didn't say it, because he wanted to get this storytelling over with; he was already looking forward to being back home alone, slumping into a book with the comforting fantasy of Zak's ongoing presence in the loft's ether. Talking about him made Jim ravenous for his secret rituals of resurrection.

"Driving back to the city, Zak tried to rationalize what he'd done. We were still arguing when we got to our place. I was telling him it was no kind of life, some inane thing like that, his back was to me and I was babbling on about how nothing was set in stone and what about all those girls who liked him so much.

"And then he got right into my face. He said, 'When are you going to drop the denial?' And before I could react to that at all, he kissed me. I'll never forget it, I'd *never* been kissed like that before. By anyone, much less a man. Much less *Zak*. I just reeled. And he said, 'I've been practicing and practicing so I'd be good at it for *you*.'"

"Jesus." Seth straightened up, his eyes wide now. "That's so *romantic*. What did you do?"

"Shouted at him that he was out of his mind, careened off to my room, and locked myself in. I spent the entire winter having a major slow-motion freak-out over it all. I won't bore you with the details."

"So how *did* you two finally get together?"

"There was a lot to it—me coming to terms with myself. But that's not what you're interested in. I'd pretended for months that I was all right with Zak bringing all these men around, because that's what people did in those days, and I wasn't yet ready to say I wanted anything from Zak for myself. But one day I couldn't cope with it anymore. I told him it had to stop.

"Zak looked at me, he was very calm, we were washing dishes, and the running water almost drowned his words out. He said, 'You know it's you I really want.' And he walked out of the kitchen. I was stunned, it took me a few moments to follow. He was in my bed, waiting for me to come to him. Which I was finally ready to do. After that we were never really apart."

He squinted out at the new crowd of tourists filing onto the ferry. The whistle boomed, gulls chattered overhead, the sticky air was filled with a bilgey, hot-doggy smell, punctuated by the almost putrid sweetness of honey-roasted nuts. All around them, these regular people having a nice day.

"We relocated downtown and for a while we lived the stereotype. The discos, the baths, The Pines in the summer, tricking tricking

tricking like there was no tomorrow. Working like mad to pay for it all. I'd quit graduate school then and taken my first agency job. We did a lot of blow to sustain the energy. Zak thrived on that life, but I never took to it the way he did; I've got this introspective streak that always does me in. Finally I said I wouldn't do it anymore and couldn't stand to watch him do it, either. I was jealous, and quite frankly frightened of the trajectory we were on. There were rumors starting about people getting sick. But Zak didn't want to give up anything he enjoyed. We had a million arguments, and they all involved Zak saying 'I want to be with you, *but*—' or 'I want to be with you *and*—' Until one day, when we were both wiped out from fighting about it, he took a deep breath, and said, 'I want to be with you.' No buts, no ands, no clauses at all. I want to be with *you*.

"We bought the place on Bond Street when there was nothing but nothing there yet, and we closed the relationship. And to our surprise, Zak's especially, it's when we began to find out what real happiness *is*. Just a little later on, while we were watching our friends and acquaintances die around us, Zak used to say that was what saved us. But really it was sheer dumb luck." He paused. "Which always ends by running out."

Seth was going to ask him about that, the end of luck. To head him off the subject, Jim got to his feet. Seth rose, too. "I want to be with you."

Christ, I fed him that line, so what did I expect?

"You don't even know me."

Seth fell back. "Nobody does, at first. Most people . . . most people don't spend their lives with the man they met when they were seven."

"Look, maybe life's a cloud of romance to you—you're young and full of fantasies. But for others of us it's shitty and short—and sometimes not short enough." He watched the effect of this remark pass over Seth's face and body like the shadow of some low-flying menace.

But Seth wasn't cowed. "Last night you phoned me. You said you wanted to see me. You sounded like you meant it. Well, here I am. *See me.*"

"I see you," he growled.

"Jesus." Seth began to walk away, then turned. "This is dumb. You're on a self-denial mission, big-time. But I know you like me. And I like you. And if you'd let me, I'd make something of it." For a moment he shimmered, upright and defiant, but he couldn't quite carry it off. "Shit." He began to walk away, toward the tall buildings. Jim watched him attempt nonchalance, his rigid back betraying him. He wouldn't turn around, he knew that. He'd keep going, dragging his steps through a swamp of mortification.

Jim never could sleep on anyone's justified disappointment in him.

"Slow down. Don't leave me alone here with all these straight people."

Seth gave him one burnt glance, which softened when their eyes met into a gratitude of ravishing sweetness that made Jim feel giddy and guilty all at once. He had too much surface, this boy, he was too easy to please or to bruise. Got up to look cool and insouciant and nothing of the kind.

Not at all.

When they got together after that, they walked the city. They ate pizza or burritos and drank domestic beer. The only immoderation Seth would consent to a part in, because Jim would not compromise, was cabs. *I do not ride the subway,* Jim told him, and the expression on his face was such that Seth did not even dare to ask why, let alone debate the point.

In bookstores, he saw Seth pick up volume after volume, dip into them and then reluctantly put them back. Sometimes he jotted down titles to look for at the library. Occasionally Jim bought books for him, which he accepted with reluctance. "I'm not trolling for gifts,"

Seth said the first time he slipped one into his hand on the sidewalk outside the shop. "That's not what I want from you."

"Consider," Jim answered, "the pleasure I get from giving this to you, not your feelings about receiving it." That silenced Seth, but afterward Jim felt vaguely ashamed of himself.

There were some occasions when they'd planned to catch a movie and Seth, at the last minute, would suggest they go for a walk instead. Over and over Jim asked himself why he went along with these restrictions, why he didn't just make the speech about how he was years past wanting to "rough it" and it was nothing for him to buy a pair of movie tickets, but he held back. Though he told himself it was in consideration of Seth's sensibility, it seemed to have something to do with how he never just grabbed and kissed Seth either. Jim wondered why Seth went on seeing him, why he was so *eager* to see him, when he held forth no promise of sex at all. Any day now Seth would certainly disappear. He'd find some other handsome kid to roll around with like two healthy puppies. Or some other older man perhaps, but one in a position to do something for him, in exchange for favors he would elicit without making Seth feel ashamed. *Something*, Jim thought, *would turn up to meet Seth's needs*, the ones he himself was still trying to ignore, and the idyll would end.

But their times together were good times, despite the restraint, or, Jim sometimes thought, because of it. He'd told no one about it, and the secrecy made him feel he was still being loyal to his mourning.

Nevertheless, having been roused this much from torpor, he looked around, during that autumn, for someone else to fix his attention on, someone older and more appropriate, although he wasn't entirely sure what he meant by that word. He even went, three or four times, to a bar, cruised halfheartedly, left, each time, alone. No one else he saw made any impression on him. His eye, his mind, his daydreams kept coming back to Seth. It would be Seth, or no one. *It would*, he thought gloomily, *end up being no one*.

5

Late one weekday evening, Jim strolled along the uneven slate sidewalks of the West Village, looking in on softly lit rooms, golden with coziness. These few blocks, bordered by Waverly and Bleecker, Bank Street and West Tenth, formed the best enclave in the neighborhood, maybe in all of Manhattan, rows of beautifully proportioned houses of the last century, many meticulously restored, offering glimpses through their windows of intricate ceiling roses, chandeliers, curlicued moldings, mantels like the stately busts of grandes dames. In summer, good tall trees shadowed these streets, affording a sense of being outside of time. Among so many pretty houses, Clyde and Billy's was one of the best: the carved double front doors painted a fresh blue, the brasses always polished. A plate attached to the brick said 1846. They'd owned the house since 1970, worked in that time to bring it back to what it had been 150 years ago. For Jim it was always a homestead, rock-solid. Amid all the destruction of the last fifteen years, nothing ever happened to Clyde and Billy's house or, mercifully, to Clyde and Billy. There was always plenty of room there for dinner parties and gatherings, for out-of-town friends to stay, for sick friends to find refuge. The bedrooms were ready all the time. Behind the house was a shaded garden where you could sit all of a May afternoon on a wrought-iron bench and hear nothing more than the breeze stirring the ivy and the ice cubes clinking in your glass.

He'd spent the first couple of weeks after Zak's death prostrated here, looked after by his friends, although they were nearly as felled by shock and grief as he. Clyde and Billy were closely associated in his mind with Zak. Their house contained so many points on which his memory caught, leaving a little bead of blood. Perhaps that was why he'd avoided it, and them, for so long now. Or perhaps it was their sheer liveliness; nothing sank Clyde and Billy. So many friends had died and yet they went on making new ones. The web of association was always patched, new strands interleaved. Whereas hadn't he, since Zak was taken from him, wanted everything to stay just as it was? No one coming in who didn't know him as he'd been before.

But he'd let Seth wriggle in. This very evening had been one of many; Seth had joined him for an early dinner, reluctantly allowing him to pay; they'd sat long afterward, making small talk for the sake of each other's company. How much more pleasant this would be if they were at home, with no need for Seth to prop his chin wearily on his hand, no need to justify their occupation of a table with empty chatter and coffee, when they could stretch out together on the sofa and be free not to talk at all. Climbing the stoop of Clyde and Billy's house, Jim hesitated, his hand on the cool porcelain bell pull. No one just "dropped in" in Manhattan. Still, here he was. He rang the bell.

Billy appeared, eyebrows raised, drew him in past the front doors and the inner doors with their etched glass, and hugged him. "Jimmy! It's been so long, we were beginning to tell ourselves you'd left town." His breath smelled of wine and garlic; he smiled a shade too kindly, even for Billy. The dark wooden foyer of the house, with its enormous gilt-framed mirror, brass chandelier, and gleaming stair rail, was hot and redolent of potpourri, just as it was every winter Jim could remember since he'd first come there at Seth's age. Twenty years ago, Clyde and Billy were handsome, fascinating men of thirty-five, lean, sharp, knowing everyone and everything. Convinced that it was witty, charming Zak they *really* liked, Jim had never left their presence without feeling sure they were summing him up with some devastating phrase. Even now Clyde's prickliness still had the power to intimidate him.

"It has been a long time," he said, "I'm sorry. I was just walking around, and I thought—you and Clyde are alone?"

"Tonight, yes, by a miracle. Come down to the kitchen. Clyde will be so happy."

Clyde and Billy had come to resemble each other, grown brotherly as they lost their looks in the same unfortunate way: faces gone blocky, chests sloping into pendant bellies. There was something comforting about their ordinariness. Jim suspected they thought so, too. Leading the way down the back stairs, Billy called out, "Can you imagine it? Jimmy's here!"

Clyde was swabbing down the kitchen counters in his meticulous way when they arrived in the kitchen. He finished the last touch or two before coming over to him. Clyde seldom smiled, and didn't now; he appraised Jim with one raking glance as he shook his hand. Clyde wasn't given to hugs, either, or kisses. People who met him more than once or twice made a point of remembering this.

"You're looking handsome, not like last time. What's that mean, I wonder?"

Ah, does it show? When there's nothing even to tell? Afraid suddenly that they'd get it out of him, despite his determination to keep himself to himself, Jim wished he hadn't come.

"You knew we were talking about you," Billy said. "That's why you've turned up."

"Were you?" He smiled, but his stomach shrank.

"You've been on your own such a long time," Billy said, bringing out a plate of exquisite little cookies that looked not at all like the kind of thing most people would have just lying around the kitchen on a Wednesday night. "Look at you now, walking alone, and at this hour! Who does that? Where were you going?"

"He's up to something," Clyde said. "Someone's been looking at him."

"No one's been looking at me," he said, as if this was the most ridiculous idea going. "I was just taking a stroll. I love the lighted windows of the houses. There's nothing like it near Bond Street."

Billy pretended to shudder and Jim smiled for him. He knew Billy thought he was wallowing in his solitude. *And I am. And I like it. Leave me be.*

"So what have you been doing with yourself? Still spending all your evenings with the Bellevue babies?"

"Why do you always exaggerate, Clyde? Two nights a week—three at most."

"I'll say it again, it's depressing. Nothing good's ever going to happen to those creatures."

"Maybe not, to most of them. Except that it's good that I show up and cuddle them for an hour or two. Good for them, good for me."

Clyde shrugged. "And in sixteen years one of those crack babies you coo over will mug you in the subway."

Jim froze. "I don't go down in the subway anymore. You know that. And *Jesus*, Clyde, what a thing to say. These are tiny babies. I like the babies, I like the nurses on the unit, I like everything about it."

"It's lovely, what you do there," Billy said, sailing between them with the coffeepot. "But we're just wondering when you're going to resume your *life*, darling."

"I categorically deny that what I'm leading is not a life. I'm at the head of a profitable advertising agency, I do valuable volunteer work in the community—"

"Oh, shut up, you know what we mean. Forget it. Billy, stop nagging him."

"I'm not nagging."

Jim thought of saying to them, *There's a boy I've met. I'm afraid he's on the verge of being in love with me, or imagining he is, which may be the same thing really, and I don't know what to do. . . . I seem to be unable to do anything, take him or send him away, so I wait and I wait, and still he's there, waiting, too. I'm waiting for him to quit me, but what's he waiting for?* But he said nothing because he didn't know how to describe Seth to them in a way that would keep his friends from turning him into a smutty Twinkie joke.

This inability to confide saddened him; it felt like a betrayal, not just of Clyde and Billy, but of himself, to have his life so compartmentalized. Ten minutes after he finished his coffee he rose to go. They both escorted him to the door, and to his surprise, Clyde as well as Billy embraced him.

"Don't be afraid of us," Billy murmured. "Sometimes I think you are."

Once he'd made this plunge, Jim went to their house more often in the ensuing weeks than he had at any time since the three months after Zak's death.

Clyde and Billy entertained often—absurdly often, as though they were afraid to face each other across the big table without the distraction of other men's voices. Every time he went to one of these parties, Jim was aware of the men who had been especially invited to meet him. They were just the right sort—engaging, attractive, appropriate in age and outlook. Jim chatted with them and even laughed, but he went home alone, clinging fiercely to his solitude as he walked across town after midnight. He resented their assumption that he needed rescuing. On those nights he made sure to call Seth after he'd gotten into bed, knowing the boy would probably be awake still, nodding over a book on his narrow futon. He'd pretend to be surprised at finding Seth at home, not out dancing or tricking, and Seth, he knew, pretended also, that there was a glamour to his struggles on bohemia's edges. They'd make another date, and murmur sleepily to each other, never straying so far as phone sex, although after he hung up Jim always jerked off thinking of Seth's pretty mouth, the line of his jaw, his neck and shoulders. His fantasies of Seth resembled those of Victorian men who saw plenty of décolleté, but nothing else.

. . .

In the garden of the Museum of Modern Art, getting the pallid November sun on their upturned faces, Jim asked, "Do you see other men?"

Seth sat forward. "Is this an important question?"

"Important? What do you mean, important? It's a question."

"I mean, I'm wondering why you're asking me. Why and why today."

"You know, it's only supposed to be Jews who answer a question with a question."

"Is that so? I'm not that familiar with Jews."

"So are you seeing anyone else? Jewish or otherwise?"

"Not at the moment. Are you?"

"You know I'm not."

"How would I know that?" Seth put a cigarette to his lips. "I see guys cruising you all the time. Women check you out. Just because you don't notice, or pretend you don't—and how can I know what you're doing when we're not together?" He flicked his lighter, lit up, exhaled.

"I told you, you're the first man I've seen since—"

"Yeah, yeah, I do know. I'm just ragging you." Seth put his hand on Jim's sleeve, squeezed, let go.

"I wouldn't mind if you were seeing other people." Even as he said the words, Jim knew he would mind it very much. He couldn't imagine that all this time the boy had been celibate, but what right had he to feel jealous? Anyway, he was curious about what Seth would say.

"I don't happen to be, right now."

He watched Seth looking around the garden, and then closed his own eyes. "Do you go to the clubs?" he asked then.

"Sometimes. Yeah. To see some guys I know. To dance."

"Do you . . . I've lost track of the scene. What goes on these days?"

"What do you mean, what goes on? What are you asking me?"

"Never mind."

"You want to know if there are back rooms and if I go in them?"

"I said never mind, Seth."

"Well, of course, there are, and I used to sometimes. But I haven't tricked since I met you. Like the actors say, I'm resting."

Jim didn't know whether to believe this. Seth didn't say it like he expected to be congratulated. But there was something pitiful about it—both of them practicing this restraint, self-denial as a game of chicken. Who'd crack first? He wanted to say, *Don't wait for me.* "How long have we been seeing each other?"

"We met around the middle of July, didn't we?"

"That's right." Jim scanned the cloudless sky. It seemed so long ago.

"You've shown me more museums and galleries than I've seen since I first came to New York. It's an education. My best pal Hannah used to be my favorite person to look at art with. But you're better than her, because you really know all about what you're looking at, and she just makes stuff up." He let the cigarette drop from his hand. "Of course, it can be funny as shit, the stuff she says."

Jim felt a little wistful, hearing Seth refer to this unseen friend. Their lives were so separate. "Oh, but it's wonderful to make things up. Wonderful to have an imagination, to get the full use of it."

Seth cocked his head, getting Jim's full attention, then paused, holding it, to light another cigarette. He exhaled a long stream of smoke. "D'you use *your* imagination a lot?"

"What do you mean?" But Jim knew.

Seth pretended to look at some people who had just walked out into the garden; he tipped his chin up to keep the smoke out of his eyes, displaying his white throat. Then he rolled his eyes playfully in Jim's direction, grinning around the cigarette and taking a long drag before removing it—with insinuation—from his lips.

"Me, I've been imagining all kinds of things, since . . . since . . ."

Jim wanted to escape Seth's words, his flirting expression, but he also couldn't look away. Seth seemed particularly fine at that moment, with the sun in his hair and that rubber-band grin of his.

"Are you chilly?" Jim said, starting up. "I think it's getting a little nippy out here."

Seth got up, too, still smiling fondly at him, and gave a good-natured shrug. "No, but . . . whatever. Let's go in." The almond-shaped yellow leaves crackled beneath their feet as they crossed the courtyard. Seth's arm brushed his, once, twice, then he jumped ahead to grab the tall glass door as it began to close behind someone's back.

Jim watched him dart into the milling crowds in the lobby. He was imagining what Seth was imagining, and didn't know whether to hang back or rush right after him.

At the office two days later, Robin brought in with the mail a large manila envelope, stiffened with cardboard. "I didn't open this one, it's marked personal. Probably someone's portfolio though."

The return address said Stanton Street. Jim's heart leapt, and he struggled with the carefully taped envelope before scissoring it. Three large sheets of drawing paper slipped out when he tipped the envelope over his desk blotter. A sticky note was affixed to the first sheet: *Does any of this look familiar to you? Yours, Seth.*

Nothing Seth had said about his work had prepared him for these. *If Egon Schiele and Aubrey Beardsley had collaborated on drawing comics,* Jim thought, *they might have looked a bit like this.* Each panel was oddly shaped or superimposed on the ones around it. The figures—spiky and loose-limbed, rendered in elegant lines—stood out from a background of dizzying detail. Jim spread the three sheets of drawings out on his desk, eyes darting from one to the next in awe. It took a little while for him to realize that what he was looking at was the story of their meeting and first date. But there, in the first panel, was Tony the photographer, the models, the snotty client, and there was Jim, who did not know that he was quite so broad-shouldered and handsome. Seth's own figure had a spare, spiritual grace, but there was a humor in the face—in all the faces. The ink Jim and the ink Seth were saying the things they'd said to each other, the words written in a tiny, round, well-defined script. The drawings also showed things Jim didn't know about: here was Seth dressing in his apartment, and there they were on the sidewalk outside the bar in Chelsea and in the cab and the restaurant. And on the corner of Houston Street, where Seth conveyed, in the stark unshaded line drawing of his face, how desolate he felt when Jim parted from him. The last panel on the last page showed Seth cinematically from above, masturbating in the bath, each tiny octagonal black-and-white tile around the tub clearly filled in. The dialogue balloon, Jim realized after staring at it for a few moments, was actually a blob of cum suspended in air. Written on it, *Never hit the light fixture before. Who's responsible for that?!?!?!* At the bottom of the panel, in spidery letters, it said: *To be continued . . . I hope.*

He wished there was someone he could show these to whom he could ask, *Tell me what it means, that he sent me this.* Taking care not to dog-ear the edges, he put them back in their envelope. They needed to be matted, preserved. Maybe he'd do that, give them back to Seth safely sealed under glass.

But Seth had given them to him.

He picked up the phone, called Tony's studio.

"Mazzoti Photography," Seth announced.

"You shouldn't be answering phones for some hopped-up advertising photographer," Jim said.

"I need to pay the rent. Anyway . . . I'm still a student," he breathed.

"These are so beautiful, I don't know what to say."

"You got them?" The question could have meant *Did you receive them?* or *Did you understand them?* "I drew them just for you." He was still whispering. *It might,* Jim thought, *be emotion or that Tony is hovering nearby.*

"May I see more of your work? The paintings?"

"Oh—you want to?"

"Of course, I want to."

There was a pause. Had he asked the boy to strip off his clothes, there would be, he knew, no hesitation.

"You really like those drawings? You don't think they're . . . silly?"

"Seth—"

"I didn't want to embarrass you, but . . . all right. I need a little time. Meet me at Cooper Union tomorrow night at seven, and I'll let you look."

Jim heard trepidation in his voice—almost fear. He wasn't naturally inclined to be ruthless, but now, staring at the drawings, he felt a flash of resentment. Here he was, being challenged to turn away from nurturing the memory of his one great love, to throw himself open again in places that were still raw.

Wasn't this an imposition?

6

A large room with skylights, lit now at night by fluorescents hung from the high ceiling. Tables, easels, sinks, walls, floors covered in multicolored spatters of pigment. It occurred to Jim as he waited that he'd never seen so much as a spot of paint on Seth's white clothes. His hands and fingernails were always clean. It seemed to him now like a small miracle.

He was early. Aware of his heartbeat, holding his trench coat folded inside out over his arm, Jim shifted from foot to foot. Outside, it was finally cold; he wondered if Seth had a really warm coat.

The elevator door opened, and there he was, unwinding a fuzzy white scarf from his throat. His cheeks were red; he looked flustered and expectant.

"Hi. I didn't think you'd be here yet." They exchanged their usual perfunctory greeting, a squeeze of the arm, a peck on the corner of the mouth.

Jim squinted at him. "All right, what did you change?" he asked. "You're wearing your look-at-me face."

Different haircut or color? No, that wasn't it. The narrow sweep of gray eyeliner was the same, too. No beginnings of a beard. "There's something, I know, but . . . I can't quite place. . . ."

"I got rid of the nose ring."

"So you did! Why didn't I spot it? Plain as the nose on your face!" He laughed.

"I thought maybe it was why you weren't kissing me more."

He brushed past Jim to go into the studio. Stunned, Jim trailed after. At the far end, in an alcove, out of view of the main room, was a canvas turned to the wall. Seth walked up to it and turned, waiting for Jim to catch up. "I came down here earlier and got this ready for you. It's just one painting. It's the only one I've done this semester that I think is really finished. It's the only one I can let you see."

"Yes, fine." He was distracted; still stuck on the disappearance of the nose ring. Seth was just perceptibly trembling, his hands gripping the edges of the canvas.

"It's . . . well . . . here it is." He flipped the canvas around and hung it on a nail at eye level, then stepped back, his gaze riveted on Jim's face. It took an effort for him to drag his eyes away from Seth's and look at the painting, and when he did, Seth turned his back with affected nonchalance and stepped out of the alcove.

Alone, he looked. The picture gave him a sense of being in a particular bright room at a particular early-morning moment, a place where he thought he could smell, despite the oily turpentine scent of the studio where he stood, light fragrances of cut flowers and ripe fruit and sleep. There they were in the three-by-four-foot still life: a clear glass jar of cheap bodega flowers, a dish with a couple of pears and an apple, a flat pale futon. The dish and the jar set on a pale gray wood floor in the foreground, catching the light, and just behind them, recumbent on the futon, Seth himself—his head and bare torso, the hair, disordered as if from sleep, seen through the distorting medium of the water in the jar, and in his hand, near his lips, another green pear. Propped against the wall behind the futon, a mirror reflected it all. The sight of Seth's face—the eyes heavy with the residue of sleep, hunger, and erotic lassitude—made his groin, and his heart, heavy. *I'm finished. Zak is gone and I'm gone, too, but I just haven't quite keeled over yet.* This idea was with him always, a dark cloud that was, to Jim's despair, both Zak and his mourning for Zak. It was also Jim's depression. At times lately, the cloud had lifted quite high, admitting some fairer weather; but here it was dropped in tight again. It did not obscure his view of Seth's picture; he could see it right through the cloud. But he could not, he thought with sorrow, see it any other way.

It was time to say something. Seth was waiting.

"I think . . ." he began, making an effort to give the boy what he was asking for, "there's great skill here, you know how to draw and you know how to lay on paint, how to make it do what you want. There's so much appreciation for these simple beautiful things. Morning light. The surface of a mirror. The skin of a pear." *Your skin. Your gleaming eyes. Your white and sculptural shoulders.*

Seth studied the picture, as though these words were changing how it appeared to him. He rested his hand on Jim's arm, and gradually tightened his grip. "You really—?"

"Yes. I'm very moved by what you've done here. You'll go on working and learning, getting better and better, but you already are what you will be."

Seth took a deep breath. "I want you to have this picture. I have to turn it in for a grade, but at the end of the semester—I want you to have it."

"Oh, no . . . I couldn't just take. . . . Let me buy it from you."

"No! No . . . that's not what I mean. I want you to have it. I painted it for you."

"But you already gave me the drawings, they were so generous. You shouldn't just give away all your . . ."

A darkness passed over Seth's eyes; he turned away. Jim knew he'd made a mistake, but he wondered if it was a mistake he'd have to let stand.

Seth's voice was calm and effortful. "I promised myself, whatever happened, tonight would be the last try. I wanted to give you enough room, but now I think I'm making myself pathetic." He slipped past Jim and took the painting from its nail, regarded it for a moment, then set it down against the wall.

"The picture's yours, anyway. Fuck my grade—take it. You can throw it in a Dumpster on your way home if you want to. But if you leave it here, I'm going to destroy it. I don't want anybody else to look at it, either."

A weird rushing sensation came over him, and after a moment's disorientation, he recognized it as longing—not just physical longing for Seth, but the need to breathe deep, to throw his arms up and inhale, expel all the banked energy of his body in movement. Which Zak would never do anymore.

He touched Seth's shoulder, turned him. "Don't be angry with me. Of course, I want your magnificent picture."

Jim felt him waiting to know what he would demand of him, what he would allow himself to accept. Stooping a little, he tilted his head to fit his mouth against Seth's, slipped his tongue lightly along the seam of his lips, which parted only little by little. Placing a hand along Seth's jaw, he felt the insistent flutter of the boy's pulse against his palm. Seth's whole body trembled, his trembled, too. Then Seth's mouth opened under his, his hands came up around Jim's neck, and he felt it dissipate, the darkness he'd carried. That first tender kiss was followed immediately by others more devouring; he pushed Seth against the wall, tipped his head back. Seth's mouth tasted good to him; the proportion of their bodies to each other pleased him. Pleasing, too, the way Seth clung to his shoulders, and the low sound he made in his throat. Now that he was doing it, kissing Seth seemed so natural, so necessary, he wondered how he could ever have thought this was something to resist.

"I'm sorry. That I've strung you along. I—" He wanted to say, *Thank you for being so persistent.* But it seemed too silly, so he said it a different way, closing Seth's eyes with kisses, biting gently on his nose.

Seth smiled and shivered, and he found this pleasing, too. "We *really* need to fuck. Can we go do that, like, right this second?"

A woozy panic lapped at him. What was to become of his dear dark cloud?

"Let's go," Seth whispered. "I'm crazy for it and so are you."

They almost ran to Jim's apartment, just a few blocks away, kissing on corners, dashing through red lights, oblivious to passersby.

In the bedroom, Jim nearly knocked the lamp over in turning it on. Perched on the side of the bed, Seth pulled his sweater off over his head; standing over him, Jim caught it and threw it over his shoulder. Seth was working on Jim's belt buckle when the large photograph on the nightstand caught his eye, and he dropped his hands.

A long-faced man with dark red hair and beard laughed out of a silver frame.

"That's Zak," he murmured, staring. Jim, dizzy, as if an amusement park ride had stopped in mid-whirl, picked up the photo.

"I'll just put him in the other room." He carried it out to the front of the loft, where the piano was already crowded with photos of the people he loved. Jim shifted a few frames around to make room amid this company who knew Zak, who knew them both as a couple. All these people—those who were still living—who would look at Seth, and seeing the bleached head, the all-white wardrobe, the tattoos and piercings, would say to one another, *Jimmy's really lost his direction since poor Zak died.*

Dropped heavily back to earth, he returned slowly to the bedroom. Seth met him at the doorway. He'd put his sweater back on.

"I'm sorry," Seth said. "I broke up the mood."

"No, it was my fault, I . . . anyway, I just remembered I don't have any rubbers in the house."

They stood in the doorway, close but not touching. Seth faced out where he could see the book-lined den, leading into the dining room and beyond that, a bit of the large front room that faced onto the street. He stared, and Jim became aware that he was holding his breath.

"God. This place is huge."

Jim seized on a tour as a way past this granite moment. But as he showed him around, he watched the boy's face grow blank; he was feeling his poverty and youth in all this space, filled with nice things acquired over years. "Never mind all this," he said. "Do you want some coffee? Or a drink?"

"I could go out and get some condoms." Seth was staring past him, as if addressing someone only he could see.

"You could do that," he said, hesitant.

"Don't you want me to?"

Jim weighed this. "Will you stay the night?"

This question seemed to surprise him. He glanced around as though he expected the answer to appear from some corner of the loft. "I assumed that's what I'd do. . . ."

"Of course. But maybe we could hold off on the condoms and just—relax tonight. What do you think?"

Seth puffed his cheeks out and blew air. "No fucking?"

"We could just take it easy."

Seth's disappointment was palpable, and he knew he'd made another mistake. He seemed capable, with him, of little else. Feeling powerless to seize control of the situation again, Jim felt the backs of his eyes burning with encroaching tears.

After a long blank moment, Seth said, "The only thing is, I'm almost out of smokes."

Standing at his apartment door, he watched him bound down the steps they'd so recently ascended arm in arm. When the street door slammed behind him, Jim thought, *Well, that's it. Bra-fucking-vo.*

There was no point now, starting a pot of coffee. Returning to the piano, he busied himself with the picture frames, reangling them, checking for tarnish. He'd been so energized a few minutes ago, lit up with frank and happy lust, but now he was heavy, slow, and old. The whole empty evening loomed before him like a horror, and all the evenings that would follow it. For a long time he leaned on the piano, staring into the crevasse of his prospects.

The intercom buzz reeled him back from far, far away. He was stunned to hear Seth's voice coming through the box.

The same elastic bounce that had carried him out brought him back. He careened in the door and pushed a grocery bag into Jim's hands. "Sorry I took so long," he said, tugging off his scarf. "There was a long line at the bodega with some jerk at the beginning of it who was trying to *return* something."

"I—lost track of the time," Jim murmured. Still incredulous at Seth's reappearance, he unpacked the bag on the kitchen counter. Two packs of cigarettes, four bagels and a square of cream cheese, a small carton of half-and-half.

"Is this all you've brought?" he said, attempting a smile. "Cancer and clogged arteries?" His heart was pounding so hard he could feel his own pulse beat in his fingers.

From his coat pocket, Seth drew a handful of gold discs. Taking his hand, he set the little stack on his palm and closed his fingers over it. The foil-wrapped condoms reminded Jim of Hanukkah gelt; he said as much.

Seth's eyebrows shot up. "Hanukkah *what?*"

"Chocolate coins that kids get, on the holiday," he explained. "They look like this."

Seth gave him what he later came to call his below-the-belt grin.

"Well, then," he said, "I encourage you to spend 'em all in one place."

Seth led the way now, quiet, confident, to the Zak-less bedroom.

Awkward but unfaltering, Jim undid Seth's belt and the fly of his chinos. Now that he was so close, he yearned to go slowly; so as to be able to remember later his first glimpse of Seth's nakedness, his first whiff of his secret aromas, the exact first touch of his mouth to uncovered skin. Seth's cock, already tight and hard and oozing at the tip, bounced out and up as he tugged down his briefs. He glanced from its rosy head to Seth's rosy mouth widening into a grin.

"I'm going to give you an incredible fuck, to welcome you back."

"Welcome me back?"

"Yeah," Seth said, "y'know, to life."

This promise made Jim giddy; he tugged him down to straddle his lap. After postponing and rationalizing for so long, his desire almost unmanned him. At the sight of Seth, clothes disarranged to reveal his charms—the skin floury pale, nipples as pink as his mouth, set on such precise lean pecs, the slightly hollow belly with its pierced navel, the pretty cock, set in its bush of hair the color of fog, a good handful, bright red at the glans and tender as an apricot over its hardness—Jim's breath caught in his throat. This boy was so entirely alive, beaming for him as if he'd just burst out of a cake— *Ta dah!*

"I need to kiss you, you're delicious," Jim murmured.

But it was Seth who cupped Jim's face in his hands, who offered his tongue first, who chuckled and then went silent as their mouths battened on each other. His hands slipped up and down Seth's thighs where the chino fabric was pulled tight, around his slender waist to the dip and roll of his back and ass, pushing the cloth farther down, exploring the smooth undulant terrain, then up again to the two sharp blades where wings would unfurl, *and for a moment, eyes shut tight, he beheld them, enormous golden wings, wings of a Fra Filippo Lippi angel, stirring languidly at Seth's back, moving the air that for too long had been thick and stagnant here.*

Jim tugged Seth's sweater up and off, breaking their kiss only as the wool swept past their faces, and resumed at once. But Jim needed to *look*, he pushed him gently back to get perspective. He was glad to see that the boy's arms connected to his shoulders like the serifs on a T, not marred by too much muscle. The delineated angles of jaw, neck, shoulders, arms, fitted together with a workmanlike neatness. Jim turned the arms a little, to run his mouth along the inner bulge, where the skin felt powdery against his lips.

"D'you like me?" Seth whispered.

He liked him so much that the liking set up an internal quivering, as though he was a tuning fork; with his hands he traced the sinuous lines of Seth's body and could not, for the moment, speak. Seth's smile broadened, and he blushed in splotches that made an exotic chameleon pattern on his milky skin.

"Let me see *you*, I need these *off*," he said, tugging now at Jim's shirt so that two of the buttons flew off: *ping ping*. "I want you inside me, I can't wait for you to fuck me—"

"Me?" He teased, shrugging out of his shirt, not wanting to displace Seth from his lap even though it was to get rid of his trousers. "But I thought *you* were going to—" The dismay that flitted across Seth's face made Jim laugh and pull him into a reassuring embrace. Into his ear he whispered, "How about taking turns once in a while, can you cope with that?"

"I can cope," Seth burbled, "for you—with *anything*. God, you've made me so miserable, waiting for you. Oh, I hate you. *Clothes off now.*"

He hadn't undressed this way before a novel audience in years. Aware of Seth's penetrating attention, he yanked and fumbled at his fastenings. His fingers had gone all thick, along with his ideas, and for one dreadful second he thought, flying in the face of all the contrary evidence, *I can't do this.*

Not being his own type, Jim used to joke that he was, for men who liked that kind of thing, the kind of thing they liked. Yet, in spite of everything Seth had done and said up until now, he still wasn't sure until, yanking his undershirt off, he heard Seth's yelp of delight. "You've sent me a real *man.* Thank you, Jesus!"

Sight of his solid bare brawn, the swart skin overlaid with black hair that grew in straight diagonals like a pelt, thickest on his chest and trailing down to another proliferation around his dark heavy cock, seemed to make Seth stupid. He stared, swaying a little, caressing himself absently.

The bed was enormous; Seth was too far away. Jim lunged for him; the gold condom packets scattered across the quilt like the remnants of Zeus's visit to Danaë, sticking to their bodies as they rolled back and forth.

Urgent to devour him all at once, to see and feel and taste all of him, Jim wanted to start at the bony callused feet, tracing each toe with his tongue, but wished for more hands, more mouths, so as to simultaneously feed on Seth's lips, on his cock, tits, hands, ass.

Seth shuddered, coming up from Jim's kisses like a drowner. "Can't we do this *after?* Please—I need—*now*—"

Seeing that it cost him something to plead, still amazed that Seth hadn't taken his twitchy, itchy self to another man's bed, Jim didn't want to tease him.

But, reaching for a gold circlet, he froze. The meaning of this crashed down on him: the Zak part of his life, until now merely on hold, would be over as soon as he had another man. Fucking Seth would make Zak truly dead.

"What?" Seth said. "Look at me, I'm *here*."

"God, you are."

"So stay with me."

"Right. How do you want to take it?" He pressed the circlet into Seth's hand.

"On my back . . . kiss me while you fuck me . . . I want you all around me while you're in me—"

He lifted Seth's legs into the air; carefully kissed each tight calf, though the boy grunted a protest at this frippery ahead of the *one thing*. But it wasn't teasing, he thought, not to squeeze the dear legs as he hefted them, not to caress slowly with lubed fingers that tight pucker that flinched, then flexed to engulf him. Seth threw his head back in a silent howl, hands scrabbling then clutching at the bedclothes, as Jim's cock prodded his balls, rubbed against the stretched perineum, then the ass.

Seth cried out when he entered him, struggling with a blind confounded look, until Jim realized he wanted not to get away, but to be gathered closer. This tore at his heart, because it was raw, an animal's distress; it stopped only when Jim was buried in him to the hilt, Seth's legs tightly clasped around his back.

Seth's whole body pulsed around Jim's cock; he swallowed hard, licking his lips, and when Jim leaned in closer, his breaths came short and hot against his own mouth. He kissed him and felt the same pulse in his heated lips, an excited mute thrumming.

"All right? Comfortable?"

Beneath him, doubled like an acrobat, Seth demanded, in a cascade of stuttered *effs*, that Jim *move*.

They picked up a rhythm, their breaths quickening, sawing, sweat forming, then flying. Seth wrapped his legs tighter and tighter around Jim's back. Then, head thrown back, Seth laughed, a reflexive bubbly outpouring that acted on Jim like fingers delicately tracing his spine: he shivered, flushed, his balls crawled. He forgot how long it had been since he'd done this, and simply did it.

After his long famished time, he finished quickly and dropped like a stone. How *exhausted* he felt, after what was, after all, so brief.

Seth, puppyish, was crawling across him now, nuzzling, sipping up the sweat from his drenched skin. His cock grazed Jim wetly here and there; still erect. He closed his hand around it, but Seth switched it away.

"Want to come with you inside me."

"I don't think so, Skeezix. Not for a while, anyway."

"Skeezix? Who's that?" Seth grinned.

"That's you. It just popped into my head. It's you." He reached for Seth's cock again. "Let me suck you off."

"No, let *me*—" With a grin, as if bursting with some desirable secret, he bent his head. And, to Jim's astonishment, made it happen. The delirious sight of him with his mouth full almost made Jim spill. But Seth knew what he was doing and what he wanted, and managed it all.

The second time was much slower, more wriggle than thrust, and they took it lying down: Seth flat on his belly, Jim covering him from shoulder to toe, mouthing the gladioli tattoo on his shoulder blade, talking happy nonsense into his ear. Seth caught his moist hand and kissed it, pressed the palm to his face to inhale its aroma like a bouquet, sucked on the fingers. Jim drew his hand away only to push it beneath Seth's belly, to grasp his cock where it was trapped against the mattress, and milk it until he came.

Later, sprawled with him in a tangle of limbs, Jim understood the saying about getting your clock cleaned. His, that had been stopped, was ticking again, keeping time.

They carved out a refuge in the space of their ordinary lives, four uninterrupted days where they both shirked everything else and settled into each other. Seth had no classes on Friday or Monday; he phoned in sick to his job on Friday morning, but only after much hesitation and Jim pinning him to the bed, saying, "That prick Mazzoti doesn't deserve you. Tell him you can't assist him today because you are assisting *me*."

Switching day for night, Jim read aloud from *Up in the Old Hotel* in bed at four in the morning, Seth listening hard as he sucked on a cigarette. Four in the afternoon found them sleeping heavily like hibernating bears. In their underwear they slow-danced to smoochy Astrid Gilberto tunes. (It was Seth who exhibited a quirky, touching modesty. He wore, Jim was charmed to see, waffle-weave boxer briefs, and put them on every time he was going to cross the bedroom threshold.) Some late seventies porn tapes Jim fished from the back of a closet sent Seth into a torrent of nervous snickering at the hair and clothes and cheesy music, even as his cock throbbed and finally thrummed against his belly until Jim captured it in his mouth. Seth drew Jim over and over in his sketchbook, and Jim, squinting and nibbling at the end of the pencil, tried to make drawings of Seth. They devoured heaps of scrambled eggs with fried kosher salami directly from the skillet, ordered in enormous amounts of Chinese food, drank wine from each other's mouths.

Thirsts arose to be quenched. Bodies existed to be tenderly mauled. Long, circuitous conversations trailed off in agreement and kisses. The sensual abundance of Jim's world, which was easygoing and free of scorekeeping, not like Charlie's at all, made Seth feel like a child, but not himself as a child. Rather some child pasha, fabulously indulged. He was both more relaxed than he'd been since infancy *and* more keyed-up. Pleasure building upon pleasure was for him an edgy proposition; like an overtired toddler who resists the necessary nap, he was aware of repressing a kind of desperation. He couldn't convince himself that he deserved so much goodness—not just the goodness of scented bathwater, abundant delicious food, without an instant ramen noodle or lentil in sight, smooth cool sheets—but the pinch-me quality of knowing Jim wanted him there. But for how long? Each new sensual delight made Seth think of how he'd feel when he was back on Stanton Street. His whole experience had toughened him for life in that tub-in-the-kitchen flat; everything Jim exposed him to, from the silky shaving cream that smelled of lavender, to his full attention when they whispered together, heads on one pillow, was unfitting him for that life. His real life. After yearning so long for that attention, having it frightened as much as it thrilled him. In the midst of the most engrossing lovemaking during that long weekend, he caught himself wishing to go off alone, to clutch his happiness like a secret. But whenever he started to dress, Jim claimed him again, and he learned quickly that he could not resist those hands on his body.

"You shouldn't have reawakened me if you weren't ready to stick around and take it," Jim said with a wolfish smile.

There was no question in his mind of not doing whatever Jim required of him. The more he demanded, the more he sheathed his tenderness in force, the deeper Seth's ecstasy went.

When he'd thought about what an authentic connection with another man would be, he'd not understood how many pulse points it would contain, how it would stretch and reshape itself from moment to moment, change face and form and odor. His imaginings had been too static, too one-sided, to encompass this dizzying reality. He'd thought in advance of the enormity of placing himself at Jim's disposal, but Jim's own mutable, humorous, vulnerable lightness-and-darkness had not occurred to him. The expression he caught in his eyes sometimes, when he thought Seth's glance was elsewhere, made him quiver.

Pillow talk was a minefield: eager to know him to the depths, Jim asked so many questions. Seth flashed on young Barnacle in *Little Dorrit*, his monocle flying out of his eye, wailing, "You mustn't say you want to know, you know!" Jim's questions, like Clennam's, were not about tonnage. Regretting his original lie, loath to embroider it further, he retreated behind an assumption of sorrow: He could not talk much about his family, his home life, it was all still too raw. His large features clenched in concern, Jim nodded, solemn, accepting. *Maybe sometime, you'll want to tell me about it. . . .*

How much easier it was, blissfully easy, to loll back and listen to Jim tell about his own childhood. What he insisted was *ordinary* and *suburban* smacked of the most Byzantine exotica to Seth: boyhood summers at a crowded Nassau County cabana club, roughhousing with Zak in a glittering pool stuffed with other shrieking children while their mothers played endless games of mah-jongg with two other women, their long painted fingernails, gold necklaces against tanned skin, and oversized dark glasses glittering in the sun. Countless weekend trips to the city with Zak and the mothers to troop lazily through museums, to try on hats in Saks, to eat fancy multilayered sandwiches and drink iced coffee at the Charleston Gardens restaurant in Altman's. Being the bar-mitzvah boy in a Nehru jacket, with the eagerly seized opportunity to get looped afterward on kosher wine while the grown-ups all conveniently looked the other way. Jim apologized at first for Zak's omnipresence in all his stories.

"It's simply that he was always there. It could have been hell, if we'd disliked each other—constantly thrown together with him because our mothers couldn't get enough of each other."

"But it wasn't like that," Seth said.

"No, obviously it wasn't. Zak and I clicked from the start, just like Miriam and my mother did."

"So . . . what was the story with Miriam and your mother?" Seth already knew that the two widows had, before their deaths, shared a house together in Boca Raton.

"If you're asking me did they sleep together—you dirty-minded thing!—this is my *mother* we're talking about! The two of them had one of those unfussy, enduring friendships women are so good at. I really believe that's all, although that's not to diminish it, a friendship like that is an apotheosis. Do you know what that is?"

Seth snorted. "Yes, I know what that is."

"Don't get snippy with me," he said, pinching him. "I wouldn't say that my parents' marriage, or Miriam and Irv's, was any grand passion, but neither do I see any other stillborn story there."

Any other stillborn story. The phrase arrested Seth's thoughts, sent them off away from Jim, whose shoulder his head rested on. How often he'd pursued that *one* stillborn story, the one that began, instead of ending, with his father. If his father had lived . . . it was a story his sister had told herself, and him, in such detail he almost believed it, that substituting one husband for another would have made their mother a different mother, their childhoods like other people's. And then there was the second stillborn story: had his last name started with a different letter, he'd not have been assigned to Mr. Hecklin's guidance list, and would almost certainly not now find himself, a graduate student, a serious painter, here in Jim Glaser's bed. How much in his life was due to the peculiarities of random chance! And extraordinary that chance had, without expectation, jumped its malign banks and pooled for him in pleasant places. The work he'd done, the effort he'd made, to bring himself here was nothing to Seth; he did not credit it. None of this life was earned . . . one did not earn chance. One merely, Seth believed, submitted to it.

At the end of a naked, mostly horizontal day (the exception being when Seth hung from the chinning bar in the closet doorway, both grunting like power lifters to finish before his biceps exploded), they took a bath together. Jim's tub would have been ample for three men. Seth had never had a bubble bath before, but decided this was something to keep to himself. Settling back with Jim in the fragrant water, he listened with abstracted interest to the noises the bubbles made, tiny worlds forming and dying all around him.

Jim sighed and sank down up to his chin. "I haven't had so much sex since the last days of disco."

Seth thought, *And I haven't had so much since the last days of Cleon Nash*. Cleon, who'd taught him physical pleasure with another man and accepted the wild gusts of love that pleasure generated, was a black satin giant, infinitely smooth and commanding; with him everything had happened fast. Wild, not subtle, with the manic pacing of a TV commercial, where the setup and the climax tagged each other closely, but there was another one and another one and another one right behind it. At their height they'd jumped each other's bones all night, not wanting sleep, making comebacks that seemed spectacular to them even though they were only twenty.

Whereas with Jim, events unfurled more slowly. After that first impetuous bout, he proved adept at getting the absolute most out of every erection before its delirious destruction. He was teaching Seth the ecstasy of patience. As when, not permitting Seth to touch himself, he'd licked his asshole, slowly, almost idly, on and on until Seth writhed, arching his back, begging for it harder, deeper, then pleaded over and over that he was ready to be fucked. Jim licked without ceasing, without rush, seemingly unimpressed with the escalation of frantic incoherent noises he made as he fell to pieces, his whole body gone soft except for his cock, which was harder than it had ever been, until finally he was keening wordlessly into the pillow, sobbing into the abyss Jim had opened inside him. And when Jim put his legs over his shoulders and drove into him, he was so perfectly filled up that he cried out and shot without anything even touching his cock, and went on speaking in tongues until he was erect again, Jim pressing into him all the while, gripping his legs tightly with both hands and giving him his own musky taste back in kisses. Leaving him exhausted and speechless with amazement at what his body had just accomplished.

Now in the bath, he thought Jim might be asleep. His eyes were closed. So he whispered, "That was really unsafe, what you did just now. Wasn't it? Your tongue in my ass." He felt this needed to be acknowledged, but hoped Jim wouldn't hear him.

Jim stirred, his big hand coming up slowly from the water, to crown him with a garland of bubbles. "More for you than for me, I think, and I'm sure I'm negative."

"But you don't know anything about me."

"It's true, God help me, I don't." He smiled with half a mouth, and closed his eyes again.

"No one's ever done that to me before. It was . . . it was sublime. But you shouldn't have just . . ."

"That's right, I shouldn't have. But I wanted to, and I thought you deserved it."

"Oh, jeez."

"Oh, jeez indeed."

Seth sat up in the water, shivering when the cold air touched his wet shoulders. "Well, it's lucky for you then, isn't it, that I went and got tested. Right after I first met you."

"It doesn't mean anything if you've been with anybody since."

"But I told you already that I haven't. I want there to be nothing between us—only skin—I don't want you to fuck anybody but me—I want it to be just us two, but no limits—promise me, promise!" In his enthusiasm Seth sent bubbles splashing up into their faces. Jim wiped his off with the heel of his hand, and smiled through half-closed eyes.

"Ah, aren't you sweet."

That little bit of condescension rankled, but he could see in Jim's expression that it was all right, that he'd done nothing wrong by allowing himself that outburst.

"I'm glad now that we waited. But I still think we didn't have to wait so long."

"I did the best I could."

Seth laid his cheek on Jim's heat-slicked shoulder. "I know you did." Then, "When I used to trick, I always thought it was supposed to be fun, breezy, light. I think it's light for other guys. Isn't it? But for me, sex never is. It's heavy. Before, or during, or after . . . the heaviness always catches up to me."

Jim was quiet long enough for him to regret venturing this confidence. He never wanted to present himself as the difficult person he knew he was. Then Jim's eyes opened. "Is this . . . what we're doing . . . too much for you? Does it make you sad?"

"No—you're the man I've been waiting . . . I mean . . . with you, I feel secure, so I can . . . this is the best sex I've ever had. . . ." He trailed off in stammers, dropping his gaze.

"Ah, well." Jim smiled. "It must be because *you* inspired me, then."

Seth sat up fast, the bubbles clinging to his wet skin, and slid around, maneuvering. "You're inspiring *me*, right now—"

"What—oh—"

"This is what you want, isn't it?" He grinned. "Me to get inside you?"

Seth watched Jim's face open up as he shifted to help him find his target. With one uncontrolled jerk of his arm, Jim sent half a dozen Kiehl's bottles toppling from the tub rim to disappear beneath the bubbles. Buoyed by the water, his big body almost floated in Seth's lap, mass without weight; easy to manipulate. Seth shoved the bubbles off to the sides, he needed to see where he was. Though he'd done his share of topping, it was always with guys as young and slender as himself. He'd never, in all his anticipatory fantasizing about Jim, imagined this *reversal*. It *felt* like a reversal of the natural order of things, almost absurd, like a Jack Russell attempting a mastiff. But that made it hotter, it was awesome to see Jim's eyes glaze over, because he was fucking him. Jim's cock, when he grabbed it in the water, was like a big slimy fish, it jumped in his hand. It was difficult to get purchase on anything; water and bubbles were sloshing everywhere, and more and more of the bath things arrayed on the tub's wide edges were now in the water with them. Jim's groans reverberated off the tiled walls and ceiling. For a moment, remembering his first impression of him back at Tony's loft, the big, slow Robert Mitchum-man in the important suit, Seth almost froze with wonder. *Here I am fucking him. Here I am with him. Jesus Christ, here I am having what I wanted for once in my piss-poor life.* Head swimming with the improbability of it all, he came.

7

Seth's eyes sprang open upon pitch blackness. Above the convulsing of his own heart, he heard the chirruping of insects outside the cabin, faint lapping of the lake, the wind stirring the treetops. The stink of dried sweat and semen filled his nostrils. The Coleman lantern must have gone out. Or they'd put it out. Where were they? Throat too swollen and parched to make a sound, he tried to wrest his sore wrists free of the damp metal cot frame—

And his arms came easily from beneath the pillows where he'd jammed them in his sleep. Like a page turning, he returned to the knowledge of where he was. No katydids trilled in Noho, the lapping of the water was only Jim breathing in his sleep. The weight he bore was Jim's leg hooked over his thigh, his arm across his back. The cabin was faraway. Hundreds of miles and eight whole years.

Seth struggled for breath, sobs rolling up his throat. He'd clung to the belief that this *thing* wouldn't follow him into the bed of any man he really trusted. And surely passion was the most powerful sorcery. It ought to protect him if nothing else could. And hadn't he, in the past nights, slept in Jim's arms without a single ripple of unease? A positive miracle, staying under for hours, remembering no dreams, awakening happy with a hard-on pulsing in Jim's glowing grip? He'd dared to think he was rid of it.

. . .

Sweat trickling from his hairline and armpits, he leaned against the wall of glass at the front of the loft, and dragged on a cigarette, looking down into the empty, brightly lit street.

At this hour, there was nothing between him and the nausea that arose not from the gut, but from that tight spot between the eyes.

It's all right, it's all right. Forcing his breathing to slow, he scanned down the length of his body, which was not the one he'd had back then—scrawny, vulnerable, pathetic. He'd changed it—shaped and marked it himself: the neat potent muscles, the tattoos and piercings, all there by his will alone, to assert his dominion over himself.

With his fingertips, he wiped the sweat from around his hairline, sampled the aroma of his armpits, which was always oddly comforting and more so the sharper it was, then wiped his hands against his thighs. The body was all right. He liked it. Jim liked it. All right.

But for how much longer?

Jim expected him to be at home here; he'd said it often enough to dissuade Seth from asking permission to look in the refrigerator, or help himself to towels, or take books down from the shelves. *All these things are for you, too,* he'd say. The loft and everything in it was all about a kind of life too foreign to him to just step into and pull up around him like a pair of jeans left puddled on the floor. Nothing here belonged to him. This was an adult place, a place that two men had made together while he was still back in Nebraska wondering when his pubes would sprout. In the silvery glow from the street the space looked even more alien; the congregation on the piano might be whispering among themselves about this interloper who would probably soon be gone.

Opening the central window on its pivot, Seth tossed his cigarette into the street. When he'd closed it again, a movement caught his eye in the loft opposite, its facade flattened by the streetlight. There was a woman, around his age, and naked, too, standing close to the glass, skin silvered in the streetlight glow.

She waved. With hesitation, Seth waved back. It was somewhere around four in the morning, there was almost no traffic on the snippet of Broadway he could see from where he stood. No lights on in the surrounding windows. Just this girl, and him, eyeing each other across a cobbled street.

She put her two hands flat together, laying them against her tilted cheek in a pantomime of sleep, then pointed to herself, and at him, and shrugged. Seth shrugged back, an exaggerated gesture she wouldn't misinterpret. She put her hand against the window, palm flat, fingers spread, and Seth did the same, thinking of how, in prison movies, the convict and his girlfriend always tried to touch hands like that through the Plexiglas barrier. Then she stepped over to the big desk near the window, picked up a marker, and began to write. In a moment she held a big sheet of sketch paper up against the glass. *Man's asleep. Feel lonely.* And there was a phone number.

The cordless was nearby. Without pausing to consider whether he wanted to do this or not, Seth held it up so she could see it, entered the number. She answered so quickly he knew no ring had sounded on her end.

"Well, hello." Her voice, languid, low, held a trace of the South in its vowels. "This is crazy, but I was so glad to see you there."

Seth was still quivering from the heart.

"Are you okay?"

"Yeah. It's just I . . . he was snoring, I couldn't settle down, and then, y'know, I got to *thinking*." She gasped out a self-deprecating laugh. "He . . . oh, you don't want to hear—"

"No, I do," Seth said, suddenly involved. "What?"

"He's . . . my college roommate's *dad*. Is that sick or what? I mean, she and I aren't close friends or anything now we've graduated, but *still*. Sometimes I'm like, what am I doing?"

"D'you like him?"

She glanced over her shoulder into the darkness. "Hmm. I don't always do things because I think I'll like it. I do it for the experience, y'know? What about you?" she asked. "You like yours?"

"Very much." He paused. "Nobody's ever been so sweet to me before."

"Oh, mine's *sweet*, I guess." The way she said it sucked all meaning from the word. The delicacy of his feelings went ashy under her scrutiny. "It's just—you look at him sometimes, and you think, shoot, he could be my dad. Yours, too, right?"

The pressure of her assumptions pummeled him through the phone. "What makes you so sure he's a he?"

"Come *on*. I've seen you both before. You hang around here in the house of windows long enough, you see just about everything. Plus, we've got binoculars."

Jim, too, kept a pair of binoculars on the piano, so Seth made no comment, but he ran the last week's activities back through his mind from the perspective of how they might look from her vantage point, and blushed. Not all the good stuff had happened in the bedroom.

"So, you were saying, about yours? Being of quite an advanced age, like one's venerable papa?" she prompted.

"He's only forty. Well, forty-two. But he's . . . nothing like my . . . I don't really have a father, anyway."

"Oh," she said. "That's tough, I guess. Still, probably saves on therapy bills that way! Unless you can get him to pay them, like I do. I figure he owes me at least that much." She shifted her weight from one foot to another. For a moment, her left breast was pressed flat against the glass. Seth had drawn dozens of different naked women in life classes, without a glimmer of physical interest, but now . . . there was something about her, sophisticated in her twenty-five going on eternal way. He was intimidated by her, but he felt it in his balls, a stirring. Like, if she touched them, something would happen. Something that would leave her feeling triumphant and him denuded and dizzy. For a moment he could imagine, with a vision too clear, what went on between her and the college pal's father—jockeying for the upper hand. . . . It was what went on behind most of the windows he could see from where he stood. New York was so full of sharp-edged people, and if you weren't sharp-edged yourself, they'd cut you to ribbons before you knew where you were. Under a thin veneer of decency that could tear at a word, there was nothing but the terrible dark.

"So," she said, "why aren't you curled up in bed with Papa Bear?"

Wishing he'd never started this, he plucked at the first evasion that occurred to him. "I woke up with that weird sort of feeling that I'd left the iron on."

"The *iron?*" Her eyes widened, then she shrugged. "And then you figured you were up, so you might as well have a smoke."

"Yeah."

"And give a little innocent thrill to the girls across the street."

"I didn't know you'd be there."

"Are you a dancer?"

"A dancer?"

"You've got that sort of body."

"What are you?" he asked.

"What *am* I?" She laughed, and put her hand through her hair. She had the kind of sharp face that turned straight guys' heads. "Some people might say I'm a wicked chick, and some would describe me as an associate financial analyst, and my mom would say I'm her little girl."

"And what would the guy—the guy whose apartment you're in—what would he say you are?"

"Oh, I think he'd decline to say."

"Because you know," Seth murmured. "You know what you are."

"I hope we all know who we are. I think I know about *you*."

"You don't know anything about me."

"Boyo, I see everything you've got there. All your stock in trade."

"You don't fucking know—"

"Does *he?*" She jerked her chin, to indicate Jim asleep in the back bedroom. "Not that he cares. You know *that*, of course."

That hot night at the lake, which was over and gone and yet

never over and gone, was in some small but real way like how this woman spoke to him, because she was trying to show him he was nothing, and seemed to feel no shame.

"We are at the age of experiences," she said. "We're taking experiences like some people take drugs." She paused. "Of course, we're probably also taking drugs."

"Don't say *we*. There's no goddamn we. Your dad pays your therapy bills . . . where you talk about what it supposedly does to your head, fucking your friend's father whom you don't even like? That how it works for you, that experience?"

Her dark hair tumbled over one eye. "*You* are asking me? What's *your* price, pretty boy? What's your going rate?"

Seth hit the off button on the phone, fumbled at the heavy cord that controlled the front blinds to shut her out. Then he sat on the sofa in the dark, his head between his legs, trying to pull his swirling thoughts out of the shit.

In the morning, Seth did not respond when Jim touched his shoulder, or even when he kissed it. Putting an ear down to his mouth, Jim felt the breath going in and out. This close, he could see the flicker of his dreaming eyes behind the white, closed lids.

Already Jim was forming a catalogue of his looks and manners, to think of which suffused his skin and mind with warmth. The idea of Seth's well-articulated hands, his belly so white he could trace a blue vein past his little pierced navel, his eel of an ass—electric and wriggling—made him achingly hard. Two years of nothing and now he felt as though he could fuck for days without stopping.

What, Jim wondered, would he be doing now if this hadn't happened? In the months after Zak died he'd often thought, with a bitterness barely contained by shredding sanity, of what the pair of them would have been doing had Zak still been there. Here was the flip side of that coin: making an inventory of the loneliness that was already feeling like something that belonged to someone else. Jim was one of those people who can't remember, in winter, what it really *feels* like to walk down a sweltering street. Now he couldn't quite get a handle on the tangibility of his solitude. *And why,* he thought, *should I? Why dwell on it?* He'd rather dwell on Seth. He'd rather dwell *in* Seth.

In another moment he was starting to do just that. When touched, Seth sighed and shifted onto his side, presenting a clear field. He did not stir when Jim kissed down his spine, nor when he caressed the dark pucker with a lubed finger. With his left hand wrapped around Seth's morning erection, Jim inched into him. He'd always liked being awakened this way himself, so wasn't ready for Seth's shriek or the sharp jab in the ribs. The boy rolled and disappeared as, with a bang and clatter, the lamp and all the books on the nightstand crashed to the floor with him.

"Owwwww! *Shitfuckpiss!*"

"Jesus! Are you all right?"

"All that crap fell on my head. *Shit*—" Seth jerked clear of his reach to crouch on the floor, holding his head in his hands. Jim got down on the floor, too, and tried to see into Seth's face.

"I'm sorry I scared you."

Seth ducked his gaze. "I wasn't scared."

Why deny it? Jim thought. It was like shrieking *ouch!* and then maintaining you weren't in pain.

"I. Wasn't. Scared." Seth repeated.

"If you *insist.*"

"I just prefer to be awake when—you shouldn't assume my consent—"

"I'm sorry. We're too new together for that kind of thing."

"It's got nothing to do with new or old. Just don't try to get over on me in my goddamn sleep, okay? Easy to remember!"

"Seth, there's no need to talk to me like that, I'm not disputing you."

He shrugged, shrank, muttered, "Sorry." Then sprang up, suddenly antic. "I'm hungry. Aren't you hungry? I'd like about two gallons of coffee and a hundred pancakes." As he spoke, he was hopping on one foot, getting his underwear on. Jim stayed where he was and watched him whirl into his clothes. "I'll cook. You wanna come watch, or are you going to sit there like a—"

"You get started," he said quietly. "I'll take a shower."

Beneath the hot spray, Jim stretched. He wasn't sure what had just happened, but it left him feeling hollowed out and bleak. Whenever he crashed into one of the corners of Seth's personality—or painted himself into one, more like—he was left with this dismay. Other men were unknowable, because other men were not Zak.

The door opened; he saw, through the distortions of the plastic shower curtain, Seth's white form. Naked again. He peeked around the edge of the curtain, then climbed into the tub.

"I thought you were making breakfast."

"I will. Do you still want me?"

"What do you mean do I still want you? No, I never want you again. Don't be ridiculous."

"Have me right now." Seth's hand encircled his soap-slicked cock, working it erect; he turned to present his back, watching Jim's face over his shoulder, bracing an arm against a corner of the wall.

"Seth—"

"Don't talk—do it." He thrust out his ass. "Fast, come on. Without thinking."

"Seth—"

"Come *on!*"

This wasn't a moment to hesitate. Driving into him, he shoved Seth against the wall, lifting him by main force off his feet. Seth let out a bleat and stiffened all over, his hands scrabbling uselessly for purchase on the slick tiles, then grabbing on to the showerhead as if he was trying to scale the wall and escape. But in the next moment he gasped, "Yeah, don't stop. Take me hard. Fucking do it—"

· · ·

Seth poured the coffee, but he didn't sit, drinking it instead over the kitchen counter, a cigarette in hand. Jim regarded him; his wet hair, gray circles under his eyes, innocent now of makeup, the stipple of beard stubble that was so fine it felt more like velvet than bristle against his own cheek.

"Why did you want me to hurt you just now?"

"You didn't hurt me."

"Don't argue with me. I did. We all like that sometimes, it isn't *that* I'm questioning. . . ."

"Then what *are* you questioning?"

Why the slow, tender fuck I wanted to awaken you with was wrong, but insisting I go into you like a pile driver when you clearly weren't ready was all right. Christ, I'm overthinking this. I just said it, we all like it rough sometimes.

Seth rounded the edge of the counter, but came no closer. "I love it when you're so gentle with me, but you know, I also love it that you're enormous compared to me. I think you hold back too much. There's other ways to get me to surrender than by all that slow hyp-notic stuff. Although that's fantastic, it is, I've never had that before. But I like being overwhelmed sometimes."

"Surrender? I didn't know that's what I'm trying to get you to do. I thought. . . ." He glanced up from his coffee cup, his vantage shift-ing once more. "Is that what you fantasize about? Submission?"

Seth shrugged nervously, and there was that blush, the eyes dart-ing and dipping. "Yeah, just . . . just, not with everybody, not with anybody but *you* really, but . . ." His breath caught, and suddenly he was sobbing.

Jim went to him. After one feeble jerk of resistance, Seth folded against him. "What's wrong?" Jim crooned. "What's wrong? I knew there was something. . . ."

Seth shook his head.

"There is. Tell me. I did hurt you. Tell me."

"No." A more violent headshake. "Not you. Never you."

"Then what?"

"Nothing. Just . . . last night I . . . had a bad dream."

"Oh. What was it? About your parents? The fire? Tell me your dream, Seth, it'll be easier."

"Yes . . . about that . . . forget it . . . I'm okay now." He was still sobbing, and in no hurry to be turned loose. They swayed together to the rhythm of Seth's choked breaths.

When Jim suggested they go back to bed, Seth followed agreeably. Jim eased him back onto the pillow and stretched out beside him. Seth fell asleep at once, as if weeping was a drug; his face smoothed out, regained its poise. His own eyelids were heavy, but he held them open, tracing the outline of Seth's profile in the gray gloom. *With what grace,* he thought, *twenty-three took storms; their violence passed over and left no lasting mark. A bad quarter hour and done.*

Twenty-three. And at forty-three, would Seth remember this, and how? While lying beside what man, or alone, or in what city, what country? Would twenty years find them still in these same places in this same bed . . . ? No, he wouldn't start down that path, not now. When a week had turned into a year, perhaps. If it did.

Meanwhile he was thankful for this much. Most thankful, amid all Seth's vital bounty, for being allowed to kiss the tears from his face. Fucking could be bought. But an approach to another's frank, unstinted grief could not, and that made it wholly precious.

In the weeks that followed, Jim continued to find his work at the agency pointless, but now it felt funny pointless, rather than tragically pointless; he tolerated it with good humor and no longer fretted about wasting his time. Everyone there noticed the lift in his spirits; he fielded many friendly questions about what had come over him.

Still, he postponed speaking to his friends. This wasn't difficult; he realized now how isolated he'd become in the last year. Without actual renunciations or quarrels, many friends had simply stopped staying in touch. Jim supposed this happened to many widowers; he was glad for it now. Eventually he'd show Seth what remained of his social circle, but it was better, in these early stages, to withhold that added pressure. What friends he had left, Jim felt, wouldn't take easily to the appearance of such a young man in his life.

Mornings, instead of heading off to the gym with an empty stomach, they sat down to breakfast together. Seth had gone back to wearing his nose ring, which Jim now found almost unbearably sexy, and revealed a pair of thick black-rimmed reading glasses he'd never brought out when they were still only dating. Half-naked at the table, still disordered from bed, eyes fixed on a novel, Seth crammed toast into his mouth. From behind the pages of the *Times*, Jim watched him, his pleasure undiminished morning after morning. Seeing Seth in such casual dishabille reminded Jim of David Copperfield's delight in learning that his Dora put her hair in curlpapers. The sight of Seth, unshaven, without eyeliner, his hair sticking up, gave Jim heartsease.

For his part, Seth settled in to his improved circumstances with what seemed like relative smoothness. He was full of conversation and laughter, with a constant lubricious gleam in his eye. His mouth was rosier, eyes more liquid. The few pounds he put on eating three squares a day suited him, made him sleeker. He smelled of turpentine and Lava soap and the baby shampoo he used on his hair, and sometimes of photographic chemicals, although he wore different clothes to work and paint, and washed as scrupulously as a coal miner at the end of the day.

In bed, he was manically active and at the same time majestically serene. He did everything Jim wanted, and brought in all sorts of new things Jim hadn't known he'd wanted.

Once, he took lewd Polaroids of himself and had them delivered to Jim's office by messenger, then turned up there at lunchtime and fucked him across his big marble-topped desk. Another time, Jim came home from work to find Seth, looking amazingly feminine and pretty in a white silk sheath evening dress and a long blond wig, eyelids painted blue, teetering on high-heeled slides. And a week after that, dressed in elaborate geisha drag he did not take off, absolutely silent and servile, he left Jim's cock and belly smeared with red and white greasepaint. He admitted afterward that Hannah had arranged the borrowing of this costume.

These games were the acting out of passion, rather than the passion itself, which they kept, as if by mutual agreement, for odd moments, when, overcome by some look or word or tilt of the head, they flung themselves together without forethought. It was then, or in the very early mornings when Seth woke him, demanding attention in the dark, that they whispered things to each other they'd have been too shy to repeat aloud in the broad light of day. By contrast, Seth's tableaux, as Jim called them, were just breezy, inventive fun. He didn't expect them to last, and he didn't, somehow, even count them as instances of lovemaking per se. They were Seth's equivalent of standing on his hands for him, saying, *Lookit lookit lookit!* It made them happy.

8

Seth had only one intimate friend in New York, a young woman he had met five minutes after arriving at his college dormitory, ragged from almost three days on various long-distance buses. She stood in the doorway of the opposite room, a bottle of Diet Coke in her hand, and watched him drag his duffel up the stairs and fumble the key into the room lock.

His first impression of her was of a fat woman with orange hair and no eyebrows. When he knew her well, Hannah turned out to be beautiful in a primal fleshy way that did not photograph. She had the large, distinct, slightly blank features of a Roman statue. Her fingers were pale and articulated, they made him think of her bones beneath the transparent skin.

As he opened the door to his new room, she said to some unseen third person, "*Someone* needs a haircut."

Here in this strange place for five minutes, and already encountering the famous rudeness of Northeasterners.

But there was no one else there, and when he met her gaze, she stepped forward.

"This place crawls with hippies, Deadheads, and other patheticos, but obviously you're not one, so you've got to lose the hair." Reaching up, she yanked on one greasy gray hank of it that was swinging into his eyes. "Yeesh. Boyo, you need a lot of advice. That's my first bit." Following him into his room, she stood back while he chose which of the identical beds to swing his bag onto, then sat on the other one.

"I got here yesterday and I'm so fucking bored that I will say *anything*. This is my third year. I don't want to be here, but my father wouldn't let me go to a real art school, and I didn't get in at Yale. And if you're thinking I look a little old to be a college junior, it's because I am. I'm twenty-four and I have a past."

Seth grabbed the soda, ignored her aggrieved "*Hey!*" and drank it down. "Thirsty boy. Why the gray hair?"

"Just lucky I guess."

"I'm Hannah."

"Seth."

"My boyfriend doesn't show up until tomorrow, the skunk. We could have dinner."

Seth said, "I'm gay." He'd never said it out loud before. No thunderclap sounded. Hannah didn't even blink. He said it again. "I'm gay."

"I said we could have dinner. If I'd meant we could have *sex*, I'd have said so. Relax. We eat at six, I'll knock for you on my way down."

That evening, she asked to see his portfolio, a word that seemed entirely too dignified for the sheaf of photographic prints and drawings he kept in a big manila envelope. She spread them out on the bed, turning them over until she'd absorbed them all. Seth kept a tense bead on her big, placid mouth and the eyes that observed so fully.

Finally she straightened up. "You know how to look at things fresh. The rest you'll learn. You'll do all right." Glancing around at him, she winced. "God, that *hair*. Don't they have barbershops in whatever Podunk you come from? Don't move, I'm getting my scissors."

She cut his hair. She gave him books. They compared notes on men and the hellishness and wonder of sex. The handful of years she had on him added to her glamour and mystery. She didn't date other undergraduates; her boyfriends were young instructors at the other colleges in the valley, local cops, slacker bartenders. There were a lot of woman friends, too, who treated Seth fondly, like a mascot; when Hannah was off with them, he imagined they were carrying out enigmatic female rites he wasn't privileged to be let in on.

She drove him to Boston and New York and walked him through art museums and galleries, talking, talking, talking. Even as bulky as she was, Hannah was a terrific dancer. When she shimmied to old soul records, there was no question that every ounce worked for her. They danced. He heard Lightnin' Hopkins and Garnett Mimms for the first time on her stereo, saw movies by Fellini and Kurosawa at her side. They stayed up late, smoking and discussing their lives. During the unstructured January days of Winter Term, their confidences devolved into a late-night game Hannah dubbed Family Hells I Have Known, which they played all of one long stoned Sunday.

In a haze of fragrant smoke, Hannah began it: "Family Hells I Have Known. Round one. My bat mitzvah party. Picture it. Banquet room at the Waldorf. Two hundred guests, relatives and my father's business associates, everyone dressed to the nines. Months of preparation on my part. Ceremony went off without a hitch, I'm up there singing Torah to the masses, feeling like a rose. Then at the party, I'm running around with a pack of my friends, getting congratulated, collecting presents, doing the hors d'oeuvre thing. And my father stomps up to me in the middle of a crowd of people by the buffet and says in his marvelous carrying voice, 'Your mother could barely pack your fat tuchus into that dress, do you really think you need to eat any *more* today?' You could've heard a pin drop. I didn't quite make it to the ladies' room before I started blubbering."

"Shit. Sorry."

"Hey, the rules of this game—which I'm making up as we go along—say no 'sorries.' No comments at all, in fact. I tell one, and you try to top it, and then I try to top yours, and so on. All anecdotes must be true. Try not to exaggerate more than you can help. Go."

Seth passed the bong back to her and took a breath. "Okay. Family Hells I Have Known. Round one. I used to have brown hair. When I was around eight, it started coming in all gray. And it happened pretty fast. Like, in March it was brown, and by September it was gray. It freaked my stepfather Roy out. He thought it was about him, like I was doing it on purpose because he knew I hated him. One night when he was drunk he locked me in the bathroom with him and shaved my head. He took off half my scalp with it; I had to wear a hat for weeks afterward."

Hannah threw him a look, but said nothing, and merely gave him the bong and began round two.

Around round four Hannah began awarding points to the stories, toting them up on a scratch pad. She deemed Seth the winner round after round.

By the time they'd reached round twelve they were whooping and laughing. Seth was so high he couldn't feel his body. The cookies and chocolate and pizza they'd scarfed down through the night had his nerves singing. He was too fucked-up to think of anything but the thrill of competition. They'd smoked all they had, and dawn was beginning to lighten the window, when Seth waved his hands in the air.

"Okay okay okay okay! Final round, and I will be the undisputed world's heavyweight champion of Family Hells I Have Known. Are you ready? Still sitting comfortably? Still whacked out of your tree? Okay. Now, I have told you many marvelous tales of my mother's excellent husband, the Mighty Roy, Oppressor Of The Weak and Friend To No One. Roy is known and dreaded by most everyone in and around Drinkwater, Nebraska, but very, very few people anywhere know this particular tale I am about to relate. It did not happen in Drinkwater. It happened in a cabin by a lovely lake in northern Minnesota. In a fishing camp that belonged to a friend of Roy's from the army, and to which Roy went every year for a week of fishing with the guys. Every year from the time I was twelve, Roy would try to get me to go along on this wonderful trip, from which he always returned all hungover and happy, but fishless, and I'd always weasel out of it. Ma in her capacious innocence would back me up, because she knew there'd be drinking and swearing, and she thought I'd never drunk or sworn yet.

"You must understand how loath I was to go on this immense pleasure trip. The year before, I deliberately jumped out of a tree the day before in hopes of getting a good sprain that would lay me up, and instead I broke my collarbone. But y'know, it was worth it."

But that year, the year, *a good week in advance, there was Ma in his room, her eyes lowered, hands twisting together. Saying*, Don't disappoint your father this year, *meaning*: Don't cross him again in this, because I'm too tired to take the consequences.

Seth was trying to do the impossible: to tell the story—and to tell it, as Hannah told hers, in an arch, brittle fashion that at once bragged of and denied the pain—without actually *remembering* it. It was a little easier not to feel afraid when he was this high. Tingling all over, the words danced off his tongue seemingly without effort, as the part of him that was not manically stoned cowered back and marveled at their utterance.

"Roy wanted me there that year, when I was fifteen, because he had a plan. A plan for me. He knew something about me that concerned him and he wanted his old pals to help guide me. Male bonding is so important for boys at that age, y'know. Especially when they don't have a real father."

The circle of orange light from the Coleman lamp after supper that first night at the camp made up the entire world, and those five men whose undivided attention he did not want were all its population.

Shocking, like being hit with a twenty-pound block of ice in his gut, to hear Roy start talking about "These local kids—boys—who like to hang around the truck stop to help out the truckers. . . . Help 'em out of their pants . . . !"

All of them then, looking at him. His name not pronounced, but they knew. The words severed the string of his spine. "These boys—they're sick. Can't control their sick twisted urges—little teenage faggots want to do it in toilets—"

"You probably aren't aware . . . well, maybe you are . . . of what kind of stuff goes on at truck stops out in the sticks. Sex stuff, I mean. I'd discovered it that year, tried it a few times. I'm talking about sucking guys off. That's all I'd done." Seth could almost see his words unfurl in the dimness. Telling what he'd never spoken out loud to anyone before.

Hannah, leaning back against a pile of pillows, listening, glassy-eyed. Her milky moon-face was perfect, receptive.

"Someone must've seen me there and told Roy. And then Roy told them, his army buddies, while we were all sitting around after supper."

Staring into the lamp glow, unable to move his eyes or his head or a single limb lest his gaze cross with one of theirs while they talked about him like he wasn't there. He'd only gone three times . . . when the yearning for the taste of men overcame his foreboding and shyness. Imagining, somehow, that everyone else there was from far-off places, passing through, never to return.

Springing up at last, mumbling, "Piss," and bolting from the cabin. Uri-nating against Roy's truck didn't make him feel any better. Not when he could hear the men's voices immediately rise in his wake. Knowing they were laughing about him.

Then loitering down by the edge of the water, hoping for some breeze to break the infernal heavy stillness. The lake smelling like his grandmother had the summer before she died. Breathing through his mouth, looking up at the stars. There seemed to be more of them here in this place far from arti-ficial light than even above Drinkwater, but they were cold and offered nothing. Gazing up and praying, with all the fervency Roy's surprise awak-ened, that he could be someone else. A boy who lived in a vast houseful of books, nowhere near Nebraska, with no one else there but Cassie, who liked him, who presented no temptation to body or mind. No men at all. Free then to think of them, think all he liked of their thick chests, the curv-ing lines of their butts, their heavy stirring sexes. Think, and wring himself out over and over, protected, by the absence of any live male creature, from both detection and the consequences of desire.

"There were four men there, besides my stepfather. Frank, Hap, Joe, and Ned. And there was Vin, Frank's son. He was just a little older than I was. At first I thought he might be all right. Not like the grown-ups."

Something cold touching him suddenly in the small of his back; wheel-ing, braced to strike out. A figure, barely discernible in the darkness. How had he crept so silently near? Not wanting the can of beer he offered, but taking it anyway, the popping of the top sounding loud in the dark. Apart from the stars, almost nothing visible save the glimmer of the viscid lake. Vin's face invisible, even the suggestion of it shadowed by the bill of his cap. Hearing him slurp from a can of his own.

"You listen to Metallica?" Vin's tone offhand, suggesting an offering. Feeling he should sound apologetic when he said no. Thinking carefully over the scene he'd just left, realizing Vin alone had remained silent through it all.

The relief of that enabling him to take a breath, pressing the cool can against his cheeks.

"Nah. Not Metallica."

"What do you listen to?"

"I like the Smiths." *At once longing to yank the words back, to name some other band.*

Vin appearing to ponder. Feeling him move, twigs crackling beneath his feet. "Yeah, I've heard of them. I know a girl whose sister moved to Milwaukee, and she saw them. But they broke up."

Standing here, chatting about nothing and sipping beer, until Frank came out on the cabin porch and called to them. "Time for shut-eye, boys." *Frank's voice scout-masterly now. Not the way they'd sounded a little while ago, drunken voices escalating to outdo one another's stories. Maybe after he'd walked out of the cabin, they'd let Roy know by signs and gestures that he ought to be a little more loyal, a little more kind to his wife's son. Maybe that burst of laughter and talk he'd heard had nothing whatever to do with him. Probably the worst was over.*

Except it wasn't.

"Once they knew that about me, once Roy made sure they knew, of course, they wouldn't leave it alone."

Roy's remarks gave them permission. Permission that night, as they turned in, to warn one another to keep their asses to the wall. Permission to tease him by snatching food off his breakfast plate, by going out of their way to bump into him and then leap back, limp wrists flailing, crying, "Oh, excuthe me, mith!"

"The next day they knocked me out of the boat in the middle of the lake, pretending it was just for fun, except no one else got knocked into the water. And when I tried to climb back in they kept prying my fingers off the side, over and over, until my hands were sore and I had to swim back to the dock. I was panicky and tired, it was a long way, but I made the swim while they shouted and hooted at me." *Roy's permission. All looking to Roy after each incident, to see what more they could get away with. Roy indicating, with his squinting, leering face, that all of this was amusing. By dinnertime on Saturday they were calling him faggypants and candyass and even cocksucker to his face.*

Too scared, too incredulous, to make any visible reaction. Their gazes burning into him, making him squirm. Feeling his lack of an ally; glancing sometimes at Vin, who had seemed so friendly at first, but Vin was an expert now at ducking his eyes, at always being conveniently stationed with his nose in the other direction. And when the men laughed, Vin laughed, too.

Wondering how he'd endure the next twenty hours out here in the middle of nowhere with these insinuating gazes, gestures, taunts, before it was time to pack up and drive back to Drinkwater. In his heart of hearts, knowing this was what he deserved; they were calling him what he was, they were showing him all he had to look forward to in life. Getting back home wasn't going to change that either. Because this was happening at Roy's pleasure: he could have stopped it with a word.

"The last night we were there. They'd been drinking beer morning noon and night, cases of it, but that night someone brought out a bottle of whiskey. They gave me some. For a little while I thought they'd forgotten about the faggot jokes; they were playing cards. Then they turned in for the night. There were a couple of metal cots in the cabin, they'd let me and Vin have those, and they slept in bedrolls on the floor. I was drunk and went to sleep. Then I woke up in the darkest part of the night and they were all awake and standing around my cot. They'd lit the Coleman lantern again, which made everything look orange, the shadows were long and spooky. Then I realized they'd shackled me to the cot, wrists and ankles."

Cutting his clothes off him with the fish-gutting knife, pouring beer over his face, telling him he was going to get what he surely must want from real men such as themselves. Terror-stricken, but not surprised. It all felt inevitable, what they were doing to him, but still full of smaller astonishments, one right after the other: the astonishment of the restraints, unable to stave off hands grabbing his long hair, yanking it around like reins, thumbs pressing his eyelids, his ears, his nostrils, as his mouth was filled.

Astonishment at just how high and rancid men smelled when they were in a lather of doing something terrible all together. Astonishment at how deeply he could gag and choke and yet not vomit. At how he could be there, shackled to the cot with Hap McWherter's cock in his mouth, and at the same time plastered in numb paralysis to the ceiling, unable to emit a sound and seeing it all happen in the Coleman lamp's glow that made the shadows long and misshapen, the bodies jerky and ghoulish.

Pushing Vin at him, yanking his pants down, poking him in the back as he tried to squirm away, chanting at him to be a man while he stayed soft, his flesh in Seth's mouth like a wad of sour cotton. Then jerking him away, their voices excoriating him as if he'd missed an easy catch in a crucial game. To be replaced by Roy, not permitting him to close his eyes, or roll them, or do anything but look right up at him all the time, while the tears poured down his face. Roy's expression saying, This is all you're good for boy, so get to it.

"They cut my clothes off me. They went into my . . . into my mouth. And then I had to pull a train for them. For Roy and all of them. Five guys on my virgin ass."

Penetration another astonishment. Astonishing that there could be a pain so deep and ongoing and dirty and bad, which yet did not make him die. Endlessly renewable pain, pain that went on separately from that of being crushed, scratched, pounded, jerked, bounced, commented on ("Oh, you're good." . . . "Doing what comes natural, aren't you?"), choked by hands around his neck, half-drowned and blinded in poured beer, pinched, yanked, laughed at, told he was a piece of shit and knowing it was true. "You want this," they said, "you love this, take it, get it," the astonishment spreading all through his aching, shackled limbs: Yes, they were right, this must be what I was made for.

Astonished to learn that no matter how deep your reluctance to do a thing, you could be forced to do it. That the worst part of terror was its limitlessness, the way it just went down and down and down, nothing to break it. And the worst part of men their ability to act in unison without pity.

Losing count of them as they used him, and time backing up in a way *that indicated it was not his friend, wouldn't pass and transport him beyond this, just as the air and his own body had turned against him, everything in league with Roy that night. The last one (Frank, or was it Ned?) about done, Roy and Hap again dragging Vin forward. Someone yanking him up by the hair so that he couldn't hide from the sight of Vin's tight, miserable figure pulled toward him. Someone saying, "You don't wanna miss a chance like this, boy. We're all in this together, right? No one else's hiding in the goddamned corner."*

At that, Vin shaking himself free; Hap and Roy stepping back, not grinning anymore, looking serious, a little apprehensive, as if sending him to win the crucial point and doubting he'd pull it off.

Unforgettable, the sight of Vin's face as he stepped up beside him, the play of orange devil light on his features gone solemn, still. The others standing around and watching, quiet. Painfully aware of his own labored breathing, sucking the hot heavy air into his dirty mouth that was about to be invaded another time. The pause in the operations making it all worse; for the moment, no one touching him, just the anticipation of being touched again.

Trying to wish it away. But his wishes, above all, meaningless here.

"They all took a turn. They had to goad Vin into it. They couldn't let him see it and not do it. At first I thought maybe he'd hold off. But then he got on me, too, and he was the worst."

Vin the only one of them not frenzied and sloppy and drunk. Conscious of being observed. Movements measured and deliberate, as though wanting to experience fully what he was doing. Performing as much for the entertainment of the other men as for his own perverse pleasure. Not hurting him at all with his hands. Not saying a word. But his invasion, his appropriation, thorough, total. The men watching, riveted, brows furrowed; someone whistling, impressed.

Pulling out slowly at the finish, so he felt the withdrawal as an agonized absence, as if Vin was drawing all his guts out of him in the wake of his cock. A pause, the briefest of delays, Vin making sure of the full attention of the company. Then patting him lightly, approvingly, on the ass. A great loud laugh going up from all of them as they grabbed Vin, pummeling him proudly, moving en masse out of the cabin.

Still bound to the cot, oozing out of both ends, the dawn chorus starting up. Hearing them on the porch, their shuffling feet, exclamations of congratulations, as if Vin had done something wonderful that won the game in a way no game had ever been won before. Hearing Roy, his voice distinct from all the others.

"All right," Roy was saying. "You're all right."

Then their feet descending the three steps, getting into two of the trucks. Doors slamming, engines racing before they peeled off down the dirt track that led to the main road five miles away. The birds the only sound now, cheerful and stupid. Exhausted, emptied, hearing it, hating the birds. Wanting a respectful silence in the world. Listening to himself breathe, and wishing that that, too, would stop.

"They got through with me in the early morning, and drove off somewhere all together. I was half-dead, which wasn't close enough to what I wanted to be. I was still tied down, but I thought they were gone and it was finished. Only it wasn't."

A porch board creaking. Everything hurt, moving had become one of those things he wasn't going to do anymore. Heart beating hard, and hurting, too. Realizing he'd dozed, or been unconscious, for some period of time, little or great: sunlight penetrating the screened window places of the cabin, and the air hotter. Lying still, face buried in the smelly mattress and his long tangled hair, alert.

The screen door opening slowly with a long screee, and someone stepping in. No sound of the trucks returning; terror flaring at the thought of being found by a stranger. Unable to imagine a stranger of any sort who would be kind to him now.

"Vin came back in. By himself."

Vin creeping up to stand beside the cot, leaning on it with his legs so heavily he felt the pressure in his body. Felt Vin's breathing change, knew he was looking at him, all opened up. Hearing him pant like a dog in this airless place. No breeze stirring through the screens.

Then Vin saying, "I bet you're thirsty."

Vin's hand in his hair. Gathering it up with a repulsive gentleness, turning his head. Putting a bottle to his bruised and puffy lips, tipping it. Water spilling not so much into his mouth as through it and onto the mattress. Vin raising his head more; groaning in protest, but then the cold water flooding between his lips, guzzling as much as he could get before Vin deprived him of it again. The bottle emptied, Vin easing his head back down, and moving around to where he was invisible, down near his feet.

"I have the key."

Trying to turn his head; needing to keep Vin in sight. Wanting to ask him to take the cuffs off, but tongue too swollen and dry, and a horror of making any more pleading sounds.

"You want me to let you loose?"

Trying to nod. Allowing himself to think that maybe now it was over, that time would begin to move again in the regular way. Vin had hurt him more than the others had, but he was just another kid really, only a little older—only seventeen—and he hadn't gone with the men when they drove off, so maybe that meant something. Maybe he'd thought what he was doing wasn't as bad as what the men had done . . . maybe he'd done it that way thinking it would be easier for him. He'd had no choice but to do it. They'd forced him; Roy had forced him. Hearing Vin move, hearing his knee touch down on the wooden floor and the clank of the cuffs as they fell away. But even then too cramped to shift his legs. Waiting for Vin to come around to the head of the cot, to free his wrists.

"At first he seemed to be helping . . . he gave me water. He had the key to the handcuffs. He freed my ankles."

Vin staying where he was, still making that panting sound that was turning into a weird singsongy hum that raced up his spine. Feeling himself being looked at. His skin bridling and crawling under Vin's gaze; Vin's breath skimming Seth's shrinking flesh.

Then something cold touching the inside of his thigh, so he yowled.

"Ssh," Vin whispering, "S'all right. I'm going to make you feel better."

A T-shirt dipped in cold water; Vin wielding it softly over his broken flesh, cleansing him, humming all the while. It did feel better, except that it was the wrong kind of better, because it wasn't being freed, allowed to cover himself and crawl off alone into a corner to die. Writhing and flinching beneath the cool cloth, knowing Vin could see and touch him, evoke noises from his bleeding mouth, filling him with a panic somehow worse than what had preceded it. Hearing moaning, and realizing after a while that it was coming from him. With every minute that it went on, frenzy spiraling; if this wasn't going to stop now, would it ever stop?

"I could barely speak . . . but I begged him to let me up and leave me alone. He wouldn't leave me alone."

Yanking his body forward, rolling onto his side and trying to kick out at Vin with one numb foot. Vin catching him by the leg, flipping him all the way over onto his back, the cuffs clanking and twisting. Vin's gaze vague in a way that was more terrifying than the feral grins of the men before. No time to figure out what that expression boded before Vin draped the dirty wet T-shirt over his eyes, blocking off his sight. Trying to shake it off, but what happened next making him freeze.

Vin's breath cool against his sweat-slicked belly. Then his tongue, hotter even than the hot air that encased them, tracing a whorl around his navel. Slow, almost contemplative. Feeling. Tasting. Then crying out, flailing, but caught, legs easily weighted by Vin's body.

"Sssh. This is going to feel good. I'll make it up to you," Vin whispering, and his breath singing through the short hairs before his lips and hand closed over his cock.

"He wanted more from me. He wanted things he couldn't do in front of the other men. I don't know what the fuck he was thinking. He said he wanted to make me feel good. He was all over me, looking at me, touching . . . he . . . he sucked me off."

In a corner against the ceiling, a big wasp buzzing. Battening on the sound, wishing it would find its way out, or fall dead, because its insistent whirring made him so hinky. Thinking he would be able to bear all the rest if only the wasp would be silent, if only the birds outside would cease their *clicking and calling. Revulsion for Vin's mouth and hands doing their slow and dreamy work, giving him what he'd long imagined getting from another boy. Proving not only what the men had said last night, that violation was what he craved and deserved and was built for, but also that his own pleasure at the agency of another man could only be hideous as well. Become that terrible thing, a fag, every pleasure was a secret rooted in filth. Vin was robbing him of it, ruining love and pleasure and him, forever. Shame spurting from him when he came, wringing the last bit of life from his wracked body. Vin uncovering his face then, looking down at him as if he was something delicate, a baby bird. The expression making no sense in this place, making him want to shriek.*

"I did that good, didn't I?" Vin's face drawing closer, smoothing his wet hair back from his sopping face. Then the last astonishing defilement. Vin's mouth softly covering his; the taste of himself given back to him on Vin's tongue. Feeling his heart stop; for a long, long moment thinking, Thank Christ, this is it, *everything rising, winging, rushing, straight toward black welcome death. Holding his breath for it.*

"And then . . . he wasn't even done then. He . . . he fucking kissed me. He put his mouth on mine, his tongue, like he thought—" Seth never had been able to figure out what Vin was thinking, although those terrible minutes were always with him.

In the silence that followed, Hannah stirred, blinking. "Are you done?"

He nodded.

Her laugh startled him. "Hell, that was some seriously fucked-up story. You are one seriously fucked-up dude to think of that. So—no argument—you win!" She scribbled on the scratch pad and held it up. A big TEN. "You're the undisputed winner and chamPEEN of Family Hells!" She collapsed on the bed, gasping with laughter.

The morning sun crested the windowsill and shone into Seth's eyes. Shrinking from the glare, he grabbed the shade and pulled it so sharply that the whole roll came down on his head.

Hannah leapt up, her giggling like running water, and tried to help him, but they were too floppy-jointed to make any sense of the window shade, and the next thing Seth was aware of was waking up on the floor with his head under the bed, and finding it was late afternoon.

"I'm out of weed," Hannah said that night. "I think it's probably just as well that we cool it with the drugs for a while."

"Hey, yeah," Seth said. Leaning in the doorway of Hannah's room, he still had that nerve-singing feeling, but now the pitch was changed. It resonated all though him, the exact weight and color of his shame. "Listen . . . that stuff I told you. . . ."

Hannah got up and began brushing her hair at the mirror. "Hey, we were so stoned. You got carried away. But it's all right, I don't care that you cheated by making shit up. You're still the winner, okay, honey?"

Seth stepped into the room and pulled the door shut behind him. "But the thing is, I wasn't making it up, Han. And if you tell anybody else about it, I'll—I'll have to—"

She froze. Her eyes met his in the mirror.

"C'mon, Seth—do you even *remember* what you said? That was some serious sick shit you thought up!"

"It happened to me."

She faced him, except that as soon as their eyes met, she glanced skittishly away. "*Shit.*"

"I'm sorry," Seth said.

"Sorry? Why are *you* saying that? *I'm* the one who—oh, God. OhGodohGodohGod. Why did you let me make you play that stupid game?" Wheeling, she grabbed up the scratch pad and flung it at him. "You let me give you *points*—!"

She burst out crying. Seth hadn't imagined this reaction. He watched her for a few moments, but when she did not master her tears at once, he sidled out of the room.

. . .

A book she'd lent him, which she wanted to give to her boyfriend, brought her to his room in the middle of the night, and thus saved his life.

The door was locked. He never was in the habit of locking himself in. Hannah knew he hadn't hooked up with anyone. There was no answer when she knocked. Once her boyfriend applied his shoulder to it and broke through, the first things they saw were the bottles on the floor: a big one emptied of vodka, a small one of aspirin.

Another hour and it would've been too late.

Through the whole thing Hannah stayed with him like a mother. At his hospital bedside, she asked what he'd been thinking.

"What the fuck do you think I was thinking?" he said, too listless to raise his eyes to her or return the squeeze of her hand.

"I think it was that if you slit those pretty white wrists of yours, every man you ever date for your long life will know you're a whacko. Whereas this way, you'll have a chance to get laid first before they figure that out."

He made no response. It was too soon for jokes, however affectionate and gentle. He had not intended to survive this.

Soon he was back in his dorm, under the care of the campus therapist, taking antidepressants that didn't seem to do anything except add Technicolor to his dreams and make jerking off impossible.

Hannah stuck with him all the rest of that winter he spent on the bare edge of another breakdown.

"You don't really want to die. I'll prove it to you."

"I did. I still do." But afraid he'd botch it again, he never made another concerted attempt. As the weeks went on, he began to think that this must mean, in however meager a way, that even if he did not particularly want to live, neither did he want anymore to die.

He made Hannah swear, repeatedly, not to tell anyone about the rape. To silence her anxious inquiries, he lied to her about telling his therapist. To himself, he swore never to tell another soul.

The depression that seemed endless inexplicably lifted in the spring. House-sitting for a faculty member that summer, working three part-time jobs, Seth scrambled to finish his incompletes and retain his scholarship. In the fall, painting flats for the drama society, he met Cleon Nash and fell in love. When that ride was over, two years later, he'd accrued more pain and disappointment, but also learned better how to hold himself, to keep it inside.

The urge for death at his own hand was gone.

Now Hannah was an artist teaching printmaking at the School of Visual Arts, living in Cobble Hill with her boyfriend, a lawyer in the public defender's office. Seth liked Eric because he was easygoing and very good to Hannah. They both agreed that she was a goddess and worthy of worship.

Hannah and Jim had met twice. The first time was by accident in the days of their hands-off period, on one of those long afternoons of roaming around with no particular objective in mind. After dawdling in the first room of a large gallery, Seth caught up to Jim to find him deep in conversation with a woman—with Hannah. Seth stayed put in the doorway, trying to think it all through before one of them turned and noticed him. He wanted very much to show off his creditable-looking friend to Hannah. But here was where his two worlds, his two *selves*, collided. Hannah knew all about him.

But it was all right. Eric appeared and was introduced, too. They drank coffee together. Seth said very little, and Hannah gave him secret looks expressive of surprise and query at the company he was keeping. Jim talked in his easy, charming way that had so impressed Seth from the first with his skill at making people comfortable, and paid for all the coffees.

Late that night she'd called him, demanding to know what he was doing with someone so much older, and what were Jim's intentions? Abashed by her concern, Seth played the whole thing down. After all, what *were* Jim's intentions? He had no point of reference for what they were doing. Courtship, that decorous and slow-moving anomaly, was something he recognized only in Victorian novels. He couldn't bring himself to tell Hannah how much in love he was when there was so little to show for it.

The second meeting, at Hannah's for dinner around Thanksgiving, when they were in the first flush of their physical intimacy, was definitely about mutual inspection. All the dinner conversation was between Hannah and Jim, and as wine loosened her tongue, she asked more and more of the questions a mother would, friendly but penetrating.

"I'm glad," Jim said with a nervous laugh, "to see that Seth has such a passionate advocate in his life. He'd led me to believe he was quite alone in the world."

Seth's throat tightened as he waited to hear Hannah's response. With a pleased smile, she said, "I've tried hard to make him feel less so."

The next day Seth met Hannah for coffee and debriefing.

"He's not the type of man I'd have pictured you with. But . . . well, how can I not like him? Eric did, too. We both saw how much *he* likes you."

Seth responded with the beatific smile he never saw in his own mirror, which made him look simple and sweet, like a lovely dog. "I can't get enough of him. I don't mean just in bed, I mean I want to be around him all the time. And—I dunno, I'm afraid to say it—I feel like I make him happy. Do you think so?"

"How's your work?"

"I'm working. A lot, in fact. Why?"

"Well, I don't know how you can see to paint . . . your eyes are all misty."

Seth smiled. "I can't help it."

"Oh, honey," she said. "that's all right. You deserve someone who'll really be good to you. But, Seth . . . there's one thing that concerns me. He's so much older than you are."

He drew himself up in his chair. "Not really, Han. I feel like I've lived at least forty hard years' worth already."

"I know." Then, "What does Jim say about all that?"

Seth turned his head, as if trying to rid himself of a crick in the neck. "Nothing."

"You haven't told him? Oh. . . . So you've stopped having the dreams."

"Oh, God . . . don't ask me. Hannah—Jesus Christ, how could I tell him? He can't ever know what kind of . . . dirt . . . I come from."

She grabbed his wrist. "You're not dirty! I *won't* have you think of yourself that way!"

"I don't believe you can control how I think!"

"All right, all right! We don't have to talk about this anymore."

"That's fucking right. We don't fucking have to talk about this. I'm sorry I ever told it to you."

"Sweetie—can we ease up on the profanity?"

"*You* want me to ease up on the profanity? Half the bad words I know I learned from you."

He laughed, and after a moment she did, too. Hannah reached across the table and cupped his face. "I can't help worrying about you. We worry about each other, that's what we do."

Seth caught her hand and kissed the palm. Then, his face burning, he recounted what he'd told Jim on their first date.

"Am I supposed to nod and approve of that?"

"No. No, you're supposed to scold me. I'm stupid and I'm bad, and if I'd had any sense I would've said it all differently or said nothing at all. I *can't* go to him now and unsay any of it. I *can't*. And I don't want to. I don't want him to know about my mother and Roy. That they even exist."

"Oh, Seth—"

"Anyway." He frowned. "It's disgusting to talk about . . . about that kind of thing. Disgusting and undignified. I hate people who do that, go trolling for pity, goddamn professional victims. They go on TV, they write *memoirs*. It's revolting."

"It's revolting on Sally Jessy, yeah . . . but that's different than telling those you're close to."

"No, it isn't. Give me a break, Hannah! I'm not going to let my whole life be about that forever! Which is what it would be, if I went around telling it to people!"

"What people? We're talking about Jim."

"Especially Jim. How could I ever fuck him again if he knew that? I. Could. Not." Turning his coffee cup around and around in his hands, he said, "You don't know this . . . but I told Cleon. He'd taught me how to make love, how to love getting fucked. He rescued my life. I wanted no secrets between us. So I told him. It seemed like the only thing I had to give him in return, my trust, since he had everything and I had nothing—"

"Not true! Seth—not true!"

"Don't interrupt me! This is hard enough as it is!" He dropped to a whisper. "So I told him one night, and . . . he was good. That night, he was good. His reaction was just . . . enough. Like he cared, like it hurt him to know, but not like I had to comfort him about it. So for a little while after I imagined I'd done the right thing. But then there it was with us all the time. In bed. And out of bed. I knew he was thinking about it. Once, he questioned me, he wanted more details. I think he was turned on by it. That was our first big fight. And then . . . well, I always knew he was seeing me as The Boy Who'd Been Raped."

"Honey, I don't know that I'd equate Cleon with Jim—"

"It's none of his business! It's no one's business! It's over!"

"I hope it is. I really do."

When they parted she hugged him hard.

"However ancient you feel, lovey, you are still just sweet twenty-three. You're just starting out. Take care of yourself . . . but be good to him, too, okay?"

For the first time, Seth had to resist an urge to wipe her kiss away with the back of his hand.

9

"Can I open this?" Seth, fresh from the shower, with a towel wrapped around his middle, held up a sealed window envelope he'd picked up from the kitchen counter. Jim was cracking eggs into a bowl.

"That's my pay statement."

"I know. I'd like to look at it."

"Why?" Jim said, his tone neutral. "What's it going to tell you that you don't already know just by looking around you?"

That was the thing, nothing. *Put it down and make a pot of coffee,* Seth thought. *Don't torment yourself with this.* "I don't know," he said. "But why can't I look at it?"

"You really want to look, so look." Jim took it, ripped into the envelope, unfolded the sheet before Seth's eyes, and put it into his hand. "Of course," he said casually, "it doesn't really tell you much. The paycheck's only a part of my compensation. Last year my partners and I sold the shop, so I've got my share of the payout coming in over five years. The car, the cell phone, my laptop are all agency perks. There's stock, profit-sharing, a hunk of money in my retirement account, various other investments. And then there's Zak's estate, which except for some charitable bequests, was willed to me.

He was in venture capital—he did quite well in biotech startups. I don't even touch those assets."

Jim's tone wasn't boasting, but it wasn't circumspect either. Seth didn't know how to take it.

"Jesus. So how much *are* you worth?"

"Right now, today, around twenty mil. Once I've got my whole packet from the agency sale, it'll be roughly double that. That's not including Zak's money. After the taxes and charity disbursal, that's another fifteen or so, depending on the market. Considering who's out there sitting on what these days, I'm really a small-potatoes millionaire."

"I see. Huh. Well. Okay." He was ashamed of himself for starting this, as he'd known he would be.

Taking the paper from Seth's slack grip, Jim returned it to the envelope with an air of having gotten over an unpleasant task. "Now let's get to what this is really about. Are you worried about money? I'd be happy to give you some if—"

Seth stopped him. "Have I ever asked you for anything? Or— more to the point—acted like I *expected* anything?"

"No. In fact you're the only man I've ever heard of who brings his own toothpaste and razor to every overnight. But perhaps you're concerned about your finances. Are you in debt?"

"I don't even have a credit card." He avoided Jim's gaze by shuffling through the pile of mail and catalogues.

"But the rent. You said Charlie was moving out."

"I'm *kicking* Charlie out. I've decided. But I can find another roommate lickety-split."

"Why should you do that? You said it's a terrible apartment. You should live here anyway."

Seth couldn't bring himself to look up. "What did you say?"

"You're here almost every night. I hate it when you're not. Let's make it official. How much more time do we need to wait to know what we want? We know."

Seth let out a quick bark of laughter, more like a hiccup. "Whoa. I always thought, if this moment came, that it would be . . . romantic. Not just some diversion from talking about how rich you are and how poor I am."

Jim left the eggs and came to his side. "It's not romantic that I just looked at you dripping on my mail and realized I need for you to be here all the time?" He fitted his hands around Seth's face, ran his thumbs softly along the cheekbones, the eyelids, the curve of the mouth. "I think it's very romantic."

With Jim's hands on him this way, Seth felt he was being sculpted. Everything in him rose to that touch. It was hard to detach and think. He reached up and took Jim's hands away.

"I don't think I can move in here. It wouldn't be right."

Jim's hands hovered before him, Seth saw that he wanted to put them back into contact with him, because they told their own story so well. But instead he tucked them, with an air of fairness, into his pockets. "Given that you used every ounce of your persuasive abilities to yank me out of my hibernation, and that you are obviously—beautifully—*delightfully* happy when you're here with me, how d'you figure?"

"I've got to live within my means."

"Your means will go a whole lot farther if you're not shelling out rent for that dump downtown."

"No, you don't understand. I can't live off you. That can't be part of what we're doing together, because it would ruin it."

"This again. It's charming, but you take it to a ridiculous extent—"

Jim's fond smile made him explode. "I'm not *charming* and I'm not *ridiculous!* I'm a grown man with *standards* about my life! I love you, but it's meaningless if I forfeit my self-respect!"

Jim was still smiling, but differently now. "Seth. You love me?"

"What?" But he knew what he'd said. He looked down at himself, his chest and belly, dry now and getting chilly, sloping into the clammy towel. This was the most important conversation they'd ever had, and here he was caught by surprise, and naked.

"Look, we can't just—"

But Jim's hands were on him again, and his mouth, and they were sinking to the floor, to do again the thing that was a discussion in itself. Jim's tenderness rolled him flatter than anyone else's force ever could.

Afterward, stretched out with the legs of the counter stools pressing into his back, Seth traced Jim's mouth with his fingertip. He struggled to find something to say to that waiting face.

"I wish you'd grow a beard."

Jim laughed. "Is that all you'll let me do for you?"

"A mustache and a beard—a good one, not one of those stupid goatees."

"All right, if you like." Jim closed his eyes. Then, as if they were sighted, his fingers brushed Seth's skin: the shoulders, nipples, belly, the spent cock, the hip and thigh. Seth held his breath, vibrating against this searching touch that read him like Braille. "Seth," Jim whispered, "here we are. Here we are. You've thrown me wide open, you've won."

"Don't try to give me things," Seth whispered back. "Make demands on me instead. That's better."

Jim opened his eyes and looked at him carefully. "Then I demand you tell me you're not going to get up and go. Not now, not later, not at all."

The next night, to celebrate Seth's arrival with all his things in two duffel bags, Jim made a coq au vin.

When they'd pushed their plates away, Jim touched his hand. "So here you are. I'm so glad."

"I'm glad, too." Glad, and nervous. He'd barely tasted the dinner.

"Listen to me now a minute. It's been my good fortune always to live well. Not, when I was younger, extravagantly—I think we come from the same sort of home. Our parents earned a nice living, there was always enough. Yes? I know you're not used to having to eke along on so little, since your parents' deaths. I know it's been painful."

Seth realized this was a hole he'd dug himself into, so he just nodded agreement, though Jim's assumption made him squirm.

"I've consulted with my attorney, and decided that the simplest thing, the best thing, is just to give you joint access to some of my accounts—" Jim reached behind him to the sideboard, where a manila envelope Seth hadn't spotted earlier was sticking out from beneath the fruit bowl. He tipped the envelope onto the table, spilling out fresh checks imprinted with both their names, and a colorful assortment of plastic cards.

Seth looked at the things spread before him. The holograms on the cards glimmered and gleamed. Bile rushed up into his throat. "Jesus Christ! You're out of your mind! I'll never get another goddamn hard-on if I take any of this!"

Seth shot up, slammed into the bathroom. He didn't realize he was going to puke until the boiling stuff splattered into the sink. Hiccupping, still heaving, he pulled off his shirt, and stuck his head under the cold shower jet.

Afterward, he almost expected to see Charlie sneering back at him when he looked in the mirror. But, skin reddened, eyelids raw, he was still himself. Whoever that was now.

He thought of gallery rooms full of handsome, clever people in black clothes, drinking wine, chattering about his pictures and him. The little red dots appearing on the exhibition list. Sold. Sold. Sold. This was the same fantasy he'd had since he'd first gone down to New York and seen where important painters showed their work. For years he'd tried to peel back the layers of his self-regard, to come to a final decision about himself, whether he was, in the last analysis, worth everything or nothing. Living on Jim's money, would he even know anymore whom he was supposed to be?

A tap at the door. "Seth? Are you all right in there?"

"Just a minute." He brushed his teeth, spitting over and over into the sink, put his shirt back on, then came out briskly, brushing past Jim and returning to the table.

"Christ, Seth."

Seth flipped the cards and checkbook over. "I'm sorry. I feel like an ingrate. But you can't expect me just to sponge off you like this. It's not a good position for either of us to be in, don't you see?"

"No," Jim said, "that's not it. That's not it at all. You don't want to be grasping, and I respect that. But don't you see that it's incredibly *selfish* to place yourself above me this way. How can we be intimate on these terms you insist on? If we're partners, that means we pool our resources. That's what love is. It's not yours or mine, it's *ours*."

This speech left Seth terrified. "I'm yours, you know that—but *can't you see what fucking you becomes for me if I'm dependent on your money?*"

Jim's expression then was terrible, and Seth knew one of them was missing something.

The phone rang, and Jim snatched it up, turning his back on Seth to wander up and down the length of the apartment, talking for a long time. After a while Seth went into the bedroom to unpack.

When all his things were neatly in their places ten minutes later, more than three-quarters of the space allotted him was still empty. Feeling small at the foot of the vast bed, he told himself, *I live here. I'm home now. Jim is my partner, and this is my home.* The words meant nothing. Flopping back, he looked at the white ceiling, blank, like a fresh canvas. *No one knows me. . . . I don't belong anywhere. . . . I could fall out of my life and disappear and no one would really notice, nothing would change for anybody else. . . .* These were the verses of his song of dread, which had played in his mind since childhood, beginning when he'd figured out that his mother would not send horrible Roy away no matter what he did or how Seth cried to her about hating him.

The white ceiling undulated as he trembled beneath it, too spacey to feel the mattress under his back, fighting the drifting sensation that made him feel sick in his head and guts. *I puked and I'm dehydrated, that's all this is.*

A voice jerked him back into his body. "Why don't you answer me? I've been calling you and calling you!"

Seth looked up. "What?"

"Were you asleep?"

"I . . . I'm not sure. What is it?"

"There's a good Robert Mitchum movie on TCM, starting in five minutes. *Out of the Past.* D'you want to see it?"

"Will you watch it with me?"

"Of course, I'll watch it with you," Jim said, already going out of the room.

Snuggled against him on the sofa, Seth's focus dulled and he lost track of what was happening on the screen; his whole awareness was concentrated on feeling Jim's pulse against his cheek, Jim's arms around him. Making them mean something, making himself feel safe.

Then Jim was kissing him and lifting him and the TV was off. "You went right to sleep," he said fondly, putting his fingers through Seth's hair. "You missed the whole thing."

"Sorry."

"This evening didn't really work out like I'd planned."

"Not like I'd planned either. Not that I, um, really planned anything."

A little later, in bed, Jim said, "Try to relax." And in a few minutes more, "Never mind, Skeezix. Let's just go to sleep."

"Maybe *I'm* not what you'd planned," Seth mumbled, mortified.

Jim was silent for a full thirty seconds, and Seth, lying close enough to hear him breathe, heard nothing except the beating of his own heart.

"I like to think I chose you with my eyes open. Trust me that I like my choice."

While Jim slept, Seth lay tense beside him, telling himself over and over how lucky he was, and also that if this all went smash, Hannah and Eric would likely let him sleep on their couch for a few weeks until he could find someplace else to stay.

10

The next day, a Saturday, found Seth as hungover from the previous night's drama as if he'd been on a drunken binge. It was difficult to keep up with Jim's long stride as they walked together after brunch in the West Village. He'd have preferred not to go out at all, to eat toast at home and go back to bed for a much-craved nap. But that would've meant admitting he hadn't slept all night. Anyway, it was a sunny day after a long run of gray ones, and Jim's enthusiasm for getting out wasn't to be overridden.

Jim came to a sudden stop in front of a boutique window. "Why don't you try that on?"

A vicious wind off the river whipped through the narrow streets, and Seth, shivering in his thin coat and scarf, couldn't imagine taking them off, let alone to put on the teensy slip of a swimsuit that had Jim transfixed.

"I don't need a bathing suit."

You might."

"This summer, yeah, but I'd never wear *that*."

"How do you know unless you see yourself in it?"

Seth thought it should be obvious. The fabric, a silvery pale blue, would go transparent when wet.

"Oh, come on, that suit would be perfect on you." Jim was going into the shop, and yanked him along through the door. A bell jingled merrily as they went in. The young men behind the high counter grinned down at them in welcome. They were a pair: one looked like a photographic enlargement of the other in blue Oshkosh overalls over thin, skintight T-shirts, identical cropped haircuts, gold hoop earrings, and clean smirks. The smaller of the two, who had been watching them through the glass, brought out the bathing suit without waiting to be asked, dangling it on its little hanger in front of Seth's face. "This size should do for what I can see of you."

Seth turned from it. "Why is it so important that I get a bathing suit *now*? It's the middle of winter."

"We might take a little trip at Christmastime. A couple of weeks in Tortola, maybe. You'll need bathing suits. When we're not skinny-dipping." Jim's seductive smile was a private look, wrong in this stupid shop full of Day-Glo fabrics and underwear packaged like porn videos. "Try this on. C'mon, Seth, humor me."

"C'mon, Seth, humor him," the clerks parroted. "Humor us *all*."

Snatching the blue suit off the hanger, Seth threw himself into the back of the shop, where the two miniscule changing booths were.

He peeled out of his coat and hooded sweatshirt, leaving the thermal shirt he wore next to his skin, and leaned against the wall to try to wrestle his chinos off without unlacing his boots. Too late he realized this wasn't going to work; the right leg of his chinos would neither come off over the boot nor go back up, and he cursed, hunched over and hopping on one foot, almost losing his balance before he got free. It was cold back here, gooseflesh rose up on his legs. Feeling like an idiot in his socks, he got the bathing suit on, then realized there was no mirror in the booth. How could a gay boutique not have mirrors in the damn changing booths?

"How're you doing?" Jim called from the front of the shop. "Let's see."

"I'm *not* going to wear this suit. It's obscene."

"Don't be so Midwestern modest. Just come out a minute. There's nobody here but us."

The salesclerks hooted. "Nobody here but you-hoo-hoo!"

Sidling out of the booth, Seth confronted his full-length reflection. This suit was like the cellophane wrapping a piece of hard candy. He'd feel less naked if he was actually naked. Charlie would be all over a suit like this, just as he'd be all over two free weeks in Tortola, wherever that was.

"Get a quick eyeful, then I'm getting dressed. I'm freezing."

"We have a heater up front," the tall clerk cooed.

"You can't tell anything with your top *on*," the small one chimed. "Give it a chance."

"Yes, step into the light and let me *see*," Jim beckoned. "Just please take this *off*." When Seth came within reach, he grabbed the thermal shirt and yanked it up. With his head caught, he heard the bell sound, and when he was free of it, a crackle of static making his hair dance, he was confronted with two stone-faced crows—fifty-something men in identical black chesterfields, who stared at him with greedy severity.

"We were passing and saw you and we said to ourselves, 'What would Jimmy be doing in *there*, maybe fifteen years ago—*if then*'"— with a blinking survey of the shiny schmatta all around—"but not the sort of place you'd shop *these days*, hardly, so we just stepped in to see what was going on."

Now Seth recognized them as the men who'd eyed him so sourly from their restaurant table that warm night in early September. "We didn't realize you were *accompanied*." Eyes behind tinted lenses riveted on Seth's body, avoiding any glance at his face. "Could this explain why we see so little of you these days, Jimmy?"

"Well, when there's *so much* for him to see of others. . . ." his companion murmured, staring openly at Seth's groin like an appraiser confronted with goods billed as better than they were.

"Don't be ridiculous. I'm glad," Jim said, "that you two have turned up, because it's high time I introduced you to"—Jim put a hand on Seth's bare shoulder and urged him forward just as he was about to bolt back to the dressing room—"Seth McKenna, these are my friends—"

"Clyde and Billy, I know," Seth said, drawing himself up and pointing his chin at them with as much spirit as he could muster. The way they were looking at his bare body made his balls shrink up. "Or is it Billy and Clyde? Does it really matter?"

"Only to *us*," said the one in the glasses, his eyebrow shooting up.

Yanking his shirt out from under Jim's arm, Seth retreated to the changing booth, where he stumbled out of the bathing suit and into his clothes. Goose bumps from the cold warred with the burn of shame that Jim's friends had come upon him this way, looking like the trickiest of tricks. Dropping the repulsive suit on the floor, he deliberately trod on it with his boots. He couldn't hear what the men were saying, although the buzz of talk was continuous, punctuated by laughter from the salesclerks, who were unabashedly enjoying the scene. Dressed again, Seth followed the narrow corridor to the back, which ended in a close bathroom and a window too small to escape through. If there was a back door, it was entirely hidden behind a tower of corrugated boxes. Huddling into the toilet, Seth lit a cigarette and took a few frantic drags.

"You can't smoke in here! What are you *doing?*" It was the small clerk, who advanced on him now, waving his arms in the air ostensibly to clear the smoke away, but really as an excuse to yank him down suddenly and kiss him with a swift, slippery, tongue. "You are so *hot* and you don't even know how much, do you? You really *don't know.*"

"Leave me the fuck *alone!*" Seth shoved him off; he tumbled against the boxes.

"Oh, if *that's* the way you want to play, I'm perfectly willing." The clerk reached for Seth again as he got back on his feet. He fled back to Jim and those two square, severe faces at the front of the shop. How could Jim be friends with such a couple as that? They looked like bureaucrats out of Kafka.

At his approach, they fell silent. Clyde was sifting absently through a basket of rainbow trinkets on the counter, bracelets and key rings that clattered together as he grabbed them up and let them go. Billy stood at attention, as if he was waiting to take Seth into custody.

"We're going to get some coffee, all right?" Jim said. "Get better acquainted."

He didn't want to do that, almost cross-eyed with anger as he was, but short of making a scene, there was nothing to do.

When they reached the coffee bar on Christopher Street, Seth dropped into the corner of a sofa and put his feet up, not caring whether he had any coffee or not, but determined not to be the least bit forthcoming.

At first, ignoring him ostentatiously, Clyde and Billy talked to Jim, tag-team fashion, about a universe of people Seth had never heard mention of. Jim barely replied, until, seizing a rare pause, he said, "You know, I really hope you and Seth get to know one another, because—"

"Well, dear," Clyde said, "he seems to be *asleep*, which isn't surprising really, it is certainly exhausting to try on those teensy nothings all afternoon, after probably simply *hours* at the gym toning those little muscles, I'm sure—"

"Seth, you're not asleep, are you?" The private affection in Jim's tone cut through Seth's disgust; he felt he had no choice but to open his eyes and engage at least a little.

"Clyde and Billy met Zak when he was your age, and helped introduce him to the gay world. They were always very special to us— practically our guardian angels."

Oh, great, Seth thought, *the sainted Zak's fairy godfathers. They're going to love me.* "Is that right?" he said, trying, for Jim's sake, to sound courteous.

"Have you two been acquainted—for a *long* time?" Clyde demanded.

"We met in the summer, through my work. We've been . . . looking after each other . . . since just after Thanksgiving." Jim's tone made Seth glance up; could he be afraid of Clyde and Billy, too? "Now I find that everyday is Thanksgiving." He glanced up at his round-eyed friends. "Seth's only just moved in with me though."

"He's *living* with—Jimmy! When were you going to let *us* know?"

They were stricken, to find themselves so prominently left out of the loop; this was the first satisfaction Seth had out of the encounter, but even so he was almost sorry for them. Perhaps he should have urged Jim to introduce him to his small circle. Except that he'd always feared it would be this way, that Jim's friends wouldn't welcome him. He'd been in no hurry to be snubbed.

Jim passed his hand over his face, and sat back. "I guess I was leaving it to chance. Like this. Because I didn't feel I could rely on you to be gracious—"

"Gracious! When you follow darling Zak with someone who is so—and so *soon!*"

"Clyde," Jim pointed out wearily, "it's been over two years. Aren't I to be allowed any more life? . . . I'm only forty-two, after all."

The crossed swords of shame clanged loudly.

Billy leaned forward. "But here we were introducing you to all those *lovely, suitable* men . . . and all along behind our backs you were seeing this . . . this. . . ." He glanced uncertainly at Seth, and in his watery eyes, unlike Clyde's, there was tentative curiosity along with the dismay. "Why didn't you at least tell us there was *someone?*"

"You can see perfectly well why he didn't tell us," Clyde said.

"Stop this. Clyde, stop," Jim said. "You're judging by appearances and you have no idea—"

"Yes, I'm judging by appearances and I have *every* idea!"

"But what you saw just now—"

"Was very instructive! You'd have bought him every dreadful bit of lingerie in that ghastly shop if we hadn't come along. Jimmy, it's one thing to take on a piece of ass at your time of life—it happens to the best of us—but it's not necessary to move it *in*—"

"Jesus!" Seth jumped to his feet.

Billy clapped a hand over his partner's mouth. "Now you've gone too far! How could you? To the poor thing's face!"

Clyde ripped the restraining hand away. "*Poor* thing—not anymore! That's what I'm afraid of!"

"Fuck you. I'm not going to stay and listen to this shit." When he tried to stand, Seth was as wobbly as a newborn colt. Steadying himself on the sofa back, he turned to Jim. Was he really no better than these two? Looked like it. "*Humor me, you said!*"

Stumbling among the café's jumble of chairs, divans, and low tables, overturning one in his haste, Seth made for the exit. Jim came after, but Seth outran him, finally scrambling down into the subway at Sheridan Square, like a fox diving for cover.

At Hannah's that evening, the phone rang as they played Scrabble after dinner. Seth tensed. She answered it, spoke without glancing at him. "Sure, fine, that's all right." Hung up and returned to shuffling her tiles.

Not Jim. Seth subsided again into distracted silence and too many vowels to do anything good with. The doorbell rang an hour later.

"That'll be for you."

Seth leapt up. "You told him it was all right for him to come out here!"

She went to the intercom and buzzed.

"Hannah, you *bitch!*"

"Manhattan and Brooklyn have mutual extradition treaties."

"What the fuck does *that* mean?"

She left the apartment door ajar, and putting an arm around Eric's shoulders, led him off into their bedroom. Jim walked in. Escape cut off, Seth faced him in the middle of the cramped, overfurnished room.

Jim approached slowly, stopping just out of reach. He rocked a little on his heels. "Sorry you had to be exposed to that. That either of us did. After you walked out this afternoon I really gave it to them for being such turds. I came to bring you home. I thought you might be hoping I would."

"Well, I wasn't."

"I hope you know that if it came to a choice between Clyde and Billy or you, I wouldn't even hesitate."

"You really think *that's* what this is about?"

Jim raised an eyebrow. "Isn't it?"

Mouth arid as chalk, Seth said, "No, it isn't."

"What then?"

His heart juddered. He wanted to cough. To lie down on his face and stop breathing. To never have imagined he could have anything good with another man. "If I have to tell you . . ."

"Seth, I'm not a mind reader." Suddenly they faced each other as duelists.

"It's about . . ." Shallow sipping breaths, all he could manage, ". . . what happened before . . . before they turned up." He tried to look into Jim's face, but failed. "The idea you must have of me, to imagine for one minute that I'd wear that disgusting swimsuit, that my *no* goes for nothing at all. And it's about what happened last night, too. . . . I thought you understood me, but you've got me confused with some Twinkie slut I'd sooner die than be. If I have to tell you that, if everything I've ever said and done with you hasn't shown you what I am and am not—then this—you and me—is a big mistake." In the balloon of silence that followed this last word, portentous and difficult to go back on, Seth managed to raise his eyes enough to glimpse Jim's face.

He looked, Seth thought, hope bobbing up amid his dread, appalled.

"I—forgive me." Jim put his hand to his forehead, which was suddenly glistening. "I didn't think—I do know you, Seth. I *do*—I know and I admire your seriousness, your purpose, they're what I love in you, I mean, just part of what I—I really had no idea, earlier, that what I was doing caused you so much pain. I should have, but I was too self-absorbed." He gazed at Seth as if from a great distance. "But why—things that are light and frivolous and fun—why are they so heavy to you? Last night, and today, when I tried to give you things . . . because I want you to be happy and comfortable, because you're beautiful to me . . . you react as if it's a violation. Such a strong—overreaction, isn't it? Really? Because another man . . . if he objected, *if* he did, another man would not behave as if he was being so terribly oppressed. Would he? Tell me."

This was clearly a question awaiting an answer. But none of Seth's belonged to the college professors' son.

"You are a delight to me, Seth, you've given me back my vivacity, but I must be missing something here. What are we doing together if I'm not allowed to share with you what I have, if I'm not permitted to help you in what little way I can? How the hell are we supposed to be partners in life if you hold me at arm's length?"

This appeal left Seth quivering to his core.

"I can't live off you." He wanted to say it out loud, with confidence, in a reasonable tone, and follow it, soften it, by a temperate explanation that would make Jim see and agree with his point of view. Instead a dry whisper was all that resulted. He repeated it as if it were a foreign phrase he was trying to memorize without really comprehending. "I can't live off you. I just . . . can't."

"You can't. . . ."

Seth winced, hearing, in Jim's toneless echo, reference to last night's failure in bed.

"How can I explain it to you again," Jim said, "how I see what you call, with such horror, living off me. I feel I'd be browbeating you. I'm already too far in the wrong . . . and I suppose it *was* a despicable, inexcusable weakness in me, dirty old man that I am, wanting to see you in that silly little swimsuit. . . ."

"Oh, for God's sake!" Seth found his voice, and then his legs revived enough to propel him to where Jim was. "The fucking bathing suit would be *nothing* if not for all the other! But it's *not* silly to me, my cock and my ass are for *you*, not for those idiot salesclerks, and not for everyfuckingbody on the fucking beach. Why did you put me through that, after I'd said no? And then of course your friends saw me and thought . . ." The memory of it made him color violently.

Jim touched Seth's hot cheek with the backs of his fingers. "I'm sorry I humiliated you. It was never my intention . . ."

There should have been sweetness in this apology. But in his head, as if reflected in fifty mirrors, Seth saw the same conflict happening, in slightly different ways, over and over between them. And each time it would be worse, because each occurrence would further erode the bit of ground they were trying to stand on together. When he raised his eyes to Jim's, he saw it there, too, the fear that they had given themselves nowhere to go from here.

"I don't know what to say to you. We were so happy, and suddenly . . . look, I've got to attend a meeting in Chicago tomorrow, maybe I'll stay on there a couple of days. Your head'll be clearer if you're on your own. Have a good think . . . I will, too. And then we'll talk."

"You're going to Chicago? When . . . when were you going to tell me?"

"I would have told you this afternoon. It was just for the day. Try not to look so stricken."

"Oh. Well . . . can we—" He wanted to go home; Jim might mean to slip away from him tomorrow, but tonight was a chance at least to overwrite last night. Before he could say it, Jim glanced around Hannah's cozy, disheveled room, and asked, "Can you stay here while I'm away? I'd prefer to know you weren't alone."

In the bright flare of panic he saw Jim throwing his possessions into the alley, changing the locks and phone numbers before going off, maybe to Chicago but probably not, and not just for a couple of days . . .

He started when Jim touched his hair. "Seth, honeyboy . . . how red your eyes are!" He smiled, but it was a smile that still held nothing for Seth to grab on to. "You are such a . . ."

"What? Such a freak? I *am* a freak. If I wasn't we'd be—"

"If you weren't—but freak is *your* word, remember—if you weren't, we'd never have found each other, would we? I mean, never caught each other."

"But you . . . you're throwing me out . . . *jezuz* . . . because I won't— we can't even fight fairly on this lopsided basis! My way or the highway, that's the choice I've got! Fuck it, you're right. *They're* right—fucking Clyde and Billy. This isn't going to work out. How the hell can it?"

"Sssh. Don't talk like that. You know you're exaggerating now. No one's throwing you out."

"Then take me home. Take me home to bed, that's where we belong, not standing here jibber-jabbering at each other."

All the time Seth was saying this, Jim went on smoothing tenderly the tendrils of his bangs, but there was an expression in his eyes, as if he was regarding a child he'd come to adore, but must now bid good-bye. Then he stopped Seth's mouth with a brief kiss, squeezed his shoulders, and murmuring a promise to call the next evening from Chicago, was gone.

Hannah appeared and started at the sight of him.

"You're still here? I thought I heard you both leave. What happened?"

"Why can't he let me just . . . just love him without *things* getting between us?"

Hannah pulled him down to sit beside her. "The world—and New York City especially—is all about *things*, sweetheart. Your self-denial is a little puzzling."

"People here dissemble and whore and steal for those things, yeah. Like Charlie. I'm not like Charlie."

"Oh, gee . . . you are a hardheaded little bastard."

"If my paintings are any good, they'll bring me the things I want, somehow or other."

"Perhaps. I hope so. I also hope that you haven't, in that poor, prideful, frightened brain of yours, made it impossible to accept a good man's love. Because that's what you've got, you little twerp, and your convoluted scruples are likely to ruin it if you're not careful."

11

Jim sounded distant the next afternoon on the phone, as if chary of being either too friendly or too much the reverse. How was he, how were things at his job, what else was he doing? How was Hannah? Chicago: cold, snowy, lake steel-gray from the hotel window. Meeting all right, looking up a couple of old friends, not a bad meal the night before. No reference to the reason for their separation, no leading questions asked. Five minutes and then a good-bye without an endearment. Seth wished Jim hadn't bothered. Before the call he'd been able to imagine that Jim might be missing him, wanting him. But that collected, distant voice just left him dangling.

The next day Seth was too hungover to move and spent most of the day on Hannah's sofa with his sketchbook and an ashtray.

Just before his hosts were due home from work, he dragged himself up, showered, and went out for what he meant to be a long walk. At an ATM he learned that he'd have to begin the world again, if it came to that, on $779.32. Tony owed him another $479. Before he'd met Jim, it was just a matter of course to him that he'd live almost on air. Why, all of a sudden, did it feel so difficult? Was it because he'd been so extravagant of himself, and was about to find all the shimmering diamonds he'd heaped on Jim turned to gravel?

That evening he helped Eric get through a couple of six-packs. They played cards, the three of them, and didn't speak much. No phone call came from Chicago.

Seth signed for the FedEx delivery at Tony Mazzoti Photography and sorted through the various envelopes with half an eye while fielding one phone call and keeping an eye on the blinking light of another. Tony was out of town on a job; alone in the studio, he was free to choose the music and blast it as loud as he liked, and to evaporate into the absorbing pile of details; invoicing, ordering supplies, paying bills. Even scrubbing out the toilet wasn't so terrible, because it kept him moving.

He didn't get back to the FedEx envelopes until the end of the day. The last in the stack was addressed to him. Must be a mistake; he wasn't expecting anything that might come this way. Someone's assistant must have carelessly addressed it to Tony's assistant. The return address was Kaufman & Stern, PLLC on East Forty-eigth Street.

Maybe somebody's gonna sue Tony, the fucker. Seth tore into the envelope with gusto.

But the thin sheaf of papers bore a cover letter that was distinctly addressed to him. Seth checked the signature first—Stern's—then scanned down the paragraphs, skipping every other word, until his eye hit a number that so startled him he went back to the top and started reading afresh.

By the third time through the letter, and after glancing at the attached papers, each with its stuck-on pointer for where he was supposed to sign and notarize, Seth's heart was hammering. *Jesus Christ on a pogo stick. This is insane.* Stuffing the papers into his coat pocket, Seth rushed back to Hannah's.

Hannah read the documents with a glazed attention, shaking her head and murmuring. Seth was surprised when she looked up smiling.

"Oh, this is only just every grant you could ever apply for getting handed to you all at once! When you need it most!" Raising her voice, she called, "Eric! Come see what Seth's sweetie has done. Doesn't this make you feel all warm and jiggly inside, like half-set Jell-O?"

Eric read the letter and whistled. "Free and clear! You could walk off with it tomorrow, if you wanted to."

"So it says," Seth said. "The point is, how can I possibly accept it? I mean, would you? Really?"

Eric and Hannah exchanged glances. Eric said, "An out-and-out gift . . . no strings."

"Of course there are strings!" Seth said. "Every time I do anything for Jim, how is he to know—how am I to know—it's not in exchange for this money?"

"But it isn't," Eric said in his reasonable counsel voice. "Once you sign for it, it's not his money anymore. That's why he's giving it to you like this, instead of in a trust that he would still ultimately control. A gift transfer like this has considerable tax ramifications for him. It's really costing him more like twice this—ten million maybe, because he's had to pay an enormous tax on it that wouldn't have been the case if he'd just made a trust. Obviously he wanted the money to be solely yours."

"Oh, Christ. Oh, Christ. Christ Christ Christ. This is Zak's money, you know. It's got to be."

"Zak's not here anymore, honey. It's going to be yours now," Hannah said. "That man . . . just loves you."

"Oh, God . . . does he? How can he? He must be out of his mind." Seth hid his face in his hands, then started up as if scalded. "Oh, no!

He must've thought I was angling for this all along! That I refused the other so I could get this! Oh, my God, what he must think of me!"

"Whoa! Seth. Sanity check here. Lovers give presents to their loves. Poor lovers give modest presents, and rich ones give big extravagant marvelous humanity-confirming ones. It's what love is. Don't fight it."

He was starting to wish he'd not brought this problem to his friends, although it would have been impossible to sit the evening out with those papers seething in his pocket and not say anything. But now they knew about it, he did not feel free anymore to reject what was offered, because they'd think he was a fool, whether they said so or not. The limbo he'd fallen into since Jim left was deeper than ever.

He went out to smoke. Hannah followed him onto the stoop in the cold, bumming a cigarette and inhaling it with furtive pleasure, hugging herself against the wind. "Don't throw Jim away. Not for this reason, anyway. Not because your pride says you have to grub along like a cockroach. They're mighty survivors, but I don't think they have much fun or get much accomplished."

"Goddamnit. Don't get all metaphorical on my ass." He stared numbly out at the street, feeling her eyes on him. "I don't want to throw Jim away."

"What bothers you about receiving this money is that it means you're being taken seriously, which you desperately want but which is also freaking you out. This gift is a sort of dowry. It makes you marriageable—by anyone, or if you choose, no one. You're set free— now you really can leave him. So if you stay, it's because you love him, not the security he can provide, and that's what he wants to know. Actually, he knows that already—he's making sure you know it."

"He doesn't need to buy me. Anyway, I know he doesn't need me like I need him."

"Seth, don't be so sure. From your point of view, still a long way from thirty, life's still a series of open-ended episodes. But for older people, especially after something horrible like the death of a lover, life narrows down. I know, because I've seen my brother go through it since he lost his wife. He's through experimenting. Things mean more, he's aware of what he's missing, what he needs to be happy, and what it means to be really unhappy. Despite your being twenty-three and full of all sorts of weird notions, this grown man's put nothing short of his peace of mind in your hands. Don't fumble it."

Jesus. Here came a speeding train, all lights and horns, displaced air and hot steel bearing right down on him. How obtuse could he be? Everything Jim had said to him the night he moved in replayed through Seth's head, but now he heard it differently, now he understood. With understanding came a flush of almost unbearable chagrin.

She put her arms around him, her lips against his ear. "Sweetie, believe me, I'm your best friend—there's nothing heroic about turning this down. Your kind of self-reliance is brutally lonely. Take the gift, be an artist, love your man. I, Hannah the Magnificent, give you permission."

On the way to the subway, unsteadied by wine and emotion, he spotted that rare thing, an empty yellow cab in Brooklyn, and on impulse, got in. It cost him all the cash in his wallet to be delivered back to Bond Street, but then, he reflected, in the morning he could make it so there would be plenty more.

"This came while you were gone," Seth said, drawing the folded envelope out of his pocket. It was two days later, Friday night, and Jim, walking in unannounced, had said, "Good, you're here," and kissed him hard.

Now he was ambling away toward the refrigerator.

"Of course you know that." Seth followed. "You planned it that way."

"Those papers are getting pretty dog-eared," Jim said.

"I feel like they own me."

"Fighting with you is hell. Please let's not fight again tonight."

Seth tapped him on the arm with the envelope. "No fight. But you just can't fathom what kind of difficulty this is for me, can you?"

"I thought I did. I thought that's why I had Stern draw up those papers. So you can buy your own bathing suits, whatever kind you like. So you'd feel free to say screw you to me when I'm out of line. What have we got to eat?"

"Nothing new since you left."

"They barely feed you on airplanes anymore, even in first. Not anything you'd want to eat anyway." Jim spoke into the open refrigerator.

"What if I took this money, and then never let you touch me again?"

"Hmmm?" Jim took out rye bread, swiss cheese, and peanut butter.

"I said—what if I took the money and never let you have me anymore? Did you think about that? What if I took it and began bringing other men here and fucking them in your bed? What if I took it and spent it all on Ecstasy and rent boys? What if I took it and lit out for the territories and never saw you again?"

"I'd miss you so much," Jim said, slathering peanut butter on two pieces of rye, and carefully layering the cheese on top.

"Yuck, how can you eat that?"

"You like things I wouldn't eat either. Those dreadful lentils, for one."

"I don't really like lentils. They're cheap and nourishing is all."

"This is good." Jim cut the sandwich in half and held one piece out to Seth. "Try it."

"I'm talking about ripping you off and betraying you and you're trying to feed me a sandwich!"

"Seth, sweetheart, honeyboy," Jim said, taking a bite of the sandwich, "this is it. This is our real life together, Jim-and-Seth-in-the-kitchen, eating a snack. Don't make a production out of it. Just enjoy it, because nothing lasts forever."

"But—"

"Drama in the bedroom is one thing, that's wonderful," Jim went on, opening the fridge again for a beer, "but here in the kitchen, no."

"But you haven't answered me! What if I take this money—and I know it's really Zak's money—and skip out on you?"

With the sandwich plate and beer balanced in one hand, Jim blinked at him.

"Are you going to skip out on me?"

Seth met Jim's mild gaze in a way he hoped would seem temperate yet cautionary.

"Because I think if that day comes, you won't hang around pestering me with a lot of questions. You'll just be gone."

"Yes, and—"

"Well, and if so, it'll be because things between us have come to such a pass that you won't care anymore what I think. So there's no point speculating about it, is there?"

They were at the table now, and Jim sat down. "As for whether it was Zak's money or not, my darling Zak is dead, and the dead don't have possessions. He left it to me to do with as I saw fit, which I have. Eat half a sandwich, Skeezix, you look sort of peaked."

Seth took the half and chewed thoughtfully. It wasn't bad—just gluey. He liked the earthy taste of the rye, the sourness of the cheese. Jim offered him the beer, and he took a long swallow.

"Are you going to sign the paperwork so we don't have to talk about this anymore?"

"I already did, yesterday. Those are my copies I've got in my pocket."

"Well, good." Jim picked up the pile of mail that was lying on the table, and Seth saw that for him, the topic really was closed. Watching Jim eat and scan the envelopes, Seth found it reassuring to be half-ignored this way, to sit near him while he did ordinary things. It was just as Hannah said, Jim wanted order and peace of mind as much as he wanted passion. Indeed, he'd just said so himself, in that sleepy way that made what was essentially a scolding go down without a flinch.

Order and peace of mind were not the preoccupations of men Seth's age, but he craved them the way others craved the thrills of excess. Just as he craved proof that his own fervent desire to matter to someone was taken up by this man calmly perusing the cover of *Harper's*. "So," Seth said, "anything interesting in Chicago?"

"Nothing," Jim said, dropping the magazine, and leaning toward him with a smile. "Except that I hadn't realized quite how crazily I could miss you. Or how miserable I felt at the thought you might not be here when I got back. He hooked a finger into the neck of Seth's T-shirt and tugged. "C'mere, you."

When Seth was restored to his physical self-confidence and both were too spent to so much as lift a finger, Jim sighed.

"What?"

"Are you all right? I mean, really."

"Didn't I just show you?"

"Yes, but I wanted to ask. You are so mysterious. I've never met a man like you before. Things that ought to please you frighten you instead, and things that ought to frighten you . . . you take for granted with a shrug. I wish I understood how you organize that mind of yours."

Seth let a few beats of silence go by. Jim didn't move or tense; anything could be said now and it would be all right. "I dunno, that's just the way I am. You shouldn't have given me all that money."

"Yet you took it."

"Hannah said I had to."

"She's a good friend to you. Speaking of which . . . can I possibly ask you to give Clyde and Billy another chance?"

"Oh, God."

"I know . . . only they are dear to me, too. Would you agree just to have a drink or something with Billy and me? Without Clyde. Billy wants to meet you again."

"He does, huh?"

"Billy is a very sweet man, honestly, Seth. I spoke to him at length from Chicago. About . . . about everything. I was so frustrated, afraid I'd lose you. He got me to talk it all through, he was very sympathetic—to both our viewpoints—and he was the one who suggested I give you the gift."

"No way."

"Really. It was his thought. I mean, he threw it out as a sort of joke . . . but I saw right away it was the thing to do. And he asked me to say he feels terrible about what happened, and he really is eager to put things right."

"I don't like it that you told him all that about us. I know the kinds of things guys discuss among themselves. You've told him about my cock, haven't you, and what it's like to fuck me."

"No, I haven't."

"I don't believe you."

"Seth. I give you my word."

"But he asked you, didn't he?"

"Well . . ." Jim laughed. "He did. But I promise you, I didn't tell. C'mon . . . once you've got Billy in your corner, Clyde will come around, he always does."

"Remind me why I should give a shit about whether this man likes me or not."

"They're old friends. I wish you'd just keep an open mind about them."

"I'll try. For you."

"It's all I ask."

After that Jim didn't say anything, and Seth thought he must be dozing, until his hand moved up to stroke Seth's hair.

"As long as we're talking this way, there's something else I've wanted to mention. It goes with the gift. Right now it seems to you that I'm all you'll ever want, but I want you to understand that—"

Seth touched Jim's mouth. "Don't talk shit."

"No, listen. We've never discussed this before. I don't know if we'll be together in six months, let alone in ten years. I hope so. But I want you to know I've no intention of putting a stranglehold on you. You're going to have success, and new friends, and other lovers. So—"

Seth stopped him again. "I told you that I'm faithful to you and I expect—I demand—the same of you."

Jim's breath was warm against his hand; he kissed the fingers. "You make me very happy when you say that. Nonetheless—"

"No. You told me you and Zak were monogamous. That you weren't really happy together until you were. That his sleeping with other guys made you miserable. It would make me miserable if you went with anyone else. Or if I did."

"Honeyboy, Zak and I were thirty when we made that decision. We were both complete sluts before that."

"And you think that's all I'm capable of? Being a complete slut?"

"You misunderstand me. I don't want secrets and lies building up between us because you fail to uphold a promise I didn't ask you to make. You don't have to be a slut to meet other fascinating men and want to be with them, you just have to be human. Which we both, thank God, are."

"You fucked someone else in Chicago."

"What?"

"That's why you're saying all this. You did."

"Seth, no." Jim got up on one elbow; his movement sent a breeze of cool air against Seth's face, and he shivered.

"You did! Or else why are you talking about me cheating—to make yourself feel better! I will never do that to you!"

"Seth, I didn't."

"Then why not? You certainly could have."

"It never occurred to . . . oh, all right. Point taken."

"Good."

"We're going to be okay. You know that now, right?"

Seth snuggled down against him, pressing his forehead against the massive warmth of Jim's biceps. "Right."

It wasn't until a day when Tony was being particularly stroppy that it occurred to Seth that he could quit his job at anytime. He abandoned a shoot in progress, walking out as Tony shouted at his back, and went straight to the School of Visual Arts, the sidewalk like marshmallow beneath his feet. He waited for Hannah to emerge, tailed as always by a little pack of her students all vying for her attention.

Seth cut through them and took Hannah by the shoulders. "I need a half hour."

"Not just any half hour, apparently you need the half hour that starts now."

She smiled at him, wriggling free of his imperious grasp. "Can we also, during this half hour, drink coffee?" She began to walk toward the corner.

"Listen to me, listen—" Seth said, trotting backward ahead of her, to keep a bead on her face. "There's something you've got to do for me."

"Yes, darling, but first coffee."

"No, listen—I just told Tony where to stick it—I mean, I would've had I said anything, but I didn't, I just walked out on him. I'm not going back. Hannah, I want you to let me pay your debts."

"I was wondering what you were doing here at this hour—" She stopped walking so abruptly that a man bumped into her from behind. "Wait. What? What did you say?"

He was almost prancing around her now. Her expression stirred him up all the more. "Let me pay your debts! And—you and Eric are always talking about buying an apartment—I want to give you the money for a down payment. Don't say no don't say no don't say no—I have to do this! You have saved my life—not just the one time, over and over—Hannah—you are the dearest friend of my life—don't say no!"

"But Seth! My God . . ."

"Don't say no!"

Jim's eagerness to give him things made perfect sense now. "Please, Hannah."

Hannah leaned back a little, squaring her big shoulders, and smiled all over her face. "Eric won't like it."

"Make him like it. He's got no choice. He's my friend, too—because he takes care of you! So it's settled. C'mon, let's get some coffee. And donuts! With sprinkles! Because I'm celebrating the end of Tony Mazzoti in my life." Seth threaded an arm around her neck, loving the frizz of her orange hair against his coat sleeve, the softness of her cheek. Hannah loomed so large for him that it was only at scattered moments like these that he discovered he was taller than she; he made the most of it now, guiding her along, looking down into her beaming, upturned face.

Hannah cooked a big roast chicken dinner, to make a ceremony around the gift, but Eric and Jim were not invited; she knew that their presence would overwhelm Seth, who did not want to be thanked, or made much of. Afterward, drinking coffee while the check he'd written out to her lay—facedown, so as not to embarrass them—on the table, Hannah said, "So, that's me taken care of. Now what about your sister?"

Seth winced. "You always do go for the jugular, Han!"

"Look, I know things are really weird between you."

"Things are not really weird. There are no *things*. We aren't in touch. She stopped answering my letters from college after she found out she wasn't going to be able to go to college herself."

"Well, I know. But I also know that you used to be very close to her. And she's still only, what—twenty? Twenty-one? Too young to write off entirely."

"I haven't written her off. She's written *me* off."

This wasn't the first time in the last couple of months that he'd weighed the question of Cassie. Angry as she'd made him, he was used to loving her, from the days when his grandmother taught him, when barely out of babyhood himself, to dandle and distract her. She'd always been his ally. The day he found out for sure about his scholarship, she went out with him to meet Roy coming home for supper, and break the news. They didn't discuss it beforehand, but each knew that it could go easier if done outdoors, where the neighbors might see, where Roy might hold himself in check.

Roy's business—the business that had once been their father's, that Roy had taken over as he'd taken over their mother, and them— sat at a T-junction; the short road that formed the top of the T was lined with squat little porched houses that gave way quickly to unbroken fields, shaded here and there by a big tree like an alien presence. It ran straight out onto the prairie so you could stand in the middle of the pavement and see clear to the northern horizon. They stood there together, shivering in the early April thaw that promised little more than a return of frigidity. There was no one in sight. At their backs, clouds piled up in the south.

There they stood, again in his mind's eye, shoulder to shoulder, while the quiet that naturally ruled over everything was broken by the crying of somebody's cat, in heat and locked out. Little by little the wind came up, soughing around their ankles and then rising to lift their hair, his straight and hers curly, but both long and gray as cigarette ash.

He knew Roy and his mother saw their gray teenaged heads as a personal reproach. When the subject came up, as it often did, Mary came over moody and more prayerful, skittish with a premonition of

judgment. Roy reminded her, with sturdy resentment, that he'd promised to raise these children, and he *was* raising them. What business
they had to grow gray hair, *he* certainly didn't know. But he knew he
didn't deserve to have the whole town thinking he'd driven those kids
gray. But Mary said you couldn't dye children's hair, it wasn't nice.

"Now no matter what he says," Cassie said, "you're going to go."

"I'm going to go," he repeated.

"Here, touch this for luck." She always wore the metal service tags
that had belonged to their real father, Seth senior, when he fought in
Vietnam; now she held them up at the end of their chain. He closed
his hand around the bits of metal that were already slick from her
touch.

"Now," she whispered, "kiss them."

"What? C'mon, only Catholics do that stuff."

"Please. Do it."

"I'd rather kiss you for luck, you're the only luck I've got."

"If he knew what had happened to us, how we were being raised,"
Cassie breathed, rubbing her thumb over their father's embossed
name, "he'd be so angry. He didn't want this for us at all."

That was her fantasy, one he didn't share.

"But he would've been so proud of you, Sethie, and your scholarship, and your track trophies and all. So proud."

"You think?"

"I know so. I know it deep down."

"The things you know. I wish I knew 'em, too."

Roy appeared then, skirting the gas island, crossing the road, and
she drew closer to him.

"What are you two doing out here? Where's your mother?"

"She's in the house," Seth said, putting his chin up in the air as if
that would do anything to command Roy's respect. "I've got something to tell you."

"Well, what is it?" Roy put his grease-blackened hands on his hips.
"Quick, I want to go wash up."

"It's . . . it's . . . that I'm going east to college in September. I've got a scholarship. It's all going to be paid for."

With his sister's anxious eyes on him, Seth tried to stare Roy down, and failed. Instead, he stuttered out more information. "The college is called Hampshire, it's in Massachusetts. It's all arranged. You can't keep me from going."

"I can keep you from pissing yellow if that's what I want to do," Roy remarked. He rubbed a hand across his belly, squinting at them. "Cassie, you go in the house."

She'd tried to stand her ground, but there was nothing at all she could do to intercede. They both knew it. When Roy took a single step toward her, regarding her out of his lizardy eyes, she took off into the house. After that Roy marched him, as so many times before, around the house and into the cellar.

And as so many times before, when he didn't appear at dinner she'd knocked on his door afterward, and he'd called to her to go away, and she hadn't gone away. She put Vaseline on the marks Roy left, lit cigarettes for him, smuggled food up from the kitchen.

"Always when I had a Popsicle, I gave her half. She never had to ask me. When I left home, I had nothing at all to split with her. I had everything she wanted, and that drove her crazy."

"'Folsom Prison Blues.'"

"Um, right. But, when I first moved in with Jim, and my finances loosened up, I sent her a big box of books I thought she'd like. I stuck a bunch of money—cash—in between the pages of the books. Five hundred dollars. I put a phone card in. I sent her my cell number."

"I'm going to deduce, from the fact that this is the first I'm hearing of it, that she didn't call you."

"Hannah, the package came back. Like ten days later."

"Unopened?"

"No. She'd taken all the stuff out, looked at it. The money and phone card were gathered into an envelope."

"Shit. She returned the *money?* No note?"

"From her, no. The note I'd enclosed wasn't there, probably because she tore it into bits and peed on it." To his amazement, tears sprang to his eyes as he spoke. He rubbed them away. "She's treating me like I'm dead. Fine, I'm dead. So's she."

"And I suppose you haven't told Jim about any of this?"

"I try to keep my past from becoming a topic. Which is how it has to be—I mean, Cassie hates me because I got loose and she couldn't—can you imagine if she knew how I live? What I am?"

"You never thought to come out to her? I find that so hard to believe."

"Hannah. Where I come from—it's *unspeakable.* I needed my sister, she was all I had. When I was fourteen, and she was twelve, I wasn't going to tell her I was jerking off about other boys. When I was seventeen and she was fifteen, I wasn't going to share my truck-stop adventures with her. Give me a break—anyway, did you tell your brothers when you lost your virginity? What kind of boys got you hot? Be real."

"Seth, she might realize more than you think."

"She might. But I really, really doubt it."

"So she doesn't know about—"

He held up a hand. Shook his head hard.

Hannah shrugged. "Okay, okay, okay. I'm sorry I asked."

She carried the platter with the chicken carcass to the sink. When she came back to the table, she scooped up the check and looked at it.

"You're sure? You're sure you want to give away such a sum?"

"If you don't deposit that the minute your bank opens in the morning, I will be mortally wounded."

"All right. I just . . . all right." She put the check into her capacious bag and came back to embrace him.

. . .

The gift to Hannah, once accepted, satisfied something in Seth that allowed him to begin to live with the money. He was at last able to spend liberally on his muse. He chose sable brushes delightful to hold, the best linen canvas, fine pebbled papers, Conte crayons, German pencils, a watercolor box from England of ingenious design that absorbed him in a new pursuit so different from the scope and feel of working in oil. Drawings bloomed from his hand all day, and not just in the sketchbooks of varied sizes that he kept; Jim came across tiny portraits, little comic strips, intricate abstract designs inked onto junk mail envelopes, Chinese menus, the margins of phone book pages, ATM receipts, the endpapers of softcover books. Seth drew in bed, at the dinner table, in taxis and restaurants. At the movies, he made contour line drawings in the dark while the trailers ran. He planned a new series of large pictures, more ambitious than anything he'd attempted yet. With a little gentle prodding from Jim and Hannah, he rented a studio in a West Chelsea warehouse building.

A rapprochement took place with Clyde and Billy. The first part of it staged, to Seth's bemusement, over tea at a tony East Side hotel one weekday afternoon. In the brocaded hush of the room that seemed to be all cul-de-sacs set with divans and low chairs, as if scenes from *Les Liaisons Dangereuses* were to be played there, Billy was, as Jim had promised, wholly benign. Over his initial surprise, and without his partner's lowering presence, Billy could exercise the full force of his tendency to think the best of everything.

Billy's gaze, though friendly, was intense; he leaned across the tea things on the low table and really watched Seth as he spoke. He subjected Seth to a rigorous interrogation, sometimes alarming in its nosy specificity, but all of Seth's answers were received with beaming murmurs of "Fabulous!" or "Good for you!" or "Aren't you clever-lucky-sweet!" When Jim left them for a few moments, Billy slipped out of his own seat and sat next to Seth on his small sofa, placing a confidential hand on his arm.

"Now just tell me quick—not that I don't know, because I see it written all over that sweet viz of yours—but tell me how much you care about our darling Jim."

Seth ceased to be intimidated. Billy—and Clyde, too, probably—were just Jim's friends, and as anxious for him as Hannah was for Seth himself, and he for Hannah. Seth looked directly into Billy's inquisitive eyes, and pitched his voice low. "I can't tell you."

"You can't—?"

"Because there are no words."

"Ah! You good boy!" To his amazement, Billy kissed him on the forehead. "Next week—we'll arrange it with Jimmy—we'll come to you for a little dinner party. I promise Clyde won't snarl at you. It'll be fine. We'll all be such good friends."

That dinner party wasn't easy with Clyde being polite as if at sword's point. But Seth was on home territory, Hannah and Eric were there, and by the time the second bottle of wine was emptied, Clyde had unbent so far as to talk directly to Seth, rather than addressing him obliquely through Jim. Then Seth had a brainstorm. Bringing out a pad and pencils, he began, without remark, to draw. The first sketch—made quickly and flung onto the table amid the remains of dessert—was a flurry of graphite strokes from which Hannah emerged, laughing. Next he evoked Eric's conversational intensity out of some dark masses and thick lines, an image entirely unlike the first one. Instead of turning frankly to Clyde, Seth began his next drawing while looking across the table at Jim, stealing only sidelong glances at his real subject, and barely even lifting his pencil from the tablet; all his practice making contour drawings surreptitiously on the subway came into play in a portrait that was at once merciless in noting every line and sag of Clyde's face, and astute in finding and fixing the piercing intelligence of his eyes. When he tore it off and skimmed it after the others, he took care not to look up, but just started in on Billy. In his peripheral vision he was aware of Clyde taking up the paper, looking at it for a long time, saying nothing. When Billy tried to peek at it, he defiantly rolled it up. But as they were leaving, he asked for a studio visit. This resulted in a sale, his first ever: three small pencil studies of dogs, each made spontaneously in the street, each charming yet entirely unsentimental.

"This is a start," Clyde said, as he wrote out the check. "Eventually I may buy a painting. I'd like to look again in six months."

He said no words of praise beyond these tepid ones, but his lack of warmth made the sale feel more significant. Seth carried the check around for almost a month before he cashed it. There was a sense of accomplishment in looking at it, his name and Clyde's spiky signature linked. It seemed almost too bad to turn it into mere nondescript money.

After that life took on a placidity Seth had never experienced before.

After taking the prints of Jim's right-hand fingers (for a "little project," he explained with a mysterious smile), he had them tattooed on the small of his back, just above the curve of the buttocks. When he revealed this new decoration, still raw from the needle's bite, Jim was appalled and embarrassed. Seth thought he was only pretending to be angry. The gesture was too flattering. And though he claimed not to care for tattoos, saying Seth's pale skin needed no pictures to be still beautifully illustrative, Jim certainly looked at it often enough after it healed, and not just because of where it was placed. Seth felt it was a successful gift. And he liked bearing his lover's mark; it gave him a sense of primitive, nearly indescribable security.

Part Two

12

"Set another place for supper," Roy said, coming through the kitchen door.

Cassie turned from the stove. Behind her stepfather stood a man, face shadowed by the bill of a dark cap. The men Roy drank with at the Tap all wore feed caps, but he'd never brought any of them into the house for a meal. She didn't think she'd seen this fellow anywhere before. There wouldn't be enough food.

Mary came in from closing up the café. Seeing the stranger, she shot a look at her daughter.

Roy washed up. The young man in the cap—not a feed cap after all, but a felt baseball one—waited his turn in the posture of someone about to be handcuffed. He wore blue twill work clothes; there was grime on his hands.

"Cal here's Frank's boy. He's come down from North Dakota to work for me," Roy said. He'd had back trouble lately that made his work slower. Since most people in Drinkwater didn't like dealing with him anyway, it gave them another excuse to take their cars up to Flanagan if they could. Maybe he thought the advent of a new face would turn things around. The café couldn't survive without the gas station, and the gas station wouldn't make it without the repair work.

Roy thrust a can of beer into the young man's hand. "I set Cal up in the trailer out back. He's going to take his meals with us."

Cal nodded slowly first at Mary, then at Cassie. His brownish greenish eyes were curiously light, like the fair brown hair that poked out from the cap. At the table he balanced the cap on one knee, like a young boy unsure of his welcome. He put a hand through his hair to ruffle it up, then smooth it down, until it sat like feathers on the neck of a chicken.

Cassie saw her mother was alarmed, wondering if the young man's arrival was good news or a sign of some trouble Roy would assign to her, as he did all his troubles. Cassie also wondered whether this Cal was going to pay for his meals and if Roy was going to increase the housekeeping allowance. He was rigid in his dislike of leftovers; they shopped for, and cooked, just enough—enough for *Roy*, in any event—and beer in sufficient quantity.

She set a plate before him, containing what would have been her own dinner.

Roy motioned for beer and Cassie brought it. As she set the cans down, Roy caught her by the elbow, a light touch; an IOU for the others that were not light. Cassie flinched, and Roy smiled. "I didn't hear you say hello to Cal here."

"I said hello." She yanked her arm free. "Hello, Cal."

"I want you to be nice to Cal. I said you'd show him around town."

"That won't take but a minute." His plate was already empty. Too bad there was nothing more to offer him. When Seth still lived at home, and ran for the school track team, Mary had contrived meals with seconds. But those days were long gone.

Mary leaned forward. "What church do you attend, son?"

"Never mind that," Roy said. "He's only taking his meals here, he don't need supervision from you. He's got a mother of his own, back home."

Mary bowed her head. "Well," she murmured, "I am glad to know *that*."

Roy tapped Cal on the shoulder. "Got to finish hooking up the water on that trailer before it gets dark."

Alone with her mother, Cassie began to wash the dishes.

"Seems like a nice young man," Mary said, drying them. "Respectful."

"Respectful? Why? Because he didn't put his feet up on the table?"

Mary jerked back. She shied at everything—a door slamming, a dog barking, her own daughter's thoughtless words. The whole world took part in Mary's danger—or mocked it.

"A quiet boy," Mary said.

"Catatonic, you mean. How long you reckon he'll last?"

"Don't stay up too late," Mary said, as she hung the damp dishrags on the oven door handle. Alone, Cassie ate two pieces of toast with grape jelly. When she heard her mother shut her bedroom door, she followed her up.

Stuffing the keyhole of the bathroom door with toilet paper, Cassie ran a hot bath. Braiding her heavy hair, she pinned it up in a lush chignon, then looked at herself in the mirror, sucking in her cheeks and full lips, trying to look like her idol, foxy-faced Colette, or one of her heroines, Renée Néré, Claudine, or a young Léa, who had not yet applied all the arts and sciences of seduction to her career as a courtesan of the Belle Epoque. Smart, sensuous French women who knew about suffering and sex and style. She wanted to be like them. Turning from her reflection, Cassie eased herself into the water, slipping down to escape the cool air coming in the window.

Once the watery heat penetrated all through her, she reached for the bar of chocolate balanced on the tub rim. Eyes closed, she bit, imagining its sweetness to be, first, that of an entirely superior French confection, such as Léa would keep for her own consumption; then as the velvet stuff melted, it became the tongue of Chéri, slipped, light and worshipful, between her lips. The dripping of the tap was his fevered whispering to her: *Nounoune, Nounoune,* that pet name that looked so sexy on the page, that she couldn't quite figure out how to pronounce. She eased the Hershey wrapper down farther, handling the candy with only the tips of her fingers.

Since she was fourteen and stumbled across *Gigi* at the library, Cassie had been intoxicated by Colette, her Paris, with its music halls and scheming husbands, and her lush countryside of fruit, flowers, and tall silent forests. Her women with the beautiful names and faces made themselves free, then wrestled with freedom, throwing it away, snatching it back out of embers that often burned them. Cassie admired the tendresse with which Colette's women nursed their own hurts; a tendresse infused with ferocity, and a refusal above all to be erased. Cassie thought of Colette's narratives, which came to her by interlibrary loan from across Nebraska, as the blueprint for a proper life as a woman. The great thing, in order to experience all that, was to get out.

But getting out—of this house that had no locks, even on the bathroom door—proved difficult. In high school, she'd earned, by bleak diligence and only the palest of official encouragement, a state college scholarship. But on the eve of departure, her mother fell—or most likely was pushed—down the stairs, breaking her right arm and collarbone. There was no one to keep the café running but Cassie. The smidgen of money she'd put together to get herself to Lincoln disappeared into medical bills. After that crisis passed, the scholarship had lapsed. She postponed applying again, semester by semester, as Mary whispered about not being able to cope without her, as Roy reminded her, "You know you're not going anywhere."

Cassie slid farther down in the water, holding the melted chocolate on her tongue, the heat against her skin and the images of gleaming fixtures, fresh flowers, delicate scents, in a gracious old house on the Avenue Bugeaud near the Bois de Bologne. Right now, right here, was beauty and sensual pleasure, just as described on the page. It was of a stopgap, ersatz type, but for this moment, prolonged with a holding of the breath, it worked.

If Mrs. Muller in the next-door house, or the Bergssons across the road, looked out and saw the light from the tiny bathroom window, they would not realize they were gazing upon the illuminations of Paris.

Again Roy mentioned showing Cal around Drinkwater, and this time Cassie understood him to mean: as soon as dinner was finished. He followed her out of the kitchen door, into the spring evening, like a dog.

As they passed around to the front of the house, Cassie said, "I guess you're Silent Cal, huh?"

He squinted beneath the bill of his cap. "People say that to me sometimes. Don't know what it means."

"The president of the United States! Calvin Coolidge. In, like, the twenties. That was his nickname."

Cal shrugged. His clothes were yesterday's; she wondered when Roy would make her and Mary responsible for washing them.

"So what's North Dakota like?"

"About like here." There was a huskiness to his voice; had he meant to speak much, he'd need to clear his throat, but apparently he didn't mean to. They turned into Drinkwater's business district.

Cassie had long since stopped seeing the place through her own eyes, and surveyed it only coolly through those of someone else. Her head was always full of characters. Famous writers, masters of observation and analysis, had visited Drinkwater under her auspices, sucked it dry in just one sip, and pronounced: Leave here or perish. Colette had. Edith Wharton. Charles Dickens and Anthony Trollope, improbably arm-in-arm and in decided unison. Charlotte Brontë, scuttling close to the storefronts in horror at the stark light, the flatness. Henry James, dour-faced and fond of her, perched on the last stool at the café counter, nursing tea with lemon, murmuring portentous judgments laden with subsidiary clauses.

Now she tried to imagine how Cal saw it. The prairie, in its compromised grandeur, was the prairie, as was the great screen of sky that seemed to smother the littleness of what it overspread. Drinkwater had one commercial strip, cut by three cross streets; their business— the gas station-café—was apart from it, at the crossroads, catty-corner to the electrical substation. The unambitious buildings could have been anywhere from Manitoba to Texas. The bank, having gone bust in the 1930s, was now a tavern. The movie house had closed for good when Seth was a baby. You could, had you not minded what people would say, do all the yoga positions in the middle of Main Street beneath its one traffic light, without threat to life by vehicular traffic. Cassie had borrowed a yoga book from the library last year, but she'd given it up now.

"Did you always live in the same place? In North Dakota? What is it called?"

"Calvin."

"I said where you're *from*. I know your name."

"Calvin," he repeated. "Calvin, ND."

"So they named it after you, huh?"

He smiled a little, not at her, not, apparently, at anything. He wasn't ugly, seemed neither markedly gentle nor fierce. But the smile gave him a gormless look that put her off. Once in a while he paused to adjust his cap, or his crotch, or to run a finger around the collar of his T-shirt.

He'd paused outside the thrift shop, which had once been a small drugstore with a soda fountain. Cassie touched his arm, and pointed straight up. They had to step off the curb to see what she indicated: Drinkwater's only piece of municipal statuary, perched atop the cornice of the bank building, three stories up. A muscled nude man, stooped under a great but absent weight. Cal squinted.

"Atlas. It's supposed to be Atlas. He holds up the world. Y'know? It's a myth. Only he's lost his world."

"It's a ball he's holding up?"

"A globe, yeah, the world. Nobody I've asked knows what happened to it."

"Maybe it rolled off and killed somebody." Again that gormless smile.

They gazed up at it. Cassie didn't say that it was one of her few favorite things in the town; she secretly loved his outline against the deepening blue of dusk, enjoyed the irony of his strain to uphold nothing. Were the statue ever to be repaired or removed, she'd grieve for it.

They resumed their walk, past the Lutheran Church, the Catholic Church, three empty shopfronts, the Tap, the IGA, the Masonic lodge.

The light was slanty and golden, the best it was all day; closing her eyes, Cassie smelled gardens. *If I could live my whole life here standing out in a field under a tree, at just this time of day, it would be all right.*

Cal swallowed audibly. "Your dad said you'd go to the movies with me. Tomorrow night."

"Roy is *not* my dad! D'you hear me?"

He nodded. She started to walk away. "And he doesn't keep my social calendar." As if she had one.

"Tomorrow night?" Cal said.

Get into a pickup and drive off with this man, who walked with an idiotic contentment that judged nothing? She was in judgment every waking moment. "What are you doing here?" She was suddenly angry. "If I may be so bold? Where'd Roy find you? Can't you see there's nothing here? You're not going to make any kind of living. This place is dying by inches. Why don't you go to some lively town and get a job there? Anyway, Roy's a rat, nobody wants to deal with Roy unless they have to."

He stared at her for a moment, then dropped his eyes to where he was scuffing the ground with the toe of his boot. "I reckon it'll be all right."

"It's not going to be all right. Last night? When he dragged you in without notice? That was my supper you ate. You think, come Friday, he's going to pay you? Don't count on it."

"Tomorrow night," he said. "After supper. Show's at seven."

He scuffed a bit more, then walked off.

She shouted at his back. "Don't count on it!"

Her mother and Roy disapproved of movies: she on religious grounds, he as a waste of money. Therefore, Cassie had seldom been to the pictures. She was childishly transfixed and repulsed by the shootings, the language, the fast cutting and loud flashes.

Cal kept his hands to himself, although they were surrounded by spooning couples whose smooches and murmuring competed with the soundtrack's quieter moments.

Afterward they drank shakes in the pickup outside Dairy Queen. Cassie had not dated in high school, when she'd hovered uneasily between the group of "nice" kids who wouldn't have her, and the skells who would've absorbed and ruined her had she not held herself apart. By now she was used to living in her head.

So this is what all the fuss is about—getting to ride in some guy's truck, having him buy you ice cream. Cal leaned his arm on the open window and finished his shake in one loud slurp. She offered him the rest of hers, but he waved it away and started the engine. The ride back to Drinkwater through cornfields took a half hour. Cal stayed at the speed limit, other cars and trucks passing them with a flash of the high beams. When he dropped her off, it was barely ten P.M.

During the mid-morning lull at the café, Mary asked her daughter if she liked the new young man.

"I don't hate him."

"He wasn't fresh."

"What does that mean?" Cassie snapped.

"I believe," Mary said, as if repeating a lesson she'd been taught, "that he's a decent boy."

"He's not *in*decent, as far as I can see."

Mary showed her watery smile. "Maybe . . . who knows? Maybe you and he will get along."

Cassie stared.

Mary was wiping the food prep area with a gray rag. "Roy said—"

"Oh, I can just imagine what Roy said. But you. You agree? You agree I should get tangled up with some stranger picked out by Roy, that fine judge of character?"

"It's time for you to think about settling down," Mary murmured. "You're at that age."

"You know what it's time for, Ma? It's time for me to finish my education and start my *life*. Do you think I'm ever, ever, *ever* going to get to do that, or am I down on the indentured servitude list forever?"

Cringing, Mary rinsed the rag and draped it over the faucet to dry. "It's what every girl wants, to be taken care of, a husband, a family of your own. He's got a good trade, that young man. He's a good-looking boy. Better than most girls expect."

"I should try to get that scholarship reinstated. I'll be old to be a freshman, but I could still do it. You could get Mrs. Hinneman in to wait tables here. She'd do it just for the gossip." Even as she issued this threat, Cassie was stymied by what it would involve. She was almost penniless. She had no transport.

Mary's eyes flickered at the door that connected the café to the gas station office. Roy might come through it and catch her daughter proposing insubordination.

"I'm not dating that dork," Cassie hissed. "That's final."

"Don't say that to Roy."

"I'm not dating him. I'm not dating *anyone*. Not here. You think I want to end up like you?"

So many of the girls she knew from high school who weren't destined for college did things to themselves. Eileen, who was pregnant and had to get married, stuck herself with pins. Marla, who got pregnant but didn't marry, binged on junk food and stuck her finger down her throat. Annie drank at bars in Flanagan with scary men and looked bleary all the time. Josie got a job at the IGA and put on seventy-five pounds in six months. Liz lost a leg when her boyfriend's meth lab blew up in their basement. Maggie followed her boyfriend to Omaha, where, so they'd heard, she got hooked on drugs and totaled her car.

Cassie wondered what people said about her. She'd never touched those things that got other girls into trouble—boys, drugs, beer, sharp objects—although she thought about them when she raised her eyes from the reading that transported her, but did not, finally, remove her from this place. Some nights she cried, having learned since a child to do so without sound. Lately, too, she took long walks out of town, and screamed at the sky. Neither was a real outlet, because what troubled all her days and nights was a hunger for true conversation, an outlet for all the words and ideas she took in and could not pour out again. When her brother was still here, she'd had that with him. They'd been a pair: loners, secret sufferers, imbibers of imagined lives.

She missed him, but didn't know who it was she missed. Missing him seemed wrong, when she was so angry at what he'd done. All their lives he'd shared with her, until sharing really meant something, and then he'd bailed. When she did hear from him, after long silence, he sent consolation prizes.

There was no longer even pleasure in memory.

The day Cal came to the supper table with a black eye was the first day Cassie felt any real interest in him.

One glance at her stepfather, who could not restrain a smirk, told the source. No point wondering what had happened. Roy's reasons had no logic and taught no lessons useful another time. But this mark on Cal's face made possibilities come into her head.

After the meal, when the men had gone, Mary made her help with the coupon envelopes and the list for tomorrow's trip to the Hinky Dinky. When she finally said good night, Cassie slipped out the kitchen door.

She'd never meant to go anywhere near the rust-streaked trailer or its occupant, but here she was, knocking. Bluish TV light shifted through the windows. Then the TV was off, and Cal was there. In the twilight his chest glowed the color of a peeled banana.

Cassie hesitated, then climbed the two steps and pushed him aside to go in. The trailer smelled of mold and socks. An old plaid couch. No table or chairs. A bed that didn't bear looking at.

"Is this the kind of thing you're used to?" She hadn't intended to start this way. Cal didn't surprise her by replying. She went up to him and pushed back the bill of the cap. Even in the light of the sixty-watt bulb dangling just over their heads, the eye looked bad. He shied away from her.

"Your own father treat you like that? C'mere." Drawing him over to the sink, she ran the water, which failed to get hot. There was no cloth or paper towel. She had to use the hem of her T-shirt, making him kneel so she could stay modest.

"Doesn't make it feel any better," he said. But he was as patient as a good dog while she cleaned his eye. His hair grew in a swirl pattern. When she traced the whorl with her fingertip, Cal sighed and let his forehead rest against her belly. His face felt hot, and gave her a feeling she didn't know how to dispose of, of wanting to press it there, of wanting to cry, of wanting to touch her lips to the top of his head.

"What did you want to come down here for?" She backed up to the sofa and sat down.

He was still kneeling. "Job. Place to live." He shrugged. "They told me—"

"Who's they?"

"My father. Your father."

"He's not my—"

"Said there'd be you."

"He did, huh?"

He spoke more or less like anyone, when he could be bothered. Presumably, he fixed cars with some competence. Yet there was about him a suggestion, intermittent, that he wasn't all there. It occurred to her that she was alone with a half-naked man, with wide shoulders and a slender white waist that disappeared into trousers that hung low, showing his navel and a trail of hair below it. His nipples were light brown and flat, his hand, dropping down from the eye, brushed one, paused for a moment. Colette had described Chéri thus, the hard curve of his bare chest. Cal didn't seem to be thinking that he was alone here with a young girl; he wasn't, Cassie considered, thinking at all.

Springing up, she went to the door. "Keep that clean," she gasped, and jumped out, skipping the steps altogether, landing in the mud, running.

What she'd meant to say to Cal: *They want us to get together and stay. But what if we get together and go?*

They wouldn't, or couldn't, keep a young couple back, prevent them from setting forth for pastures new. Right? Away from Roy, all things seemed possible. Cal had a pickup truck, Cal had a marketable skill, Cal, for all she knew, might have a bit of savings. Cal had, also, a biddable nature: It was that which gave her courage to go to him in the first place. But it was that, too, which gave her pause: how he set his hands on her hips, his boyishly simple look, unconscious of the comeliness of his long body. The sight of the top of his head: He was a man. A real man, whom she began to suspect she could maneuver. But the intimation of that power, inherent in her hips and belly and long hair, was double-edged. Because once she started to drive Cal Dunkett, there was no knowing how long her control might last. Hadn't Mary—here was a new thought—hadn't Mary believed, before she let Roy slip a ring on her finger, that he was her creature, because she could move him with a smile or a kiss? Had she believed that, if only for a month, a week, or a single moment, the moment right before she said yes, and handed over her right to say no forever?

Cal's blankness made her hesitate. She did not trust it, did not trust her own ideas about what she might make him do.

But Cal Dunkett was all she had to work with now.

A few days later, when she'd stepped out the back door of the café for a breath of air, he appeared from the garage. Stood off from her, while she pretended he wasn't there, and a rivulet of sweat trickled down her neck.

"'Nother hot day," he said. He sidled closer, reaching into his pocket. "Got something for you."

"What?"

"C'mere and see."

"Don't you have work to do?"

"C'mere and see."

From inside, the clatter of crockery. Cassie felt her mother might be watching them. She backed up a couple of steps, but Cal came after. Pulled something from his pocket, held it up in front of her face.

"Had these made for you."

Two keys. Shiny clean keys. Newly cut keys.

"So you can drive to the library, up to Flanagan. That's where you like to go, right?"

She watched the keys dangling from his hand in front of her eyes.

"What's in all those books you're always into?"

"Life is, that's all. Real life." The sun struck globs of light off the keys.

"So you can go. Take 'em."

The kitchen noise behind her, the gunning of an engine, the weedy expanse on which Cal's trailer sat, all narrowed down into just that mesmerizing brightness. She reached for them.

Cal's hand closed. Cutting off the gleam. She blinked.

"Kiss me first."

Throwing him a look of contempt, she wheeled and barged back into the kitchen. Cal knew better than to follow her.

As she worked, Cassie was aware of her nipples, of a tingly, tugging sensation *down there*. Nothing new, but more urgent now as she pictured Cal's mouth, his big nimble hands. For once, none of her imaginary friends was present in the café: Henry James's usual stool stood empty. It was just her in her head, alone with the idea of Cal's body, Cal kneeling, Cal's stupid, calm patience.

That night she waited in her room to hear Roy come in from the Tap and clomp up the stairs to bed. Then she slipped down, barefoot, out the kitchen door, closing it without a noise. She imagined bursting upon Cal, inflicting with her fist a blow she could then tend to as he knelt before her.

She fell against him where he sat in the dark on the trailer step. Heard beer spilling from the bottle she'd overturned, heard also his low chuckle as he settled her across his knees.

She'd been going fast, but now everything slowed down. He hummed, holding her. It was a moonless night, and back here away from the lights of houses, things were just dark shapes. His mouth, when she got at it, tasted of beer, but good. He kissed slow, but his hands moved, not fast but thorough, up under her T-shirt, down the waistband of her jeans, leaving trails of brightness on her skin. Remembering his appalling bed, she wanted to be in it with him.

When they moved inside though, the bed was made up tight as a drill instructor's. The thin, tatty sheets smelled of detergent when he spilled her across them, tugging her jeans off, catching her flailing legs under his arm. It was darker in here than outdoors; Cal became a blacker shape against black, standing at the bed's foot.

Then he kissed her knee.

She froze. Tried to see him in the dark, see an actual grown man, holding her leg up in his hands and touching his mouth to the kneecap, the side of the knee, the ticklish back. Sliding his mouth along the calf. Not seeming to care about its unshaven down. Tongue tracing the dust on the bare sole; exploring the toes. This was not a capability she'd have attributed to Cal Dunkett. She wanted the big thing gotten over with first, and exploration afterward. Like when she'd had her ears pierced—watching the girl fuss with the accessories, anticipating pain, wanting it over. *C'mon, you big Casanova, just pierce me.* But it was awesome too, to have your toes kissed. *Chéri,* she thought, *probably kissed Léa's toes.*

Her other foot rested against his chest. She slid it down, pressed it against his flat stomach, and then past the heavy belt buckle against a firm bulge that returned the pressure of her foot. She knew it was there because of her, that mysterious thing, and yanked her leg away, rolling, giggling, hearing the *clink-clink* as he undid his belt buckle.

He was, from standing over her, suddenly *there*, all around her. She listened to his short, hard breathing; heard it get shorter and harder when her hand sought that pulsing knot and found it now a different shape, a wilder temperature against her palm. She dropped it before it burned her. He put her hand on it again. It was too dark to see, but she closed her eyes anyway, taking the tour. Rough hair and skin soft-over-hard, dry some places and others slick, shapes she'd never touched before. The sound of his breathing told her what she was doing. His own hand worming its way between her pressed thighs. Then he withdrew, fumbled for something under the pillow. She heard the torn packet hit the floor as he turned to her again.

It felt better than she'd expected, but not as good as she believed it was supposed to. His back went from powdery to sopping as it rose and fell beneath her clutching hands. She was loose, flushed, but even so, grew sore. It seemed to take a while, yet also to be done too quickly. When he rolled off, she was ready to begin again. Trapping her wrist, he moved it firmly from his shrinking flesh. After a moment of holding her hand, he pressed it back against her side.

"You're nice," he said.

She barely heard him. She was thinking, *So this is it!* She wanted to compare notes with Colette, with Charles and Anthony. Still, lying here beside Cal, her pride in owning this experience, having chosen it, was already ebbing. After all, here she was, right where Roy and her mother wanted to put her. When they got wind of this, they'd force her and Cal together until they took, or something exploded.

This might be the last moment's peace they would get.

She touched his shoulder. "Cal?"

He began again to kiss her.

"Cal—wait—" Interposing her hand between their mouths, she pushed him back.

"Wanta do it again?"

". . . Yes. In a minute. Two things first."

"Two things?" He sounded just slightly affronted.

"Two things. One—don't tell anybody about this. Don't tell Roy, especially, but don't tell anybody else. At the Tap. Anywhere."

Even as she said this, she felt a little foolish: when had he ever been heard to boast, or even talk? But Roy could get blood from a stone.

"I won't tell. Thing two?" He was stroking her thighs. She parted her legs and gasped.

"Have you got any money saved up?"

He became still. Was this the unsound of Cal thinking?

"I need to get out of here. We need to get out of here. Some garage in Lincoln might hire you—you're a good mechanic, aren't you? You don't want to work for Roy. He's probably cheating you. He blacked your eye."

"I made a mistake."

"That's no excuse."

"It's all right here. It's all right." His hand was moving again. It happened again for her, so quickly she bit her tongue, and again almost as soon as he was inside her, so that he chuckled and said, "Hey, you're really into this, aren't ya?"

There was no use pretending not to be. She snuck back home near four, a scant few minutes before her mother rose to open the café.

Cassie expected everything to be different now she'd been admitted to the sex mystery—and found it was and wasn't. Sex made the sky more wondrous, the air taste sharper through her nostrils. It also made Drinkwater dingier; it made her look at people and wonder what fucking was like for them, except that she didn't want to apply her new secret knowledge to the familiar faces around her. The pleasure she wrung from her body made it worse to be trapped here. There ought to be other men for her, who would be more than sex, men like Renaud and Jean and Chéri, and sex ought to be part of something else, a life filled with great loves, great work. A Colette life. Cassie pondered that, as she went doggedly about her usual duties involving toast, damp rags, bacon grease, coffee rings on chipped gray Formica, suggestive jokes from men she had to face over and over, hot steam and dirty dishes.

The keys Cal had given her didn't do her much good. The cobbler's children went barefoot. Half the time his truck was in pieces awaiting unspecified adjustments. As the summer wore on, Cassie's restlessness deepened into an itch so far inside that she couldn't hope to reach it; at first it seemed that fucking would ease it, but that quickly became, like the reading, just a stopgap.

She tried talking to him again, in his bed, where he seemed most amenable.

"Why don't you want to go to Lincoln?"

"What's so great about Lincoln?"

"The university is there. And don't you think you could earn a whole lot more than Roy's giving you, practically anywhere else? You're good."

"Dunno."

She lifted her head from his chest, tried to engage his eye. "People—nice, regular people—around here don't bring their cars to Roy because they hate him. Haven't you figured that out yet? You're not the only person he's decked. He's doled out plenty of black eyes in this town. He's bar-fight central. Every year the businesses lose more money. We owe all over town for supplies. We only eke along like this because people feel sorry for Ma, because she's lived here all her life."

Cal made no reply.

"You and I could start over somewhere else, it would have to be better than this. We wouldn't have to sneak around, either."

Cal sat up.

"What?" she said.

"I'm not going to leave here, okay? So drop it."

"Why? Who's stopping you? Roy can't *stop* you. Put the truck back together and *go*."

"No one's going, okay! So shut up!" He slammed a fist into the wall, right through the flimsy paneling. The whole trailer shook, and there he was with his hand stuck in the jagged hole.

Cassie leaped out of bed. The wall one minute, and her face the next? She didn't want to find out.

Cal retrieved his hand, which by some miracle was barely scratched. "Where're you going? It's still early."

She didn't answer, jumping into her jeans, stuffing her bra and panties into the pockets.

She avoided him for three days, as much as she could, having still to face him across the supper table every night.

What, besides her own favors, did he get out of being here? His answers were so obtuse. Roy gave me a job. I have a place to live. Have you.

She wanted to say, *What if you didn't have me? What if I up and left?*

But she couldn't say that out loud, it would hurt too much, since she hadn't done it yet.

Coming and going to him, she'd been discreet. But now that she'd stopped for a little, she realized that everyone knew, and probably had almost since the beginning.

At the supper table, Roy gave suggestive jabs to Cal when she served them both, made remarks that caused Mary to beg him to hush. People in the café began to ask her if the date was set. Josie at the IGA, when she handed the change, asked her if she had her ring yet. No? Maybe for Christmas, she said. Christmas engagements were so nice.

Was this how it happened to everybody else? Did marriage rise up to meet them like floodwaters, while they thought they were just minding their own business? It would befall her, if she stood still. That seemed to be all anybody wanted of her, Cal included, that she just stand still.

At first she caught up on sleep, but the urge to go to Cal was relentless, it built through the night, night after night. After five nights apart, he came and threw pebbles at her bedroom window, but she didn't open it.

"You still mad at me?" he asked her the next morning, coming into the café kitchen with a startling boldness. "You know I'd never mean you any harm." She backed him out the door. Touching him made her knees feel watery. She'd thought, at the outset, that she could drive him with sex, but it hadn't occurred to her that sex would end up driving her. Women, she'd been brought up to believe, weren't like that. But it was a lie.

"I miss you, nights," he said.

"Take me away from here, and I'll come back to you."

Roy appeared in the back doorway of the garage, and Cassie skittered back inside.

· · ·

But that night her resistance was over; she snuck out as usual after Roy was asleep.

Cal, waiting outside as if he knew that tonight she would return, guided her to the truck. They drove into the hot night, the high beams lighting up a stream of flying bugs that squashed against the windshield. Parked up a dirt road, they climbed into the pickup bed. Above their heads the sky stretched away, pinned in place by a million white points, with a slice of moon making a single rent in the fabric. He settled her against him, his back propped against the truck's rear window. They picked out the constellations.

"How come you know so many?" Cal asked.

"My brother taught me. He learned them from books, I guess. We used to spend a lot of time at the cemetery at night, stargazing."

"Your brother."

"Yeah. He went to college."

"You see him?"

She shook her head. "He lives in New York. He has a whole other life. He never came back—" *for me.*

"You think New York is so great?"

"I dunno. I'm more interested in Paris." This lay between them like a fart. He ignored it, politely.

After a while she felt the tenor of his breathing change. His arms were wrapped around her tight. "You scared me, when you stopped coming."

"You scared *me,* when you freaked out like that. Don't do that shit, Cal. I get enough of that at home."

"Cass . . . you know I love you, don't you?"

This was news, not uninteresting, not unaffecting. His words made an emotion well up that she couldn't—didn't want to—name.

"I'd like to take you out of here. I'd like to take you anyplace you want to go. Anyplace those books talk about."

She waited.

"Or anyway, to Lincoln, if that's what you want. Only . . .

your dad—I mean, Roy—he didn't tell you anything about me, did he?"

Cassie started to turn, to see his face in the meager moonlight, but Cal put an arm across her chest to hold her gently still.

"A while ago, I helped a couple guys knock over some convenience stores. All I did was drive. But they shot up one place, and we were caught. . . ."

A dank sensation, the opposite of surprise, came over her.

"My dad was able to pull a few strings to get me released early, but my parole says I stay here and keep this job with Roy and check in every week, for the next eighteen months. So if you'd wait for—"

"You were in prison."

Now he was the one spinning silence. His face was invisible under the cap bill in the dark. She pushed it up until the faint starlight caught on his eye-whites.

"Never again, though. That's the thing, Cass. Never again, not with you to look after."

She couldn't bring herself to say her first thought, *You've got to be kidding*. He took her head in his hands. She let him push her backward, let him come over her with kisses. Her head raced around what he'd said. *All I did was drive*.

She put her fingers between their lips. "How long were you in there?"

"Too long. Almost a year." She felt his breath against her ear. "I couldn't stand it. I was gonna crack up, then my dad managed to—he's knows a guy in the state capitol—they fixed it so I could get out if I had a job I'd stick to."

"What was it like in there?"

He chuckled. "I didn't meet nobody like you, Cass." He began to kiss her again, his hands straying.

"No—what was it *like*?"

He got up on one elbow and looked down at her, although there was no telling what he could actually see. When he spoke his voice was changed. "There's some questions you just don't ask. It was just bad, okay? Bad. I'm not gonna go back."

"Okay."

"I mean . . . some guys never change. But not me. I've changed all over. I'm not doing that stuff anymore. It's been rough, but I'm okay now."

She wanted just to take what he said as he said it. His hands were so welcome on her body. "You make me feel lucky. I'm gonna be all right . . . with you. Everything you want, I'll get it for you." He kissed her nose, and she could feel him smile. "You'll see. You and me, it'll be good."

While they fucked, Cassie wondered at her own power; a couple of months ago she didn't know this man at all, and now he was making earnest pledges to her. Again she thought of her mother, lured into the snare by some charm Roy must once have possessed.

Afterward, she drifted in his arms, breathing the night smells, the odor of their commingled sweat. One fuck drifting into another, one day into another, and that way the years piled up. She could feel them already. The years for her brother, who'd packed that box full of wonderments for her, did not pass as hers did. His must be spangled, high-stepping.

And when Seth found some girl to lie in *his* arms, she wouldn't whisper in his ear about promises of reform.

Because it was her birthday, her mother cooked, panfrying a chicken and making mashed potatoes from scratch. When she came down, Cal was already sitting at the table like a totem pole. Mary looked up from the stove and smiled at her, her face shining from the heat, her hair fluffing weakly around her narrow shoulders. She'd put on eye shadow and a Sunday blouse that only accentuated her thinness, her stringy neck of a much-older woman. Cassie kissed her. They hardly ever touched anymore, since she was grown-up, but

Mary stood on tiptoe to press her lips to her daughter's forehead.

"You're taller than me, when did that happen?"

"Guess I'm still growing."

Mary put a hand through Cassie's long ashy curls. "Oh, you—twenty-one. I can hardly believe it." Her voice dropped into a whisper. "You're so like your father. Of course, he was gone before you came. Never got to see you."

"Am I really? I wish there were some pictures. Isn't Seth like—"

"Hush now, here's Roy," Mary said, bringing bread and the tub of margarine to the table.

From the doorway, Roy regarded them, eyes narrowed. "You were in some kind of hurry to get your supper," he said to Cal. "You didn't finish up on the Chevy, did you?"

"It'll be ready when he wants it, in the morning," Cal said.

"That's not what I asked you." He made as if to go over to Cal, but then took in the rest of the scene: Cassie sitting, Mary standing up frying chicken. "Oh. The birthday, right." He washed and took a beer from the fridge. Usually he brought one for Cal, but today he didn't. Cassie got up and gave him one, then resumed her seat.

Roy rubbed his hands together. It was a gesture that in most men would have been avuncular. "What were you all talking about when I came in?"

Cassie opened her mouth, and Mary rushed to answer, "Cal was telling us about his mother's fried chicken." She began serving, Roy first.

As they ate, Roy chuckled, throwing glances at Cassie that made her keep her gaze fastened to her plate.

"So, twenty-one," he said. "All legal." He exhaled a giggle. "Guess I should take you to the Tap for a drink now, huh? Twenty-one's the age."

"Roy, now you know you're not going to do any such thing," Mary said, her voice thin.

"Well, maybe *someone* should," he said, clapping Cal on the back and roaring.

When it was time to clear, Cassie helped, although her mother tried to keep her seated. She wanted something to take her out from under the direct gaze of the men. Roy's face was a snigger, and Cal had a woebegone cast to his eyes that would have made her laugh if it had been directed at anybody other than herself.

"Ready for your cake?" Mary lit the candles and began to sing. The men didn't join in. She persisted, her voice quavering, to the last *you*, and pressed another kiss on Cassie's forehead. She blew out the candles. Mary handed her two wrapped presents.

"From Roy and me."

"Thanks." She took the packages without hope. The first box held a little white plush dog, wearing a T-shirt that said I WUV YOU. The other was a hardcover book; for a moment, seeing the top edge, she thought maybe for once her mother might've gotten it right. But it proved to be a Christian romance. "They told me up at Wal-Mart that this one is a big seller right now," Mary said.

"Looks great," Cassie replied. She piled the dog on top of the book and started to get up, but Mary touched her arm.

"I think someone else's got something for you."

Cal was on his feet, holding out a small square box wrapped in white tissue paper. As soon as she saw its size and shape, she knew she didn't want even to touch it.

It was well-wrapped, done at the store. A gold ribbon, curled at the ends. She pulled the wrappings off. The box was covered in something that was supposed to approximate dark-blue velvet. She couldn't bring herself to open it. Cal came around the table and opened it for her, and she saw what she'd been dreading. The stone was tiny; she suspected it wasn't even real, not that it mattered to her. Her hand spasmed. Mary and Cal both dropped to fish for the ring under the table, and she was left to Roy, who faced her with his hands resting on the table.

"You sure are one lucky girl. You're going to be all taken care of now."

Cal bobbed up, the ring held in his fingers; taking her hand, he began to slip it on. She pushed him away; the ring went flying again.

The only thing any of them said that she could recall later on came from her mother, who should've known by then when to keep her mouth shut.

"Maybe," Mary said, "maybe it *is* too soon for Cassie to take such a big step."

Time crunched up against itself like the pleats of an accordion. When it expanded again into normality, she was alone, staring at a smear of Mary's blood on the sharp edge of the kitchen counter. Roy always faulted her, afterward, for being so clumsy, for managing to get herself so badly hurt by his gestures that, he maintained, he meant nothing by.

Cassie looked at the red mark for a long time. The light was dim; her eyes stung, the mark seemed to shift its shape and distance from her as she fixed on it.

"Cass."

She turned to see Cal beckoning from the doorway.

"Go away! This is all your stupid fault! Go—go—go!"

He came in, put an arm around her. His embrace and his voice were gentle, but her skin rebelled in gooseflesh.

"Don't stay here tonight. Don't be here when he comes back."

She let him lead her to the trailer. He sat on the couch and pulled her down onto his lap. She sat there, straddling his leg, his arms around her waist, through a string of sitcoms and loud commercials. Sometimes he kissed her on the back of her arm, which was nearest his mouth. He put his hands through her hair, and she let herself be soothed. He said nothing about the ring, or about anything. At eleven he turned off the TV.

"Come to bed."

"No, I—I'd better get back. I need to see if my mother's all right."

He didn't try to stop her walking out. She wondered what she'd have done if he had.

In the kitchen, everything was as she'd left it. Roy was in the sitting room, watching TV, a can of beer in his hand and a few more at his feet. Her hands tingled at the sight of him. She thought of murder. Surprise might do it—surprise and then a sofa cushion. When the volume jumped up for the commercial, he looked at her over his shoulder.

"You are some kind of troublemaker."

"How's Ma?"

"They're keeping her there overnight. Observation."

"Observation of what?"

"Concussion. That woman falls over if you puff air in her direction." He shrugged at her and raised the volume on the TV.

Cassie went upstairs, crept into Roy and Mary's room. Eased open the top drawer of the bureau, felt among Roy's folded y-fronts for the thin envelope that held the weekly house money. With the little she'd managed to hold back over the years, there might be enough. It would have to be enough.

She waited until she heard the TV go off, Roy's heavy tread on the stairs, the bedroom door shutting on him. Then she continued to wait, one hour, two. Quietly, she began to gather things together. All she had by way of luggage was her old high-school backpack; it wouldn't hold much. She mashed in some clothes, a few of the books.

Boots in hand, Cassie eased herself down the stairs. Moving smoothly, holding her breath, she opened the kitchen door, slipped outside. Her bike, which had been her brother's, was in the storm cellar. She wrestled it up the stairs.

It took almost an hour to pedal to the truck stop outside Flanagan. A couple of times headlights came up behind her and she was so sure it was Roy, having discovered her theft, that she just tipped over into the tall corn and lay hidden there, her right leg half-crushed under the bike's crossbar, until the vehicle passed, until she couldn't even hear it anymore.

She left the bike leaning against the wall of the little shelter where the Greyhound buses drew up. She was the only person to board the 5 A.M. eastbound bus. She kept her eye on the bicycle as long as she could as the bus moved out, wondering whose property it would become by the end of the day.

13

The driver's announcement startled Cassie awake. After two days and nights, the coach was about to slip into the tunnel, into the island of Manhattan.

When the bus pulled into its berth in the Port Authority station, all she could see was concrete pilings and other buses. As the passengers filed off, Cassie stayed planted in her seat. How could she go out there? New York City was a black maw! What if the phone number Seth had sent her didn't work or was disconnected? She'd never find him: she had no idea where he lived. What on earth had she been thinking, coming here like this?

Not to mention the distinct possibility—likelihood—that, *if* she found him, he wouldn't be glad to see her.

As she stared out the coach window at the grimy glass of the bus gate, Cassie flashed on herself as a child in the schoolyard, anxiously watching the jump rope whip around, feeling its backdraft on her skin, gathering her courage to make one fluid step into it, and become one with its intense beating. Done correctly, it was like stepping through into a different dimension; if miscalculated, the rope left a red stinging slash across the cheek, the brand of the graceless. You mustn't be aware of the rope, mustn't let yourself be hypnotized by the whispered *thuck thuck thuck*; you must just slip in. Once you were within the whipping rope, you could not stop, but you were safe, too, in a pocket of ordered calm.

It took a couple of tries to find a pay phone that worked, and then she flubbed it, reaching someone who shouted at her in Spanish. That mistake cost her a quarter, a twelfth of all the money she had left.

She tried again, referring to Seth's note, which she'd kept wadded up in her pocket through the whole journey. After six rings the phone was answered by a sultry man's voice that said, "Hello lover. How was your night without me?"

Another wrong number! It was like the dream she sometimes had where the only thing between her and an engulfing monster was a phone that failed over and over to work. But no wonder, the way her fingers were shaking. As she reached up to hit the cradle and try again, the voice said,

"Hey—hello? Are you there?"

This time the intonation felt familiar. "Seth? Is that you?"

A pause. Then— "Oh, my God. Cassie?"

"Yes. It's me, it's Cassie." Stomach clenched, her gaze whirled over the ugly space, the dull brown tiled walls and floor, the neon signs, masses of moving people. An aroma of cinnamon buns, almost pure sugar, wafted at her, and her gorge rose.

"I'm in the bus station. Can you come get me?"

A silence. Then—"Jesus, *what* bus station?"

"The—what do they call it? Port of Authority? In New York City."

"What the hell are you doing here?"

What the hell am I doing here? Cal's face rose up before her, his ground-down dinner-table look, his passive half-smile. The sensation of Cal's arms settling around her waist, holding her like she was a ventriloquist's dummy, even though she was the one who made up the scenario, fed him his words, and bought the illusion she'd created. "I . . . needed to see you. So can you come fetch me out of here?"

In the Burger King opposite the bus terminal where he'd told her to wait for him, she got coffee and potatoes and took a seat in the corner where she could see the door.

At the table next to her a young Indian couple chatted together. Urdu? Cassie was proud of knowing the name of that language. Although maybe it was Hindi? The woman wore a pink sari over a fuzzy acrylic sweater in the same pink; the end of her sari kept slipping down off her shoulder, and she brushed it back up without pausing in her talk. She had long red fingernails and big gold hoops in her ears, but to Cassie's disappointment her chin receded and her upper teeth stuck out.

Glancing around as she blew at the coffee, she noticed she was the only white person in the entire crowded place. She ate one of the Tater Tot things, squishing it hot and greasy between her tongue and the roof of her mouth. This first hot food since leaving Drinkwater awakened a wild hunger; she bolted them and wanted to get more, but nothing remained of her money but some coins. This really was the end of the line. If Seth hadn't answered that phone . . .

Okay, but he had.

At the door, three homeboys made their swaggering entrance, each wearing the baggy jeans, unlaced sneakers, huge jerseys and do-rags she'd seen on television. One of them had gold teeth. Their booming talk and laughter drowned every other sound. At first she didn't notice the young man who slipped through in their wake. But when she did, she realized he was much more exotic: he wasn't just white, but *white*: milky skinned, unnaturally blond, dressed in close-fitting whitish clothes that showed off a sculpted body. Burger King didn't seem to be his kind of place; he stopped just inside the doorway, his body almost rippling with impatience, and scanned the tables. She dropped her eyes so their gazes wouldn't cross and then checked the street through the big windows for her brother's high-shouldered slouch.

A hand came down on hers, almost upsetting the coffee, and she jerked her head around, right into the faggy guy's face. Snatching her hand back, she was astonished when he called her by name.

Her stomach heaved against the wodge of potatoes. Seth . . . Seth? When she'd last seen him, six years ago, he was a teenager hiding his skinny, pimply, pasty self behind greasy gray hair and a shapeless gas-station coverall with his name machine-stitched on the breast. It never had occurred to her as she endured the long bus ride toward him that he'd look any different—she'd barely anticipated that he wasn't going to be seventeen anymore. Aware of the hot gazes of brown people fixed on them, she shrank back; not wanting to be identified with this . . . *creature*.

"What's the matter," he said, "can't you speak? All right, let's get out of here. C'mon." Grabbing her things, he tugged her up. She let him steer her out into the moving mélange of humanity on the street, holding her arm so tightly that it hurt. What had happened to him? Maybe this getup was a joke? But who made jokes like that at eight o'clock in the morning?

In the cab, he turned that intense gray gaze on her again, "I can't believe this. What are you doing here?"

"You are wearing eye makeup." Even as she saw it, even as she *said* it, she still couldn't make sense of it. Maybe he *wasn't* Seth. Maybe this was Seth's roommate, whom he'd sent in his place. Maybe this was Seth's zombie, the one that ate him when he got here, and took over his soul. Of course she knew his voice, and those snapping eyes—they'd been Seth's one beauty when all else with him was acne and moroseness.

"What have you *done* to yourself?"

"What's happened to *you?* For chrissakes, Cassie! Coming all the way out here with no warning, what am I supposed to—has something happened to Ma?"

"No more than the usual." She knew this was not the way to proceed with him, not when she had to depend on him now for everything, but she couldn't bring herself to stop.

The cab drew up, he paid and herded her out. She followed him unseeing up steps to a metal door, into a vestibule and through another metal door, then in and up a flight of stairs. Watched him fumble at the lock on a third big door, unable, after three tries, to get the key into it. He swore under his breath, stopped and leaned against it.

"Cassie."

"What?"

"This is not what I planned for today. I had my whole day mapped out and it did not include the sudden mysterious appearance of my bitter, hard-hearted sister."

Her exhausted mind presented her with snapshots of the last half hour: the dark eyebrows seen through dyed blond bangs, the pointy sideburns, the hard body in its pale clothes. These fell into place in her system of understanding, connecting with other details that had, before this, contained more idiosyncratic meanings: the drawings he was always scribbling and burning, the Russian and English novels, his brooding isolation, the little fires, maybe even Roy's punishments. They were all signs that pointed to this, which he'd hidden from her. So, those stupid girls in the locker room, talking about him while she pretended not to be able to hear, were right. And he wasn't just gay, he was an extra-weird, hyped-up, show-offy kind of gay.

"When that box came, I thought, fuck you, don't do me any favors *now*."

"Cassie, when I left home I was eighteen, what was I supposed to do about you? I . . . I could only save myself! Some things—you just have to manage by yourself, no matter how scary or difficult they seem."

He fitted the key now, turned it, paused.

"What's in there you don't want me to see?" she said.

"Huh? N—nothing."

"So open up. I need to pee."

He steered her straight into the bathroom, hustling her past any chance to look around at the loft's decadences, and shut her in.

Jim was with clients in California, a miraculous bit of good fortune. Cassie was a ticking bomb, to be removed with gingerly dispatch. He'd have to put her up somewhere that was decent but not too nice, and pretend he was maxing out his Visa card to do it. Seth drew the heavy shades over the front wall of windows. She mustn't see his pictures—narrative paintings that would make her head spin—hanging in the front room. The less light he let in, the less details she'd grasp before he could hustle her out again.

Balancing two mugs of coffee, he knocked on the door.

"Do you want me not to look?"

"Come on. I guess it's nothing to you, anyway."

She was up to her chin in scented bubbles, wrestling a comb through her long wet hair. Amid the half-full bottles of lotions and potions from Kiehl's, loofahs, brushes, sponges and plastic bath toys, she'd found the very bubble bath he and Jim always used together. Its scent evoked a complicated olio of sex and confidences that made her presence in it all the more confusing.

"So here you are with your hair still gray," Seth said, sitting on the rim of the tub. The self-contained, windowless room felt safe, like a sterile clean room. He'd get her out of here in an hour, and all would be well.

"I like it, it's my own. Roy hates it, so if for no other reason . . . but never mind that. Look at you. Your skin sure cleared up."

"Uh, yeah, thanks. I guess." He wished he was wearing something with sleeves.

"So . . . this is very fancy. He's very rich, the guy who owns this place, right?"

"Well, yes, but you see, he—I mean, I'm just here—"

"You let him do stuff to you in bed, and in exchange you live here and he pays for you. Is that it?"

Seth started. "No! No, that's not true."

"Well, that's you, isn't it? And the man?"

Seth glanced where she was pointing. *Fucking hell.* He'd forgotten about this picture, which, just last week, Jim had insisted on framing and hanging in here. An ink drawing, gothic with layers of crosshatching and wash, in which his own sprightly kneeling figure, a lick of phosphorescence amidst the shadows, was coupled with Jim's as an immense, possessive, dark sort of minotaur, hugged tight to the curve of his back, inside him to the hilt, gripping his sex in one massive hand. Staring at the picture, Seth remembered his excitement as he'd made it, late at night, in bed beside Jim asleep. As he drew with the pen and brush on the pebbled surface of the paper he'd still felt an after-resonance of being impaled by Jim in just that way, the undoing ecstasy of it, and watching it in the mirror as it happened.

A melting, undoing sensation gripped him now, with a difference. His machinating plans of five minutes ago collapsed. Absurd, unworkable lies. Shameful. Shameful to be so ashamed of himself.

"Yes, that's me. And . . . and Jim."

"So have you been doing this ever since you got to New York? Or even before that? Did he take you right off the street, or—"

"What . . . what are you talking about?"

She craned around and looked at him, grave and unflinching. "I get what you are, Seth. You're like a . . . a courtesan. You have an arrangement. That's why you look like that, how you get to live in a place like this, why you had all that cash to send me all at once."

"Cassie . . . my God. What have you been reading to get these lurid ideas? Jim is my partner—my lover. This is our home." Her accusation was not so wide of his conscience's mark that he could defend against it without a pang.

"Sure it is," she said. "Oh, yeah. I really get that."

He watched her, perched on a kitchen stool wrapped in his terry robe, devour two toasted bagels, four fried eggs and bacon, two tall glasses of milk. She kept shaking her head, as if she couldn't believe the depth of her hunger. Seth smoked and drank another cup of coffee, unable to take his eyes off her. In six years she'd become lush, with real hips and tits, a behind, round arms and shoulders. Her face was different too, sharper, with something veiled about the eyes and stung, or stinging, he wasn't sure, about the mouth. Sometimes she looked almost old, and then he could see the little girl still peering out of her eyes. The changes spooked him, because unlike so many of his, they surely weren't deliberate.

"So okay," he said, trying to sound nonchalant, "You said on the phone that you wanted to see me."

"Yeah." She gave an angry shrug.

"But now you've seen what you've seen, and drawn your conclusions—you don't want to talk to me?"

With a sigh she plunked her arms on the counter and cradled her head.

Seth said, "Okay . . . you finally just had enough, you said good-bye and off you went."

"I didn't say good-bye." She sat up again. "I ran away. I stole the house money out of Roy's drawer and rode your old bike at three in the morning up to the truck stop to get the bus. I had to leave it there, but I guess you weren't coming back for it yourself either."

He blinked. What a getaway. "If you'd kept that money I sent you, you could've flown—"

"Look," she cut in, "I dunno what you thought I was going to do with five hundred dollars. It wasn't enough to get me off to college on, was it, even if I could've kept it. I sent it back because Roy and Ma were right there when I got the box, and it was either return your wages of sin, or Roy was going to confiscate it, like he confiscates everything else I ever earned. Okay? I didn't think you really wanted Roy to have your money." She glanced meaningfully around at their surroundings. "Your money which you must've worked so *hard* to get."

He ignored her implication with an effort. "I worked hard for that photographer for just enough to keep body and soul together so I could go to art school and paint. I was barely getting by. As soon as I could, I sent you what I could spare. If I'd heard any little word from you, I'd have sent you every penny I had."

She frowned his sincerity away, examining the end of her braid as if there was an oracle in the tassel.

"Anyway, why didn't you at least let me know you were coming? I might have been out of town, and then what would you have done?" The vision of Cassie disembarking from the bus, knowing not a soul for hundreds of miles around, calling him and getting no answer, made him queasy.

"Look, I knew you weren't going to want me here. I'm not wrong, am I? I didn't phone you from the road because you'd have told me to go back. And I just couldn't hear that, okay? I just couldn't. You're all I have . . . except I don't have you, do I?"

"You have me. C'mon, Cassie . . . you have me. You do."

She barely acknowledged this. Cassie occupied her stool almost deadweight, the circles under her eyes, the almost imperceptible quivering of her whole body projecting her exhaustion.

"Come lie down before you fall down. C'mon." Now was the time to herd her out of here, but instead he led her to the loft bed in the guest room. She hesitated, glancing at him, then stretched out. Seth sat on the top step beside her.

"I feel like I'm still on the bus. I can still feel it moving."

"Just go to sleep, sugar. I'm right here."

"No, you're not," she said, her voice faint. "You're nobody I've ever met before. . . ."

14

She woke, as on the bus, with a jerk, bleary and still tired. Seth was gone. She wandered out, shivering in the clammy robe she'd worn out of the bath, speaking his name into the still indoor air. The darkened loft had an empty echo to it, like the inside of an enormous seashell. Thin pencils of intense light showed beneath the heavy drawn window covers, illuminating here and there the rich colors of the Persian carpets. The piano and sofas were dark lumps, the pictures on the walls in twilight too obscure to make out.

Now she was here, feeling herself washed up on an acid shore, she missed Cal. He'd not quite been what she'd thought . . . but compared to Seth, he was as pure and transparent as well water. Helpless, too, which maybe made him easy to forgive. And then to leave.

An envelope was propped on the kitchen counter. It was a piece of junk mail; Seth's note was written on the back.

I've gone to my afternoon class, will be back by dinnertime. Stay inside and rest. If the phone rings, let the machine pick it up. Hope you feel better now. Try to adjust your attitude a little, okay? S.

Even Seth's handwriting was different—he'd abandoned his jagged school script for a self-conscious kind of block printing, triangles for *a*'s. *Adjust your attitude.* It was adjusting by the second.

Pulling up the blinds, she blinked in the sudden glare, and began to look around. Seth's paintings, big full-blown canvases, stunned her: it hadn't occurred to her before that her brother could be a real artist. It was only something other people did, people that people like her didn't know at all.

The largest picture, some seven feet square, drew her like a traffic accident. There was a large bed in it, and naked male figures. Even though she was alone, she felt furtive about examining them. It seemed like the kind of thing that ought to be hidden, not hung where people lived, where light poured in from the street.

The painting showed a room: large, white. A bed, also large and white, seen from above and to the side, as if from a high ladder. Diffuse light, making soft gray and blue shadows. In the bed, the covers drawn up to their waists, two men lay at the extreme edges. One, her brother, faced the viewer, wearing glasses with heavy black frames that made him look scholarly despite the earrings and the tattoo, was reading attentively with his head propped on his hand, an arm curved around the book. The other, an older man contrasted in almost every way, by his dark hair and beard, the muscular bulk of his body, appeared to sleep, fleshy lips parted, cheek resting on one doubled-up arm. All around these two solid, oblivious figures, pale nude ghost images hovered, interacting in a state of partial transparency. Most notably to Cassie's rapidly blinking eyes, the pair, clearly Seth and the same dark man, coupling in the space left in the middle of the bed by their solid doubles. The other figures surrounded them, in ones and twos, silent witnesses: she saw her brother again, gazing steadily, stoically at a slender, bearded, red-haired man, who returned the look with an otherworldly calmness. And there was the red-haired man again, standing in the corner, embracing the big dark man, their two heads turned to regard the bed. Perched atop the dresser, one leg drawn up, a cigarette dangling from his mouth, her brother appeared once more, aloof, squinting at the scene, drawing in a sketchbook; the graduated pebbles of his spine reflected even more palely in a watery mirror at his back. And stretched on the floor, face buried in hands, back muscles hugely knotted, was the figure of the dark man, convulsed by pain or grief. The final figure, child-sized compared to the others, was the red-haired one, who floated above the headboard of the bed, near the ceiling, arms spread as though about to dive, or bless. The figures, even the two entwined on the bed, had a static, waiting air, as though they might dissolve into pure light.

Everything she'd assumed about Seth fell to pieces as she looked. Here was her long-gone brother in a new mask, playing a part in a complex drama beyond anything she'd have guessed real life could hold for him. In the space left by her collapsed assumptions was sadness and curiosity and fear.

She knew what she really needed to see and decided to go get it over with.

Just inside she hovered, gazing at that enormous bed. It was the one in the painting. She counted six pillows jammed up against the headboard, where Seth must have pounded them in his sleep. The night tables were stacked with tantalizing books and magazines; on the near one a pretty glass ashtray, overflowing with butts, vied for space with a juice glass whose bottom was smudged red with wine lees, and a paperback novel, its spine cracked where it lay sprawled on its belly. She recognized her brother's old habit of reading and smoking in bed long into the night, the narrow beam of the lamp bringing the page up white in the darkness. It was the first familiar thing about him she'd encountered here.

Having seen the painting first, she could not help staring at the bed, placing those grappling bodies in it. The thought made her feel faint. And here she was having to rely on him for her next meal.

The bureau drawers were crammed with sweaters of cashmere and cotton and beautiful shirts in every imaginable style. These must be Jim's—even as little as she'd already seen of her brother, she knew these didn't match his austerity.

Seth's things took up only a couple of drawers—everything looked newish, but lacked the sheen of expensive self-satisfaction of Jim's clothes.

The drawer of one night table stuck; when she forced it, it disgorged condoms, their green packs linked in snaky profusion, a couple of tubes of something disquietingly called Astroglide, some Polaroids bound together with a rubber band, and—she blinked—a hard rubber object the use for which she did not care to guess.

Slamming the drawer, she turned to the closets.

A faint waft of cologne greeted her as the door opened, and she was confronted by a dark row of hanging suits, and on the floor a neat line of polished loafers and wing tips. The suits were serious and substantial, such as she had only ever seen in *New Yorker* ads at the library. Nobody in Flanagan County wore clothes like that. With hesitant fingers she parted the even row, so she could see one from the front. Slate-gray, double-breasted, with a blank impregnability that awed her. The man who wore these clothes was tall and built solid. The man in the painting and the drawing—the minotaur. How much bigger he'd be than Seth! Older, too, which was creepy all in itself. If she'd found Seth being a faggot with some other boy his own age, that would be bad, but a different, less critical, bad than this was.

The next thing she knew, her fingers were slipping in and out of the pockets of the gray suit. Two ticket stubs for a movie with a French title, an ATM receipt for a $200 withdrawal, a business card for a designer of Web pages, and—what was this?—an old-fashioned looking oval locket without a chain. Unlike the pocket's other contents, this fancy thing fit into her vocabulary of objects, and for that reason she held it for a few moments, letting the gold warm in her palm, while the temptation to see inside it spiraled up from the part of herself she was purposefully keeping dumb. As she pried it open, she bit her tongue and looked up at the ceiling, disowning what her fingers were doing. The catch gave with a little snap. Expecting to see some stiff sepia ancestral faces, she found instead, on the left, a man with a reddish beard in regular Kodacolor, and on the right, Seth. Her brother's head looked so fragile shorn of its long hair. She stared at the image, Seth sentimentally twinned with a stranger.

Then she realized she'd seen the other man in Seth's painting.

"Hey—what are you doing?"

She started, and the open locket flew out of her hand to land at his feet. Seth bent slowly to pick it up. "What are you doing in there? Looking for money?"

"No! No . . . I was just—" She stopped. Seth was looking at the locket.

"Where did you find this?"

"In . . . in the pocket . . . right here. I wasn't going to swipe it. Or anything. I was just . . . curious."

A rapt smile appeared on his lips as he gazed at the two little pictures, but it wasn't for her, she could see that. "You didn't find this in the dresser?"

"No! No, it was right here." Emboldened by the change in his demeanor, she crept closer to him. "Who is that in there with you?"

"Zak."

"So who is Zak?"

Seth gazed at the locket a moment more, his face curiously smooth. "Oh—he was the love of Jim's life."

The painting made a little more sense now, in light of that. The dead boyfriend . . . and of course it was AIDS that took him . . . didn't it, eventually, take all those people?

"I knew when I left you here that you'd snoop around. I kind of wanted you to, so maybe you'd have less to wonder about. But I thought you'd find the porn stash or something. I didn't think you'd have the nerve to actually rifle our clothes." He shut the locket with a brisk snap. "Show me exactly where this was."

"Here." She pulled the gray suit out so he could see.

"You're sure? You're sure you didn't take it out of the cuff link tray in the dresser? Don't lie to me."

"I swear, it was right here. What?"

He'd turned his head sharply, but not so fast that she didn't see again that smile of private delight.

"Seth?"

"Never mind what. Just put it back exactly where you found it, and come out of here."

It all seemed so precarious, this unmapped adult world. She didn't want to know about her brother as a man; in her thoughts they were still children together, partners in subterfuge and fantasy, smarter than the grown-ups who punished them, and better, but just that, just children.

She followed him out of the room. "Seth."

"What?"

"This . . . this . . . way you are," she whispered, "Do you think it's because our real daddy died?"

"No."

"But . . . don't you like girls at all? Have you tried?"

He rolled his eyes. "Are you reading this off of some kind of script? I didn't have to try in order to know myself. I was gay back home, too. Just like all the jocks said I was."

"Oh! So, who . . . um . . . did you . . ."

"Look, I'm not going to tell you who I messed around with in high school. When did you get such a dirty mind?"

"Dirty mind? *Me*? But I mean . . . was there anyone I know?"

Suddenly he *wanted* to talk: after all, whom was he protecting? Her? Certainly not anyone back there. He shuffled through his mental images of the locals he'd known below the waist. "Remember Todd Hopkirk?"

Cassie frowned, pretending to be unsure.

"C'mon, *Todd*—quarterback of the varsity football team. Dated the homecoming queen. Senior year, he was constantly after me to let him suck me off in his parents' storm cellar. He never wanted to be seen with me in public, the big macho jerk, but when he could get me alone, down he'd go. I didn't even have to reciprocate." He still sometimes thought of big tough Todd, who was trying even harder than Seth himself to live undercover. The handful of others Seth had fooled around with acted as though they were doing him a big favor, letting the pervert service them, but Todd, when they were in the cellar together, barely tried to keep up his charade of dominance, of straightness. Once, about a month before graduation, he'd begged Seth to fuck him. Afterward he started to cry. After failing to joke him out of it or comfort him at all, Seth got spooked and left him sprawled there, weeping in a pile of his family's dirty laundry. "He was really something, Todd. And he was not the only one." He grinned, just to get at her, although it was far from a happy memory; there were none from Drinkwater. He'd disliked Todd and feared him, as they met more and more frequently, just as Todd returned that dislike and fear. He'd gone to Lincoln to play football for the U—where was he now?

Cassie shuddered, and turned her head sharply away. "I really would rather not know about that kind of thing."

"If you don't want to know about that kind of thing, then you have thrown yourself on the mercies of the wrong brother."

"You're the only brother I have."

"Then if I were you," he said, "I'd try very hard to keep that in mind."

"Did you know that guy?" Cassie asked.

"No."

"But you smiled at each other as if you did."

"Come on, let's make this light." Seth took her arm and trotted her across Second Avenue. It was a mild night, balmy as June, no sign of winter in the sultry air, the young trees, the strollers' costumes. That felt wrong. In his white chinos and tank, Seth was a pale pillar in the lit-up nighttime street. Cassie noticed that he had a different way of walking that made him seem taller. Gone, with the weighty gray hair, was the self-effacing slouch. That felt wrong, too.

As they cleared the curb, another young man, leaning against a graffiti-covered mailbox, commanded Seth's attention. The stranger's gaze traversed her brother's body, he met Seth's glance with an expression that was dark and wistful, and broke it off with a little smile. Seth had slowed down during this mutual inspection; his head turned and then he was walking sideways; she had to wait for him to catch up.

"Is *that* someone you know?" she demanded.

"Nope. Tragically, he isn't."

Her mind balked. "What is going on here? What are you *doing*?"

"Nothing."

"But if you didn't know those guys, why were you looking at them like that?"

He stopped her. "Now just let me ask you something. Are you *really* that obtuse, or are you trying to wind me up?"

Her throat was closed up tight, so she only looked at him, blinking.

"C'mon."

She forgot the problem of the men in her first sight of East Sixth Street. Confronted with the bright awnings, festooned with signs and fairy lights of the Indian restaurants that occupied every one of the tenement houses on the south side of the block, she was seized by a curious pleasure that was almost alcoholic.

"There's so many! How do you know which one to pick?"

"Everybody swears by one, but so far I haven't heard any two people swear by the *same* one. I forget which one Jim likes. They all have pretty much the same menu. You choose."

"Am I going to like this food?"

"*I* like it."

She paced slowly up the block, looking in at every restaurant. They were all narrow and seemed impossibly small, viewed from the street. A couple of them had turbanned sitar players crouched in the windows, looking cramped and industrious in their exotic robes. She passed these by quickly, afraid to meet a stranger's eyes. At the corner of First Avenue, she sighed. "How can I pick when I don't know anything about it?"

Seth took her elbow and steered her into one, and in the next moment she was seated, with other couples hemming her in on each side. After he ordered for them both, they were left to wait and eye each other across the bare table.

Seth said, "Does Ma . . . ever talk about me? At all?"

"No. Not so's I heard, anyway."

She thought he flinched. "So Roy still reigns?"

"Nobody's staked him yet, so yeah."

Their gazes slid past each other like two cars barely avoiding a collision on an icy road at night. There was nothing either of them wanted to say about Roy; they'd never, at home, talked about his ways. Everybody else in Drinkwater did. They'd always known this, by the way people fell silent when they walked up to the counter at the IGA, or the way they didn't stay silent as they came out of the post office, dropping remarks meant to burn young ears.

"Okay," Seth said. "Let's move on. Here's what I'm prepared to do for you. Tomorrow you'll move to a bed-and-breakfast for a few days, and we'll get started finding you a decent sublet where you can live until we can get you into college somewhere in January. I'll take care of the tuition and your rent until then and clothes, whatever you need, but I think you should get a part-time job in the meanwhile. The rest of your time you'll need to get your transcripts and do your applications and all that, but you'll be happier—less isolated—if you've got somewhere to go most days. If you want to take a couple of evening classes at the New School or something in the meantime, you can do that, too."

She blinked. "You're going to take care of my *tuition* and my *rent?*" She leaned over the table, dropping her voice. "Seth, explain something to me. I've been trying to figure it out all afternoon. Your arrangement with that man in the picture . . . how exactly does it work? You let him do that stuff to you, in bed, and then he pays you each time? Or does he just keep you—like, on a retainer—"

Even in the dimness she could see the ferocity of his blush. "Cassie, *Christ*—! Shut up!"

The waiter was advancing on them now with his laden tray. She averted her eyes. Seth began to eat as if it was his first meal of the day. She picked at the colorful stuff on her plate. The chicken was bright red, the rice like confetti.

"I don't think I want to take any of your hard-earned money."

He answered without looking up. "I don't see how you've got a choice, unless you want to live on the street and beg for small change. Which, if you keep this up, is going to become your only option."

"You can't tell me that the way you live isn't wrong."

"It's true, I can't tell you that. Because you won't listen. Your little mind is closed. Eat your murgha tikka."

"When you went away I thought you were going to be all right. I knew you had to go. But now you're into all this weird disturbing shit, those paintings I saw, how can you *draw* stuff like that? It's nasty."

Seth set his fork down. "Listen. You are just about on my last nerve. You want to live like Jerry Fucking Falwell is king of your mind, you can do that. Now, I will do what I promised to do for you, because you came to me for help, you are my only sibling and I acknowledge that I owe it to you for old times' sake. But the less you say right now about me and mine, the better. Okay? Now eat your food."

She couldn't stand the silence. "So tell me about that man. Jim—Jim what?"

"Glaser. He's what Roy would call a Kike Faggot from Jew York City."

She blenched. Whispered, "He's old."

"He's forty-two, since you're so interested. Not old." In a different tone, he said, "Jim is incredibly kind. I love him like crazy, but he deserves more love than I can give him, a hundred thousand times over. Yet I seem to make him happy. I don't know how. I'm just lucky, for once in my life."

The smile he wore was the same one he'd beamed into the locket before, its simplicity echoed by the twin curves of his lowered eyelids, the mascaraed lashes making spidery shadows on his cheeks. Then he glanced up at her and the look was gone, but he wasn't blushing anymore either.

She held his glittering gaze for a moment, then looked away.

On the street, he took her hand, and after a couple of frozen seconds of picturing where his hands had been, she gripped it tight. They walked; it seemed he meant to show her the neighborhood, but she was too overwhelmed to take anything in. The lights made the sky invisible, but it seemed very low; she thought it was warmer now than before, the air closer. After a while he let go her hand and put an arm around her shoulders instead. The movement released a light cologney scent from his body that she inhaled with unease. He stopped and bought an ice-cream cone, mouthed a little off the top and handed it to her. "I just wanted a taste. Go on and finish it." Again she hesitated, but the initial touch of sugar on her palate overcame her.

"Hmm, some dinner," Seth said.

They went in and out of shops where small garments were laid out on marble slabs, like precious relics.

In one, the clerk smiled at her, and said, "You have the coolest hair. May I touch?" She inclined her head, and the boy (dark, slender, eyebrows that arched), placed his hand on her crown, and drew his fingers down along the side of her face through the tight curls. "Mmm. It's like when a cigarette just burns down in the ashtray, that silvery-gray, that perfect roundness. Fabulous. How do you get it to do that?"

"It . . . it just does. It just is."

"Fabulous," he repeated.

Seth bought her what he called "a few bits of clothing to start with," while assuring her that they weren't really shopping, that he'd take her, tomorrow, to *really* get what she needed. Cassie blanched. If they weren't shopping, what were all these bags she was accruing, of tissue-wrapped garments with staggering price tags? Seth handed over a glimmering credit card without even glancing at the totals.

"So now you're with that man, you don't work a job anymore?"

"Stop saying *that man*. You know his name is Jim." Seth lit a cigarette with an angry flourish.

"I don't think I can take any of this." She prodded the shopping bags at their feet with her toe. "It doesn't feel right to me. Anyhow, I only needed a couple changes of—"

"Of course you'll take them. They're nice things, they look good on you. I want you to enjoy being a pretty girl in the big city. Being yourself. Nobody's going to give you a hard time about that anymore."

She ducked her head. "You think I'm a pretty girl?"

15

The tall glass-encased candle weighed heavily in Jim's briefcase as he climbed the inside stairs to the apartment. It was past one in the morning; the last hours of Zak's yartzeit had expired while the plane circled Newark above an electrical storm, finally landing, more than two hours late, at Philadelphia. He'd decided not to try for a place on a commuter flight to JFK, and rented a car instead. Almost four hours later, he was home—the whole point of cutting the last meeting to get back early defeated. He'd have been better off doing what he'd preferred not to, lighting the candle for Zak in his L.A. hotel room. Well, never mind that the day was over, he'd light it and say Kaddish anyway—Zak had never been on time for a thing in his life, and he'd probably think it appropriate, wherever he was, to have the anniversary of his death marked a little late.

There were no lights on when he opened the door. Good—Seth was asleep. He needed to do this alone. In the morning he wouldn't mind explaining the memorial candle to Seth, but now he didn't want to talk to anyone but Zak—and God.

This anniversary wasn't just Zak's remembrance day. It marked Jim's mourning for all that lapsed with him: the child he didn't get to adopt, the departure from the business world he'd so looked forward to.

He was still there, at the agency, going through the motions, having postponed not just his resignation, but all his vague plans for travel. Seth wouldn't talk about taking off together—not just on account of graduate school, but because he wasn't ready yet for the luxury of idleness. It seemed wicked to him. Jim could commiserate.

The other thing that bound him to New York was those evenings at Bellevue with the babies born to mothers too strung out or helpless to even take care of themselves.

Holding a friendless infant, walking up and down and crooning to her, was, Jim believed, more important than anything else he did—including helping Seth's artistry to bloom. Sometimes he had a dream in which he was all alone in the nursery, the nurses disappeared, and he coped, feeling extraordinary elation in what was his natural domain. When he woke from this dream he felt helpless and stupid, because he'd lost in real life that amazing capacity for knowing what he had to do.

You could get some part of your life fixed and certain—Seth, whose love still astonished him—but it didn't have enough of an effect on the other parts. Why hadn't he learned that with Zak? Perhaps, until the end when they'd lost it all, they'd been *too* blessed.

Slipping off his shoes, he moved quietly into the library to look for the prayer book. Back at the kitchen island, the compact blue book fell open to the Kaddish prayer for the dead. Before he started,

Jim stared into the yellow glow of the little flame, breathing deep, and tried to conjure Zak again—not just his appearance, but his distinctive smell, the sound of his voice and laugh. Except, on the boundary of sleep, these things were less and less available to him. Looking at photographs barely brought them back any more sharply. It was only at times like this, when he was tired, defenses down, that Jim could bring forward again something of the grain of Zak's ginger skin, the mealy timbre of his voice. Looking into the flame, Jim worked at it, and finally felt a presence behind his left shoulder, something almost like breath against his hair. Closing his eyes, he could feel Zak in the rigidity of his spine; he hovered just behind him, almost within him.

Holding this delicate connection, Jim opened his eyes, centering his sight on the bold Hebrew type on the left-hand page of the prayer book. He began the prayer, in a low singsong chant. His father had rocked his body as he prayed, but even though he was alone, Jim felt too self-conscious to do that. He wasn't really a praying man, but the Kaddish felt like an obligation, one he didn't care to shirk. When he reached the end it felt that he was atoning for his own failure to stop living. He began the prayer again, in English this time.

But as he worked through the words, already he was coming back to himself, aware of the ache of the endless day on his shoulders, the pull of the time zones he'd spanned. A yawn caught him before he got to amen. He left the candle and the book, turned off the light. Flickering shadows turned the dining room into a sepulchre. The flame would flicker and ebb for a day, and like the life it represented, go out. Jim walked back toward the bedroom, tugging off his tie, undoing his cuff links. All his business was concluded, there was nothing else to do but go to bed. They weren't expecting him at the office, he could stay in bed all day if he liked. With any luck, light-sleeping Seth wouldn't stir when he joined him; Jim wanted no greetings, just to clasp the boy spoon-fashion and pass out. At the bedroom door he glanced back for one more moment with the shifting golden radiance.

And cried out, his cry at once echoed by an overlapping one that was higher, shriller. The figure stood frozen between him and the glow, a female shade with streaming hair that looked as gray as Miss Havisham's over the streaming white shroud, pale arms luminous in the near-dark, face blanked by shadow. His startled mind reminded him that for a few years before the Civil War, the building contained a coffin works. This tidbit fit perfectly into the shape of his wonderment, explaining all. *She must be from then.* He stared, waiting for reality to reassert itself in her vanishing. Then the shade let out another sound, a sort of long low *hunnhhh*, and dissolved into movement, not toward him, but away. In the next instant she was gone, and something slammed. Jim stumbled backward onto the sofa, grabbed the lamp, turned it on.

The bedroom door opened and Seth peered out, squinting and scratching his head. "What's all the—Jim!"

"Honeyboy, I'm sorry I woke you—" He staggered up, his legs gelid, heart still rushing. Reached for Seth's bare shoulder, warm and moist from sleep, and tugged him in. "I gave myself such a scare just now . . . I thought I saw an apparition, a girl—" He tried to laugh, "Maybe we have a poltergeist. . . ."

The sound of the toilet flushing silenced him. He grabbed Seth closer. "What was that?"

Seth put a hand up against Jim's cheek. "My sister's in the bathroom."

"Your sister? In the . . ."

"She arrived this morning. I wasn't expecting her. She must've come out of the guest room and you saw her in the dark. Wow, your heart is pounding." He pressed a kiss against the pulsing vein in Jim's neck. "I didn't know you were coming back tonight. You weren't supposed to, were you?"

"No . . . no, I made a change, at the last minute, because of Zak—Zak's. . . . Oh, there she is."

He turned with Seth in his arms, as if they were dancing something stately and slow, a gavotte. In the bright light the shroud was revealed to be a cheap cotton nightie that did not do enough to conceal the form of a girl just out of her teens. Her face, framed in its streamers of corkscrewing gray, was fresh and fine, and very like her brother's, but in her eyes he saw a concentrated hardness directed at him as surely as a laser beam. She shook herself like a dog coming out of the rain, her hair shimmying around her body, and bolted back into the guest room. The French doors came together with a clatter.

Seth stepped toward them. "I'm going to talk to her. Don't worry, though, she'll be gone in the morning."

"Gone in the—but wait a minute. She . . . what's she doing here?"

"I don't really know. I've been trying to find out. But she's not staying, so . . . so . . . I'm taking care of it." Seth tapped on one of the glass panes with his finger. "Jim, you can go to bed. I'll be with you in a little bit."

After a pause, the door opened and Seth slipped through. Jim stood where he was, bewildered, curious, still spooked, although now it was the effect of her look that made his spine hum.

Without thinking, he returned to the kitchen.

Jim's eyes went to the yartzeit candle, and focused on it. *Zak, if you were here, you'd be laughing at me. Thinking I saw a ghost! No— if you were here, Seth wouldn't be.* He saw with a pang, that the idea of no Seth was terrible. Which didn't make sense, because if Zak was alive, he'd have wanted or needed no one else. This was a kind of blasphemy. Once more he appealed to Zak. *He never speaks of her, this sister, and now she's here, with that look in her eyes.* Her arrival wouldn't have seemed portentous in the light of day, yet he could not shake off the idea that there was no such thing as coincidence. This girl appeared to him first in the glow of Zak's burning remembrance, and the emotion she churned up in him was not still yet. Turning from it, he put the kettle on to boil, and went about making a pot of tea. He had no idea anymore what time it was, felt beyond the need for sleep, coasting on these extraordinary events, out of time. He set butter wafers on a plate in a fan pattern, took down cups and saucers, brought out the sugar bowl with its tiny spoon, sliced a lemon, poured milk into a glass creamer. When the kettle boiled he warmed the pot and made the tea, decaffeinated Irish Breakfast, watching the steadiness of his own hands. Then he went to the spare room door, knocking softly. "Come out now, let's see you. I made tea."

Seth, looking too naked in the pajama trousers he seldom wore, emerged first. The girl, wrapped now in her brother's robe, crept behind him, hiding in her Victorian hair. Seth took her arm and coaxed her forward.

"Cassie, this is Jim. Jim, my baby sister."

Jim caught the wistful pride in that adjective. What had they spoken about together just now, brother and sister? This *baby* girl still looked at him as if he was a thief—of what? Her brother's virtue? Seth claimed his parents had been okay with his sexuality, but the sister seemed to have missed the memo. Offering his hand, he said, "We scared each other pretty well, didn't we? Let's start our acquaintance again, all right?"

She didn't know how to shake hands or else she didn't want to. Jim let her tepid fingers go.

"There's tea. Come have some."

They took stools. Seth turned on all the lights so that the glow of the yartzeit candle was almost invisible. Jim's eyelids felt wooden.

"So," he said, glancing from Seth to the girl, "what's brought your sister to the big city? Has she lost Belle Rêve?"

Seth shrugged, the *Streetcar* reference sailing over his head, and told about the phone call that morning.

"Ah," Jim said. Turning again to the girl, he said, "So what brings you here?"

"Bus."

Rubbing his eyes, Seth said, "She's not going to stay long, she's trying to figure out her next move. Her life's been a little . . . disorganized . . . the last few years. Now she's ready to start college, so once we get that sorted out, she'll be off. Meanwhile she'll stay at a bed-and-breakfast, I've got that arranged. If you'd stayed away as long as you were supposed to, she'd have been there already and none of this hoo-ha would've happened."

"Wait a minute, please—" In the midst of this confusion, here was something he clearly understood. "She's visiting New York for the very first time—it is the first time, isn't it?—and you're going to put her all alone in a room? Whatever for?"

"Jim, it's her choice. She needs privacy."

"Our spare room is plenty private."

"She doesn't want to be in our way—"

"She wouldn't be in *my* way."

"Jim! Do I have to spell it—she doesn't approve of—"

"I get that. But a gentleman doesn't let certain petty details obstruct his hospitality. She's your only kin. She's . . ." he paused, then decided to chance it. "She's my only in-law."

At this the girl, who had been staring mutely into her tea cup, raised her face.

"Cassie. Wouldn't you rather stay right here with your brother and me? You'd be less lonely, don't you think?"

Still staring with that acid gaze, she gave one slow nod.

Seth touched her arm. "Are you sure? I want this to be your choice. So later on you don't hold it over me that we kept you here against your will."

Her eyes now moved from one man to the other, expressionless.

"She'll stay here," Jim said.

Again, the one nod.

"Good. Settled." A yawn caught Jim; he checked his watch. "Christ, it's almost three. I'm ready to drop. Let's go to bed."

Seth got to his feet.

"Cassie, I can see that you don't think I'm a suitable man for Seth," Jim said, since she was still staring at him with the intensity of a child watching a cartoon. "But you should know I love your brother very much. Maybe you could keep that in mind while you get acclimated."

She let his remark pass as though spoken in a foreign language.

"Anyway," he added, tired of her and everything else, "you'll just have to get used to it."

Seth led her away. Jim put out all the lights, and took the yartzeit candle, now restored to its full radiance, and set it on the dining-room table.

It guttered, casting tall shadows up the walls. It was already burning down, already becoming less. Maybe Seth's sister would get used to them, but there were some things, Jim knew, you never could get used to.

Alone again in the guest bed, Cassie's muscles were bunched and painful no matter how she turned on the mattress. Impossible to relax.

She couldn't, for one thing, get that man out of her head. He'd loomed out of the shadows looking horribly like his inked image in the bathroom picture, dense and immense and dark. And then when she came out of the bathroom, there he was clutching her brother to him as if he was going to swallow him up. Men shouldn't touch each other that way. They shouldn't have touched each other like that in front of her. It wasn't right.

Before they'd come out for the weirdo tea party, Seth had crowded her against the wall in here, making her look him in the eye, telling her in a fierce whisper to follow his lead and say as little as possible.

There was a big lie here, surrounded by a bunch of subsidiary lies. Lies shooting out in all directions. She'd told Seth that he didn't have to run this charade on her, about being in *love* with the man. Any idiot, even one from Drinkwater, could see what their ménage was actually about. No matter how he tried to couch it, it was clear: Seth lived on the man, and she, now, was to live on Seth.

Lying back, she felt herself moving again, the miles slipping by beneath her as the bus covered the road. Toward the middle of the trip, she'd settled into it, began to feel content just to travel and postpone arrival. She, who had never gone anywhere, felt herself gradually remade by distance covered.

Then somehow, despite all that distance, she was in the kitchen with her mother. Mary was sitting at the table with her coupon envelopes, shuffling the little slips of paper into piles, murmuring to herself, about how the take was less and less every month, how Drinkwater itself was fading away before their eyes. Through the glass of the closed kitchen door, Cassie saw Roy outside, his face cramped with resentment that anything should be shut against him. He was knocking to be let in, but Mary did not look up. Cassie couldn't move from her chair at the table as Roy darkened, keeping up that steady thumping, so that she began to feel it was shaking the whole house, over and over. He might knock the door off and get in, his rage filling the room, and they wouldn't be able to stop him because she couldn't get up and Mary wouldn't stop shuffling those little slips of paper. *Thump, thump, thump*, over and over, harder and harder. . . .

Then her eyes were open and she remembered where she was, but the rhythmic thudding was still going on, it made the wall behind her head vibrate, and she heard a voice through the plaster.

"Uh uh uh *UH*—uh uh *UH*—"

Clutching the pillow, she tunneled down under the quilt so her head was where her feet had been, and covered her ears. The thumping soon stopped, but the vibrations of what her brother was doing rippled through her, like a rock tossed in a pond, lapping lapping lapping right out to the edge.

Seth bit down on the wad of sheet in his mouth and forced himself to hold still. The cock was an enormous file sawing slowly inside him.

Every instinct of his body screamed to fight off the crushing weight on his back. *It's Jim, just Jim, and you began it, he just wanted to go to sleep, let him finish, he's half-asleep already, it's okay, it's okay. . . .* So why was it Roy's stink he smelled, Roy's hands squeezing his throat so he could barely breathe? Jim's hands were nowhere near his neck. Counting his pulse beats, counting Jim's strokes, willing him to be done quick so this could be over. Because he could *feel* them all there, massed around the bed, their heavy breathing, fumes of whiskey and beer and hatred pulsing off them as they waited their turns: Frank, Hap, Joe, Ned. And Vin. Always Vin, always the last, always always always the worst.

Jim kept trying to push his hand under Seth's belly, but Seth didn't want him to touch his erection. He shouldn't have one, not now. Not for *them* to use, to mock. No one was going to touch it, no one was going to have that ugly satisfaction. Grinning around the pain, he tried to grind back, to get Jim off quicker. Why did he have to be so damn langorous about it?

There—at last. Jim stiffened, groaned. It was over.

He pressed a last appreciative kiss against Seth's shoulder as he slid off his back straight into sleep. Freed of his weight, Seth was immediately lonely and afraid. Roy, Vin, and the others were still all around him in the dark. They'd invaded the room and settled in like waiting vultures.

This was Cassie's doing.

Somehow she'd brought them here with her, renewed and strengthened in every dimension. The sight of her, the tones of her voice, her gaze, evoked them. She was the first person he'd seen after returning from the fishing trip, and he'd had to hide himself from her because her questioning gaze was unbearable. And today, just the way her gray hair squiggled away from its center part reminded him of a hundred things he'd wanted never to think about again.

Seth burrowed against Jim, who was sprawled on his belly.

"Jim," he whispered. "Let me in. Let me in."

With a little grunt, Jim shifted; his arm found Seth and curled across him.

"Hold me tighter. Tighter—"

"Ssh. Sleep." Jim shifted so they were spooned together. Still Seth was afraid to close his eyes. His heart beat fast and thready. He forced himself to stay still, to inhale Jim's heavy postcoital aroma. Sleep was a lurking predator. He dreaded the nightmare, and what he might do or say in it that Jim would overhear.

When Seth came in to rouse her, he was dressed and looking like butter wouldn't melt in his mouth. If her brother had no slender ring in his nostril, or had colored his hair something a little more decent, like plain brown, or had cheekbones just a shade less sharp, she could have spoken up about the thumping. As it was, she kept quiet, and felt herself blush.

"Where's that man?" she asked, afraid to scoot from the guest room to the bathroom lest she encounter him, perhaps in some state of rampant undress.

"He's fast asleep, my poor Jim, worn-out. The flight, and all that rumpus last night. With you."

"So, what's the big lie you've told to this great love of yours? That I have to go along with or perish?"

Seth dropped his saucy gaze. "That our parents were English lit professors, in Lincoln, with a big Victorian house full of books and lots of friends. That they loved each other. That they loved *us*. That when I was away at my first year of college, our house burned down in the night and they died."

"Oh. That." They'd often shared this fantasy, in various shades of bitterness and longing.

"And . . ." she could only whisper, "and he believed you?"

"Yeah, he did. Does. Has to. Cassie, he has to. You're not going to do anything to change that."

Seth brought her by subway from West Fourth down to Canal, where they emerged, amazingly, into Asia; the streets stinking of fish, sidewalks crowded with Chinese people jostling along, the white faces, seeming rarer and whiter for being here, gawking at the merchandise, creating eddies and blockages of movement. Heaps of fruit and vegetables spilled out of shopfronts, their colors distinct and shiny; she saw glazed and blackened ducks hanging in restaurant windows, like victims of an oil slick. The smells were staggering. At every street corner that wasn't obstructed by a construction site, there was a woman presiding over a table heaped with stacked blue-and-white china bowls and soup spoons, each divided from each by a bit of excelsior, flat cotton slippers paired up with rubber bands, folding fans made of flowered paper with sharp metal edges, tiny cat figurines. She stared at all this exotica, too overwhelmed for desire.

Seth stopped at a sidewalk cart and bought scallion pancakes and turnip cakes packed in Styrofoam boxes. They took them around to the steps of a high-rise jail, where they sat amid the indistinct hooting of the inmates many stories up. Cassie closed her eyes and forced herself to taste the funny-looking food without protest, thinking to chase it quickly with Coke and hold her gorge down. She was hungry all the time lately, anyway. But the black oily-looking sauce was delicious, and she ended up competing with Seth, who wielded chopsticks with amazing agility, to spear the last bit of turnip with her plastic fork.

He was friendly, holding her hand as they walked, yet she thought she caught him sometimes looking at her with a cold eye. He'd be talking, then stop suddenly and drop his gaze.

Finally she said, "You hate this, don't you? You want me to disappear."

She was afraid—of him, of that man, of the city, of her future, of everything. But she didn't look away. It seemed terribly important to *look* at him right then, to see what he would do.

Seth broke their stare first. "I'm glad to know you're safe. I'm glad you're away from *them* now. Don't read so much into every little way I hold my head."

This didn't quite satisfy her, but it was all she could get.

Hannah overwhelmed her. They met for coffee near the art school where she taught. She was so *big,* and took up space in a way that was different from the fat people Cassie knew at home. She talked and gestured continually, used words Cassie had only seen in books, and said things that made Seth laugh, but didn't seem funny to her. When they parted, Hannah hugged her, congratulated her for being in New York. "We'll get to be good friends," she said, as if she was sure Cassie would want that, too. Cassie pretended she did. Maybe eventually she would, although it was hard to imagine.

There was a crowd in Father Demo Square as Cassie and Seth walked west along Bleecker Street. A small, muscular man with long dark hair, wearing a spandex bodysuit unzipped almost to the groin, was riding a unicycle. Behind him was a property trunk set up by the flagpole, and all around him, on the benches and in rows behind the benches, tourists and passersby had become an audience. Cassie stopped, and Seth, with a murmur of annoyance, stopped too. She shouldered quietly through the ranks to be near the front. She'd never seen a real live man on a real live unicycle. New York didn't need television, she thought, because New York *was* television.

The performer asked for a volunteer from the crowd, and before she quite knew whether she meant it or not, Cassie put her hand up, and found herself reeled out to the center of the ring. The performer, now she was close to him, radiated a compact, tightly wound power. He smelled musky.

"Don't worry," he told her, pitching his voice to the audience, "I won't hurt you—unless you *ask* me to. Do you have a boyfriend?"

She shook her head.

"Who's that guy you were standing with?"

"Brother," she whispered.

"Brother! Right! I can see that!"

Cassie wondered whether there was some insult intended to Seth. But when she glanced toward him, his whiteness blazing out from the crowd, he gave her an indulgent nod.

"What's your name?" the performer asked.

She said her name. She said where she was from. He called for applause for her, for the state of Nebraska, and mimed the bow he wanted her to make.

The next thing she knew the performer's head was poking between her thighs, and he was standing up with her on his shoulders. She let out a little scream, and screamed again when she saw him kick the unicycle into the upright position. The crowd was clapping rhythmically now, and she looked for Seth, found him, his arms crossed on his chest, his mouth open in a jeering laugh. Then the performer's shoulders seemed to glide away from under her, she flapped her arms and grabbed the top of his head. But he sailed smoothly in a wide arc around the flagpole, pattering on to the audience all the time, and Cassie began to enjoy her vantage point, and the way the wind drew out her long hair. The tops of people's heads were visible to her, and she could see over them down Sixth Avenue, up Sixth Avenue, down Carmine Street and into Bleecker as she was borne around and around. The gliding sensation centered in her stomach, and she was aware too of the man's head gripped between her thighs and the solidity of his shoulders. Raising her arms up, she acknowledged the audience, and when her feet were back on the ground, felt it was over all too soon. Now the performer was passing his hat, saying, "This is how I make my living—please be generous. Special price for tourists, twenty dollars. Those of you who are from New York, you know how much to give." Seth put a dollar into the hat when he reached them, and she tried to catch the man's eye, to reconfirm for one little moment their connection, but his gaze slid past hers without pause as he worked the crowd for money.

"How did I look up there?" she asked Seth as they walked away.

He paused to light a cigarette. "Like you were losing your virginity."

"What the hell do you mean by that?"

He shrugged. "You'll know when the time comes."

"How do you know it hasn't come already?"

With a fond snort, he pinched her arm. "Yeah, right. I know *you*, Miss Priss."

As they walked back to Bond Street, Seth said, "Listen, it would probably be better if you didn't say anything to Jim about going into the subway."

"Why?"

"Well, even though I told you that you'd be fine down there if you use common sense, he likes to worry. So, if it comes up, it was just buses and cabs, okay?"

"Um . . . I guess I've got no choice but to go along. Am I allowed to say we ate Chinese food from a cart, or is that a secret, too?"

"You can say anything you like about the Chinese food."

"There's an awful lot of secrets around here."

"Maybe, but this particular one isn't like the others. Trust me."

16

When Cassie crept out to the kitchen in the morning, wanting only to gnaw some toast in solitude, Jim was there.

"Good morning," he said. "Want some Cream of Wheat?"

It was too late to bolt back to her room. "Where's Seth?"

"Gym. Here, you stir the cereal while I do the toast."

Slipping down from her stool, she came around into the kitchen and took the wooden spoon he held out to her.

"Just keep it moving, so it doesn't stick to the bottom."

"I know how to cook cereal." *I do it for a living.*

"Seth's got school stuff to do today, so I think it might be nice if we went somewhere together. It's a good clear day, we could do the Empire State. Or the Cloisters. It'll be a chance for us to get to know each other. We should, don't you think?"

The cereal was erupting now in little plorping bursts. She turned down the heat. At her elbow, Jim spread butter on thick slices of white mountain bread, and sprinkled them with sugar and cinnamon.

"We could go up to the Met, or—now, you might really like this—the Frick. Small, manageable museum, you can see the whole thing in a couple of hours, it's a jewel. Seth said you're interested in pictures, too."

"I don't wa—what kind of pictures?"

"Different kinds. There's a whole room full of Fragonards, pretty pink-and-white ladies in beautiful fluffy gardens—they look as if they'd shit rose petals if they shat at all. Eighteenth century. You see those pictures and you understand the entire French Revolution. And there's some Lawrence and Gainsborough portraits, beautiful women with big hair and big jewels and sweet little mouths. And— have you ever heard of Ingres? French painter, nineteenth century. There is a Comtesse of his, a beauty in a blue dress, with the most serenely haughty face you ever—"

She wanted to hear about these paintings, she wanted to *see* them, but instead she found herself cutting across his words. "I just have to tell you something. The day I got here, I went through your things. The desk, the closets, the drawers. Even the pockets of your suits." Her lips tingled as the sentences passed them.

"I didn't touch so much as look," she added.

"And did what you saw allay your fears? Or make them worse?"

She thought of the shirts and sweaters enough for five men, the contents of the nightstand drawer. No, none of it made her feel better. She said, "I saw your locket. You must have forgotten to change your pockets over that day."

He faced her. "You're right, ordinarily I carry it with me. But I was packing for a business trip, I was distracted, I left without it."

"It's a girl's locket," she breathed. Of course, there was no such thing as a boy's locket.

"Ladle out the cereal before it gets lumpy." He put the bread slices into the toaster oven, and wiped the butter from his fingers with the dishtowel. "Zak's mother gave it to me. I'm sure Seth has told you something about Zak. You've seen his pictures around the place.

"Zak's mother had the locket from *her* mother-in-law when she was married, with a picture of Zak's father. It goes back farther than that, it's a family tradition. Of course Zak didn't marry a wife—he married *me*. But that was all right with Miriam, she was a wonderful woman. I wore the locket on a watch chain, carried it every day in my pocket. Then just after Zak died, the chain broke, and I put the locket away in a drawer. I only just started carrying it again."

She wondered if he was making fun of her. Were there really mothers who would do something like that—treat a son's boyfriend like a real daughter-in-law? The Cream of Wheat glopped off the wooden spoon in thick clots.

"You want to ask me what happened to Zak," he said. "I can see that you do. So ask."

The words forced themselves up from the tightness in her chest. Her face half-turned away, she whispered, "I don't have to ask. I know he died of AIDS."

"Seth didn't tell you that!"

"He didn't have to tell me."

"Oh, you just assumed it?" He didn't wait for her response. "What *did* Seth say about him?"

"Nothing. . . . Only that he was the love of your life."

"Is that what he said?" Jim wrenched the refrigerator open, slopped some milk into a small pitcher, and then with easier motions, put it in the microwave.

"You don't have to tell me anything about him," she said. "You don't have to talk to me at all." He spoke to her as a fellow adult, as though she had consequence, and this was new, intoxicating—it scared her, as everything about him scared her.

"Zak was as healthy as a horse. Do you hear me? As a horse. Although I don't know why we should say a horse is especially healthier than anything else, or—"

She moved to cut him off. "I'm really sorry I—"

"Listen. You wanted to know, so listen. One morning, a man—a lunatic—came down into the subway. The morning rush, all those people, it could have been me or anybody else. But he picked Zak, rushed him like he'd hated him for a lifetime. Pushed him off the platform into an oncoming train. Right around the corner," Jim said, gesturing, "at Bleecker Street, the fucking six train tore Zak apart."

What he remembered most strongly about the whole thing afterward was the small wiry fellow, not young, but made strong and solid by compassion, who forced him back and blocked his view as he struggled to follow where Zak had gone. *Don't look, Mister,* the stranger said, his sour breath rising to Jim's nostrils. *You really don't want to look at that.* But even so Jim had an idea in his mind, of Zak with his clothes, his face, his limbs, in places where they ought not to be. His splattered blood. The image came to him not in dreams, but at odd times, flashing upon his mind's eye in the middle of a presentation to clients, or when he was on the bench press. Of course, he'd never set foot in the subway since.

The microwave dinged. "The guy who pushed him had escaped from a psychiatric hospital in Queens. All they did was put him back there. For all I know, he's on the streets again, wandering around right now. And the idiotic thing was—any other day Zak would have been on the opposite platform. But that day we had an early-morning appointment together uptown." He took the pitcher out and set it on the counter next to the sugar bowl, and then without pausing peeled a banana and sliced it, half into her bowl and half into his. Seeing the bread darkening, Cassie reached around him and sprang the toaster oven door.

When their arms touched, Jim said, "We saw so many of our friends get that *thing*. I personally know easily fifty men who've died or are sick. Yet somehow Zak and I escaped. And we felt so lucky—and guilty for being lucky—because we were just as likely to get it as anybody else. But we hadn't, so we thought we were safe, that we'd have our full span of years together. I guess we felt kind of invincible. Hubris. Gets you every goddamn time."

Cassie didn't know how to respond. Finally she murmured, "That explains why Seth said not to tell you we were in the subway."

"Did he? That's ridiculous—everyone I know is now inoculated against anything bad ever happening to them in the subway. Lightning doesn't strike twice in the same place. Take the subway all you like."

"I'm so sorry about what hap—"

"Sit down and eat your cereal while it's hot."

She didn't want to eat. She didn't want to face him. The plain cereal stuck in her mouth like paste.

Jim pushed the milk and sugar toward her. "You might find these helpful."

"I'm so sorry for you, about . . . Zak."

"Never mind that now."

Big tears ran down her nose; one plopped into her cereal.

Jim put down his spoon. "All right," he said, as if he was gentling an animal. "All right. I see you're sorry. You don't have to do that."

But there was no stopping now. She sobbed and sobbed. He made no move to comfort or quiet her. But neither did he walk away. After a while she was able to raise her head. "I wish I hadn't come here. It's not right for me to be here."

"But here you are. I think you'd better make the most of it. Eager kids pour into this city every day, and they have a pretty good time, I guess. You can have a good time if you let yourself. Seth does. I did."

But she felt like a child who, forbidden to cross a busy street, has crossed it anyway, and finds herself stranded on the other side as the huge cars whiz by. It felt daring and bad and also immensely liberating just to *talk* to Jim.

"Anyway, I think Seth missed you terribly. I don't think he knew how much, until you turned up."

The sobs backed up, making her throat ache. "He . . . he doesn't want me. He's changed."

"I'm sure he has. You got here, expecting to see the same Seth who came home to bury your parents—"

She started, but caught herself. "Yes . . . that was stupid, though. . . ."

"What was he like, then?"

"Nobody *you'd* have looked at twice!"

His sudden loud laugh made her jump. "You're so sure you know what appeals to me. . . . Now you've really got me wondering!"

She stared into her cereal.

"He *is* lovely, your brother. If he'd stop wearing eyeliner and all those earrings, and dress himself better, he could be really stunning, but he doesn't know that yet, and it isn't for me to tell him. Mostly it's not important, except inasmuch as it may keep him from being taken seriously, and that's what he wants from other people the most. I think your brother is going to be a major painter, if he keeps up the way he's going. You looked at the paintings?"

She nodded. Clearly, he knew all about art, so she didn't mention how they'd befuddled and perturbed her.

"Anyway, he's gifted, your brother, and serious and smart and charming and beautiful, but his secret idea of himself is that no one else will agree. He needs to make big sweeping displays of selflessness to convince himself he's deserving. For instance, his maddening method of proving he loves me was to refuse to take anything from me. I'm not sure why exactly I found that so touching, but God knows I did. Otherwise I don't know that we would've gotten over that hurdle. But, I'm glad to say, we have."

Her heart fluttered high in her chest. "You talk as if you really *love* him, or something."

"I told you that the other night."

She blinked. "But I don't know what love *means* to you people."

He let off a woof of disgusted laughter. "*You people?* Good God. I wonder what it means to *you.*"

He glanced at his watch, suddenly irritable. "Let's leave all this—this food's cold now anyway. Come. We'll have brunch uptown and go to the Frick and look at nice serene pictures."

By now she believed—being on sufferance—that she hadn't any right to refuse. But as she bathed and dressed she listened out for Seth, hoping he'd come back and prevent this from going forward.

In the new clothes, she was self-conscious. When Jim complimented her on them, she blushed again. "Seth gave them to me," she whispered.

"I know."

When they were ready to go, she saw that Jim had left her brother a note, and this reassured her. During the cab ride uptown she became absorbed in the drama of changing neighborhoods, every seven blocks a completely new environment. They had brunch in a small restaurant on East Sixty-sixth Street where everybody looked to her like George and Barbara Bush. Jim relieved her of the necessity of finding things to say by talking about the city and the gallery they were about to see. She ate her eggs Benedict in small, precise bites, and then she walked beside him to the Frick, telling herself that all she had to do was be polite and look at things, and it would be over sooner or later. People glanced at them as they passed, and she wondered what they thought Jim was to her: a youthful, handsome father?

An older lover? Or could they all tell with a New York glance that he was queer, that they really didn't belong together at all?

As she followed Jim into the gallery, Cassie felt herself standing up straighter, placing her feet more delicately. Her silence changed from apprehension to awe in the dark polished lobby.

"People *lived* here?"

"Yes. But not for very long. Frick died three years after he built himself this place, and after his wife died, it opened to the public." Jim bought the tickets and handed her a brochure that she held in hands suddenly moist with anticipation.

At first she couldn't see anything, because it was too enormous to just be in this beaux arts palace where everything was decorative and old and *good*, like *The Spoils of Poynton*. She moved from room to room in a numb rapture, and made a complete circuit without pausing. Jim made no comment on her methods; he strolled beside her, looking dapper with his hands in his pockets. Even without looking at him, she could tell he was observing her more than the pictures, which he must have seen already many times. She stared at the elaborate mantelpieces, the heavy, roped-off furniture, the chandeliers. The fountain—indoors!—stunned her.

"This . . . this is the sort of place Edith Wharton writes about, isn't it?" she whispered. "I never thought I'd—"

"You like Edith Wharton?"

"Very much. Better than Henry James, even." Her eyes were fixed, trancelike, on the little bronze frog who spit an elegant stream of water toward the center of the fountain.

He watched her breathe it in, trying to be equal to it. She approached each painting with a humble, blind look, as if she was waiting to be introduced to an important dowager, and she looked at them thoroughly. Jim had to catch himself from rushing her. Some paintings released her easily, others held her so that she had to back away from them and wrench her gaze away.

Observing her against the backdrop of so much art, Jim tried to find her in the pictures that surrounded him. But after a while, he realized that what she was, and that uncannily, was a girl straight out of Julia Margaret Cameron—pale-browed, features full and delineated as if by a sculptor's small chisel, the confident jaw giving way to a strong columnar neck. It was a profile of an old-fashioned beauty, unconscious of itself. And all surmounted by the kind of hair that was the glory of an ignorant parlor maid posed as every noble female of British myth. Its grayness only added to his impression of her being somehow a little out of time.

She stared for a long time at *Lady Peel,* at her satin sleeve, her three immense jeweled bracelets and the delicate pink-and-white hand. Glanced from this to the ruddy-cheeked patrician face beneath its red plumes, over and over, swallowing hard.

"I think," she speculated, "the guy who painted this was more interested in her arm than in the rest of her."

"Maybe she—or her husband—wanted a record of her jewels just as much as a record of her own beauty. Do you think?" Jim asked.

They were going through the collection backward now, against the flow of spry white-haired lady tourists in bright-colored clothes and quiet European pairs in tweeds. When they came into the Fragonard room with its tall windows, it was flooded with light, and, for the moment, empty.

In the opposite doorway, a young man appeared, elegant in black Italian sunglasses and a white linen suit, the collar tabs of his white shirt buttoned, his hands crossed over a museum brochure. She looked at this self-possessed and mysterious young man, whose hair and clothes gleamed in the long shafts of light, and it was only after she thought how very like he was to her idea of a French film star did she realize it was Seth.

He crossed to them, smiling. "Are you having a nice time, Cassie?"

"This is a beautiful place."

"Yes, it's very beautiful. Have you seen the Vermeers? Come, I'll show you." Seth introduced her to *Officer and Laughing Girl,* told her about the light, the way stillness and vibration coexisted in it, contradictory and not, and held her there, when she was ready to turn away, insisting quietly that she look again, more deeply. He scrolled sentences into her ear as she stared that were full of learning and delight; he brought her to *Mistress and Maid* and *Girl Interrupted at Her Music,* made comparisons. He explained to her how the paintings were made, he pointed carefully to certain details he wanted her to notice. All the time he held her hand lightly in his, and behind her she was aware of Jim hovering, not too close, waiting.

This was beginning to feel like a masquerade: dressed up to look unlike themselves, she all in black and he in white, pretending in this palace of beauty to have no relation to Drinkwater, Nebraska, to Roy Jenkins or Mary McKenna Jenkins, to a run-down gas station-café or a drafty clapboard box of a house, with a muddy yard and torn plastic sheeting over the windows. To bruises and black eyes constantly blooming on too-pale skin. To laundry baskets full of soiled clothes bought at the St. Vincent De Paul. The monotonous wind off the prairie. No relation to tracts printed on thin paper, studded with Bible quotes in red ink, which Mary brought home from church and left scattered about the house; to meals eaten in a violent silence; to her brother's unspoken-of errands in the cellar with Roy.

As though there never had been a Roy Jenkins or a cellar, Seth told her, in a calm educated voice, of what he knew about the life-work of Vermeer. While behind them hovered the man to whom Seth allowed an access to his body too repugnant for her to think about, and too immediate *not* to think about.

"Come on, Cassie, there's another thing I want you to see, now you've understood something about these."

He brought her to stand in front of a very small painting of the *Virgin and Child, with Saints and Donor* by van Eyck. He'd threaded his fingers in with hers; his hand was cool and pleasant to hold.

"*He* told me about this one already," she blurted, suddenly unable to bear how Seth ignored Jim. She turned around to look at him. "You told me—"

"Van Eyck is Jim's special favorite," Seth said. "But sometimes I think what he likes about him is only the same thing you'd like about a little dollhouse filled with uncanny miniatures."

"The deliberateness of his vision is very moving to me, yes, but that's not all there is to it. Besides, I know you love van Eyck, too."

"In one way it's silly, really," Seth said, "to make favorites when it comes to art. Paintings aren't pop songs, they're—"

"Maybe, but how can you help it?" Jim said.

Seth had turned a little toward Jim, although they were still not really talking to each other, but directing their artificial-sounding remarks only at her. A strange little smile played on Jim's lips. It made Cassie uneasy; she suspected he was making fun of her.

"There are so many things we do," Jim continued, "that we can't help. Yet we just try to make allowances for one another. To be, you know, accepting. Of one another's tastes and foibles."

Seth looked at the picture, bringing his face quite close to it, squinting at the background scene of a bustling little Dutch city, carrying on its workaday business unconscious of the presence of its savior.

Suddenly Cassie realized that they were behaving this way because of her. So she wouldn't be embarrassed to be with them in public, a male couple. They were indulging their conception of her, even though they didn't approve of it, out of kindness. The understanding made her flush with shame.

. . .

The wall-knocking, often at night and always in the morning, was a constancy she began to find comforting. Awakening to it, she'd think, *Seven A.M., and all is well in Seth's little world.* Her world, being a subset of his, depended on that.

And at eight she'd be at the breakfast table with them, feigning complete unawareness of what she'd heard. But it was impossible not to see, as he wolfed eggs and drank coffee, holding the cup with both hands, a cigarette burning unheeded between his fingers, that Seth glowed like a bride. For a while she thought it was disgust that made her cheeks burn when she met his eyes. But finally she had to own to herself that it was really envy of her brother's physical happiness. She missed her own, cramped and dead-end as it was.

Seth's felicity made him more distant. She'd imagined, on the bus, that as much as she needed his help, he would still need hers, too. The way he'd needed her company as they rode their clattery bikes for miles around the back roads, making ever wider circles around the center of their private griefs, always returning there in time for supper. The way he came to her to share his resentments—and later his smug triumphs—at what went on in school. And when Roy had finished with him in the cellar, the way he'd hover around her wherever she was, red-faced and speechless, until she gave him something to do: her math homework or weeding the vegetables or helping to clean the oven: anything so that they could be together, yet not have to talk.

Any reference to that was taboo here. Everything she used to give him, he claimed not to need. Jim met all his needs now—at least, all the needs this reinvented Seth would admit to.

Cassie watched Jim sternly scanning the Op-Ed page of the *Times*, feeling around behind it for his coffee. She wondered whether he'd ever seen Seth broken up, his face contorted beneath a sheen of sweat, tears, and snot. He certainly hadn't seen Seth on that early morning when Roy, with Mary hovering, anxious but not disapproving at his back, made him haul all his music magazines, Walkman, and tapes out behind the service station, pour gas on the pile, and set it alight. *This'll burn the devil out of you*, Roy had sniggered, prodding him in his shrinking back while the cassette boxes melted like salted snails, the Morrissey T-shirt went up, and their mother prayed aloud. Jim certainly hadn't seen—*she* was the only one who'd remained to see—Seth jump into the dying flames, pogo-ing up and down in a clenched white rage until his sneakers and jeans legs were half-seared away and his feet blackened and blistered. Jim hadn't seen him either, just a few months after that, when he got back from the fishing trip with Roy. He hadn't been there when Seth climbed down, not from the cab but, oddly, from the *bed* of the pickup, his blanched face half-hidden in dirty hair, and just walked away, ignoring Ma's greeting from the kitchen door, ignoring her, too. She'd searched for hours, all over Drinkwater, and finally found him at the Frawley place, a boarded-up old farmhouse they'd gravitated toward as children, four miles outside of town. Seth had crawled under the big deep porch. She could see him, when she knelt to peer through the broken lattice, lying on his belly, his eyes glittering like a feral dog's. He didn't answer when she called to him. Something about his stillness, his stare, prevented her from squirming in after him; she was frightened of him, as if he would bite her if she got close. She wasn't sure if he really stayed in the crawl space all the time, with the live and dead rats and bugs and all the other filth, but that's how she found him every time she went there to check, for three whole days. Three days of relentless baking sun and no wind, when it was no cooler for him wedged there than it was for her, squatting to look in and plead with him, offering water in a jam jar and cheese sandwiches snuck out of the café when no one was looking.

Jim, serenely self-absorbed after his morning fuck, intent on his breakfast and the news of the day, wasn't there for all that, nor at the end of the third day when the sirens sounded and the whole town rushed to see the Frawley house and surrounding stubble fields in flames. He hadn't felt her loose-ribbed terror that Seth was in there, in the very heart of the fire, nor heard her screams when the bottom floor collapsed and the whole structure caved into a white-hot maw at just the place where Seth had secreted himself. And then how she fell down sobbing and shaking in the dirt when Seth came calmly through the crowd, grimy but unharmed, walking away from the conflagration as if it was a carnival sideshow he'd gawked at enough.

After that he swatted her away more and more. Their intimacy was at an end.

What would happen, she wondered, *if I started to talk about that day? I could just open my mouth and say, "Did my brother ever happen to tell you, Jim, about how be burned down the Frawley place . . ."* Would Seth shout, or leap up and hit her, to shut her up? And what would Jim do if he knew about Seth's lies? No more wall-knocking in the morning, she guessed, if he found out.

No more anything.

17

After a run of raw rainy weeks, there was a spate of freakishly warm days. Days when people abandoned their coats, when flies were born months too soon, and flew into windows flung open in overheated apartments and offices. Jim could barely sit still at work; on the third day of the thaw, he impulsively took a bus to midtown instead of a cab and saw a poster left over from the previous spring, promoting the cherry blossoms at the Brooklyn Botanic Garden. Seized with an urge to walk in the sun amidst bare trees, to wander into the glass houses and inhale their loamy air, he went instead to the garage where he kept his car.

Behind the wheel, he headed first toward Chelsea. It was a day when Seth had no classes, and went to his studio first thing in the morning. Jim hoped he could catch him before he began his work, and spirit him off.

As he turned off the avenue, Jim spotted him on the sidewalk. Striding along in the warm air with the sleeves of his sweater pushed up to the elbow, knapsack over one shoulder, ears plugged with headphones. Jim slowed the car to a crawl at his back. Seth had a carton of take-out coffee in one hand; he paused to sip, and Jim cruised past him. Seth had only seen Jim's Boxter a few times, as they seldom used it; there was no reason now for him to notice it here. In the rearview mirror, Jim drank him in, the unaccustomed treat of seeing Seth from a distance, unaware. Going, with purpose, to his work. His face already bore a look of concentration and inwardness. Jim envied him that strong good purpose. He felt sheepish, playing hooky from the career he'd stopped caring for. How long would it be before Seth grew impatient with his lack of direction?

The last few nights, without prompting, Seth had fucked him. He did it with a cool air, almost arrogant, as if he was asserting his right to something that might, if he was too tepid, be in dispute. In the midst of it, Jim felt that in his head Seth was replaying some boyhood game of king of the hill against a lot of other kids bigger and meaner than he was. Afterward, having had the stuffing pulled out of him, Jim slept, but when he drifted to wakefulness an hour or so later, Seth was still sitting up, a cigarette dangling from the corner of his mouth, drawing with a rapid fury in the big sketchbook propped on his knees, a propulsive humming coming from his throat.

This tigerishness was for the night: most mornings Seth still demanded and got the slow, deep coring, accompanied by sticky kisses and locked gazes (impossible to look away from those serious gray eyes when they engaged his, or not to shiver with lust at the intensity of them). Lately Jim got the sense that Seth derived more from these fuckings than pleasure and the reassurance of his love; Jim was stoking some intricate, magnificent engine that would run the rest of the day off the energy he infused it with.

Seth wouldn't want to forsake his painting that morning to go to the Brooklyn Botanic Garden. He would hide that, Jim knew, and get in the car with a smile. Seth was always attentive to his whims, his moods. An attention that was pleasing, but also betrayed how far Seth had still to go to be entirely relaxed with him.

Seth trotted across the next avenue, tossed the coffee cup into the corner trash can, and broke into a run for the last block.

Life seemed so narrow now. He let Seth go.

Jim spoke into his cell phone. "Be on the stoop in ten minutes. I'm going to take you to see something nice."

He could feel her reluctance in the dead air of phone space, but Cassie was the only person he knew who was absolutely free to make this last-minute excursion, and he didn't want any fuss. She seemed to have no idea that what she'd stepped into so innocently—a room of her own bigger than a great many Manhattan apartments, three good meals a day, a new wardrobe and all the books she could read, no pressure to earn a penny—was *not* the usual thing for girls of twenty-one who disembarked at the Port Authority with nothing in their pockets but a phone number. In exchange for his hospitality it was time for her to sing for her supper.

They were not alone; the warm weather brought people out with the same seeming mystery as it brought out flies: Cassie wondered aloud at the circumstances of all those they saw not working on a weekday. But she fell silent when they entered the Japanese garden, casting her awe out over the still lake with its serene torii arch floating in indelible outline against a sky so blue it shimmered. They leaned side by side on the wooden balustrade of the viewing pavilion and took it in.

This was a place—there were so many!—that he'd visited with Zak, that final autumn, clutching their excitement about their soon-to-be-parenthood, to watch other people's children brought there to see the changing leaves, the big turtles entering the water with a *plop*, the late-blooming flowers. Bringing Cassie to see it was the closest now that he could come to that. Now she breathed out, blinking. "This . . . this is *amazing*."

"Isn't it? There's a tag of verse Zak used to say whenever we came here: 'I can't even enjoy a blade of grass unless I know there's a subway handy, or a record store or some other sign that people do not totally *regret* life.' "

"Who wrote that?"

"Frank O'Hara. A poem called 'Meditations in an Emergency.' It's a line I'll always associate with Zak because it describes him so completely."

"I'd like to read it."

"You told me the other day—well, you bit my head off with it, actually—that Seth wasn't anybody I'd have looked at twice, back home. What was he like?"

"You brought me all the way out here just to ask me that, didn't you?"

Despite the heat of her smoldering displeasure, Jim stayed amiable. "You caught me."

"I don't really see why it matters. He's what you like now, or else you wouldn't have him. You can't have his past, and nobody knows the future."

Instead of the little light anecdote he'd wanted, something fond and simple that he could turn over and over and enjoy, she'd clapped a block of lead into his palm.

"Okay, okay—my brother as a teenager. Let's see. He was skinny—painfully skinny. He had lots of blotchy red whiteheads that kept him from shaving himself neatly, and he was always picking at them. He wore his hair long, in a ponytail, and it was gray like mine, and usually not very clean. His eyebrows grew together in the middle, and his Adam's apple stuck out a mile. He had a narrow little chest and sunburned arms and dirty fingernails. When he sweated he stank, and his breath was bad."

Jim raised a cool eyebrow. "Bad breath? Really?"

"Well, maybe. Mostly I said that because you piss me off sometimes, you know?"

"Do I? Why?"

"You're so—sure of yourself. Everything is the way you like it, and that just seems normal to you."

He couldn't help admiring her a little for the courage of her convictions, exasperating as they were. She was not like Seth in this, she didn't care about pleasing.

"I suppose you're right. Although exaggerated. Everything isn't the way I like it all the time."

Cassie sighed.

"We used to read together, okay? I mean, he'd read to me. He was very good at it. Charles Dickens, mostly. Or Tolstoy. And *Vanity Fair.* Those were the ones we liked. I don't know how we found out about them, nobody told us."

"Well, they were in the house," Jim said.

"Oh—yes! I just meant, no one *made* us. . . . And he'd draw things for me, on scraps of paper. Teensy pictures of animals he made up. Like happy monsters. He'd leave them for me under my pillow, or in my schoolbooks . . . or in my shoes." She smiled. "I hadn't thought of that in a while."

"You two were very close."

"I thought so at the time." She amended this. "Yes. Yes, we were close."

"That's good." Then quickly, "Tell me about your mother."

Cassie was in the act of pushing her hair away from her face when he said this; she froze. Everything froze, as if she was holding her breath, and even holding her blood back from moving.

Jim touched her on the wrist. "No, I'm sorry. I see it's too raw."

"Too raw," she repeated, sucking on her lower lip. He saw a nervous movement in her throat, beneath the skin. "I wasn't there on the night when . . . I was staying at my girlfriend's house. I'd had a fight with her, and I went to my friend's." Cassie left him, hastening up the path.

This went a good way to explaining the unspeakableness of all this. It was as if he'd quarreled that morning with Zak, gone down with him into the subway in a red silence. Determined to let him stew for the day. He was sorry for the way he'd handled her, but didn't know how to say so.

The day was already drawing in; clouds scudded over, bringing the bite of winter back into the air. The way she was walking away from him in the gloaming, as if she might dissolve at any moment, with her gray hair unfurled to the waist, she made him think again of those mysterious monochrome beauties who modeled for Julia Margaret Cameron.

Catching up, he offered her his arm, and after a moment, she took it. She liked him, he recognized that, but she bore her fear of the Other with the same ordinariness as her hair; she'd not yet made up her mind to cut it off.

They walked for a while through the chill green stillness. "This is nice," she said. "I like it here. I feel—don't laugh at me or I'll die—I feel like little Maisie walking with Sir Claude in that London park, what is it called?"

"Hyde. Or Regent's. Or Green Park. I forget."

"He was the first bright spot in her little life, wasn't he? Even though she didn't really understand at all who he was or why he was even *there* in her life . . . and of course he wasn't there for her at all. Not at all. The whole thing was going on so very far above her head. . . ."

"That's amazing, I was just thinking about Henry James before."

"I think about Henry James a lot. He was one of my regulars in the café, I kept a stool for him, the last one at the end of the counter, by the coat hooks. Nobody sits on it, really, because there's always coats hanging in the way—I used to have long conversations with him. And with Colette, of course, and Charles Dickens, too, but I always thought Henry James was the nicest to talk to, somehow, even though you wouldn't exactly think so from reading him. Sometimes I think—"

"Don't stop. Tell me. I'm not laughing, am I?"

"You are so *nice!* You really listen. Why do you want to spend so much time with a couple of oddball kids like Seth and me—don't you have any grown-up friends?"

He didn't like the picture of himself he glimpsed in her question. "Of course, I have grown-up friends." In her naïveté, she was too astute. "I don't think you're an oddball. All the most worthwhile people have an imagination. Your mother and father must have taken a lot of pride in your imagination, when you were a little girl." His own had, in his; he felt on confident ground with this. "So tell me. You used to work in a café?"

"Not a café like here in New York. More like a luncheonette. Y'know, with a counter, and a few booths, and a deep fryer."

"You were a waitress?"

"Yes. . . ." She hesitated. "Look . . . we should go. It's going to rain."

There always came some moment like this, in their subsequent outings, which Jim dubbed the Daring Daylight Robberies—time stolen from what he *ought* to be doing—when she would change the subject in a way meant to conceal her reticence. You had to let people move away from their individual horrors, Jim reminded himself, you couldn't keep calling them back, not just to assuage your curiosity. He loved Seth and wanted to know everything, but because he loved Seth, he did not ask.

Days later, at the highest point in the Guggenheim, looking down into the rotunda, he had a strong sense that she was thinking intently about these things she refused to share.

Below them people were truncated, pates with feet, moving in ones and twos and threes across the lobby. He wondered what this all looked like to her, these whited sepulchres of art and money; she trotted through them with such an accepting mien, keeping her avidity for telling her brother about what she'd seen in the same spilling-over way a child retells a cartoon show.

It always seemed easier to question when they were looking out at some view together, and not at each other. He asked her where she most wished, at that moment, to be.

"Promise you won't laugh at me," she said, no hint of a smile in her face or voice. He never laughed at her, but she made him promise, this way, over and over.

"Of course."

She darted a sidelong glance, to make sure first. "Paris. I think about living in Paris."

"Paris," Jim repeated. A thousand tired clichés bloomed and died in a moment. He repressed his sigh of disappointment.

Then she said, "I think about scraping along there on my own, just wandering the streets in wintertime, slinking along in the rain."

This was startling—the slinking, the rain. "To what end?" he asked.

"Does it have to have an end? It's my idea. It's what appeals to me." She paused. "I once read this book by Jean Rhys, about this girl in Paris, who was absolutely wretched and alone, penniless, sick, but when I finished it I thought, I'd like to try that sort of life."

He knew the book, and a chill touched the back of his neck. "Oh, God, Cassie, be careful what you wish for."

She was silent for a while, gazing down. Then she said, "I *am* very careful what I wish for. I've had a lot of time to consider my wishes, and sort them out. And I'm sure I'd rather be free, absolutely free, on my own, in a place that is ancient, beautiful, and difficult, than anything else. I might change my mind later on, but right now, that's what I wish for."

"You say you want your freedom—but freedom to do what?"

"To find out what I *can* do . . . who I can be."

"Well, wouldn't it be better to go to college? You could find your-self and be as unhappy as you please." And he added, to placate her, "There's always junior year in Paris."

"I don't really see myself doing that."

"You'll have to make some decision . . . not that it isn't delightful to have you stay with us. Of course."

"I will have to decide, won't I." She didn't phrase it like a ques-tion. "But I need to wait, to see. . . ."

"See what?"

"Oh," she mused, drifting back from the balustrade, "see what happens. You know."

18

The evening after that first excursion to the Brooklyn Botanic Garden, Cassie pulled Seth into her room after dinner and shut the door.

"Did you notice I didn't eat much just now?"

"Huh? Why? I thought that stir-fry I made was pretty good, Jim had seconds."

"I didn't have much of an appetite. Because I told a lot of fibs to-day. For you. And that kind of turned my stomach."

Seth's expression, bland and distracted before, hardened.

"He wants to know all about you. It's sickening really. Well, it's sweet, but. . . ."

"And you told him—what?"

"Hey, I stuck to the party line. I know what's good for me, Big Brother."

"Cassie . . ."

She'd expected him to be sharp with her, but he melted into her desk chair, and laid his head on his hands. "I didn't *mean* to lie. It was our first date, but I already knew he could be *the one,* if I could convince him *I* was the one, and I was afraid, so I said just what popped into my head. Now I have to stick with my story, and yes, I'm ashamed that I've lied to him, you can't *know* how much I hate it." He slipped an arm around her waist and pulled her closer. She could only resist for a second before she curved around him, her cheek against his hair. "Sugar, you don't know what it's like to be me. You think you do, but you don't. I'm just not any good really, I'll never be any good. I think I can keep that from him, but you've got to help me. I need you, you've always been my friend. I haven't always been very nice to you—"

She pressed against him. "Stop, *please*—" He was the best of brothers, he was the only person she loved or had loved for years, he'd made up to her for their dead father, he'd made up for their mother's vagueness, and for Roy. It was unbearable to hear him humble himself to her. It was unbearable that he might think she would betray him.

The Daring Daylight Robberies quickly changed from sporadic occurrences to standing appointments. She took to getting up earlier, getting ready. She scanned the *Times* and the weekly magazines Jim took, so she'd be prepared with suggestions about what they might go see. She didn't question Jim's devotion of so many hours to her cultural education. No adult, except maybe the librarian at the Flanagan County Free Library, had ever paid her such steady attention. Cassie began to feel entitled to it. She read the books he put in her hands, practiced her spotty high-school French on him, learned to eat all sorts of previously unthinkable things: sushi, pho, satay. Jim brought her to the dinosaurs on the Upper West Side, the New York Diorama in Queens, Patience and Fortitude on Fifth Avenue, the manuscripts of Pierpont Morgan and the tapestries of the Cloisters. Finally, one evening after the galleries on Fifty-seventh Street closed, he even brought her to the babies.

He hadn't told her about his volunteer work, and he supposed Seth hadn't, either. Her apprehension was palpable as she followed him into the hospital, looking askance at each empty gurney or marooned piece of equipment in the halls, averting her eyes from people slumped in wheelchairs.

When they arrived at the nursery, she let out a *huh* of relief.

"What, did you think I was going to make you wash the feet of AIDS patients? I wouldn't inflict you and your prejudices on anybody that weak."

"I guess you think I deserve that," she said with little resentment.

"You've a ways to go, kiddo." Turning from her, he greeted Pearl, the nurse, with a kiss on her wide cheek; introducing Cassie as his friend.

"She can visit this once," Pearl said, wagging a finger at him, "but this is not a cocktail lounge, you don't bring your dates here!"

Washed and gowned, he took the baby Pearl handed him to a rocking chair in a dim corner of the nursery. Perched on a desk chair the nurse rolled up for her, Cassie cradled her hands in her lap and stared at the blanket-wrapped infant.

Her expression reminded him of his impression of her, a choked, affronted misgiving.

"You have," he said dryly, "an opinion."

But she denied it with a vehemence just a tad overdone.

After that he forgot her, became absorbed, as always, in the drama of the baby face. Some nights the child of the moment fussed continually, as though fully cognizant of the dubious future before it.

Others, like the baby now—LaKeesha was her name, he'd held her the last time, too—seemed to catch his own thought, that here was the opportunity for a delicious hour of repose, snug in human warmth. His pleasure in the babies felt selfish; one could never, as long as one had arms and a heartbeat and body warmth, be in the wrong with them. Jim liked to feel the child's heartbeat against his hand. He crooned and whispered the same whimsical nonsense he'd heard from his own parents, grandparents, aunts and uncles. So much of what he passed into the tiny dark ears was in Yiddish, but the babies never seemed to object. It was Cassie whose eyes widened.

Shifting LaKeesha in his arms, kissing the top of her head, he looked again at Cassie. She was staring into space, lips parted, watching a movie only she could see.

"I bet you can barely stand to give them back when your time's up, can you?" she said.

"Some nights," he said, avoiding her little sorry-for-you frown, "it's almost beyond me." He cleared his throat. "Tell me something. How does Seth speak of . . . us . . . himself and me . . . to you?"

He could see her calculating, wondering. "I think you know already."

"Maybe so. But humor me."

"He adores you. He can't get over it that you care for him, too."

"He's told you this? Out and out *told* you?"

Again that suspicious squint. "Um, yeah."

"I take it it wasn't what you wanted to hear."

"We're talking about *you* now."

"Okay, yes. So that's what he said."

"Jesus, you don't need to ask me! He's like a dog—he follows you with his eyes, he's always wagging his ta—" She bit this off, and colored.

Jim laughed, and this made LaKeesha stir; her wet anemone of a mouth opened, and Jim took up his crooning again.

Behind them, a door opened, and the quiet of the dimly lit room was exploded. Rubber soles squished across the floor, two voices were upraised in Spanish, and all the while a squall worse than any car alarm or horny cat jagged the air. It was a sound that made them both wince and arch their backs, it was impossible not to writhe with it.

"Jim, Jim, you come see what you can do with this one." It was Pearl, gesturing from the doorway. "All day, all day he's been like this."

Before she could object, Jim thrust LaKeesha into Cassie's arms. In the corridor, another nurse held the keening infant. Pearl said, "Jim maybe will get this baby to sleep. He's good at it." The other nurse shook her head as she handed the squirming, flopping thing over; she looked like she wanted to drop it and run. Other babies in rooms off the corridor were screaming now, too, and LaKeesha, who had been so quiet, wiggled in Cassie's grip, trying out her escalating notes of distress. Cassie wanted to hand her over, but the nurse was gone, and Pearl was focused on Jim, talking to him in an undertone as he jogged the little body gently up and down.

The screeching baby he'd taken to himself was abnormally small and thin; its skin was a terrible purple, its flailing limbs seeming to bend in the wrong direction. It looked flayed. Cassie stared at it, wishing she could drag her eyes away; against her own body, LaKeesha was crying now, all but ignored. This was absolute hell! How could they all stand to listen to that ugly thing, or touch it when it was so repulsive, how could they resist smothering it with a pillow? Jim walked up and down with it, but it wasn't human, it didn't know enough, as LaKeesha did, to cuddle down against him and nap, it was like dandling a monster. Jim, remaining calm, managed even to smile, as he bounced the grotesque little body that didn't respond at all to his singing, his humming. Which he kept up anyway, as if it didn't matter. This was the worst thing she'd ever seen.

Then Jim brought that *thing* right up against her almost, and she jumped.

"What are you doing? You're not going to quiet her down like that. You need to really hold her."

She tried to gather her baby closer. He turned his back on her and resumed his pacing, and she knew she'd slipped in his estimation.

Pearl coolly relieved her of LaKeesha. "You don't like babies, hah?"

The horrid whooping went on. After a couple more trips up and down the corridor, Jim stopped opposite her. "Maybe you'd better go home and have supper with your brother. Tell him I'm going to be later than usual tonight. I can't just put this little fellow down until he's asleep. Could be a while."

"Oh, God," she stammered, "I'm sorry, only I—"

"Never mind," he said, already moving again, "this isn't for everyone."

"I can't imagine how that baby *could* ever get to sleep. It looked like it could only scream and scream until it died. I guess Jim will stay with it until it dies."

"You're hyperventilating," Seth said.

"It made me so afraid."

She waited restlessly all evening for Jim to come back; she'd left him at six, and at nine-thirty he hadn't returned. Seth asked her to come out and have a drink somewhere. But she wouldn't move from vigil.

Just before eleven they heard the key in the lock and both leapt to the door. Cassie threw herself against Jim and began to cry.

"I'm sorry, I'm sorry, I didn't know it would be like that—" She wanted Jim to hold her, she wanted to know that he still liked her even though she'd failed. Seth interceded between them, peeling her off into his arms.

"Sugar, don't you see how exhausted Jim is? C'mon, cut him a break. Hey . . . it's all right. It's all right." Over her head, she felt Seth was looking at Jim, in a way that had nothing to do with her, made her nothing. "She thought it was going to die," Seth was saying. "She couldn't stop thinking about it." She felt Seth's hands on her body, he was trying to hold her up as she gave way. She couldn't feel her knees. It was wrong for her to be this way, it made her no better than the thing she was crying over, she wanted all the attention to be on Jim, who was exhausted, who was so very, very good. Suddenly she was caught. Swung up.

"I don't know," she heard Seth mutter, "what's the matter with her really. S'probably got the rag on."

"All right, Seth. Why don't you make a pot of tea?" Then to her, "Hey, I thought I was finished with this for the night when I left the hospital." He set her down gently on the chaise; after one glimpse of his face, drawn and weary but still good-natured, she turned hers against the cushion. She wanted him, both of them, to just leave her alone now to get over her embarrassment.

"It was all right," Jim murmured. "Not *all right* all right, because the poor little guy will never be that. But for tonight, he was okay when I left him. He was asleep."

"I am so sorry," she whispered, "I just lost it, I—I—I don't know what happened."

He squeezed her arm, but then, thank God, left her. She heard the men talking quietly in the kitchen, and pretended to be asleep until they'd drunk their tea, turned out the lights, and went to their room. A moment later someone moved toward her in the dark. Seth threw an afghan over her, tucked it around her body. He said something, but she didn't know what it was until she heard the bedroom door close.

"Why are girls so damn crazy?"

In bed, Seth said, "You don't have to do this. She'll go out on her own quicker if you don't baby-sit her all the time."

"Quite frankly, I need to escape from the fucking office. And I like showing things to your sister."

"It's not that I wouldn't *love* to go around with you all day, but I've got to paint in the afternoons," Seth said. His tone half-aggressive, half-apologetic. "I mean—if I'm going to take my classes, and be here in the evenings, I need to—"

"Seth, of course. The last thing I want is to pull you from—"

"But what would you be doing if Cassie wasn't here to drag around with you?"

". . . I don't know, exactly."

"Your really should chuck the agency if you hate it so much. You've wanted to as long as I've known you. Find something else to do. I mean, it's not fair to yourself. . . . And I guess it's not fair to them either, you flitting in and out of there the way you've been doing lately."

"I don't know, Seth. I could still retake the reins. I think that's probably what I ought to do."

"No, it's not what you ought to do." Seth sat up, lit a cigarette in the dark. He hesitated. "I think—hell, I don't know anything about it."

"No, you're my partner. I want to hear your counsel."

"My counsel!" Seth giggled; the tip of his cigarette glowed red. "I think you should start another career. You used to love doing advertising, and you don't anymore. So you should do something you love right now."

"What I love. What I love is you. Apart from that . . . what I love is going to the babies, because they need me." He paused. "What I'd love is a baby of our own."

Another silence, longer, broken by a laugh from Seth that reminded Jim how he was just a kid himself.

"People start breeding awful young where I come from," Seth said. "Guys my age, it's not unusual for them to be saddled with two, even three kids. It's crazy."

"Seth, I'm not your age."

These words fell into the dark between them. Jim was afraid Seth wouldn't answer, that they'd lie there with nothing cushioning their echo. An idea came to him, a little burst in the blackness like the red tip of Seth's cigarette. He could break it off with Seth, he could find a woman who wanted marriage and children, the city teemed with them, and he'd be a consummate catch. Someone intelligent, sweet-natured, hopefully a bit undersexed, but a good friend, a loving mother. Two children, three. Maybe twins! Maybe four! A nice, low-key life, a nice family. The children would carry him through the rest of the forties, fifties, into his sixties, and then . . . grandchildren. No more men, of course. But life was all about trade-offs, wasn't it?

Seth's cigarette glowed bright orange; the vision faded with it as he exhaled and Jim pictured the plump curve of his mouth, the plush tongue peeking between the teeth, the sleepy grin. The way his eyes shone beneath half-lowered lids when Jim pinned him in the mornings, the musk from his armpits, kisses tasty despite the staleness of sleep. Oh, God.

Switching on the light, Jim plucked the cigarette from Seth's lips, and tossed it into the ashtray. For a moment he hovered to take in with his eyes all he'd just seen in his mind, knowing there would have to be some other way to make sense of his life because what he'd just imagined, giving Seth up, finding a *wife*, was a laughable absurdity. Then they began to kiss and he forgot everything else.

19

They were rounding the corner of East Eighty-third Street on their way to the Met when a woman called after them.

"Jim! Is that you? Jim Glaser! Hi!"

Fran Monti always had an air about her as if she didn't expect to be remembered. With her was a little girl of seven or eight in a red coat and hat, whose Pocahontas backpack was heavy with toy key-chains hanging off all its corners.

She hastened to close the distance between them, shaking Jim's hand with an eager swiftness and looking at Cassie sidewise, like a bird.

"Fran," Jim said, and introduced Cassie as a coolness blew through him.

"Oh, it's very nice to meet you, very nice. This is my daughter Lucy. I don't think you've ever seen her."

"No, I haven't," Jim said. "Hello, Lucy."

The child craned her neck far back to look up at him, then at Cassie, then back at him. She didn't speak, but her eyes, large and brown, narrowed.

"Everything's good?" Fran Monti asked. "You look just terrific. I wish we would hear from you. There are opportunities—"

He shook his head, smiling that sage little smile he hated to catch himself at, the one that said *no, no, all that is over* to a chorus of violins. He hoped Cassie took Fran for a real-estate agent or an art gallery owner.

But she plunged on, her speech, as always, staccato and somehow slippery. "Oh, yes, you know it's getting easier all the time, and you were always so beautifully qualified, I always knew you—I mean you *both*, of course—knew you were *so ready* for parenthood. It was just heartbreaking."

"You were very kind to us," Jim murmured.

Cassie turned to him, brow creased. "You never told me about this."

The hurt in her voice surprised him. "There's a lot you don't know about me. Why should you?"

"But—" Cassie placed her hand, so lightly he couldn't actually feel it, on the sleeve of his coat. "I thought—"

Lucy pointed at Cassie. "She looks like Gretchen's au pair. Don't you think she looks like Gretchen's au pair, Mommy?"

"I don't think so, dear." To Jim she said, "Tell me what you've been up to lately—"

"Gretchen's daddy doesn't live with her and her mommy anymore, and Gretchen only gets to see her au pair when she visits her daddy. Gretchen's mommy says her daddy is robbing the cradle. I know what *that* means, it means—"

"Lucy, that's enough." Flustered, Fran gripped the child's shoulder. "No one wants to hear about this. Mr. Glaser and his friend don't even *know* Gretchen."

"Gretchen's au pair is going to have a baby boy. It's in her stomach, just like yours is. Is yours going to be a baby boy, too?" Lucy was pointing at Cassie's middle.

"Lucy,. this is very, very naughty!" Fran bent over her daughter and began tugging hard at her jacket, and hat, and the ends of her braids, as if this fierce straightening would shake the whole subject out of her. In a hot whisper she said, "We don't speak that way to pregnant ladies unless they tell us about it first, Lucy. Because we can't always be sure by looking. It's very important for you to remember that and not embarrass Mommy." In a moment she was dragging the girl away. "We'd better be off! So sorry! Good-bye, Jim—so nice to see you—do call if—" Disappearing in a hurry around the corner, yanking the reluctant Lucy behind, still pointing with her free hand.

Jim glanced around at Cassie, smiling. "Four going on thirty-four, huh?"

Face drained of color, she pressed her hands to her belly. "Oh, God, I didn't know it showed *already*. . . ."

Showed? *It?* He looked at her. She seemed the same as ever, but now he spotted, beneath her breasts—and had she always had such round breasts?—he wasn't, of course, in the habit of noticing, but wasn't she usually more, well, less?—framed by the edges of her unbuttoned coat, her sweater certainly did fall over a decided . . . bump. Now he saw it, he was amazed he hadn't noticed it before.

Under his scrutiny, she flushed red, tugged her coat closed, and turned her back. Jim followed her, trying to look her in the face, but she kept turning, and for a minute they made, he felt, an odd spectacle, circling on the sidewalk. It was as though he was tailing his own startled ideas round and round.

"Stand still, *please*. Would you like my hankie?"

She took it, and backed up to sit on a stoop.

Heart jumping in his chest, Jim sat down heavily at her side. "Are you all right?"

"Not exactly."

A car alarm started up. As if by mutual agreement, they waited for it to stop. It went through its four changes of tone twice, then cut off mid-bleep.

"I don't know what to say."

"Well neither did I . . . or I'd have said it already. I meant to tell Seth as soon as I got here, only I didn't know he was going to be such a—"

She left the word unsaid. The wind sent a few dead leaves and bits of litter along the sidewalk. Jim traced with his eye the fancy draperies on an oriel window across the street, and wondered at himself for not taking charge of the situation. Feeling around in his overcoat pocket, he found a half-roll of mints, and offered her one.

Cassie slipped it between her bloodless lips and began at once to chew it. The crunching was surprisingly loud, as if her teeth were chipping.

"Be careful," Jim said.

"I thought you just liked to hold the abandoned babies—because it's a good work, charity. Why didn't you tell me . . . you and Zak were about to adopt?"

"It was none of your business," he stammered. "Your brother knows about it, of course. We were on our way to meet Fran that morning, to sign some papers, when Zak was . . . The baby we were to get was due in just a few days."

She winced. "So he was killed, poor man, and instead of a baby *you* ended up adopting . . . Seth."

He shot up.

"Well, it's true, isn't it?" she said.

"No, it is not true! C'mon, we can't stay here all morning, let's go . . . let's move."

When he'd bundled her into a cab on Fifth Avenue, he began to feel the inner clouds parting a little, and some of his managerial self returning. He guessed what the story must be: pregnant, nearly broke, probably needing to escape an uneasy relationship—or the lack of one entirely—she'd come east, hoping Seth would help sort things out for her. And then seized up, as she'd said, at the sight of him, and kept quiet all these weeks. "When . . . when do you expect . . . ?"

"I'm not sure exactly."

"You need to see a doctor. Had you thought . . . I suppose you came here to get an abortion."

She went big-eyed.

"I'm not getting rid of it before it's born." She was quiet for a while. "We used protection every time, but once it came off. Inside me. I guess that was the time."

"Who is he? The father?"

She shrugged. "Nobody I need to see again. I was sort of glad it happened in a way, because otherwise I wouldn't have had any good reason to leave him. To leave there. It's easy to just . . . where I'm from, people just kind of drift into . . . shit happens and then you're stuck. People don't think."

Jim supposed that, once orphaned, her brother far away, she'd fallen in with a bad crowd. "But," he said gently, "that's not you. You think. I see you thinking, all the time."

"And you guessed you always knew what I was thinking."

"No. Don't be absurd. Okay . . . sometimes, yes, I thought I knew."

"Well," she conceded, "You were right, sometimes. I—I've

changed my mind about a lot of stuff, since I got here." She paused. "Seth always thinks he knows what's in my mind. And he's not right even half as much as he assumes he is."

"Young men are often arrogant about their sisters, aren't they, though?"

"I guess." She paused. "But I'll bet I know what *you're* thinking right now."

Jim put up a cautious hand. "Now, Cassie—"

Her gray eyes sparkled as she turned to him. Suddenly she was glittering and dangerous. "I can read your mind—it's right there on your face." She reached out and stroked his bearded cheek with the tips of her fingers. The gesture astonished him. She was so enchanting, her expression so like one of Seth's that always made him go soft and hard at the same time. He wanted to jump out and walk home alone.

"I know what you want. Help me get what *I* want, and you can have it."

His heart was beating so hard, he could barely speak. "And what would that be?"

"I've told you already. I want to go away to Paris. If I could just *get* there . . . if I were free to go . . . I wouldn't expect anything else from you. I *want* to manage there on my own."

The driver sounded a long horn blast that made him wince.

"Don't you want to keep your baby?"

"God, no! I don't. I can't. It was all a mistake, I've known all along that someone else would have to—I want it to be you."

"You might change your mind. You might change your mind at any time. When it's born, when you see it—"

"No. No no no no *no.*"

"Then you must be aware, Cassie, that there are thousands of couples in this city, well-to-do, happily married, *straight* couples, you could choose. . . ." He trailed off.

"Is that what *you'd* like to see happen?" she said.

The strength had drained out of his body; he could think only of the anonymous weekly babies, the powdery smell of the tops of their heads, the webby mottling of their silvery skin. How he always had to go away empty-handed. Slowly, Jim counted backward from twenty in his head. He'd last felt this excited when he was about to have Zak for the very first time, all those years ago. He didn't trust his own motives, and his mouth was so parched he could barely get the words out.

"This is so sudden, you can't have given any *thought* to this. . . ."

"You'd prefer," Cassie pressed, "that I give away, to *strangers*, Seth's nephew, Seth's niece?"

The driver shot the partition with a bang that made him jump. "We're not going anywhere. Wanna try for the FDR?"

"Yes," Jim said, "whatever you think best."

The partition banged shut again, and they turned east.

"You don't *really* want to do this. You can't. I mean—you've gone a long way toward loosening up about us, it's true—but why would you want to do this?"

"I think you'd be good to my kid, the way you're good to me. You'd give it everything it needed. And I think you'd cherish my brother more because the kid was his flesh and blood."

"Don't you think I cherish your brother already?"

"You do now. I hope you will all the time."

"Cassie, sweetheart, these sentiments . . . they do you credit, they really do. I—I'm very moved." He had to speak slowly around the lump in his throat. "But it's a serious thing you're proposing, so spur of the moment, and—"

"So you're refusing?"

Their eyes met, and held for a long time. Then Jim tapped on the Plexiglas. "We've changed our minds," he said to the driver. "Take us to Chelsea. Eleventh and Seventeenth." A towering fear had sprung up within him. Bringing this about, getting Seth to agree, making it all feasible . . . would require the delicacy of a neurosurgeon.

· · ·

Seth was oblivious at first to the intercom buzzer, so filled was the long studio with rolling, thrumming music. He was absorbed by the canvas in front of him and the ideas in his head, ideas that had an oily, scented savor to them: they filled his thoughts even as he'd made love with Jim that morning, even as he'd eaten his breakfast and glanced through the *Times* and written his customary letter to Mr. Hecklin.

When the buzzer did penetrate his awareness, he ignored it. Sometimes kids from the housing project nearby mashed down the buttons; he'd heard them shouting obscenities into the intercom in the first week he'd had the place.

But the buzzer didn't stop. It wasn't being mashed, but rung in a systematic, insistent way. Finally he threw down the brush, went to the wall and pressed the talk button.

"What?"

"Seth, it's me. I'm with Cassie."

It wasn't quite eleven in the morning. They'd said, at the breakfast table, that they were going to the Metropolitan Museum; Jim was going to teach Cassie how to look at Chinese scroll paintings. That would keep them busy all morning, they'd have a late lunch, then, probably, knowing Jim, do some shopping somewhere, and arrive home just before he did, laden with booty, agreeably tired and in good humor. Seth froze. It could only be one thing.

Fuck, this is it, she's told, it's over. Ever since his sister's arrival he'd feared this disaster rising up like the ground to meet his falling body.

The buzzer sounded again, a long, strident demand. Seth again pressed the talk button, again said, "What?"

"Seth. You know I wouldn't come here like this if it wasn't important. I've got to talk to you."

This was like trying to stay upright in heavy surf while the sand was sucked from beneath your feet. He looked back at his canvas, the pencil lines of the drawing not yet obscured by the initial under layer of paint.

The buzzing resumed, short and sharp, little screams.

Fuck fuck fuck, what's the use? He knows and it's over and I can't keep him out. When Roy used to beckon to him, jabbing a thumb down in the air to indicate the cellar, he always went. He never did try to protest, to run, to fight. Just walked down the stairs, time after time.

Seth pressed the door button.

When he stepped up onto the landing, Jim didn't seem blatantly angry. No, it was worse: his face was doubtful, drawn, with a sharp little indent between the brows.

Glancing around in an odd, blindish way, Jim said, "Why wouldn't you let us in?"

He's so disgusted with me he can't even express it. He's just white.

There was no point denying anything . . . Jim would think what he would think. It was all over now anyway. "Cassie isn't coming up?" The words came out in a twelve-year-old's squeak.

Jim moved toward him; Seth fell back. They passed into the studio. He retreated before Jim until his legs bumped the sofa in the corner, and he sat.

"Seth, I don't know how to say this—I can't imagine it's going to be something you want to hear—"

Jim loomed over him, looking, to Seth's bewilderment, apologetic. *I'm sorry to do this, I know it's not what you want to hear, but I hate you now, you fucking liar, and I want you out of my life.*

"Your sister told me something just now. Something very . . . well, startling. I had to speak to you about it right away." Seth opened his mouth. Jim forestalled him. "The thing is—your sister is going to have a baby. She wants to go away and start her life. And she wants the baby to be ours."

"She—what?"

"Of course, I told her you and I had to decide together, but—Seth, for God's sake—I've got to have this. *We've* got to have it. This is manna from heaven."

He jerked. "Are you sure she's really pregnant? Why didn't she say anything before? *Jesus*. She's only twenty-one! You can't just manipulate her into—"

"*I* haven't manipulated anything!" Jim sat back, affronted. "Seth, this was all her—I tried to talk her out of it."

"Oh, yeah, I'm sure you tried really hard!" Seth sprang up and began a panicked pacing.

Jim steered him back to the sofa. "You don't want a child. You hate the whole idea. I know that." He brought his mouth close to Seth's. Whispered, "But this baby, do you realize, will actually be a part of *you*. *I* find that immensely appealing. Think of it, we'll be daddies, and it'll be your real nephew, or niece. We'll help your lovely sister out of her jam, and be a family."

A family. Jesus Christ on a pogo stick.

"Your routine won't have to change much," Jim said. "I'll quit the agency, stay home with the baby, I can't imagine anything I'd rather do. You can be like *my* father, who would always just kiss me good night after he got in from the city, and take me to the zoo once in a while. It'll be great. It'll complete us."

Seth's mind was starting to work again. *Complete us.* Seth already felt complete . . . at least, as complete as he'd ever feel, given that big parts of him were broken off and bobbing in the frozen straits. He was much too young to be a father. And *way* too fucked-up.

Jim's eagerness touched that part of him that was always prostrated at Jim's feet.

Looking into his glowing, expectant eyes, Seth knew he had to be very careful. There was so much to this, most of which Jim could have no idea of; understanding it was like trying to grab hold of the frayed ends of a snapped metal cable as it whipped through the air, any one of them might slash you right through.

Cassie was pregnant and hadn't told him. She'd offered this baby she didn't want to Jim, as if she'd always wished to strike a blow for gay couples becoming parents. It *had* to be because Jim had money—the money to send her off to chase her impractical Parisian dreams.

She'd done her best to make *him* feel guilty for accepting Jim's largesse—yet she'd penetrated to Jim's very heart, found the exact spot to press to start the arterial fountain of funds spurting. No moral nausea there. Just cash on the barrelhead and here's your baby and I'm out of here. But the last ten minutes had already turned his priorities upside down. He was not ruined, Cassie had not betrayed him, and in fact appeared out of the blue with the one thing necessary, had he only realized it, the child Jim pined for.

It meant he could still get it right. If he was very very careful from here on out.

Jim put a hand up to touch Seth's mouth, tracing its contours with the tip of his finger. "What d'you say?"

"Why's she out on the stairs?"

"She wanted me to tell you first. She thought you'd be angry with her."

"Poor Cassie. I have to talk to her."

"Talk to her, yes, you should." Jim caught at his arm. "But for God's sake, don't try to talk her out of—please, just tell me we can have the baby. You haven't said yes yet."

Seth hated it that Jim had to plead to him for anything. It should all be the other way. "It's what you want, so—of course."

"Seth, it's not quite enough that you want it for *me*. You have to want it for yourself, too."

He heard the justice of this. But he only wanted Jim, and Jim wanted the baby: that's how the equation stood. "I will. I need to adjust to the idea, that's all," he said with a nervous laugh, "but I promise I will."

"You're not just telling me what I want to hear?" Jim laughed. "Who am I kidding? Of course you're just telling me what I want to hear."

"Yes, but you know . . . it'll be all right." Seth's chest expanded as he said the words. *Maybe it really will be.* "Your happiness is really important to me. You know that, right? So it'll be okay, you'll see."

Jim rose and kissed him in that slow, intense way that melted all reluctance and always made Seth throw a boner.

"This . . . you have no idea . . . I hope the kid will be like you," Jim said through more kisses, "You'll see, we're going to have the most marvelous life, the three of us." It wasn't until Jim had yanked the coverall zipper all the way down and had his hand in Seth's briefs that he broke far enough out of his daze to pull away.

"I'd really better go speak to Cassie, don't you think?"

"Oh. Yeah." With wistful, tipsy concentration, Jim watched him trying to put himself away. "But you can't go to her with that sticking out of your—let me help you, Skeezix."

Abashed, relieved, apprehensive, Seth stood with trembling knees while Jim sucked him off. It troubled him sometimes, how much power Jim had over his body, what he could do to him with a look or a touch. Life had just done a one-eighty toward the unimaginable. *But Jim still loves me, and all I have to do,* Seth thought, *is let him steer.*

Jim was gone. Seth washed as best he could at the sink, hopping about in the gritty puddle he was making on the dirty floor, trying to rid himself of the reek of sex before putting his street clothes back on. He drank for a long time from his cupped hands, the torrent of water from the utility sink abrasive and cold.

When he returned to the studio, Cassie was on the couch, gulping seltzer from a can when she wasn't holding it against her hot cheeks and forehead.

He sat beside her, determined to be kind, to put her first, as he should have done from the moment of her arrival. The words *I* and *me* were unpleasant on his tongue; he'd been saying and thinking them too much. He hoped he could leave them alone for a while.

"So are you mad?" Cassie said. "I mean, how mad are you?"

"Not mad. Surprised. But it's not important. How are *you*?"

Her face was shuttered. "Relieved. Glad to know I'll be going."

Seth took her hand. "You're really serious about that. Going to live in Paris."

"*You* think I'm crazy, but yeah. I never thought I'd get out of Drinkwater, but now I've got this chance, thanks to you. I want to go there where no one knows me and be somebody new. I may not stay there all the time, but I don't think I'll come back here."

The arguments he wanted to make shrank in the face of her cruel determination. And the *I*, *me* ban he'd just imposed prevented him sharing his sadness over this trade he'd never looked for—his sister for a baby. Now that he knew how determined she was to go, he wished she'd stay on with them indefinitely. He'd come to rely on her presence: Jim, Hannah, Cassie; the three anchors of his small life.

"You've been so lucky, Seth. Don't begrudge me *my* luck."

"Oh, God. I don't. I totally don't."

They sat, both looking straight ahead, getting used to each other now that everything was different.

The elongated rectangle of sunlight moved slowly across the wooden floor. When it touched the leg of the table, a thought came to him that made him gasp.

"Cassie! You haven't said who the baby's father is. It wasn't—"

"The baby's father is no one you know." Then she was on her feet, the half-full can of seltzer bounced hard off his shoulder, spraying him. She screamed, "*Roy!* You think it was Roy! All this time you thought Roy was putting it to me—and you never did *anything* to get me out of there, you sack of shit!" Her pummeling fists felt like golf balls hitting him. When he ducked her and sprang up, she recovered and flew at him again, slamming him against the wall.

A voice in the doorway arrested her. "Hey! What the fuck—?"

From his half-crouch, Seth recognized his next-door neighbor, a man who ran a gallery out of the adjacent room on the landing. Cassie turned her back, and Seth hastened to get rid of him.

"My sister and I were having a little spat—sorry we disturbed you."

"A *spat?* Man, she was howling like a banshee—"

"Yes, but it's over. We'll be quiet now. Sorry." Seth closed the door in his face. "*Jesus.*" He rubbed his shoulder. There would be bruises. "When did it become okay for us to hit each other? We picked that up from *them*, it's filthy."

"You thought—all along you thought—"

"No, I didn't. Really."

I know Roy's taste in rape doesn't go that way.

She didn't know about that, because he'd protected her from it. But if she knew she would never speak to him like this.

"He's got some woman in Joralemon he fucks on Tuesday and Saturday nights. Suzy, her name is. She's a barmaid. Everybody knows it. He leaves Ma alone mostly. I mean, he still knocks her around whenever he's pissed-off or drunk, but he hardly ever wants to fuck her."

Seth winced. "Y'know, you don't have to talk so—"

"Don't like it? Then get another sister, get a sister who grew up in a fancy house with a couple of sweetie-pants college professors like *you* did, you lying bastard! *I* grew up in Roy Jenkins's house, and I'm sick of pretending! I'm sick of the way you've wiped me out of *your* version of our life, because according to you and your big honking *lie*, you didn't *need* me! And you know if I hadn't been there for you then, you'd probably be *dead! Nobody else loved you, Seth! Nobody else!*"

Her rage sucked all the air from the room. Only when she flung herself at the door and disappeared could Seth breathe again.

"The thing about being pregnant is that I have to pee every half hour. I hate that."

She threw this olive branch ahead of her as she reentered the studio, hoping he'd take it. She wasn't sure if she was really over her anger. Maybe if she let herself be as angry with him as she could be, there would be no end to it.

He went to her. "I know you loved me. I always knew that. And you were the only one I loved, really. You know me, Cassie."

She went into his arms.

"I'm stupid. I thought you were just the same as when I left you. I never thought you'd have a lover, or—or—anything."

"You are stupid," she said, rubbing her cheek against the solid ball of his shoulder.

"Was he a lover? Or just a one-night mistake? I hope he wasn't like most of the louts we knew in high school. I hope he was good to you."

"He was good. Very good."

"He *wasn't* one of the louts we knew in high school, was he?"

"He was new in town. He's . . . actually he's this mechanic Roy hired last summer. I know—don't say it, Seth. But he was kind of different." She was embarrassed to say what had attracted her to Cal, what had made her feel safe enough with him to lose her inhibitions. His silent oxen passivity. Men weren't supposed to be like that, after all, but thinking of him still gave her a twinge between the legs.

"What kind of glutton for punishment would work for Roy? How could Roy even *afford* a mechanic?"

"He . . . I don't know." She didn't want to tell too much. Cal was good, in his Cal way, but she knew he wouldn't hold up in a frank description. "He just showed up one day with Roy. Roy put him to live in the trailer behind the gas station. He ate dinner with us every night."

"God, what a life. That frickin' garage all day with Mr. Personality, and then Ma's cooking at the end of it."

"It was my cooking, actually."

"What was he like?"

"He was . . . a young man. Quiet, and sort of sweet, and . . ." This was inadequate, but she couldn't find better words. Her memory of Cal resisted words; it was mostly tactile.

"So—was he good-looking?" They'd drifted to the window. Stood side by side looking out at the ailanthus trees.

"Tolerable."

"Huh. What sort of cock did he have?"

"Seth! You can't ask me that!"

He slipped an arm around her shoulders. His mood had gone from dark brown to pink. "I could if you were a guy. That's what guys ask each other."

"That's gross!" She began to laugh, and leaned into him. "It was— I don't know! I didn't have much to compare it with . . . it was perfectly fine. It did the trick."

"The trick. Which was an accident, right?"

She rolled her eyes. "It was *such* an accident. God, yeah."

"I'm sorry you thought you couldn't tell me what happened to you," Seth said. "You came here expecting me to look out for you like I used to. And I didn't."

"You didn't. But Jim's been doing it for you, so you're off the hook this time."

A cigarette and lighter appeared in his fumbling fingers; he laid the cigarette on his lip, flipped the Zippo, cursed under his breath, and stuck the cigarette instead behind his ear. "Guess I shouldn't smoke around you anymore. I'll have to quit before the kid comes."

"Oh, just light it for chrissakes. It doesn't matter."

He dragged hard on his smoke, then said, "I just want you to be sure about what you're doing. Because you can still change your mind today . . . but if you change it later, when the kid's born, after all that anticipation . . . you'll wreck him."

She grabbed his face and printed quick hot kisses on his cheeks and chin and forehead. "Sethie, it's not *me* who's going to break that man's heart—it's not me!"

They walked home. He took Cassie's hand, curling his fingers between hers. Used to holding Jim's, her hand felt so small, he could feel the individual bones pressed between his. When they were children going to school, Mary always sent them on their way into the dark snowy mornings holding hands through their mittens. They stood apart from the other children at the bus stop, and sat together, whispering to each other in their elaborate charade of pretending not to care that no one else coveted their company. Pretending that the other children didn't know they were shabby and scabby and had a stepfather with fists like windmill blades.

Cassie hung on to him then, and she hung on now, tucking his cold hand with hers into her coat pocket.

"Where are your gloves?" she asked.

"Forgot 'em today."

"Jim's going to get the kid those mittens on a long string, y'know, that thread through the coat sleeves, so you can't drop them? That's the kind of thing he'll always think of. Maybe he'll get *you* a pair while he's at it."

"He takes good care of me," Seth mused. "You'd think that would be something that's easy to get used to, but . . . the weird thing is, it's not. Not for me. It makes me feel so fucking low sometimes, I don't know what to do with myself. Even after what happened to Zak, he still thinks people are good and life is mostly sweet." He shook his head at the enormity of Jim's naïveté.

"Seth, seriously. You should just tell him. Now more than ever. Just sit him down and tell him all about yourself. He'd understand. He'd forgive you. You know he would."

"Yeah," Seth said. He lit a cigarette, but slipped his hand back into her pocket at once. "Probably."

"So?"

He took a long drag, blinking up at the sky. "He'd forgive me, all right. He'd be forgiving me every day for the rest of our fucking lives. That would be one goddamn beautiful thing to live with, y'know?"

Part Three

20

Once he'd made his arrangement with Cassie, Jim's other hesitation gave way. He gave his partners a month's notice, time that seemed, despite the heaviness of winter, to skitter by, so he found himself tumbled all of a sudden into freedom.

Seth was working on a large portrait group of the three of them; his way of reconciling what was about to happen to their lives. For the last week Jim spent mornings at the studio, sitting. Most afternoons were taken up with Cassie—rounds of shopping, doctor visits, childbirth classes, trips to the library to look at pictures and hear music.

That day, Seth had appropriated her to pose, and Jim was on his own. Someone was leaving a message on the answering machine as he let himself into the loft. He grabbed the phone.

"Hello? Wait a sec!" He pressed some buttons on the machine, which often whirred on even when the phone was picked up. "Are you there? Hello?"

The voice on the other end was breathless and not loud, it took a moment for Jim to tune in on it. "... number I have for Seth McKenna and I didn't want to intrude on him but it's important I speak to—"

"Seth's not here right now," Jim said, rooting through the take-out menus, screwdrivers, and old postcards in the phone-stand drawer for something to write on. "I'll take a message."

"It's . . . oh, dear. Maybe . . . maybe I could talk to the tape again."
It was an elderly man, perhaps a little confused. He had a heavier version of the twang that came into Seth's voice when he was sleepy or talking amiable sexy nonsense.

"Well, if you want to," Jim said, patience straining, "you can call back, and I'll let the machine pick up."

"It's . . . oh, dear. I'm not sure what party I have reached."

"This is Seth's home number."

Again a silence. Then, his voice rallying, the caller said, "You perhaps are Mr. Glaser?" He spoke with a precision that was nearly queeny.

"Yes, I'm Jim Glaser. May I know who's calling, please?"

The old man chuckled. "Oh, he's written to me about you."

"I didn't quite catch your name?"

"My name is Lucas Hecklin." He paused, clearly expecting Jim to respond with recognition. "Seth must have told you about me." He sounded disappointed.

"No. No, I'm sorry, he's never mentioned that name." Jim began to be interested. Kicking off his shoes, he took the portable over to the couch and sat down.

"Now that surprises me," the man said. "Seth has written me all about *you*, and your life together."

"*Has* he?"

"Now don't get the wrong idea, young man. I was Seth's guidance counselor, you know. His mentor, in a way. Of course, I'm retired now."

"His *high-school* guidance counselor?"

"Yes, indeed." He sounded absurdly proud, and Jim began to feel oddly annoyed.

"I'm sorry he's not here right now—he's at his studio. He paints there, afternoons and into the evening."

"Well, isn't that fine. Ordinarily, I'd just write to Seth with any news, as I do, but . . . you probably don't know what small community

life is like, Mr. Glaser, but we all know one another's business out
here, sooner or later. The thing is, I'm not as mobile as I used to be,
so I don't hear all that goes on as quick as some people do, and in this
particular instance—"

"I didn't realize Lincoln was as small as all that," Jim said.

"Lincoln! You've got the wrong end of the stick there, young
man. Lincoln's a good three hours from here. Three hours if you
speed, that is. What made you think I was in Lincoln?"

"Well, I—"

"No, I'm phoning from my home, I'm in Joralemon, that's just
seven miles from Drinkwater—Seth's hometown. It's all small farm
towns here. The county seat, Flanagan, is pretty small, and getting
smaller. The schools are there, that's where I worked before I retired."

"Of course," Jim said. "I don't know what I was thinking when I
said Lincoln." These place names sounded like the fake ones in the
children's books Jim had read thirty-five years ago; they were meaningless, except that it meant something—something ominous—that
Seth had never pronounced them. Lincoln was the only place he'd
ever mentioned, as if it was the only town *in* Nebraska.

"Well, as I was starting to say. The unhappy news. It was only this
noon, when my niece Maddie—she's a nurse over to Saint Bonny's—
that's St. Boniface Hospital to you, it's our hospital here in Flanagan
County—when Maddie came over to see me and check my blood
pressure, that I heard about it. And I was so startled that it wasn't until just now that I realized I'd better call and tell Seth about it. Because I'm the only one knows where he is now. The family's got no
idea."

The family. What family? Jim's mouth went dry. "Tell him
what, sir?"

"About his mother. The poor woman has been in the Saint
Bonny's ICU since last Wednesday, she had a terrible heart attack.
Can you imagine? At her age? Mary Jenkins is—why, she's no older
than *you* are!"

Jim heard all this, but it didn't make sense; he groped up the string of words as if it was a rope he was climbing hand over hand out of a pit. He might get to the top into the light, but it didn't seem likely. "Are you sure we're talking about the same person here. Seth McKenna? He hasn't any—

"Of course! I know *you*, don't I? Mr. Glaser."

"But . . . Seth's . . . *mother?*"

"A massive coronary. She's barely alive. She's always been one of those itty-bitty delicate women. But I'm sure it didn't help any that her daughter up and disappeared a while back. I only heard about that today, too. The girl snuck away in the night, no one knows where. I wanted Seth to be aware of all this. I expect he'll want to come see his mother."

"Sir, excuse me, I'm not entirely following you here . . ." Jim said. "You're speaking of Seth's actual biological *mother?* The mother who raised him?"

"Of course I am, what other? The children are McKenna, although Mary is Jenkins. Well, surely you understand, Mr. Glaser, that Roy Jenkins never did *officially* adopt the children. Although he certainly was the man who brought 'em up; their real father passed before the girl was born. Seth has barely any memory of him, unless I'm much mistaken. Roy and Mary've been married upwards of twenty years."

"I see," Jim said. These names, the way the old man repeated them, were blows to the gut, small but sharp. "So you're saying that Seth's mother is—"

Glancing up then, Jim saw Seth planted in the doorway, a wild, sick expression on his face.

"What is that? Who are you talking to?"

"Wait, he's just come in, sir," Jim said. "I'm going to put him on the phone. Just a moment."

Seth was at his side now, skin greenish against the white of his sweater. Jim held the phone out, but he didn't take it. "It's someone to say my mother's dead, isn't it?"

"No. It seems she's—I don't know exactly. It's Lucas Hecklin. You talk to him."

Placing the phone in Seth's hand, Jim walked into the bedroom. Sitting on the side of the bed, he saw his reflection in the mirrored closet doors. The waxen face of a man who first realizes he's been made an entire fool of.

None of it was true. The story of himself Seth had told from the beginning, of the bookish supportive parents in their gingerbread Victorian full of books, all snatched away by fiery accident. The shattering loss they supposedly had in common: not real. Was anything true, at all? He'd seen no corroborating evidence for anything. Not a single snapshot. Not a single document—he'd never, come to think of it, even seen Seth's college diploma.

Emerging, he found Seth perched on the sofa, staring into space with a cigarette dangling from his mouth, the ash dangerously long. Couldn't look him in the face, so Jim stared instead at his trembling hands.

Hands that had caressed him in every way. Hands he had kissed hundreds of times. A deceiver's hands.

Jim cleared his throat. "So?"

"She's very very sick. Mr. Hecklin didn't seem to know much about what happened, or if she's expected to—"

"When will you leave?"

Seth looked around, as though there might be some helpful clue in the piano, or the potted plants, or the pictures on the walls.

"There probably isn't any such thing as a direct flight to Nebraska," Jim said.

"I don't know. I left there by bus and I've never been back."

"You'll just have to get on the phone and see what you can arrange."

"Yeah . . . I'll call. . . ." The long ash fell then, and rising unaware, Seth smeared it across the carpet.

"Christ, would you look what you're doing! I don't know why I let you smoke in here at all, I—"

"Sorry. Sorry, I'll clean it—" Dropping to his knees, Seth moistened his fingers with spit and started rubbing at the gray stain.

"Stop that, you're making it worse—I don't want your filth ground into my Persian rugs—"

The way he knelt there made some previously unknown hinge in Jim open. "You lied to me. From the very beginning, you just calmly lied and lied and lied. Every day, in every way, you've lied to me. Every single goddamned day."

Seth was crying in that silent motionless way that was like rain sluicing down the outside of a windowpane. *In his fucking waterproof eyeliner, so he can stay pretty even while he pretends his weeping means anything.*

Seth's abject pose made Jim itch to hit him. He retreated again to the bedroom.

When he heard Seth on the phone, making travel arrangements, Jim leaned on the front window, looking out. He was still there when Seth came from the bedroom carrying his knapsack.

"Jim?"

Seth came up behind him and touched his shoulder. He could see the boy's reflection beside his own. How like this was to their first conversation, in the photographer's studio, when he'd been aroused by Seth's image in the glass. He should have, that day, listened to his better sense.

"Jim, please, one thing."

How could he have been so trusting? And why did this have to happen now when things were so good? The goodness all shown up as hollow.

"Please . . . don't tell Cassie where I've gone. It will be better for her not to get involved."

Jim turned to confront Seth's chalky face.

"How can you say—"

"I *know* it's not right. I know. But it would be even more not right—for her—if she got sucked into going back there to—"

"This woman—your mother—is her mother, too, isn't she?"

Seth nodded.

"What then?"

"If . . . if it looks like there's any real good she could do . . . or if, you know . . . then I'll send for her. But meanwhile, please don't—"

"And what do you propose I tell her, about your whereabouts?"

"I'll leave that to you, you always know the right thing," Seth said. Without giving Jim a chance to argue further, he walked out.

Jim saw him pass out through the street door, and hasten to the corner of Lafayette, where he hailed a cab. Almost as soon as the cab was gone, Cassie turned into the street from Broadway, laden with grocery bags. No matter how often he told her that the store delivered, that there was no need to schlep, she went on dragging the shopping home like a frugal peasant. She walked slowly, her long open coat flapping behind her. Jim was always trying to get her to wrap up warmer, and she was always complaining, her cheeks and mouth ruddy, about feeling too hot.

How vital she looked, her hair and skin and flowing black clothes seeming to crackle in the clear air. The sight of her had become almost as precious to him as her brother's. Even before she promised her child to him, he'd grown attached to her. Even now that disappointment clung to him like a sour stench, he couldn't bring himself to regret it.

She, of course, had lied, too, on strict instructions from her brother, no doubt. Who now expected him to compound lies with more lies by withholding this information about her mother back in Nebraska. His whole being recoiled from this miasma. But if, as Seth had pointed out, he let Cassie out of his sight, let her go out there to those mysterious Jenkinses, who knew what influence they might exert to rob him of the infant—he already thought of her as Ruby, the name he'd chosen with Seth when they learned the baby's sex. Seth's reasons for holding out on her, being entirely self-serving, were wrong, but . . . *Well*, Jim thought, *I'm selfish, too. I'm selfish for myself and my child, so I'm going to keep her quiet here. And after Ruby's born the two of them can go to hell for all I'll care.*

Jim pulled away from his station at the window, feeling as if he was leaving his whole top layer of skin behind, and went down to help her with the groceries.

The only way to reach Omaha that night was by first flying to Atlanta and changing planes. In the waiting area by the gate, Seth felt he'd already left New York; many of the people seated here had southern accents, and they all looked scrubbed in a way no one in Manhattan ever quite did, whether dressed in suits or the casual uniform of Dockers and polo shirt with tiny tasteful corporate glyphs embroidered on the breast. No one was reading anything other than *USA Today* or *The Wall Street Journal* or the latest Tom Clancy. No one looked gay. A couple of video screens suspended from the ceiling projected a continual buzz of images and chatter into the sterile space, impossible to tune out. People stared at him.

People stared at him; and his mother, who'd never protected him or acknowledged what Roy did, was gravely ill. People stared at him; and Jim was so angry that he'd not even turned from the window to look at him when he left the apartment. He slumped down in his seat and crossed his arms. There was nowhere to smoke, there would be hours and hours and hours to endure before he'd get to smoke again.

In his window seat on the plane he curled up as best he could, his face turned to the wall so the man in the aisle seat wouldn't see that his eyes were wet.

His mother, five miles from town, struggling through the churned-up snow at the side of the road at six in the morning. That's how she was found, according to Mr. Hecklin, by a farmer driving in, who gave her a lift back to her café. Where some hours later, at her usual post between the grill and the deep fryer, she collapsed. She'd given the farmer no explanation for her presence on the road at that hour, in only the light jacket she wore to run between the café and the house. Seth couldn't get that image out of his head. Mary laboring along, wheezing, hunched over, alone. Alone. Because when was she ever alone? There were always customers, always Cassie, always church ladies, always Roy. Mary never was, never wanted to be, alone.

Or the other detail Mr. Hecklin had supplied, that once she was at the hospital the doctors had found she was suffering from malnutrition. A woman who cooked for a living.

Time after time, Roy put his hands through her like cheesecloth to get at him. She'd never rescued him, and now he felt unable to rescue her; he imagined going in to see her in her hospital bed, and finding they both were mute.

Seth thought he'd stopped loving his mother long ago, but now he wasn't so sure. Perhaps all this would be easier if he really had. The thought of her taking that literally heartbreaking walk in the freezing dawn roused in him a serrated pity that was even worse.

Not usually much of a drinker, Seth was sure that getting liquored-up was the thing. He had some time for the bar at the airport in Atlanta. Vodka was the elixir of the moment. Except that no matter how many drinks he had, he couldn't stop thinking.

Why hadn't he spoken in those first shining weeks of lovemaking, when it would've been the easiest thing in the world, clasped in Jim's arms, to murmur, *Forgive me, I wasn't straight with you, but I was afraid, I was ashamed, I thought you wouldn't care for me. . . .* He needn't have said anything about the rape, or the worst of Roy's other abuses. Just admit to Drinkwater, to Ma, to the basic *truth*.

If only he hadn't been such a stupid jerk.

And if only Mr. Hecklin hadn't called when he did, and run his mouth quite so much.

But what did Mr. Hecklin know? Seth wrote to him about the wonderful things he had now—a home with his love, a studio, the space and time to paint, a groundedness and security he'd always craved—but nothing to indicate the lie on which the whole edifice perched.

And soon he'd see him. Stay in his house. Accept his hospitality and say nothing to spoil it, not let on that his well-meaning phone call—how he must have enjoyed talking to Jim, whom he'd been told so much about—had set his world on a sharp slant toward the shit.

Fortified with another couple of vodkas, he joined the crowd at the Omaha departure gate. Here were mostly young families, returning from Disney World laden with trademarked product. When the plane landed, they would load sleepy kids into Explorers and Broncos and melt away into the Omaha suburbs. Had any of these people ever had occasion to drive through Drinkwater, stop, perhaps, for gas at Roy's, eat a hamburger or a grilled cheese sandwich from his mother's hands? Fewer and fewer did all the time. Once, when he was fifteen or sixteen, a couple of college girls with Illinois plates, in black clothes and sunglasses, had appeared and exclaimed over the octagonal metal sign that swung out from the low building, the words

E
GAS
T

picked out in white paint and thin neon tubing. He'd been working the pumps that spring afternoon, as always, and they'd spoken to him as if he was a half-wit. Wanted to know how old the sign was, and if anyone had ever offered to buy it, and what people did around there for fun. They'd snapped pictures of it, and the two abandoned storefronts on the other side of the road, with their desiccated whitewash and splattered plate glass, and the facade of the old IGA, and laughed at everything he said, although he was sure he'd spoken no differently

than they. Then they'd driven away without entering the café or buying any gas. They'd have forgotten him completely before they passed
Joralemon, but they left Seth feeling like a feral beast they'd teased
through the bars of its cage.

The Omaha flight was full; once more in the window seat, he
found himself beside a little boy of nine or so, a quintessential
Poindexter with thick glasses and a cowlick, who, once buckled in,
pulled a thick book of crossword puzzles out of his knapsack and set
industriously to work. Seth couldn't help glancing at the clues and
filling in the answers in his head; the wrong ones the boy jotted in ir-
ritated him more and more. Finally he muttered, "It's oast."

The boy glanced up.

"Thirty-three down. Oast. O-A-S-T. A drying kiln."

Without comment, he wrote it in.

"And that one there," Seth detached himself from his slump
against the bulkhead and stretched in his seat, "that's not Rhine, it's
Rhone. The Rhine does not flow through France."

"Oh." The kid made a big deal of erasing the entire word, even
though it was only a letter different, and writing it in fresh. His geeky
earnestness aroused Seth's pity, and contempt. Seated on the other
side of him and occupied with another child across the aisle, the boy's
mother was stolid and solid in neat pink sweats, fair hair strained
back with a clip.

"Do you know this one, mister? Blank und drang. Five letters."

Seth leaned in closer to see where the skinny finger pointed, although he already knew the answer. "Sturm."

"What's it mean?"

"Sturm und drang. It means . . . like, a big fucking hoo-ha."

Seth wasn't sure if it was his words, or perhaps a whiff of his
breath that made the kid recoil, but he pulled back and smiled uncertainly. At the same time, Mom, not in fact as oblivious as she'd
seemed, shot Seth a killing glance, lumbered up, and changed places
with her son.

He rode to Omaha with her elbow in his ribs and didn't protest.

When he'd emerged from the men's room, where he threw up the liquor and replaced it with as much water as he could slurp out of his cupped hands, the sweat-suited families had mostly dispersed, everybody knowing where they were going. No more flights were coming in or going out that night. A digital sign showed the local time and temperature. It was forty degrees colder here than New York. Seth realized he'd brought nothing with him warmer than his lined leather jacket. No hat, no scarf, just a pair of thin gloves jammed into one pocket. Plowed snow was piled up outside at the edges of the parking lot, lit up yellow by the sodium lights.

A couple of the rental-car desks were dark, but the Avis and Budget stations were stuffed, each by a solitary clerk, leaning on their counters and exchanging perfunctory remarks. He hesitated before them.

"Last year he got me this, like, granny-gown. Like a flannel granny-gown up to my *neck*. I thought, *what is he trying to tell me?*" the clerk at Avis said, laughing.

"So what do you think he'll give you this year?" Budget asked.

"Well, I hope not that again." Avis looked up. "Need a car, sir?"

"Uh, yeah." Seth still hesitated; Avis had claimed him first, but he thought Budget might be a little cheaper; he was acutely aware that he was spending Jim's money here, money he'd received under false pretenses, and he ought to be frugal with it until he could refund it all. He approached the Budget counter.

The clerk there straightened up, yanked at the hem of her blazer, and dismissed her friend at the other counter with a wave.

Seth took his credit card and driver's license out and laid them on the counter. "I need, basically, the cheapest car you can give me."

The young woman was typing. Her name, Cecilia, in gold script glinted at her throat.

She picked up his cards with the edges of her long nails and examined them. From the driver's license she glanced at his face, then back at the picture on the card.

"Don't tell me I've got to be twenty-five or any of that bullshit."

"Seth McKenna? Wow, *you've* sure changed. Are you, like, a rock star or something now?"

Despite the stares he'd gotten all along, it was only now, confronted by her smirk, that he remembered how he looked, hair dyed, eyes lined, ears and nose pierced, neck and clavicles displayed in a silk boat-neck sweater, Jim's gift.

"D'you think you could just take care of the car? It's late."

She recoiled, and he remembered that this was not how business was transacted in Nebraska. Clearly, this young woman had gone to Flanagan County High School with him, and she expected to be filled in on his life since graduation, and to fill him in on her life.

"You don't remember me?" she said. "Mike Stepic's twin sister? Mike was on the track team with you."

"Oh, sure, Mike. Yeah."

He recalled Mike, who hadn't been quite up to snuff for the football team, and took out his frustrations on Seth, when he dared, in the locker room after practice. A real Neanderthal. And liable to let the squad down in the relay race.

She was still examining the picture on his driver's license. "I saw you at all the meets," she said. "You sure were fast."

The jocks used to say, behind his back, that he was so fucking fast because if they caught him they'd kick his homo butt clear to Omaha.

"Mike will be amazed when I tell him I saw you."

"Mike's still around, is he?"

"Sure, he works with Dad at the dealership. Wow, you live in New York now? Do you ever go to that restaurant where they all hang out on *Seinfeld*?"

"No."

"What do you do? I bet you're like, a musician or something, right? You look like those guys on MTV."

"I'm not on MTV. I'm not on *Seinfeld*. Can I just get a car, please, Cecilia?"

The false bonhomie evaporated, and she began to type. "Guess it's true what they used to say about you."

"Yeah, what was that?"

She didn't reply, except to ask him curtly if he wanted extra insurance, and if he'd return the car with a full tank or an empty. When he'd signed and initialed the form and she'd torn off the perforated edges and folded his copy into the rental brochure, with a local map, all by the procedural letter, she pushed it, and the key, across the counter. Seth noticed she didn't place them with her hands into his hand. She wanted him to notice that.

"I used to hear all kinds of things about you."

"Really. Well, you can tell *them*, if you still talk to *them*, and I'm sure you do, that I'm no rock star but I *am* a big screaming faggot, just like they always suspected. Be sure to tell Mike. He used to mention it from time to time; he'll be so glad to know he got it right."

After phoning St. Bonny's ("No change in Mrs. Jenkins' condition, which was graded as serious"), and Mr. Hecklin ("I've got a bed all ready for you, you just come on out when you've seen your mom, I'll be here, don't worry"), Seth couldn't, in the end, lie down without making one more call.

The phone was picked up on the first ring. Jim didn't even say hello, but Seth could hear him breathing. For a few moments, all he could do himself was breathe; it felt as if he'd resumed it after a long period of silent choking.

"It's just started to snow," he whispered. "I'm watching snow falling on the parking lot of the airport Hilton in Omaha." There was no loneliness, Seth was quickly learning, like the loneliness of a crappy airport hotel room far from all you love.

"So you got there."

"Jim, kiss me."

"I told your sister you'd gone on a last-minute trip with your professor, to see an exhibition in Chicago."

"You're so good to me. Please kiss me."

"How's your mother?"

"I don't know yet. The same. Whatever that means."

"I've been lying here thinking—"

"No," Seth cut him off. "Don't think yet. Wait until I get back. Until I can talk to you."

"You never really described her to me. You never said anything concrete about her or your father. Except how wonderful they were, and how bereft you were when they died, when you lost them and your childhood home all at once. I really identified with that horror, Seth, and I thought it was too painful for you to go into detail, so I didn't press. I was in love with you so I didn't think how really fucking *odd* that was."

"Jim, I'm all by myself here. I need you to kiss me."

"Go to sleep, Seth. Go to sleep so you can do what you have to do in the morning."

"Please. Just kiss me good night. You have no idea how I feel right now."

"I think I have a pretty good idea, actually. It's just about the only thing I'm pretty sure I know about you right now. That you're feeling pretty damn bleak because your big tower of lies has come crashing down, and you're fucked."

"Jim, you're scaring me. Don't talk like—"

"Good night, Seth."

"Please just don't *think* until I get back. Please."

There was a pause before Jim replied, during which the snow looked to be falling upwards.

"Enough," Jim said then. "Enough of this nonsense. I've had enough."

With the whirring phone still cradled at his ear, and his belly grinding with hunger, Seth stared out at the snow. He was exhausted but afraid to sleep; how much worse here, closer to their source, his dreams would be!

When he was small, four and five and six and on until the change in his voice and the zits on his face withdrew her even further from him, his mother would come to him sometimes in the night, when it was very bad, sit in the dark on the side of his bed and rub his back, teaching him by example not to cry or discuss the trouble, but know-ing it, even if she never admitted anything, even if, the mornings af-ter, she looked through him again the same as ever, always harried and two orders behind. She'd never done anything for him, Daytime Mary, never even tried to defend her son from what she'd brought into her house, but those times at night he'd been able to fall asleep clinging to her bewildered sympathy.

With each mile he drove north on 275, thinking about his mother, Seth grew fainter. He'd arisen at dawn, not sure whether he'd slept or not, and stood under the ineffectual warm dribble of the shower for ten minutes, until his fogged brain understood that he wasn't going to feel any better than he felt right then. In the harsh light of the hotel bathroom he removed all the rings from his ears and nose, losing one down the sink. After staring at himself for a while, he decided that his reddish beard stubble added more to his masculinity than it detracted from his neatness; the decision not to shave was reinforced when he discovered that he'd forgotten to take his shaving tackle. He'd also failed to pack anything really suitable for a prairie visit; the other sweater he'd grabbed had a high turtle-neck, true, but it fit his torso like a second skin. He hadn't realized how much Jim had encouraged him to give way to vanity about his body—even the soft old chinos were, in this place, revealed to be all about his butt. These were clothes to get bashed in.

Instead of leaving Omaha right away, as he'd planned, he drove around until he found a Wal-Mart, emerging in a version of the local uniform: baggy blue jeans, a thermal top beneath a plaid flannel shirt, a hooded-down parka in a dull khaki; all oversized and entirely unremarkable. New work boots rubbed at his heels and toes through heavy socks. Inspecting himself in the rearview mirror, he wrinkled up his nose and sneered. *Who are you trying to kid?*

Not much in Flanagan had changed, except that everything looked smaller and plainer and shabbier. The absence of tall buildings made him feel small; not the reaction he'd expected. He noted, as he drove through town, that there was a new Subway sandwich shop, an empty storefront where the Woolworths had been, and a few shops had changed hands. No new buildings. The wheat fields he drove through on the way to Joralemon, under gray snow, were the same.

Joralemon, like Drinkwater, had very few of what little it did have: few trees, few stores, few houses. Getting out of the car in front of Mr. Hecklin's, it occurred to him that he'd neglected to bring anything to mark this enormous reunion. But what: flowers, a bottle of wine?

There he was at the door. Seventy passing for eighty. Grayer and fatter than Seth remembered, blinking behind thick glasses. The same cardigan and rumpled shirt. He held the storm door open and said nothing until Seth joined him in the tiny entryway, and he'd shut them in.

Then he folded Seth into an embrace that at first startled him and then filled him with such terror that he began to sob. He hugged the old man back for a moment, then dropped his arms.

"My boy, I'm so sorry."

For a moment, he thought news was being delivered; Mr. Hecklin saw his mistake and hastened to assure him. "You haven't been there yet? There's no change, no change. She's still in intensive care, but there's no change. I called over there this morning. Here, let me take your coat. Come, there's coffee ready."

Seth felt like a giant in these tiny rooms; the house seemed fragile enough to be leveled by a few punches.

In the kitchen Hecklin peered at him hard through his thick glasses, shaking his head and smiling. With a tentative gesture, he reached to grip Seth's biceps, squeezing a little. When Seth didn't immediately move away, he squeezed harder.

"You know, when you first pulled up, I wasn't sure it was really you. . . . You've become such a handsome boy. I can say that to you *now*, can't I? Wouldn't have dreamed, back in the . . . but then, you weren't yet . . . but you're not a boy anymore either, are you? My my . . . how time slips by . . . it does nothing good for me, though."

Blushing, Seth offered to pour the coffee; this recalled the old man to his hostly duties; he pressed Seth into a kitchen chair, coaxed him to eat an anemic cheese sandwich and some carrot and celery sticks that he laboriously cut up, over Seth's protests, and watched him consume as though he was a toddler.

"You've certainly changed," he said, unconsciously echoing Cecelia at the airport. "Gotten rid of that tattletale gray," he added with a laugh. "Hair looks awfully . . . bright. So nice and bright." The way he said it, Seth knew he should've bought a box of brown dye along with the new clothes, and doused it down. Except that he didn't think he'd ever be able to douse himself down again far enough to pass muster here.

"I was surprised," Hecklin said next, "to hear your sister had gone out there to you. Surprised, but relieved, of course."

"Yeah, she's all right." Seth coughed. "We're glad to have her with us."

"He sounded, on the phone, like quite a . . . quite a man. Your Jim. You must have a picture of him?" Mr. Hecklin suggested.

Seth considered shaking his head and trying to change the subject. But there was such hunger in Hecklin's eyes, distorted by the thick lenses. Taking his wallet from the unfamiliar denim pocket, Seth showed the snapshot they'd asked a passerby to take at an outdoor restaurant table. Here they were, arms draped around necks, beer bottles in hand on a balmy autumn night, each giving the camera the expression they reserved for each other. Hecklin looked at it for a long time, and returned it with a sigh.

"So, what've . . . what've you been doing with yourself lately?" Seth asked, knowing as he spoke that this was the wrong question, that there probably wasn't any right question.

"I wish you'd call me Lucas."

Seth did not want to call him Lucas, but he nodded. He wouldn't call him anything now. "Please tell me about my mother."

"Aren't you going to go down and see her? Should be about a good time to go, lunch over and all."

"I—"

Mr. Hecklin's face took on that same expression he'd had in the past right before he began a harangue, the mildness disappearing under the exhortation to do what needed to be done, to do it right. Seth knew what he'd say even before he said it. That whatever had passed between them was in the past, Mary was his mother, and he must not waste another precious second because who knew what would happen?

"Can I, I dunno, drop you anywhere on the way? Do you need to do any shopping, or . . . the library?"

The old man shook his head. "You just go. Only thing is . . ." He leaned forward and peered at Seth, squinting. "That how they're wearing their sideburns in New York these days, hmmm?"

"Uh . . ." He'd been, for the last couple of months, shaping them into long stylized points that touched his cheekbones.

"Didn't get to shave this morning, I see. Maybe you'd—?"

"Yes. Yes, I'd like to get a little cleaned-up before I go."

He followed the old man's halting steps up the narrow staircase, to the bathroom, where he fussily found him a new disposable shaver, brought out the can of Barbasol and a towel, held his finger in the running water until it was sufficiently hot, and only then, reluctantly, left Seth alone. He waited until he heard Mr. Hecklin descending the stairs before he began to shave.

The sideburns, offending or fascinating, he wasn't sure, he whisked off with the rest. With wet hands, he combed through his hair, pushing the fringe back off his forehead, exposing the bare beginnings of gray roots. Last night was when, had Mr. Hecklin's phone call not come, he would have touched them up. With his hair pushed back, his head devoid of jewelry, he saw himself at seventeen, too wary to look even into his own eyes.

21

Mrs. Rausch at the high-ledged reception desk hadn't changed a bit from the way he remembered her; the only surprise was seeing her at the St. Bonny's reception desk, because she'd been one of the high-school secretaries, ushering him in and out of trouble before his big turn around, and then cheering him on, in her small way, afterward. Seth watched her, across the expanse of the lobby waiting area, talking on the phone, half-glasses poised on her nose. It would be impossible to get by her to the ICU without stopping, and impossible to speak to her without being recognized. The dismal prospect yawned before him of unwanted reunions proliferating into infinity, like images in a three-sided mirror. Not just his mother, not just, unless he was awfully lucky, Roy. But all these neighbors who'd known him as a kid, and whom he'd have to deal with, one by one by one. They'd all be expecting him to be polite, to say a few words about himself, to ask about them and theirs.

Christ, I can't do it. I should never have come here.

In the overheated vestibule where he hung suspended, between the inner and outer doors of the hospital, he began to sweat beneath his copious layers.

A man entered behind with an onrush of frigid air and jostled him.

"Jeez, kid, of all the places to stand around in—"

It was Roy.

Seth's body knew it before his eyes could relay the image to his brain; he started back, an army of microscopic ants marching across his vision. Roy in his dark-blue work clothes, with a three-day growth clinging to his hollowed cheeks, blew past him without a glance.

At the desk, he conferred with Mrs. Rausch. Talking to her, he looked a little cowed, but Seth didn't see him that way. For years, the idea of Roy was linked in his mind with that of a looming cobra as big as a man, the result of the many times Seth had seen him, severely foreshortened, from the cold cellar floor.

No way, no way could he go in to see his mother now.

Instead he asked the way to the billing office. Once there, he wrote out a large check to cover Mary's care, large enough to ensure she wouldn't have to leave the hospital before she was fully recovered. The payment felt like a slim sort of atonement, an atonement he shouldn't have to make at all. He handed it over without any sense of satisfaction, doubting that, if his mother knew the source of the money, she'd permit its being spent on her at all.

Jim's money. He still couldn't think of it as his own, no matter what Jim said. And now that Jim knew he was a fraud, how would he feel about having given him such a generous gift, about any of it going to the support of a woman he'd supposed didn't exist?

After that, it seemed like a good time to drive over to the old place. He didn't really want to, but there was nothing he *did* want— not food, not sleep, not even to go home. Thinking of Jim's as home only made him uneasy, as if he was claiming stolen goods as his own. *I don't want your filth ground into my rug.*

He drove through Drinkwater three times, knowing, as he passed slowly down the streets, that the presence of a strange car was being noted by people behind the windows of houses and shops and other vehicles.

It had always been a bleak shithole, but now it was a veritable *black hole* of shit: all the humiliation, pain, and boredom of his first eighteen years compressed and crammed into one small geographical point. A headache formed behind his eyes, the kind that comes from oversleeping on a cloudy morning. The sky was low and uniformly gray, the light diffuse; the edges of things seemed to boil. When he pulled up under the sign at Roy's Service Station, he was afraid he'd be sick, his mouth filling up with gooey saliva. Slowly, he rolled the window down. The cold wedged in at once.

A young man appeared; at first glance it was like seeing a ghost of himself, in twill work clothes, a quilted jacket hanging open, red scarf looped around the throat. Big mirrored sunglasses and a wool hat with earflaps hid most of the face. He leaned in the doorway with an indolence that Roy, had he been here, would never have tolerated.

This must be Cal. Who else could it be? The guy Cassie did it with. Who made her get that funny little smile on her face when she talked about him. Ruby's father. A vein in his temple began to throb.

"Café's closed," Cal said.

"I'm not hungry," Seth said. He'd once seen a porn video that started off like this, only in the video it was high summer in some place where the light was flat and grueling: Arizona, maybe, New Mexico, and the young man in the gas-station doorway wasn't wearing a shirt.

From where he sat, he had a whole vista of the facade of Roy's, the office with its dirty window, a clock advertising motor oil hung in it, the two bays of the garage, icicles hanging down, the tow truck parked off to the side. The attached café, with MARY's painted on the smeary window, was dark, the blinds drawn. His mother must have been in more-than-the-usual distress for a while; she never allowed the windows of the café to get like that—her cleanliness was a marked contrast to Roy's side of the business.

Seth tried to parse out his separate strands of feeling, but all he felt was crushed. He wasn't the boy who had lived and endured here anymore, but neither was he the man he'd turned himself into in Manhattan. Sitting in a car he didn't own, in clothes he'd chosen for their invisibility, on money he'd taken under false auspices, persona non grata with his hometown on one side and his lover on the other. Where was he going to go when he left Nebraska this time?

"Gas?" the young man emerged now from the relative warmth of the office. Seth knew he'd be depending on a temperamental electric space heater that would roast his ankles and not much else. With an arm propped on the roof, he leaned over to peer into the car.

The glasses reflected Seth back at himself, oddly stark without eye makeup or piercings, gray circles under his eyes extending halfway down his nose.

"Fill it up?" His voice was reedier than Seth expected.

"Yeah," Seth said. "Regular."

Despite the cold, Cal's movements were languid. He eased over to the pump, teased the gas cap off, and stood without even drumming his fingers while the tank filled. Seth kept an eye on him in the rearview mirror. When Cassie had spoken of him, she'd grinned and blushed. Watching him now, there was something familiarly repellent about him: he was like boys he'd gone to school with, boys he'd had to defend himself against. But that didn't mean that this Cal hadn't been gentle with Cassie, hadn't given her good reason to feel fond of him though she never meant to see him again.

He was back at the window. "Nine seventy-five."

Seth took out his wallet. "You like it here?"

"What d'you mean?" Cal frowned in at him.

"I mean, you like it here? Here in—what's this place called?"

"Drinkwater," Cal said, after a suspicious pause.

"I used to work in a place kind of like this," Seth said. "S'why I ask." He looked, not at his dual mirrored images in the guy's face, but out the front windshield.

"Sure. Like it all right."

Seth held his open wallet on one knee; he could feel Cal's impatience to be paid and allowed to get back to his space heater.

"Not much to do around here, I guess. Got a family?"

"Girlfriend. She left town, though."

"Where'd she go?"

"Dunno." A pause. "Nine seventy-five. For the gas."

Seth took a ten out of his wallet, but didn't pass it over. "Were you in love with her?"

"What the fuck's that to you?"

Seth handed him the money. "Just making conversation."

Cal studied Seth for a moment, and then what Seth could see of his tanned face went white.

"Shit. You're her brother."

Seth nodded. "How'd you know?"

"Jesus." Cal reeled back, and stood regarding him now from a little distance, like a spooked cat. "You *look* like her. Shit."

Cal backed blindly toward the office, and didn't reemerge with the change. It wasn't until he'd lost sight of the EAT/GAS sign in his rearview mirror that Seth paused to wonder why the guy was so freaked-out. Did he think Seth was going to get out of the car and challenge him for interfering with Cassie? *Christ, I've got enough going on without that.*

On the long straightaway toward Flanagan, a familiar pickup barreled toward him—Roy was hunched over the wheel in the way Seth knew by heart; at the sight of him, he jerked and the car swerved; he heard a whistling, then the truck was gone. *God, I could've put us both out of our misery, right here.* He coasted to a stop. This was a no-place, fields on both sides, a few trees contending in the distance with the sky, plowed snow heaped up against the barbed-wire fencing on either side. Here was very likely where his mother had been walking that morning last week, toiling along in her house shoes over irregular heaps of rock-hard snow that made a narrow channel of the road. *That fucker. That fucking, fucking shithead arrogant fucker.* He dug down on the accelerator and the car shot forward.

He got past Mrs. Rausch fairly cheap, thanks to a ringing telephone that let him slink off before having to recount to her the whole story of his adult life. Following her directions to the ICU, his steps slowed as he approached it. He still had no idea what he would say to his mother.

At first glimpse, he thought he had the wrong person: this was an old woman, a very sick old woman with tubes running in and out of her.

He hadn't known, until he saw Mary's small head, the thin hair pulled back, that anyone's skin could be that color, a white that was really blue. It was as if her blood was azure, and cool as stone. Her eyes were open, trained on nothing, and her hands, lying outside the covers on either side of her body, were balled into bony fists that showed the raised tracery of veins on their backs.

With numb fingers, Seth peeled back the paper from the flowers he'd picked up at the Hinky Dinky, along with the pound and a half of grapes, and stepped forward.

"Ma."

Her movements were minute and clipped, as though she had clockwork inside. "Ma. How are you? I came as soon as I heard."

He was sure she'd seen him, or at any event, heard him, but she closed her eyes. Closed them tight, like her fists. What kind of effort must it be for her to make those fists, debilitated as she was?

As a child he'd once picked up a dead baby bird that was like her hand now: curled in on itself, blue and knobbly, hardening and cooling. He'd held and examined it for a long time, repulsed and fascinated, until she appeared, and seeing it, slapped it away from him. *Why am I here? What do I want with her? What the fuck do I expect?*

"I guess you can't really talk," Seth said, "Here's some grapes. Could you eat some grapes?"

No movement, no response.

Roy had been angry at her for not giving him any children of his own. That anger was a big part of the litany of every cellar visit. What a goddamn pony-ass he was, not a proper son at all. Seth stood in the place of the *real* son he'd been cheated of by Mary, who, if she thought a couple of insolent gray-haired freaks were his idea of a decent family, needed to think again. And don't go imagining, Roy always said, that your real father would've liked you any better than I do—

Ma, why don't you end it, why don't you leave, why don't you kill him? Why don't you douse him in hot fat and bash his head in with a skillet while he's writhing one the floor? Why didn't Cassie? Why didn't I? Should I do it now? Would that end all this for you? Would you look at me and talk to me if I did it? Would you visit me in jail? Would I be your son again?

Still touching that terrible crabbed hand, he felt behind him with his foot for the chair, and dragged it forward to sit. Feeling like a fool, but resigned to putting in the time.

"Why do you come here?"

Seth had to lean in to hear her voice, raspy and low. "Mr. Hecklin got in touch with me and told me to."

She shook her head. "Your sister—"

"Cassie's with me, she's fine."

"With you?" Mary craned her neck, looking.

"Not here. Cassie is living with me in New York. She sends her love. She . . . she couldn't come with me, though. To see you." On the table was a cup with a straw leaning out of it; he offered it to her, but she turned her face away.

"Where's Roy?"

"What were you doing walking the roads at that hour? Where were you going? Where were you coming from?"

"Tell Cassie . . ." She tried to lick her lips; he offered the straw again, and this time she took a pallid swallow. "Tell her . . . stay far . . . from this."

What this, Seth wondered. *This place? Or this state of health? Or this kind of life?*

"She wanted me to say she's sorry she couldn't see you," he improvised. *Would she be sorry? What will she say when she finds out where I am?*

"Why . . . why did you come here?"

"Because Mr. Hecklin called me up and told me to come." It hadn't occurred to him there was any choice. Not when Jim was practically shoving him out the door.

In New York he didn't think about it so much, but here it came upon him full force: the futility, the sheer heartbreaking waste of loving her when nothing came of it, no comfort, no protection, no commiseration, no understanding. She'd never understood him, or her daughter, and he, thinking he knew her all too well, didn't understand her either. The silence around them was clammy with things that could never be spoken, or if spoken, never really be *heard*.

What was there to wish for, for Mary? Her recovery, which meant a return to Roy's house and Roy's justice? A peaceful sleeping death? To hope she might undergo a spiritual awakening that would transform her into a different woman, a stronger woman, determined to free herself and live some other life? She lay sipping air like a caught fish, thrashed out and about to expire. There was nothing he could win back—all Mary had to bestow was rejection, or dependence.

"Well, look at who's here, Mary. Your beautiful boy's come home to see his mama."

Seth flew around, knocking the chair over. Recognizing that he was a couple of inches taller than Roy, and broader in the shoulders, did nothing to make his presence less belittling. A look from him still might make him lose control—spew or wet himself or start mewling.

"How d-d-d-did this happen?" Seth said. The stutter made him blush, but even when Roy edged closer to him, he didn't step aside.

Instead, Roy moved around him, righting the chair.

"Woo-wee. Grapes *and* flowers. If that don't beat all. You must be mighty pleased with your long-lost boy, Mary."

"What did you do to her?"

"Now if we just knew where that gorgeous girl of yours had taken herself off to, why, we'd have ourselves one fucking marvelous family reunion."

Mary turned her head away, as if to keep a breeze off her face.

"He doesn't mean any harm," she murmured.

"Harm? Of course he don't. Who's he gonna harm? He couldn't—"

"Roy." Seth was amazed at the volume of his own voice. He wasn't sure what he was doing, but he wasn't whispering. "I asked you a question."

Glancing over his shoulder, Roy smirked and put a finger up to his lips. "Ssssh. Don't you know you're supposed to be quiet in a hospital?"

"I want to know what you did to my mother."

"Where you been the last six years? I haven't seen you around. But now all of a sudden here you are, and you're asking me *questions?*"

"I want to know—"

Roy shook himself, and began to walk around Seth, steering wide. "You want to know what's the matter with her, damned if I know, there she is, ask her . . . shit, what do I look like, a goddamn doctor?" Each word carried him farther away. Seth threw himself at Roy's back and knocked him down.

"What have you be-be-be-been doing to her? Why can't you fucking leave her alone?"

Roy uncoiled, shaking his head slowly as he rose. Seth felt his fist connect with Roy's cheekbone. And then Roy hit him, and as he tumbled backward some woman was saying, *Oh, Christ, Oh, Christ—Get someone—Get someone!* He saw blood in the corner of Roy's mouth, and swarmed toward him again. Then he was grabbed and saw that Roy was taken, too. Seth struggled against the man who held him, struggled with the huge unfairness of not being able to finish what he hadn't quite meant to start. Why was this happening? No one had ever held Roy off from him, all those countless times. And now he had his chance, when things might be different, and they wouldn't let him go. "I oughta kill you! You're fucking lucky I haven't killed you yet! Leave my mother alone—why can't you just fucking leave her alone?"

Their captors were already hustling them down the hall. Roy's marched him straight out the doors to the parking lot. Seth twisted around to see his own in the green uniform of the sheriff's department.

"Good thing I happened to be here," the officer said, in a voice whose amiability didn't match the tightness of his hold on Seth's arms. He let go then. "My aunt's hip fracture is your gain."

"How the hell d'you figure that? Why can't you arrest him, for chrissakes?" Seth said, yanking his clothes back into place.

"You're lucky I didn't just arrest *you*, kiddo," the cop said. "Now get out of here." As he turned away, Seth heard him mutter, "Anyway, your old lady never prosecutes the sumbitch."

In the hospital lobby he tried the phone again. He'd been in Nebraska less than twenty-four hours, but already the exhausted powerlessness he'd lived with as a teenager was settled down around him as dense and smothering as the heavy parka he wore. His face where Roy had punched him was stiff, the clothes he'd bought only that morning at Wal-Mart felt as if they were caked onto his body. Once again, he reached the machine. Not wanting to alarm Cassie, he managed only, "It's me. Everything's okay. I love you." He no longer knew what he meant by the first statement, the second was untrue, and the last one didn't seem to matter anymore.

With five beers dangling on their plastic rings from his left hand, Seth knocked on the aluminum storm door. The trailer, dirty white in the dark against the gray glow of snow, was right where Cassie had said it would be, out behind the service station on a piece of waste ground where Roy had once piled bottles and cans up for target practice.

No sound came from within, just a diffuse light stealing from the curtained window beside the trailer's door. He heard some stumbling movement, and the inner door opened. It was difficult to see through the storm door's angled glass slats—but he could feel the other man's scrutiny.

Seth held the beers up. This worked. The metal catch rattled, and the door swung out toward him.

Even though he'd already drunk one beer on his way over, the malty stench inside hit Seth the moment he crossed the threshold. The place smelled as though a keg had been drained on the floor, and a lot of dirty socks thrown down to soak up the spill. In the dim light, he saw the place was strewn with empties, discarded clothes, porn mags, trash. *Jesus, this is where Cassie got her cherry busted? This disaster area?* She'd said her nights in his trailer were a respite from home. Seth began to suspect it was a story she'd concocted to cover a far more sordid reality. Which was what they did, the both of them. Probably she'd let the guy get to her once, maybe when she was drunk, and that once had done the trick He couldn't imagine Cassie wanting to come back here again. Or maybe she hadn't wanted Cal at all. Maybe he'd forced her. The whole place felt to be about force. Despite the chill that hung in the stale air, Seth began to sweat, and realized he was afraid. That he'd begun to be afraid as soon as he knocked on the door. Cal was clearly on alert, too, his movements and motives were difficult to predict. Seth tried to look into the guy's face, to get some sense of what he was about; but he was wearing a long-billed baseball cap, and the room was so dark. He felt for the light switch beside the door, and flipped it. Nothing happened.

"Power's on the fritz right now," Cal said. He was kicking things out of the way, shoving them with his foot under the couch, and into corners. "I kept it nice when your sister was still here," he muttered. "She'd tell you."

"She . . . she said that, yeah," Seth ventured, edging farther into the room.

Now Seth saw that the light source was a battered old Coleman lamp set on the kitchen counter. It threw more shadows than anything else; Cal's climbed the wall and crossed halfway along the ceiling as he lurched about. The stench, the changing light, the tall shadows, he didn't like anything about them.

They replicated his dreams.

"I came here," he announced, very loud, "I came here to ask you if you know anything about what happened to my mother."

Slowly, Cal straightened up; his shadow loomed and distorted as he turned, and seemed to lunge at Seth.

"I'm sorry about your ma."

"What happened in the hours before she had the heart attack? Do you have any idea?"

"No, man. Nothing happened at supper that night, and that was the last I saw of her until after that farmer brought her back to the café in the morning."

"You saw her that morning?"

"Just from the corner of my eye, y'know. When I came to work. I skip breakfast, mostly."

Seth glanced around at the lamp; he didn't like having it behind him. Would Cal think it was strange if he picked it up and set it down—where? Where would it be all right to have that lamp? He wished he could put it out altogether. His balls were crawling, and a drop of sweat made its way down the small of his back, a ghost finger tracing the spine. *I should get out of here,* he thought. *This loser doesn't know anything. This place is disgusting. I don't want to think about this when I look into Ruby's face. If I do.*

"Do you have any suspicions, though? Any theories?"

Cal didn't answer. The beer cans in their plastic nooses glimmered on the trash-strewn table, but this was not an atmosphere for two men to drink together. Seth said, "Look, if this is a bad time. . . ."

"Why'd you have to come after me? I didn't do anything bad to your sister. Let the past be the past!"

Confused, Seth stepped back against the counter where the Coleman lamp was, and after a moment, took hold of the handle and hefted it. It would be better, he thought vaguely, on the table, in the middle of the room. As he swung it around, the heavy shadows moved, and the wide flat angles of Cal's face emerged from the blind of his cap bill.

That's when Seth saw it. How had he missed it this long?

He knew Cal.

Jesus God, he was Vin Dunkett.

A hot red flower opened inside Seth. He backed up, as if moving through plasma, set the lamp down on the table, and picked up one of the kitchen chairs. Then he swung it at Cal's head. When the blow connected, and he toppled beneath it, the flower blazed up, and time speeded up into a crazed staccato. The red flower blossomed into hundreds of red flowers, flesh-eaters, popping and snapping around his field of vision. And each pop was a snapshot of what they'd done to him, Vin and Roy and the others, in the cabin by the lake, by the light of that very Coleman lamp, in just the same kind of stink as pervaded this place.

Seth dragged Cal up by the collar and hit him again and again.

Then Cal was sprawled on the floor. His cap was gone. Seth stared at the top of his head, where the hair grew out in a whorl.

"You—you bastard! It wasn't enough that you—*you dared—my sister!*"

Seth kicked him in the groin. Cal jerked, moaned, and keeled over. A circle of vomit appeared beside his profile on the floor.

Hunched over with his hands on his knees, Seth panted, glowing.

With an effort, Cal rolled on his back. His lower half was still de-
fensively curled, hands in groin, but he looked up at Seth, and all
Seth's fear and revulsion responded to that cut, bleeding face. He
itched to kick him again. He could imagine, easy, delicious, the feel
of the good steel toe of his boot connecting with Vin Dunkett's
mouth. Vin Dunkett's belly. Vin Dunkett's kidneys.

"Roy, he started it," Cal murmured, blood seeping from his lips.

The words froze him.

"I didn't want to do it." Cal sighed, coughed. "I couldn't go
against him." He was trying to gather himself, to sit up. He wiped at
the blood, slipped a finger into his mouth and ran it around the gums.
Each movement torpid and gingerly. Why hadn't he fought back?

"No one forced you to do what you did afterward, when they went
and you came back alone. That was all your idea."

Gurgling, he struggled to turn back onto his side. Seth didn't help
him. Cal stopped moving. His eyes glazed, and seemed to be staring
into the past.

"My life fell to shit that day," Cal said.

"*Your* life, you fuck!"

"Every day I remember what Roy made me into. I hate that man.
It wouldn't've happened without him."

Seth realized Cal wanted it, craved it, this beating.

The red flower opened again. How easy, how satisfying, to step
down now with all his weight on Cal's throat. Vin's throat. Had he
thought splitting his name a different way would make him a different person? Seth could've told him that it wasn't nearly so simple.

"You fucking closet-case bastard." Seth kicked him again and began to cry. "What you did to me wasn't enough? You had to smear
your *filth* on my sister, too?"

"I was nice to her. She didn't know about that. I was good to her.
I . . . I love her."

He dove for Cal's throat. The thick Adam's apple bulged sickeningly against his pushing hand, and he knew this insane dirty rush was how Roy and his pals must've felt. This hot shit high. His whole body pulsing, the biggest hard-on of his life straining his jeans, and the foul air like wine. "You don't get that. You are permanently fucking disqualified from love. You are nothing but a worthless piece of shit who should *die*."

Cal's gaze was unwavering, soft. It said, *Take me. Do it.* The unresisting eyes nearly serene.

Shit, no.

Vin Dunkett had stolen enough of his life. Seth wasn't going to give up the rest to paying for this moment of retribution, no matter how tangy-sweet it tasted in the back of his tightened throat. He sprang up.

"You think any of this makes up for what you did?" He poked with the toe of his boot at the skin split over Cal's cheekbone, as if his face was a squashed animal in the road. "You think it makes you better than Roy and your dad and those other guys, because you feel sorry for yourself over it and they've forgotten? You think it makes you better because it was *Roy's* idea and not yours? My sister doesn't give a fuck about you, man, she never did. No one ever will. You could fucking *kill* yourself, and you wouldn't *begin* to make it right."

Cal's hand came up and grasped Seth's leg. A terrible sound, thin, impossibly eager, came from his ruined mouth.

"Then—you'd forgive . . . ?"

The question, its asker, were untenable, obscene. Tearing away, Seth threw himself out of the trailer, misjudging his distance so he sprawled full-length on the frozen mud and snow, cracking his chin on a jutting shard of ice. Fighting to get the frigid air into his lungs, he made for his car, as if some enraged and crashing thing was gaining on him, up his spine, making for the vulnerable back of his head. But he didn't look around to see what it was.

22

"You'd better come out here and get the boy."

The ringing phone had awakened Jim from one of those deep feverish sleeps that descends on an angry and agitated mind. He wouldn't have answered at all if he hadn't been startled by the jangle, and then he was so confused at *not* hearing Seth's voice he lost the next few sentences the old man said.

"Please slow down. What's happening?"

"Okay. You're right, slow down. Here's what it is. He went out earlier to visit his mother at the hospital. I didn't hear from him. Well, he came back here about eleven and said he didn't feel well, he wanted to go straight to bed, which I must say didn't surprise me. So I sent him on up, and I went to make him a mug of cocoa, I thought he'd like that, although he did smell like beer when he came in. Fairly reeked of it. Well, I made the cocoa, and when I came up with it I knocked and he didn't reply. I thought perhaps he'd already dozed off, but then I couldn't get the door of his room open. Which was very odd, as we have no locks on the doors in this house. I pushed and pushed, there was some resistance on the other side, finally it opened a little way, and I realized the poor boy was on the floor."

"On the floor?" He switched on the bedside lamp. His view, lying on his back, was principally of the ceiling, as long as he kept his eyes pointed straight ahead. By dropping them a bit he could see Seth's self-portrait with the pear, hung here where he could slide his contented gaze from the painted face to the real one on the pillow at his side. Earlier, getting ready for bed, the sight of it was tortuous enough that he reached out to snatch it down. But then Cassie had tapped on the door to let him know she was through in the bathroom, and he'd left it hanging. But he didn't want to see the picture now.

"On the floor," Mr. Hecklin confirmed. "I forced the door enough to squeeze into the room. I had to shove at him with the door, but I don't think he felt it. He . . . I guess he'd been starting to undress, because when I found him his head and arms were tangled up in his pullover, and—he was, well, it sure looked like a convulsion to me. All my years in the schools, you know, I've seen plenty of kids have plenty of fits. Well, I knew I had to get that shirt off him so he could breathe. It wasn't easy, the way he was jerking and flailing, but I did it. And then when I saw his face . . . Mr. Glaser, I don't think it was a seizure such as a doctor would recognize, because I've never seen a child with epilepsy *cry* that way. He could not speak, and he could not respond to me, and he could not control himself. I mean, not in any way. He"— the old man's voice dropped into a whisper—"he soiled himself. I didn't want to call an ambulance, but I can't lift him. . . ."

Jim kicked the tangled sheets back. "Is he unconscious? What are you doing for him?"

"Well, I filled a bucket up with cold water, and I—I poured it on him. I didn't know what else to—well, it seemed to help. He stopped that terrible twitching, and just lay on the floor, gasping and crying, but I don't think he saw me, I don't think he saw anything. I put a blanket over him and let him lie. It's a mess. I don't want to involve outsiders, paramedics or anyone, but it might come to that—"

Jim had an overwhelming desire to just put the phone down and roll over. What did he have to do with any of this strange business in the middle of nowhere, Nebraska? For all Jim knew, this phone call was part of some scheme Seth had put the man up to.

"If he's truly ill," Jim said, cutting off the next stream of words, "calling an ambulance is the best thing to do, particularly at this time of night."

Jim could hear the old man breathing, stumped.

"Of course," Jim added, "you can call me in the morning—or he can, if he's up to it—and let me know how things turned out."

"You must not've understood what I've been saying," Hecklin said. "I thought he ought to come and have a chance to make his peace with his ma, but . . . there's some things that can't be put right, only put more wrong than they are. He needs to go from here. You'll come get him. I'll tell him you're on your way."

Jim's resistance mounted as the man talked on. *I'm not going to get sucked into this. I've been betrayed, I'm the injured party here. He played me.* He was on the verge of just hanging up when a soft knock came at the door, and Cassie crept in.

"Is that Seth? Is something wrong?" She held her robe gathered tight around her big belly.

Jim covered the receiver. "No, it's not Seth. What are you doing up so late? Go back to bed, sweetheart."

She withdrew, and Jim said into the phone, "Sorry, I'm back now." Later, when he'd concluded his call and was looking over the directions he'd jotted down, he thought how strange it was that one little intrusion could change one's intentions so completely.

Leaving the loft before dawn, he set out an innocuous note, mentioning a client emergency in Chicago, which she'd find when she rose. *Call me on the cell if you need to for any reason. If anything happens, call Clyde and Billy, they'll come right over.* Nothing, he assured himself, would happen today. He'd go get Seth, they'd be back by evening, and then he'd figure out what to do with him.

Seth awoke, flat on his back, to an overwhelming smell of shit.

Without opening his eyes, he knew it had come at last, what he'd been postponing day by day, hour by hour. The outcome reserved for him—where he'd been heading all along.

Then a light whose brightness through his closed lids made him flinch. A heaviness alongside: Mr. Hecklin. The old man kneeling.

"You're awake now—good. You had a little accident, son. I'm sorry I left you like this, but I couldn't undress you or move you without you helping me a little. Come, let's get you out of your dirty clothes and—"

Why couldn't he leave him here, and stay away, and when he was dead call in the authorities to remove his bloated corpse.

"What's the matter with you? Seth, open your eyes. What's the—"

He jerked his head to be free of the man's hand on his cheek.

"Seth. We've got to get you out of these clothes and into a bath. I promise you you'll feel better when you're cleaned up and fed. Come now. Don't be embarrassed, I've seen everything. I saw it all in Korea."

Little by little, in brief jerky movements, Seth permitted himself to be undressed. When his jeans came off, the stench, already pervasive, flooded the room, it flowed into his nostrils and down his throat, grabbed at his guts and made them heave. He turned his head and vomited. More shame, shame upon chagrin.

In the dimness he was aware of Hecklin gathering the clothes up in a ball, getting to his feet.

"Now, never mind the mess, I'll take care of it. You just rest there for a minute while I get the bathwater running and take these downstairs, and I'll come back and help you into the bathroom."

The words *let me die* wended their way through his mind, grotesque eels swimming in heavy waters full of dark, undulating weed, swirling and eddying around others, *shit, black beast of shit, fuckhead, worthless scumsucking piece of shit.* He realized, with a dim astonishment, that he had no control over the words in his head. Something else, the big black thing, like a horrendous toad, had taken it over, squatting on his mind.

Far, far away, he heard a rushing sound that gradually became known to him as the sound of the bath filling in the next room. A series of thumps: the old man going downstairs. Gone. Good. But not for long. He'd promised to come back. He'd come back and see Seth's hideous naked filth-strewn body; he'd touch it.

This idea was enough to stir his heavy limbs. Slowly, slowly, he rolled over. The edge of the bed was there, giving him no more room; he must get up. In elephantine stages, he got his knees under him, got up on his hands. Began to crawl toward that rushing sound, finally flopping into the tub with a splash.

When Mr. Hecklin knocked on the door, Seth yanked the shower curtain across with a furious force. If the old man came in, if he were to look at him again, Seth would start to scream.

"I took your clothes down to the machine," Hecklin said through the door. "And your cigarettes are there, on the sink, if you want 'em. How do you feel?"

He didn't know how he felt. He could remember only the Coleman lamp's glow on Cal's face, hours ago and eight years ago: the two images mingling and becoming one. He held his breath. The hot water opened him up to more pain as surely as a scalpel. After a couple of pregnant moments, he heard Hecklin clump downstairs.

Everything was truly, irretrievably, fucked to hell.

He'd certainly made a big mistake trying to boost himself into Jim's orbit by making up all that happy-houseful-of-books horseshit. He should have trusted in his own freshness, the book intriguingly jammed down the back of his waistband, the impulse of kindness—and show-offery—in that glass of milk. That's what got him noticed, and after that, he could have gotten by, no trouble at all, by telling, not what he'd told, but just the unremarkable surface of the truth. *I come from a small town, my parents have a small business there, my dad is dead and I have a stepfather I never got on well with; it was a dead-end kind of place but I was smart and I had some help when I needed it most; I got out.* But he hadn't been able to trust in that, because all the mundane shit of life in Drinkwater was merely the setting, the superstructure, the prelude to and aftermath of the one thing, the awful thing, the thing that set him lower than every other man he ever met.

Had he not discarded the boy who crawled down from the truck after that fishing trip, who slouched off to hide himself under the old

farmhouse and ended up setting it alight with half a mind to immo-
late himself with it . . . *it was him or me. Couldn't be that kid and live.*

Hecklin didn't know about that. Seth climbed out of the tub,
pissed, wrapped a towel around his hips, lit a cigarette, thought of
telling him, connecting every dot until he saw the old man's face col-
lapse. It was the best way to punish him, and it would be worth it, un-
leashing his secret, to destroy the old fool's idiotic illusions, to make
him hurt. And then he really could just get into the car and go.

When he opened the bathroom door, Hecklin was just arriving at
the top of the stairs, a little tray in his hands with a steaming mug on
it, a plate of toast. At the sight of Seth he stopped, rocked back on
his heels. Seth imagined him going right over, head over heels back
down the stairs.

"My boy," Hecklin spluttered, his eyes growing enormous behind
the thick lenses, "you'll catch—it's cold up here—better get into—"

And then Seth understood, in the blackest part of his heart, what
was making the old man quaver. He cocked a cold half-grin, settled
himself languidly against the door frame, inhaled a sharp rush from
the cigarette. With one hand, pushed the towel just a little lower on
his hip. Never mind that he *felt* ugly and vile, he knew he was a torment before he even opened his mouth, just by being young and fine
and naked in this man's upstairs hallway. Watching Hecklin look at
him and try not to look at him, feeling through the stale overheated
air how the blood was pounding in the other's veins.

"We need to talk. There's something I need to tell you," Seth said.

Mr. Hecklin's eyes were trained now on the carpet. The hand that
held the tray shook; he ought to reach out and relieve him of it,
ought as well to relieve him of the sight of his body. The part of himself that was not black and hard and furious had curled up into a tight
reed of shame at what he was doing. He stared at the old man, willing
him to look up, until he did look up. And when he did, Seth raised
his hand slowly, and slowly traced the shape of his right nipple, pre-

tending to scratch it, on the way to taking the cigarette from between his lips.

"You're feeling better?" Hecklin mumbled. "Thank God for that.
Better get some sleep. Both of us need some—"

"I thought you wanted to know where I was tonight?"

"I think you ought to eat this—drink your—get into bed—"

"I need," Seth said, his voice low and hard, "to talk. To you." He
reached between them and jabbed a finger into Hecklin's chest.

Hecklin jumped, the tray wobbled; Seth saw the cocoa splash up
from the cup and back, miraculously, without spilling. The old man
hastened past him, into the spare room.

"*No!* . . . No . . . you need your rest. You can talk to your Jim,
when he comes. He'll be here soon—you talk to him." Mr. Hecklin
reappeared then, without the tray, his face stark white.

Seth almost bit off the filter on his cigarette. "Jim—Jim is coming
here?" He tugged the towel higher and began to shiver. "You called
him?"

Hecklin sped toward his own room, eyes resolutely averted. "Of
course I called him. That was the right thing to do. He's coming to take
you home. That's that. That's all. Good night." Gaining the safety of
his own door, Hecklin flung himself in and slammed it.

23

From the tiny regional airfield where the charter set him
down, it was a forty-minute drive to Mr. Hecklin's house, on straight
two-lane roads through a landscape of substantial whiteness: snow on
the ground beneath a white-gray sky, only the occasional grain elevator

or water tower breaking the flat line. Trees, Jim noted, were not natu-rally occurring here; those he saw had an air of deliberation about them. The knots of settlement they passed through seemed to exist in a held-breath hush. The taxi driver said nothing when Jim, spotting a billboard with a picture of a fetus and the legend Abortion is murder, grunted. Neither did she react when, after they'd passed three more of these invocations, he murmured, "Good God Almighty."

It was snowing lightly but at a good windy slant when she pulled up in front of Mr. Hecklin's house. The front door was open even be-fore he was out of the car. Mr. Hecklin, whom he'd imagined being small and slender with sandy hair gone gray, was instead tall and fat and almost bald, with thick glasses that made him turtleish. He de-scended the icy front steps with careless haste and caught at Jim's sleeve as he advanced up the dug-out path toward the house.

"Sir, I'm going to ask you to be very quiet, to make a quiet en-trance. He had a terrible night, and he seems to be sleeping now. I'd like to let him sleep a while yet." Having said this, he let go of Jim, and instead held a hand out to shake. "Lucas Hecklin. This is all very unusual, but—I hope you had a good trip?"

"Uneventful," Jim said. "Costly."

"Well, c'mon in. There's hot coffee."

Jim smelled the coffee as soon as he entered, and it awoke a crav-ing. He felt a shrunken, harsh-eyed fatigue that matched the lower-ing light here. There was an awkward moment in the cramped entry, jostling; he was acutely aware of the man's scrutiny as he removed his coat and handed it over. The cashmere coat with its silk lining gave way to more cashmere: the black sweater skimming his broad chest and shoulders, its V neck showing the collar of the silk T-shirt he wore underneath. Hecklin regarded all this with a musing intensity as he fumbled blindly in the closet for a hanger.

"I take it he recovered, anyway, from—from whatever was wrong with him last night?" Jim asked. He glanced up the narrow carpeted stairs.

"I underestimated Mary Jenkins's antipathy to her son. I thought . . . I really thought . . . I'm a sentimental idiot, is what I am." He shook his head. "It's all my fault, the suffering he's endured since he got here."

"I need to get back to New York," Jim said. "If you don't mind, I'll go tell Seth to get ready."

He half-expected the other man to object or block his way, but he only nodded. "Go on upstairs, it's the door opposite the landing."

Jim took the steps two at a time, keeping his head down to avoid the ceiling. He threw the door open without knocking and was met with a blast of frigid air. The window was wide-open. Jim blinked for a moment at the bed, then he wrenched open the closet door, and after that, the other three doors on the landing: master bedroom, linen closet, bathroom. Nothing. The cold had taken over the little hallway. He went to the window to shut it, and looking down saw the broken lattice Seth must have pulled down in his escape; the trampled snow, and the footprints, leading away toward the street. Turning, Jim found Hecklin had followed him up, and was hovering now in the doorway, his eyes swimming behind the thick lenses.

"He knew I was coming?" Jim said.

"Of course he knew. I believed it was that news that allowed him finally to sleep."

"Uh-huh. Well," Jim said, "I can't say I'm surprised, at this point."

Mr. Hecklin drew in his chin. "You are certainly angry."

Jim rounded on him. "He lied to me. He never told me about this! College professors, he said—and dead, in tragic circumstances! Don't I have the right to be angry?"

"Sir, that's not for me to say."

"Aren't you angry? You should be! He's deceived you, too!"

"Has it occurred to you to wonder *why*, perhaps, he preferred not to tell the man he wished so much to impress, that he grew up here as a whipped dog, between a mother who props her weakness against the silliest sort of muddled Christianity there is, and a stepfather so full of rage he can't control himself even when his very business and livelihood are at stake?"

"Yes, it's occurred to me," Jim said. "A great deal has occurred to me since I got your call." *Mostly,* Jim thought, *how I could have been so blind as not to have seen through his cover story right away. I just didn't want to see it.* "What galls me—he wanted to be taken seriously but he didn't take *me* seriously, he thought he could lie to me with impunity. He used my own confidences . . . my own losses . . . to manipulate me."

"He hates pity," Hecklin said. "He must have wanted you to know him without the taint of that. I'm sure he was only trying to do the best he could with what he had. Most boys like him turn into men like Roy Jenkins. Seth held on to his sanity with all his might. I know because he wrote to me—all these years, beautiful letters. He told me about you, his devotion to you, how good you are to him. A heartless liar didn't write those letters."

"This isn't a *trick* we're talking about. Seth and I were so *much.* I gave him—did he tell you this?—he made himself out to be so fastidious about taking gifts—I gave him an independence, so he wouldn't feel uneasy coming to live with me. And so that he could be an artist, without struggling his youthful energy away. Idiot that I am, I've got romantic ideas about artists. Idiot that I am, I loved his pictures, and his poverty looked noble to me, his self-denial—*Christ, what an act!* I don't care about the money, thank God I can afford to lose it, to lose more—but I gave him, as well—"

"Your heart. I see that."

"Jesus, listen to yourself! You're as dizzy over him as—Seth's a user and an exploiter and a liar! Yet you make excuses—"

"Doesn't any of this excite a little compassion in you? You're angry, yes, but if you loved the boy before I made my foolish phone call, then *think now*—"

"We've already put you to too much trouble," Jim said. "I'll get out of your way." He went back to the entry hall, yanked his coat from the closet. It was then he remembered he'd need to call the cab back. Mr. Hecklin laid a hand on his arm.

"Why go so soon? We could drive out and look for him."

"You've got a car?"

"I don't drive anymore, but yes. It's in the garage. I pay the girl next door a small consideration each week to go in and start it up, keep it fueled. You could drive it."

The way the man talked, so flowery. A *small consideration.* Did he have any idea how he sounded?

Do I want to drive around looking for him? Fuck no. But do I want to go back to New York and face his sister without him? No way could he admit to her that he'd let Seth slip away without lifting a finger to find him. *Fuck*—Hecklin was already getting his coat on, writing a note that he made a great show of affixing to the front door, in case Seth came back in their absence.

"The air will do us both good, you know."

He was lonely, Jim thought, and enjoying this drama for all it was worth.

The day had drawn in. It wasn't snowing, but wind teased the trees and bushes, and the small houses in their rows seemed to be cowering beneath the deep darkening gray sky. In the car, Hecklin directed Jim out of Joralemon onto the road toward Drinkwater.

"Perhaps we'll find Seth nearby, but at least you'll see it. You'll be interested to see what Seth came from."

Jim made up his mind to say nothing. He knew they wouldn't find Seth, who was certainly long gone by now. With one part of his attention, he began to compose the talk he'd have with Cassie about all this; the careful way he'd have to explain to her, a way which would both honor the truth, and keep her from bolting off in a panic with *his* daughter.

He drove with attention to the speed limit, between heaped-up snowbanks. It was the same sort of scenery he'd absorbed on the way from the airfield; perhaps, he thought, there were nuances and landmarks here for the natives, but to him it was just an undistinguished bleakness. A crossroads was an event.

"I know how this looks to you. It looked pretty bad to me, when I got back here after the army. Sometimes I wonder," Hecklin mused, "why I didn't stay in California after they brought me back from Korea. But at the time it didn't occur to me, my mother was hankering for me to come back, and all I could think about was her cooking and my old bed. Some of the students who go off to college and come back here at Christmas describe it, that great eagerness for home, and then it dissipates in a day, and they find themselves counting the hours until they can go back to campus."

"Have you been counting the hours all these years?"

"I've had a very rewarding career," Hecklin said firmly. "I'm respected in the community, and that's saying something. Here's the edge of Drinkwater. Seth's old home is on the other side. Slow down here."

Jim slowed down; he wanted to take it in, now he was here. The main street, three short blocks of businesses, none erected, he guessed, after 1930, and wearing an almost Soviet-style utilitarianism. He counted them off: a movie house, boarded-up; a Masonic temple, a beauty shop, an IGA grocery, a drugstore, a clothing store, a post office. There were three bars, each with pickups and SUVs parked outside.

"Turn here," Hecklin said. "The gas station café is down this way, closer to the county road."

Jim slowed down further, reluctant to reach it and really see the place behind Seth's invention. The gas station sat at a T junction; beside it, and reached first as he drove slowly up, was a small house with a sagging porch that Hecklin pointed at quietly. Jim stared at it, taking in the peeling paint and the torn plastic over the windows, the atmosphere of abandonment. An utterly hopeless house.

Then they saw the two patrol cars parked along the verge of the connecting road. Behind them was a white van with a tall antenna, pulling out; as it sped past, he saw the logo of a local TV affiliate on its side. Jim turned the corner. A white trailer set in a weedy field behind the gas station was roped off with yellow police tape; a green-uniformed deputy stood in the open doorway, and a group of Drinkwater people milled around in front. The scene had an air of being near its conclusion when Jim parked and killed the engine. Mr. Hecklin was unable to get out of the car until Jim came around and helped him. But there were people in the small crowd, who, turning to them, knew the old man.

"You hear this on your scanner, Lucas?" one man asked, coming forward to take his arm.

"No, no . . . we were just taking a drive. . . . What is it, what's happened?"

"You missed it—a few hours ago, they took Roy Jenkins out of there. What was left of him. He'd gotten his head about blown off."

"Roy Jenkins! Dead?"

"Of course dead. You don't stay alive without half your head."

"You saw it, Joe?"

"I saw them take the body out covered in a sheet." He paused to survey the effect of his words. "Hank Lupic found the body. He stopped by early for gas, and the place was shut up tight. Got out of his car and knocked, no answer. Nor at the house. So he tried the trailer, looking for that mechanic kid, Dunkett. The door was open, so he peeked in. And there he was, Roy."

"*Tsk tsk tsk.* How—who—"

"Well, I always said if this ever happened, they'd have to haul every man-jack of us here in for questioning." Joe adjusted his cap and chuckled, then pulled his face down into a more appropriate public expression. "But the sheriff's got a line on Seth McKenna. Apparently he was seen scuffling with Roy in Mary's room yesterday, up to the hospital. Was heard to threaten his life. Clara Moss works at the hospital, y'know, and she heard about it in the cafeteria afterward."

"But—that's absurd!" Hecklin said.

"They picked him up, too," Joe said. "I overheard the deputies talking on their radios. Picked him up just a little bit ago, down near Eulalia. He crashed the car against a tree, but wasn't hurt much, and they got him and took him in."

Jim listened to this from what felt like a great distance, although he was standing just behind Hecklin's shoulder, able to see over the heads of most of the people still gathered, as the few deputies left to mop up the scene made their self-important trips between the trailer and the cars. It was very cold, snow flurrying down in breathy puffs, but Jim didn't feel it, although he'd left his coat in the backseat. He stared at the dirty trailer. This was like nothing he'd ever dealt with before. He didn't understand how anyone he cherished, anyone he *knew*, could emerge from a place like this.

He wanted to get rid of Hecklin and his car, get himself back to the airport, home. It was dark, and he hadn't yet phoned Cassie. Beside him, the old man was actually crying. Jim had to pull over, because he had no idea where he was going anyway, and it was too distracting to try to drive while his passenger made such slurpy sobbing noises.

Jim waited, hoping Hecklin would regain self-control. When that didn't happen, he said, "I can't take you home if you don't tell me which way to go."

Hecklin looked up then, his glasses coming off his face crooked as he rubbed his streaming eyes.

"Of course we're going to go to the police station. We've got to see him."

"I've got to get back to New York. I'm afraid that taking you home is my best offer—you'll have to find some other ride. I'm finished here." Jim admired his own steeliness. It wasn't like him, but it was the right thing for this place, this surreality.

Hecklin mopped at his face with the hem of his sweater; Jim was surprised he didn't have a handkerchief, but felt no inclination to offer his own. "Now, which way?" he asked.

"Are you telling me that you really think Seth had anything to do with that back there?"

Oh, God, I so do not want to be wrenched around and assumed and questioned anymore by this maddening old optimist. My Seth couldn't do this, of course not, but my Seth only ever existed in my head.

"You do. You really—oh, Mr. Glaser, how could you hold any such ridiculous notion?" Hecklin put a hand on Jim's arm. "Drive. Drive us to the police station. We have to see him, Seth must be so frightened. This is a terrible, terrible thing that's happening to him." When Jim hesitated, Hecklin shouted, "*He had nothing to do with this violence! Now drive!*"

When Seth woke, warmth trickled in his eyes, and he was holding on to something hard with both hands. He was surprised to find himself not in bed—hadn't he been in bed?—but behind the wheel of a car. Someone was pulling him out of the car, wrenching him around; it was still and frigid, scattered snowflakes coming down like ash, and the gray air lit by red flickers. The flickers were from the three other cars, police cars, parked in a loose circle around his own. Beneath his feet not road, but snow-crusted turf, broken cornstalks poking through. Where was the road? There were men all around him, in green uniforms; one of them yanked his arms together, and then he was in handcuffs. When he felt their cold weight on his wrists, Seth roused; he wiped the wet stuff off his face with the sleeve of his coat and saw it was blood. His head began to throb.

There were hands on him, shoving him against the car, frisking him, turning him. He heard the men talking, but none of them seemed to be talking to him, so he kept quiet. What was this? A dream? He struggled to recall the last few hours. He knew he'd left Cal's trailer, but that had been nighttime, and it seemed to be afternoon now. Had he gone back to Mr. Hecklin's in the meantime? He must have, but he couldn't remember. They were prodding him now, away from the rented car, which, he saw now, had left the road a ways back and driven hard into a stubble field, stopping with its front corner crumpled against a tree. Had he done that? He must have. Sleep tugged hard at him; he was addled and ready for nothing but unconsciousness. These men would take care of it, whatever it was. Amidst his confusion, it seemed right to Seth to find himself with the police. This—and not the nice home, the studio, the art school, the good man's arms—was his natural, inevitable place.

Someone's hand on the back of his neck propelled him forward and down into the backseat of another car. Just as the door slammed on him, he caught, in the babble of the men's voices, the word *murder*. Murder. *Oh, fuck, he was alive when I left him. Did I kick him too hard?* Remembering the sensation of his foot connecting with Cal's body, he wretched, but he was so dry and empty that nothing came up.

They took him first to a hospital; not the one where his mother was. He'd driven miles away from Flanagan. In the emergency department of this strange hospital, Seth learned that when you are a murder suspect in police custody, you are not required to wait. The gash on his forehead was cleaned; his eyes inspected; a doctor questioned him about the date and the president and made him subtract numbers backward. The sleepiness, apparently, was related to the blow to the head. Mild concussion, but the police wouldn't hear of him being admitted; they had their instructions. The suspect was wanted back in Flanagan. In a few minutes he was in the patrol car, with the blood scrubbed from his face, and a big bandage stuck to his forehead. There was nothing to stop him stretching out across the seat and closing his eyes. So he did.

The crackling of the police radio woke him. He didn't know how much time had gone by. The car wasn't moving, but when he sat up, Seth saw they were no longer outside the hospital in Eulalia. Now they were in a mini-mart parking lot.

The two men in the front seat had coffee and sandwiches; they glanced around at him through the Plexiglas partition. "Sleeping Beauty wakes."

"I say it's pretty damn cold-blooded," the other one said. "Going off for a nap like that. When you're being brought in for murder. Doesn't look good."

He was very thirsty.

"I need some water."

"Go back to sleep, Sleeping Beauty. We're gonna be here a while."

The men finished their snack, and still they sat in the parking lot, as cars pulled in and out for gas and junk food and lottery tickets, and the radio crackled. Seth wanted to protest this treatment, but didn't have the energy. It was easier just to remain thirsty, to rest his head against the windowsill and drift. Nothing much mattered anyway, because his life was over. He thought about kicking Cal, and wanted to wish he hadn't done it, but couldn't summon up enough regret to make a hole in his loathing.

Then a voice over the radio said, "It's all set. C'mon and bring 'im in."

"All set, yeah," the driver chuckled, and eased the car into gear. "Sheriff's making the most of this," he remarked to his partner. "He's figuring to get his face on the news all the way to Chicago with this one."

"When's the last time anybody got murdered in Drinkwater?"

"Shit, who knows? I've been on the job ten years and never seen one there. So now we've got a dilly, and we wait to bring 'im in 'til the news cameras arrive." He laughed. "Sheriff wants a perp walk just like on TV."

Seth heard this but didn't really understand it until he saw the vans with tall antennae parked outside the Flanagan police station, marked with the call letters not only of a couple of local TV stations, but also of the network affiliates out of Omaha.

He kept his head down as they pulled him out of the car, but the cops had him by the arms so he couldn't shield his face, and the crowd lined both sides of the walkway; springing forward, hurling questions. It was all a cacophony, his ears rang along with the throbbing of his head. All his concentration went into not stumbling.

He heard his name in a more sober register than all the other voices calling to him, and before he could stop himself he'd glanced up and met Mr. Hecklin's eyes. The old man had shouldered his way past two cameramen and was reaching toward him; Seth instinctively shied away.

Then he saw Jim. Hanging back behind Hecklin. His tall, elegant figure a shocking sight in this context, the hooded eyes dropping when their gazes met. A face with nothing for him. Seth jerked his head around, right into the microphone of a woman in a red suit who leapt as if he'd bitten her.

Then he was inside, and the noise ceased.

24

Seth sat in a chair behind a metal table in a small tiled room lit by a flickering fluorescent. His mouth tasted putrid, and he couldn't get up enough spit to swallow. When he blinked or tried to move his head, spots marched in his vision.

A Flanagan County policeman he hadn't yet seen came into the room and closed the door.

"You led us a merry chase just now. You trying to end it all against that tree, son?"

Seth blinked at the gray metal surface of the table. He wanted some aspirin and a bed, but those weren't for the likes of him anymore.

"You made a big old mess in that trailer, didn't you? How'd that come about?" the officer said. "I guess he provoked you?" He bent to peer sideways into Seth's lowered face. He was a comfortably portly man, half-bald, round-faced. He spoke as if his questions were pleasantries. "Seth McKenna, right? I got your wallet right here. We can't say we caught you driving without a license, anyway. Seth McKenna, Two Bond Street, New York City? Formerly of Drinkwater, Nebraska. That's you, son."

Seth let his eyes fall closed. Keeping them open was too difficult.

"What's the matter with you, boy? You gonna be sick on me?"

Seth moved his lips, once twice. Tried harder. "Thirsty."

"I give you a drink, you talk nice with me? Help me get this matter cleared up so we're not here all night?" He went to the door of the room, opened it, snapped his fingers at some unseen person on the other side. In a moment, a bright red can appeared in Seth's small field of vision. The sugar tasted so bright; at first he just held the soda behind his teeth, eyes squeezed shut. He didn't swallow until he felt a touch on his arm.

"Now tell me—we didn't find it in your car. So what did you do with the shotgun, son?"

Seth's head snapped up. The cop, whose name badge said Reynolds, was regarding him with his head to one side, eyes squinting.

"What shotgun?" Seth breathed. "I didn't murder anyone with a shotgun." He'd had such a long, bad night. Maybe there was something he'd lost track of, forgotten. "Did I?"

"Well," Reynolds said in a low confiding tone, "we all sure as shit think you did. Would you like to tell me where you disposed of the gun?"

"I don't know anything about a gun. I haven't touched a gun in years. I didn't think I hurt him that bad."

"Well, he's sure dead. His head's blasted all over the inside of that trailer. If that's your idea of not being hurt too bad, well. . . . And you, son, were fighting with him at the hospital yesterday. You were heard to threaten his life. And now he's killed. So we, as they say, did the math."

Seth's eyes opened all the way at this. "Wait a minute. Who?"

Reynolds clucked his tongue. "C'mon, boy. Don't fool with me, because I'm not nice when I'm being fooled with. They must've told you when they arrested you what they were taking you in for. We are talking about your mother's husband, Roy Jenkins, whom you blew away in that trailer behind his gas station. Now, c'mon."

"Roy. Roy?" Seth shook his head. "You found *Roy* shot to death in Cal Dunkett's trailer?"

Reynolds sighed and shook his head. "This is a very nice little display of shock and incredulity, son, but it's not doing you any good to pretend—"

"I never saw Roy again after that afternoon at the hospital. When was it—yesterday?"

The cop shook his head slowly, as if to say, *You have to do better than that.*

"But—" Seth struggled with the news, "if he was in the trailer . . . that's Cal's trailer. Cal lives there. Where was Cal Dunkett? Why aren't you talking to him?"

This resulted in no affable comeback like the others. The other man's eyes narrowed, his mouth drew up into a pocket. He hitched up his gun belt, scratched his chin. Then, with an admonishing look at Seth, he left the room.

It was only when he'd sat there by himself for some ten minutes that Seth realized he should have refused to speak without a lawyer present, and that he was supposed to be entitled to a phone call. And it wasn't until he remembered the phone call that the whole thing fell in on him. Hearing the slamming of a car door outside Hecklin's house, shinning down the trellis into the frigid air. He'd had no plan as he drove off; he was only running—from Jim, from all the words coming from Cal's mouth that echoed in his head the way the thing itself echoed, their filth compounding with every repetition.

Instead it was Roy who was dead. Seth guffawed. Startled by the sound, he clapped a hand over his mouth.

Roy had been shot. In Cal's trailer. Which could only mean one thing. *The bastard freak had really done it.*

Another policeman escorted him to a holding cell. He didn't say anything to Seth, and Seth didn't ask any questions. Another uniformed man brought him some supper on a tray. He was relieved that the cell seemed to be off by itself. He'd been afraid of being put somewhere with other men, but now he stopped being frightened. He ate the greasy food, drank as much water as he could hold, and stretched out on the narrow bed that was just a shelf on the wall. For a while, exhausted as he was, he couldn't close his eyes. Stared at the gray wall, and saw there the gun-barrel-shaped shadow of Vin's twisted remorse.

In the hours they sat in the waiting area at the police station, Jim and Mr. Hecklin became intimately acquainted with the green vinyl chairs, the black-and-white vinyl floor tile, the posters about seat belts and gun safety, the humming fluorescent fixtures, the acid coffee a gurgling machine dispensed into tiny paper cups for twenty-five cents, the two dog-eared issues of *People* and loose sections of *USA Today.*

When they'd arrived, while Hecklin spoke to the desk sergeant, Jim got on the phone. First he called Clyde and Billy, asking them to go to the loft and bring Cassie home with them. It was Billy who answered, which was a relief, because he was immediately enchanted with the idea of an overnight guest on short notice, and forgot to ask all the suspicious questions Clyde would have come out with. Even so, some explanation was necessary.

"The fact is, Seth's had a little accident out here in Chicago. Now, I don't want to worry her, and it's really nothing serious," Jim said, staring at a safety poster on the bulletin board that featured two cars accordion-crunched in lurid light. "But we probably won't be back before the day after tomorrow at the soonest, so if you could—? Yes,

I'm going to call her myself, she'll be ready when you go to get her. You can always reach me on the cell. Thank Clyde for me, too."

When he reached Cassie, he'd already half-convinced himself he *was* calling from some Cook County emergency room. He told her as little as possible—accident—possible concussion, not too serious—couple days' observation—yes, quite a lucky coincidence, his happening to be there on business—he'd call in the morning. The way she gasped made Jim's heart turn over.

After that, it was just a lot of waiting. Seth, the sergeant told them, was being questioned. An officer would come out to talk to them when they were ready to charge him. When? Soon. Anytime now. Mr. Hecklin seemed to know every other person, cop or civilian, who wandered through the front doors, and spent most of the time making use of this grapevine, leaving Jim, mercifully, to his own thoughts. Jim realized he'd already begun to mourn his love for Seth. Too good, too good to be true.

He wasn't such a fanatic that he couldn't forgive a simple defensive lie. The killing joke was Seth going on with it even after he knew about Jim's own terrible experience, which was real. Going on pretending to know what it was to have the world yanked out from under you. Pretending it for months and months as their intimacy deepened, as they prepared to make a whole life of it together. That was too deliberate, opportunistic, to overlook.

A commotion at the door made Jim look up; the sheriff and a knot of deputies had entered, pursued by a news crew. The reporter, whom the deputies were trying to force back outside, was shouting, "We know you've discovered a second body, Sheriff! Tell us what you've found! Is this a murder spree?"

Jim joined Mr. Hecklin.

"This is not a spree." The sheriff turned and spoke into the reporter's extended microphone. "The other dead man is Calvin Leon Dunkett, an employee of the murdered man, Roy Jenkins. At this time, as we further our inquiries, I've no other comment."

"We know you've got a suspect in custody, Seth McKenna, the dead man's stepson. Is he responsible for this other death as well?"

"Mr. McKenna is undergoing questioning. That's all I'll say at this time." The sheriff walked curtly away, and the deputies hustled the news crew back out the door.

Jim turned to go back to his chair.

"Two murders, Mr. Hecklin," he murmured. "*Two.*"

"Mr. Glaser," the old man said, "Seth was *not* involved!"

The desk sergeant, one of Hecklin's former students, approached them then.

"Sir, I promise I'll call you first thing there's any new news. Meanwhile, if you go home and get some sleep, you'll be doing yourself a favor."

Getting back to Mr. Hecklin's tiny house wasn't much of a relief. He wouldn't hear of Jim's going to a motel, insisted, although he was blinking with fatigue, on preparing dinner. In the end it was Jim who had to throw together a skillet of ham and eggs while the old fellow, overcome, snored on the sofa. Jim spent what was left of the night in the bed Seth had abandoned, in a room that was cold and still reeked of his bodily distress.

It was Reynolds who woke him up in his cell, out of a dream of Jim the way he used to dream of Vin: as a shadowed enemy, with ideas about him that would do him harm. He was glad to wake up from that.

"We're letting you go, son," he said.

For a moment, Seth couldn't move. The words, *letting you go,* which should have been so welcome, sounded to his disoriented mind like the firing to end all firings. Like being jettisoned from the world.

"Sheriff wants to talk with you first, though." Reynolds stepped back. "Well, come on then. Don't let's keep the sheriff waiting."

Seth unfolded himself, not trusting his legs. He glanced from the cop to the toilet set into the wall of the cell.

"What?"

"At least turn your back."

"Nah, c'mon. Jakes's down the hall on your left." He pointed. Seth broke and ran.

That piss was the first good sensation he'd had since leaving New York.

Afterward, he looked at himself in the mirror. Unshaven, eyes bloodshot beneath the bandage, teeth almost furry. His head throbbed. The bandage was stuck on with dried blood. Not the young man Jim had admired in Tony's studio. Here was the old Seth back, the one who was supposed to be buried forever, risen again like something in a horror movie.

But that didn't matter, because they were finished, anyway. He washed his face and hands, then felt around in his pockets for his comb, but the cops must have taken it. Reynolds walked him into the sheriff's small, cluttered office. The morning light, reflecting off yesterday's snow, made Seth wince. He fixed on the musty buffalo head mounted on the wall above the sheriff's desk. There was a feed cap hanging off each horn, and a rosary hanging from the animal's neck. The sheriff, a stern bearded man, was brewing coffee on the credenza behind his desk, under the buffalo's nose. He poured some into a foam cup for Seth. "Black all right? S'all we've got."

"Thanks." Seth took it awkwardly. He already felt out of the habit of being treated like a normal person.

"You're in the clear," the sheriff announced. "We found Cal Dunkett last night, and he's our shooter."

"I told you I didn't do it." He was on the edge of tears; it was like those times when he was a kid and his mother accused him of sins he hadn't committed. He always was seared by her suspicions, so quick was she to doubt his innocence. *You never give me a chance,* he'd wept, five years old, six, seven, whipped for things he didn't really understand.

"You appeared to have the motive," the sheriff said with a shrug. "I'm sorry. We're just doing our jobs."

"Yeah, I know." Seth inhaled the rich smell of the coffee, but it was still too hot to drink. "Did he . . . did he confess?" Seth asked, when the silence had gone on a while. He couldn't meet the sheriff's eyes. The man would know things about him, if Cal had told it all.

"You could call it that, yes."

"Was he running away? Where did you find him?"

"Wasn't running anywhere. We found him in his truck, parked by the cemetery outside Joralemon," the sheriff said. He leaned back in his chair and cracked his knuckles so loudly Seth jumped. "We also found the shotgun he used on Roy Jenkins. It was in his mouth at the time. What was left of his mouth, anyway."

"In—his—mou—" Seth's whole being curled away from this detail.

"He left a piece of correspondence I'd like to ask you a couple of questions about before you go. It mentions your name." From the desk blotter, he took a piece of paper and held it out to Seth.

"Take your time, son, you've had quite an experience."

What they handed him was a photocopy of something written on one of Roy's garage invoice sheets. An oddly grainy photocopy, defaced by irregular black blotches.

"Original's being held in evidence," Reynolds explained. "You wouldn't want to touch it anyway," he added. Pointing to the splotches, he said, "Gore Xeroxes black."

"Reggie—" the sheriff growled.

"Just explaining it to the kid."

It was Roy started it, and Roy made me do it, and doing it ruint my life ever after. Tell Seth I hope he'll forgive me now I've done all I could to make it up. And I never did anything bad to her, she'll back me up on that. Good-bye. Calvin L. Dunkett.

With one part of his mind he took in the meaning of the note with perfect clarity, but another part was absolutely stuck, wanted to dig into darkness and deny deny deny. Pity for the miserable fuck welled up, squelching, like mud around a boot. Another one touched by Roy, smeared with the stain that never washed off.

"You're free to go, son, like we said. But we would sure appreciate knowing what that's all about, first," Reynolds prompted.

"I didn't kill anybody. I didn't ask or encourage or suggest that anybody kill anybody."

"No one's saying you did. Not anymore. But we want to know why Dunkett up and killed your stepdad, and what he's talking about there in that note. And who's the woman he refers to? Is it your mother, Mrs. Jenkins? You could fill us in so's we can close this case."

"What will you do to me if I don't?" Seth whispered. "Seems to me you've got enough to close it now."

Reynolds and the sheriff exchanged quick glances. Neither said anything. Seth got to his feet. "I'd like to leave, please."

"Look, son, we know you're tired, but we're just seeking to understand—"

"It's not a police matter, it's private," Seth said.

"So you *do* know what this note refers to," the sheriff said.

"If you're planning to sell your story to the press, it won't make any difference whether you've told us or not," Reynolds said. "C'mon, son. Give a hardworking civil servant a break."

"*Sell it to the press?*" Seth stared at Reynolds until the other man dropped his gaze. "I thought I was supposed to be free to go."

Again the look between the two men. Reynolds went to the door and held it open. The sheriff rose and started to take the photocopy from Seth's hand.

"I want to keep this," Seth said. "You said it was a copy. I think I've got a right to it." Hanging on to it felt important, like a passport he'd need to cross some border he'd not yet reached.

At the office door, Reynolds said, "The sergeant at the desk will give you your items. We'd appreciate it if you wouldn't leave town for a few days. Until the coroner's filed his report."

Seth looked into his face. "I'm not going to talk about this. Not tomorrow or the next day. Not to you, or to *the press.* Anyway, you have my address in New York." He walked out, half-expecting, until he passed the front desk, that someone would step out and collar him.

And wishing, when he saw Mr. Hecklin hovering in the waiting room, that someone would.

25

Jim couldn't process what was happening: Seth, cleared of suspicion in two deaths, stalked right by him without a glance, hands clenched in pockets, shoulders high. *He looks,* Jim thought, *like a photocopy of a photocopy of a photocopy of himself.* Degraded and pale. Mr. Hecklin was trying to keep him from the newspeople waiting just outside, and trying as well, in his pathetic earnestness, to convey to Seth what he'd been saying all along: that he'd never doubted all of this was just a mistake. Expressing that was the whole of the old fellow's mind right then.

Whereas I had no trouble believing he'd killed the man. Killed two men. I was all over that idea, more than willing to say amen.

A few minutes before Seth was released, the desk sergeant explained to them what the police now officially knew about what was being ruled a murder-suicide. The motive was still obscure, but they were to understand that no suspicion remained on Seth. Mr. Hecklin had listened to all this with his head wagging like a toy dog on a dashboard.

But, Jim wondered, *who were these people?* Seth's stepfather, and the stepfather's employee. Why had they picked this particular time—just when Seth returned to town after so many years—to erupt into mayhem? There was an untold story lowering here, and Seth was involved in it someway or another.

Seth parted the curtain on the hotel room window to look out. He saw a parking lot, and beyond that, some twin-engine planes, and the control tower off to the side. Behind him Jim sat on the bed, expectant. The day was bright, with a subtle hint of spring to come, even when the ground was covered with fresh snow, as it was now.

How had Cal lured Roy to the trailer in the first place? Perhaps he'd summoned him to look at the electrical situation. He'd said, when Seth was there, that the power was off. So Roy had come over—how unwillingly? He never liked looking after anything that was his. Swung inside demanding, probably, to know what Cal had done to fuck up the wiring. Was Cal waiting for him with the gun at the ready? Perhaps bracing himself against the kitchen counter, the shotgun half-raised as he listened to Roy trudge through the snow from his own back door. Then drawn up into position as he called out, *Door's open,* and Roy walked in, wearing that irritable rat-faced expression that used to make his mother cringe. Did he give Roy time to see what was about to happen to him? Seth hoped that Roy got a good long eyeful of the gun barrel, and Cal's face behind it, his pulpy, furious, righteous face. He saw Cal, holding the gun loosely beneath his arm, step over Roy's body, careful not to slip in the mess, calm and matter of fact as he crossed to his truck, started it up. Had he written the note in the truck, or back in the trailer, maybe even before Roy arrived? Seth imagined the gun barrel sliding in between Cal's cut and swollen lips. Pressing his forehead to the glass, he spat sudden laughter, shaky and spangled.

Hands on his shoulders, hands spinning him. He came around, still laughing, right into Jim's face.

For the first time, Seth could look right at him. It was like looking at his favorite Titian, *A Man in Blue*, acknowledging its magnificence, knowing you wouldn't be taking it with you or living with it, except as a memory, or maybe a postcard. It was easy to see Jim now, because nothing mattered anymore, they were finished. Giggling, grinning, he looked him straight in the eye.

"What is this? Just what the hell is it?"

God, you'll never know, but he really did it. Jesus Christ! The fucker went and did it like the fucking wrath of God—

Cal performed his terrible expiation, and it meant nothing he'd intended it to mean. Perhaps Cal had a glimpse of satisfaction in the minutes between seeing Roy fall and putting the gun in his own mouth. But all he'd done for Seth was to yoke him forever to that obscene plea for pardon. Still he laughed, because he was forever in the shit and right now—fuck yeah!—there was something so filthy and delicious about imagining Roy's mouth drop open right before Cal pulled the trigger and blew him away.

"Seth! Stop it! What is this?"

Jim shook him, and he stopped. The blackness enveloped him again as if a switch was flipped. He could barely see Jim, couldn't remember what had seemed so funny.

"Talk to me! What was all that? To you? That man, Dunkett? What did it have to do with you?" Jim sighed and let him go. "I guess I don't really know you at all, do I?"

Seth turned back to the window. His mind teemed with crucial messages, but speech had deserted him.

It's true you don't really know me, if you mean in the sense that you had a certain mental image of where I came from, of the people that made me and raised me, and that image was incorrect because I misled you. But in another sense, in the sense that for God's sake really matters, you know what you need to know, what you've always known. I'm the one man in all the world who thinks about you more than he thinks about anybody else. And while what I think of myself is harsh and stringent, the place I hold inside for you is nothing but benign, and that's always there for you, even right now when I'm so sunk in I can barely see. Wasn't love—real love, not the thin gruel he'd grown up on—supposed to allow for the absorption of such truths through the skin, unspoken but understood? During those times when Seth had awakened already in tears, too late to hide the way his body was betraying his discretion, and Jim pressed his ear to Seth's chest, how had he failed to hear what fluttered there?

Just two days ago he'd lain by himself in a motel room a lot like this one and begged Jim on the phone to wait, and Jim had hung up on him.

Yet here he was now, keeping a sad eye on him. They were both miserable, angry, and far apart, but here he was, standing by.

Terrible. Things were terrible. Loving was terrible. Wasn't it time to go? He felt he'd been traveling for a month, and lost his sense of departure or arrival.

During the two-hour layover in Dayton, Jim lost track of him after they'd been to the men's room. He dashed back and forth from their gate to the metal detectors, certain that this was it, Seth's escape made good. As he searched, a sensation stole over him that Jim recognized as relief. If Seth was gone, there would be no need to untangle all the reasons why he'd lied, or to try to understand why his mere presence again in his home-place caused one man to kill another and then himself. He would be spared the attempt to work out who Seth really was and whether they could go on together. Jim sat down by the gate and tried to formulate a story for Cassie about her brother's disappearance. He envisioned life on his own again, with baby Ruby. He'd probably have to hire a nanny after all, just part-time; or maybe, better idea, a housekeeper, who'd free his hands to do everything with Ruby himself. He felt jealous of placing his daughter in anyone else's care. He'd been apprehensive these past weeks about how much he'd be able to allow Seth to do; he'd found himself dreaming of spectacular, fatal accidents Seth would have with the baby, the results of the pure carelessness of a twenty-four-year-old. He'd be scoping out men on the street instead of paying attention, and the baby would be squashed by a bus or dashed into pieces by a speeding bike messenger. He'd bring her to his studio, where she'd swallow turpentine while Seth was concentrating on his picture, and die in a writhing agony. Seth didn't really want to be a father, and perhaps in the end this would all turn out to be what his mother used to call A Blessing in Disguise. The overarching scheme of things, Jim told himself as the gate area began to fill up, never did include Seth as a partner for life. He was a catalyst. He'd done his work and right now he was probably slouched in the back of a taxi on the way to downtown Dayton, losing his concreteness with every quarter-mile, dissolving into the layers of story that made him up.

This mental image came with a sorrow that was shockingly physical. How could he be so stupid? He wanted Seth: to touch him, to smell him, to comfort him if he could, to fight with him if he had to.

Jim knew his love at that moment as he'd never known it when they were merely happy.

He sprang up. Perhaps someone had seen him leave the airport. If he could find out what taxi company operated the car, then perhaps he'd be able to locate the driver, who would remember where he'd dropped the young man with the earrings. . . . Hurrying down the concourse, he barely registered the sound of his name. He wheeled around to see Seth slouched warily against the wall, holding a carton of coffee in each hand. He held one out; Jim approached slowly and accepted it. When he glanced at his watch, Jim saw that barely twenty minutes had elapsed since Seth had left him in the men's room; it felt like hours. With his free hand Seth pantomimed smoking a cigarette. Jim darted his face against Seth's, prodding his mouth, sniffing for the fresh confirming tobacco smell on his breath. Seth jerked back. A passing pair of white-haired ladies shot them an indignant look. Jim lifted the lid off the coffee to take refuge in a first swallow. He was surprised—but why?—to realize that Seth had taken the trouble to ask for half-and-half, the way he liked it best. The coffee itself was lousy, but that wasn't Seth's fault. It was a peacemaking gesture, which Jim had flubbed.

"You could've said you were going to smoke. I couldn't find you."

"I did," Seth whispered, head bowed. "Didn't you hear me?"

On the plane, Seth fell asleep, and Jim was finally able to touch him, holding his hand under a blanket spread across their laps. He was sure Seth wouldn't have permitted this if he was awake. The skin of his fingers was drawn and crisp; Jim rubbed his thumb over them, marveling at their familiar shape, even as Seth himself was so altered. This was the maker of those surprising drawings, and the superb self-portrait with the pear, the possession of which gave Jim such greedy and private joy.

A half hour before landing, Seth stirred. Jim let go of him slowly, hoping he wouldn't realize they'd been touching at all when he came fully awake. He opened his eyes with a little groan, and seemed at first not to know where he was; he tried to rise, then scrabbled at the restraining belt.

"Shh, we'll be there pretty soon. I know you're exhausted." Jim carefully kept his hands to himself, although he'd have liked to place one on Seth's arm. "Think cheerful thoughts," he said, echoing what his mother used to tell him when he was trying not to be carsick, or waiting to face the dentist; this advice had always struck him as inane, yet here he was repeating it.

The Fasten Seat Belt light came on and the plane began to descend.

At LaGuardia, Hannah waited. Jim saw her just before she spotted them. Her face formed into a welcoming smile for Seth as she came toward him with her arms out, and Seth walked right into them.

"Sweetie, sweetie, sweetie," she crooned. Over Seth's shoulder, she looked at Jim, eyebrows slightly raised.

"Hey, Hannah."

"Hello, Jim. Grueling trip, I take it."

"It hasn't been pleasant." He hesitated. "Nice of you to meet us."

"Well, Seth phoned and asked me . . . listen," she said, drawing back some and addressing Seth now, "Eric is outside in the car, so we didn't have to pay for parking. Are you waiting for luggage?"

Seth shook his head.

"Then we should go." She glanced at Jim. "We're only going as far as Long Island City, so . . . you'll excuse us not offering you a lift."

It wasn't until then that Jim understood what this meant. In his confusion he couldn't find anything to say: this seemed not to be right, but then, who was he to question it? Clearly it was what Seth wanted, what he'd disappeared at Dayton to arrange.

"Seth, your sister—"

"I'll call her as soon as we get in," Seth mumbled. "I won't forget."

"You can use Eric's cell and call her from the car," Hannah said.

"Well . . . okay," Jim said. "As long as you . . . she's at Clyde and Billy's. Do you have the number?"

"I'll get the number."

"No, it's important, wait—" Jim patted his pockets; usually he was fully equipped, but everything now was out of place. Hannah produced a pen. Jim refused the slip of paper she offered, and catching Seth's hand, wrote the number along the inside of his thumb. All the while he pressed with the ballpoint against Seth's skin, Seth tried lamely to tug his hand away.

"So, ah . . . c-c-call me tomorrow—or I'll call you."

"Yeah." Seth turned without another glance. When he'd gone about fifteen feet he looked back. His eyes were dark, as if dimmed by dirty weather. "My sister's only ever slept with one guy, you realize that. It was Vin—Calvin—Dunkett."

"She—what?"

"You heard me."

Hannah gasped; her whole face changed.

"Oh, my God!" She took off after Seth, calling to him to slow down. Hannah knew, apparently, what all this meant.

Jim watched them recede.

He wanted to go straight home, take an Ambien and forget the last couple of days in sleep, but instead, heavy with responsibility and dread, he took a taxi to the West Village. He got out on Seventh above Sheridan Square and walked slowly west toward Clyde and Billy's house. After the cold of Flanagan County, the Manhattan night was balmy; open-coat weather. He felt some private embarrassment for how glad he was to be back in the city, for feeling that this place was so very superior to where he'd just been.

He trudged up the tall stoop and yanked the porcelain bell pull.

Billy opened the door.

"Where is she?"

"We're down in the kitchen, having a round of Milles Bornes."

Jim followed him down the stairs. Clyde was at the counter, brewing coffee; they nodded at each other. At one end of the big table that seated twelve—twelve men, always, Jim had never seen a woman at a dinner party here—Cassie sat in one of the deep old armchairs, her hair pinned up, fanning herself with a section of newspaper as if she was on a subway platform in August. The game cards were laid down neatly in front of her, and there was the wine and a bowl of walnuts and a nutcracker. Jim wouldn't have believed it possible, but her belly looked even larger than when he'd left her two days ago; she was almost pyramidal in the big chair, her cheeks flushed and eyes bright. As she put her arms around his neck and kissed him, he shared her helpless bewilderment. How odd it was for her to have started out in that shabby café by the side of a featureless road, and end up here in this lush West Village kitchen, surrounded by men whose ways she'd been suspicious of a few months ago, looking to them as if they were the only people who cared what became of her.

"Coffee or wine?" Clyde asked. He was frowning, brisk—his usual self. Jim tried to smile for him. Billy, as always, was positioned between them, keeping a weather eye on Clyde, ready to turn him aside, to suggest softer alternatives to his harsh assumptions.

"Better make it wine, *then* coffee."

Clyde brought him a sandwich, too, of leftover meatloaf. He knew, just by the aroma, that Cassie had made it. Cassie went on fanning herself, staring at him while he ate, and he was grateful to her too, for holding on although she was bursting to ask questions. After a few wolfish bites, he put the sandwich down.

"The three of you been playing nice together while I was gone?"

"Tell me about Seth. He said he was calling from Hannah's. Why'd he go there?"

"He's . . . he's hurt, all right, and he wanted Hannah to look after him for a day or so. That's all. Okay? How're *you*?"

"Seth's gone to stay at Hannah's because you guys had a fight, right?"

"He's gone to Hannah's because that's where he wanted to be right now." Jim swallowed a big mouthful of wine. "And I came here, because this is where *I* wanted to be." He tried to eat more of the sandwich, but his exhaustion had caught up with him. Billy came to his side and tugged him up; he stretched out on the sofa at the far end of the kitchen, near the window that looked out on the street. A refreshing little draft off the glass bathed his face. He closed his eyes and that was it.

Part Four

26

When she heard about their mother, Cassie sprang up and began rushing around Hannah's big room like a fly looking for an open window. After a night that wasn't over for him yet, although it was broad daylight outside, Seth was barely capable of narrative. He'd told her about Mary's illness, said that Roy was murdered . . . and left it at that. He didn't want her to know about his night in jail, even had he been able to talk about it.

Slumped in an armchair, smoke curling up from the cigarette he kept forgetting to smoke, Seth didn't think there was anything wrong with what he was doing—or not doing—until Eric caught his eye, shook his head, and rose to catch Cassie by the shoulders. Hannah got up, too, and took Cassie from him.

"Don't pretend it's not the best thing that could've happened to her," Seth said, the words slurring through his numb lips. "The church ladies will probably rally round her now Roy's gone."

"But she's in the hospital and you just *left* her there? Roy's been *murdered,* and you don't even know how she is? I want to talk to her! I want to call her."

"You can phone her," Hannah said. "Sit down, though. Don't get all excited."

Cassie turned on Seth. "You shouldn't have gone there by

yourself—it wasn't fair to leave me behind, not to *tell* me! About Ma, for God's sake! *Seth!*"

Eric steered her into the other room to make the call.

Seth sighed.

"Darling," Hannah said, her voice pitched to soothe. "You know I like to help you. I won't let you down. But there's a right way and a wrong way to handle things from this point, and I—"

Seth gestured, but she shook her head. "Look, they're dead now. The best way to really put all this in the past is to confide in the people who love you. Your sister and Jim deserve to know what's going on. What's been going on."

Seth turned his head, and then he found he couldn't control his face, which was spasming into a grimace. He couldn't control anything that his body was doing, the grief jerking out. He flung himself into the bathroom and slammed the door.

Cassie said, "She wasn't at the hospital."

His eruption passed, Seth recomposed himself around a necessary cigarette. They'd all resumed their places, as if this was an ordinary visit; they were even holding steaming mugs of coffee.

"She checked out this morning. Her church friends brought her home. She said she was resting on the sofa, but they were boxing up all of Roy's stuff for the next rummage sale. The weird thing is, she really didn't sound very interested in me. She barely asked me any questions. Or about you, either."

"She's probably in shock. Anyway, I told you she'd be all right," Seth murmured. Hannah's gaze oppressed him. She was waiting for him to tell about Cal, but the more he postponed it, the more he thought maybe it wasn't necessary to tell at all. Cassie had expressed little surprise or curiosity when he'd reported Roy murdered; he'd always had so many enemies, feuds, bar fights, bad debts. It hadn't yet occurred to her to ask who'd done the deed. If she ever did, Seth was beginning to think, he could say no one knew. Cassie would never go back there or research the county newspaper, and their mother, if she kept in touch with her, would never talk about it. In her mind, Cassie had already left Cal far behind; what matter if he was alive or dead?

He knew that witnessing her inevitable grief over a man whose name she couldn't say without her lips unconsciously curling into a sexy little smile would tip him over the edge of losing himself completely.

He couldn't love a girl who'd mourn Vin Dunkett.

Seth rose. "I'll drop you at Bond Street," he said. "Jim's all itchy about you, I bet."

She looked up at him sadly. "You're not going home, are you?"

"Well, not right now."

"Jim's furious with you, isn't he." It wasn't a question. "He was acting so peculiar all the time you were gone."

"Something like that. C'mon, get your coat."

The blackness was all around him now. It was like being in a badly erected tent in a downpour; any moment now he'd be swamped. As it was, he was having trouble organizing his limbs; reeling in his coat, and his sister, and his cigarettes, and getting them all out the door was a feat.

On the subway, Cassie huddled against him, chin drawn down into her collar.

"So Jim knows you lied."

"Mr. Hecklin practically told him the story of my life. And then he was out there; he saw everything."

"So—"

"Look, just don't worry about it, okay? It's not your fault, and it's not going to change anything for you." He had to control his speaking voice, taste each word as it came out to be sure it was the one he wanted. All sorts of wrong words seemed to want to fly through his lips. His thoughts were slow and twined about grotesquely like headless eels.

"I think I'll go back to Clyde and Billy's. I'm not ready for . . . I'm not ready for Jim," she said.

He got rid of her on Perry Street, pretending not to see her importuning look.

Ducked into a liquor store, got some vodka, got a taxi, and set off to get as far away from himself as he could.

Feeling as if all the locks of his life had been changed against him, he was surprised that he could get into his studio. It was chilly inside. He didn't bother to turn on the lights. Why look at anything there now, when he wouldn't be coming back? He could hardly believe that he'd ever had the nerve to take this place, to work here as if he deserved it, as if what he was doing had any merit. The last year—hell, everything since Hannah aborted his suicide five years before—was a mania, now exploded into tiny pieces of foul trash.

Dropping onto the sofa, Seth opened the vodka and began to swallow straight from the bottle. Then he was up on the roof—what roof? any one, this one—climbing from the tarred flat surface up onto the parapet, the cement gritty under his hands as he wobbled, pushed off with his palms to stand up. For a little while he balanced, arms spread out, aware of but not looking at the blind-fronted street below, just shuttered warehouses, no one passing there. Taking cautious steps along like a kid walking the top of a fence, nothing much at stake. Maybe even doing it with eyes closed, little steps. Nothing around his body but moving air and the reassurance of the nearness of death. He climbed down, knowing he could climb back up at any moment. The world was full of roofs and bridges offering this guarantee; he could just tip his body forward, endure the bad minute of falling—he couldn't imagine regret, but he admitted it would still be bad—and then, over. Like a last twenty kept for an emergency, Seth folded this assurance and tucked it away in his mind. He wasn't yet at the point of wanting death above all else; he merely saw that time on the near horizon, as he jerked dizzily forward; he might still swerve and miss it, or he might gratefully head straight at it.

Back inside, Seth sprang at the walls, tearing down the prints and clippings, rending them into shreds. He yanked down the strings of fairy lights, seized up the standing lamp beside the sofa and swung it against the wall, where the bulb shattered, leaving him with a twisted piece of metal in his hands that he tossed away. He jumped up and down on the sofa until it collapsed, flinging him off to bruise his knees on the floor. He barely felt the impact. Throwing open the window, Seth chucked his sketchbooks, portfolios, small canvases, and art books down into the weedy waste space behind the building. Then he followed them down by the fire escape ladder, piled them up with fierce fast motions, sweating under his clothes. Dizzy from the vodka, he staggered as he worked.

Soaked in turpentine, the things went up with a fierce *whoosh* as soon as he threw the match. All his college work, his Cooper Union work, every piece of paper he'd ever marked and kept, flew up into floating ash in an instant. Watching all his things in the flames, which flared high out here where the surrounding buildings cut off the wind, brought images back of other fires. The time Roy had made him burn his albums in the lot behind the café, when he'd danced in the flames and burned his legs. The little blazes, the *hey, I'm alive, fuck you* fires he used to set under the bleachers on game days. The blaze—and what a motherfucker *that* one was!—that he'd set at the Frawley place. Oh, man, he should've considered a career as a professional arsonist after that one. And later, the little flame in that Coleman lamp that lit up what Roy and his pals did to him, the same flame that brought it all back again in Cal's trailer.

When he got bored with the burning, he left it and scrambled back up the fire escape ladder, which was harder than going down; his muscles had gone soggy. He fell in through the window and crawled across the floor toward the wrecked sofa, where the bottle of vodka waited. He finished it, tipping it back so the last drops fell onto his cheeks and chin. Then he took up a box cutter and began on the big paintings.

Each one as he'd planned and painted it flared into life for him like a match being struck. Now he held them blank side in, sparing himself the sight of them as he laid them waste. They were full of cockeyed optimism, even when their subjects were ambiguous or suffused with sadness, because they were lit with a painterly exuberance that said *there's always something that comes after.*

It was ridiculously easy to slice through the layers of paint he'd so painstakingly laid down. They turned to inane colored tatters hanging from their wooden stretchers, which yielded easily, too, to being crushed and broken. There was a crazy glee in this destruction. He could breathe deep at last, and not think. All he felt when everything was destroyed was disappointment; he could have gone on slashing canvas all day long.

Fortunately, there was more booze.

When next he became aware of himself, of his head like a block of cement, foul body sprawled on the floor, eyes refusing to open up, he knew only that time had passed. How much he couldn't tell. Impossible to focus on his watch. The diffuse light from the windows seemed to be withholding information. He half-crawled, half-staggered to the bathroom, and was sick for a long time.

Then he remembered the other pictures. Nothing was more urgent than that he yank them out of existence. After that he'd be free to go where no one would find him.

27

Jim had a feeling about the loft, that somehow, since they'd all left it, it had settled into emptiness, the life lived there dispersed. Even Zak's shade would be gone. He'd have to turn on all the lights, music, fill the air with the aroma of cooking to stir the place out of that distemper.

But the nearer he got, the less he felt up to the effort. Didn't want to be there alone, or worse, with Cassie; didn't want to think about the situation pressing down on him. He'd been responsible; rescued Seth, brought him back to his sister. This afternoon, he would check out.

He ended up at the movies. Sat through one subtitled feature, a lot of yelling and heavy breathing in Italian, then snuck into the theater next to it for more of the same in Chinese. Afterward he wandered up and down the cast-iron blocks of Soho, staring unseeing into shopwindows. Ate a hamburger and drank a beer in a crowded bar. Remembered to turn his cell phone back on.

Immediately it began to chirp at him. He called his voice mail. Clyde's voice started in without preamble.

"She's started! For fuck's sake, where are you? Her water broke all over my new stair runner! This is what I get for harboring females!"

The cabdriver caught the lights right. The trip uptown took barely twenty minutes while Jim made calls, reaching no one. To the guard at the desk in the Klingenstein Pavilion, Jim spoke Cassie's name, the words seeming to float out in front of his face. Did all expectant fathers feel so unreal? When the elevator door opened, he misjudged the distance across the threshold and almost turned his ankle. *Jesus.*

At the end of a long echoing corridor he found her with Clyde and Billy, who greeted him with wild glad cries, as if he were spelling them from a siege. Jim hadn't seen them looking so pale and out of their depths since the time they'd learned of Zak's death. These were men who wouldn't even hire a woman to clean their house, yet here they were now in the midst of all this womanly bellowing and flying sweat, holding Cassie's hands, sponging off her face, being marvelous. *For me, because they are my friends.* Clyde and Billy were present, and Seth was not. He threw off this thought so as to appear to Cassie with a glad face. He *was* glad. Frightened, astonished, and already giddy.

"I called Seth. Left him a message. He should be here—"

She shook her head, already far beyond asking or answering questions. Dr. Liebling, calm in a way that instantly made Jim feel angry on Cassie's behalf, greeted him. "Perfect timing. The last act's getting underway."

Cassie hollered and cursed in a manner that none of the child-birth classes prepared him for. Jim came around by her head and caught her hand. After a while there was a lull. Still panting, she tried to smile.

"I'm doing it, she's coming for you!"

Jim remembered that later, her scarlet face, eyes small and blood-shot, hair stuck to her sweat-slicked skin, as she promised him his daughter. The pride in her eyes, the way it shone through the pain that glazed her.

Dr. Liebling told her to push then, and she was subsumed again in her work, their private little moment passed.

At three in the morning, Jim gave Ruby Glaser her first meal from a warm bottle—a familiar task, made utterly new. After all those anonymous transitive infants, the scrunched face he looked into now was one he'd been allowed to give his name to, that everyone acknowledged was his.

Clyde and Billy, trailing congratulations and stunned laughter, had gone home. Cassie was asleep in the bed nearby. The room was almost quiet. The baby in her woolly wrappings nursed, and Jim, heavy-eyed and slow-minded, was suffused with a peace beyond anything he'd anticipated or ever hoped to know.

"What's the time?"

A raft of sentimental fantasies skittered away when he raised his eyes to her.

"What, darling?"

She repeated the question, he answered it. She moved her hands languidly on the coverlet, feeling her changed shape, and made a liquid sound when she swallowed. Her head turned and turned on the pillow, and Jim realized she was uncomfortable. Reluctantly he set Ruby in her cradle and got up. Lifting Cassie into a sitting position—she felt now as light as spun sugar, but smelled of quite something else—he unbraided her hair so the thick rope of it wouldn't press on her nape. Then he took up the baby again and resumed his chair.

"I'm glad this is over," she said.

"Billy and Clyde handled themselves all right, did they?"

"Oh, I guess." She grimaced, then giggled. "Clyde was furious about that rug, but he was trying not to show it, and then a little while after we got here I guess my hollering was too much for him. He fainted. Billy was trying to help me, but he had absolutely no idea what he was supposed to do or say and finally I told him to just shut up." She paused. "Don't tell them I said any of this, though. I know they did the best they could. They were very nice to me while I was at their house. We watched *Dark Victory* and *All About Eve*, and they taught me how to make a cassoulet."

"You will furnish them with a topic of dinner-party conversation that'll last them the rest of their lives, I'm sure."

"Oh, if that will make them happy, then I'm glad."

"Were you afraid?" he asked. "When it started and Seth and I weren't there?"

"I was at first. But then I realized that it would happen no matter who was there, and it was happening to *me*. But I wanted Seth, because Seth *knows* me. When you're in a state like that, you want someone near you who knows you. No offense to you."

Seth had cheated them both: Cassie of the comfort of his presence, and him of the experience he'd coveted—of experiencing Ruby's birth from first to last, being as close to it as he—as any man— possibly could get. Just being there in time for the baby's emergence wasn't enough.

"You're breaking up, aren't you?"

"What? No. Don't think that." He didn't pause to think whether this was true or not.

"Because he lied to you. And you saw what he lied about."

I did and I didn't. "I'm sorry about Cal Dunkett."

"Oh, you saw him? Don't be sorry, he was fine for me. For a while. He's a sweet person, really." She paused. "Oh—d'you mean you're sorry 'cause he's out of a job? Because I bet Ma might keep him on, maybe."

It took Jim a few seconds to understand that she didn't know Cal was dead. Now was not the time to tell her.

Her eyes closed. He was buzzing, lit up beyond fatigue. His eyes traveled from her white puffy face to her daughter's, over and over, marveling at all the circumstances that assembled to make this young woman give him her child. Five in the morning turned to six, to seven. A nurse came in. Cassie was awakened.

Once he'd given Ruby her first bath under the nurse's eye, a strong hint was given that perhaps Daddy should go away and get some shut-eye while he still could.

Jim kissed Cassie's forehead. "Have I mentioned that I owe you everything; that you are the heroine of my whole life?"

She turned her head, blushing, but smiling. "Don't talk like that, that's just silly."

"Ruby is perfect. Perfect. I thank you. You've done a wonderful thing for me."

"Go away now."

The bare trees of Central Park were silhouetted against a sky whose blue almost shimmered. At the curb Jim blinked, trying to clear his swimming eyes. The air was cool and still. There were no cabs. He set out walking, crossing over to the park side, striding beneath the canopy of gray denuded branches. For the first time he noticed on them the bare beginnings of their next cycle, although it would be some weeks still before the shoots appeared. Across the avenue gray apartment buildings loomed, full of sleeping people, lawyers and stockbrokers and investment bankers with the spouses they'd always known they'd have beside them and the kids they'd always known would come tucked in their beds down the carpeted hall. *My family is up there, too,* Jim thought, walking south with the giddy sense of balancing on a beam, a little trick done just for the joy of it because he was alive and Ruby was alive and they were linked unbreakably together. Could anyone tell, if they saw him, a tired man of forty-three in crumpled clothes, his overcoat flapping around his legs, that today, even as mystery and disappointment churned through him, he was nevertheless made brand-new?

At Ninetieth Street he found a taxi. Told the driver to congratulate him, and then spent the rest of the ride listening to the cabby complain about how raising his two daughters in Corona was ruining them and he wished he could send them back to Pakistan but it was probably already too late, his influence on them squashed flat by the America that seeped in though every door and window and electrical outlet of his apartment. At any other time the cabby's mind-set would've been irritating, but now he had a daughter of his own he could begin, in the vaguest and most cheerful way, to enter into the problem from the other man's point of view. He made agreeable noises and thought with satisfaction of how Ruby wasn't going to be corrupted by anything because she would have marvelous discernment and would be splendid in every possible way, all her life long.

Jim gave him a twenty for a twelve-dollar fare and went upstairs. He'd be alone; Seth gone to Hannah's or to hell. A problem, anyway, for a later time. He'd shower, climb into bed for a couple of hours, then head back to the hospital. Cassie wasn't, as they'd arranged in advance, going to do any of the baby care; it wasn't her baby. So he must rush back to hold Ruby, feed her, change her. The new life of a father was his. What he'd wanted. Even if he hadn't envisioned it quite like this.

As soon as he let himself into the loft, Jim's eye flew to the wall opposite the door, where Seth's big dream picture hung. It wasn't there now. The wall was empty, and on the floor was a mess of ribboned canvas and broken wood. Jim rushed to kneel beside it as if it was a fallen person; then glancing up, saw that every picture of Seth's in the front room and dining area had suffered the same fate. All sliced up and strewn across the Persian carpets. Seized with a premonition, Jim leapt up and rushed into the bedroom.

There, with his back to him, was Seth, the box cutter in one hand and the self-portrait with the pear in the other. Jim shouted; Seth glanced up, his face feral and hopeless. For a moment they stood, gazes locked. Then, with a terrible grin, Seth jerked the knife; Jim leapt at him as the blade bit the corner of the canvas. Seth stumbled backward, flailing out with the cutter, and the picture's frame buckled beneath their combined weights as they crashed to the floor.

Jim had expected Seth to struggle, but he lay absolutely still beneath him, as if they'd just finished an energetic fuck. He breathed like a cornered animal and reeked of alcohol. Then he tensed, and Jim was afraid. Seth wasn't himself. Where was the box cutter? Jim tried to scramble up. It was then that his hand began to throb. Flexing it made him wince and gasp, and when he braced himself on it, it slid liquidly against the wood floor. He glanced at the painting. The frame was broken, and there was a two-inch gash in one corner, but the picture was intact. It could be mended and restretched. This seemed enormously important now, when the picture might be all that remained of the boy he'd fallen in love with. Scrambling up, he looked at the deep gash across the fleshy part of his palm, sluicing blood, the skin laid open neat and deep, and his head spun. He sat down again, hard.

The thump he made hitting the floor roused Seth, who raised his head and shoulders slowly. His eyes were small and red and unfocused.

"Look . . . I seem to have cut myself." Jim held his hand out. The blood came up in the cut like oil bubbling slowly from the ground.

"It's your own fault," Seth mumbled. He scooted back, the box cutter still gripped in his right hand. "You're not supposed to be here now."

Jim blinked. "Not supposed—?"

"It's fucking checkup day, isn't it? First thing every Thursday morning, right? You should be at the doctor's office with my sister. Goddamnit to hell. I can't fucking get anything done here!"

Jim blinked, amazed that Seth remembered this quotidian detail in the midst of his frenzy. Although of course he'd not have dared, in his current mental state, to come back here if he hadn't been expecting a clear field.

There was a crash. Jim's halting mind processed the sound: Seth had thrown the box cutter, shattering a mirror on the closet door. He gaped at the shards, and the white wood where his reflection just was. "Seth, stop this. Just . . . stop."

He was bent over, holding his head. Jim thought Seth might be going to vomit, and the mere idea made his own gorge rise. He gripped his wounded hand by the wrist and tried to assemble a course of action. Just getting up seemed like an undertaking. Crossing to the door would involve stepping on the shards of mirror. The pain blossomed then, pulsing, raw.

"Look, my hand's sliced open pretty bad here."

Seth crawled to him. He took Jim's hand in both of his and squinted at it up close, as if he wasn't sure what it was he was looking at. Jim could smell him again; beneath the liquory residue was the higher note of dried sweat. He noticed the gray roots of Seth's hair.

In the bathroom, Seth washed and bound the hand with a slow, inebriated concentration. When the blood was washed away and Jim saw the extent of the gash, he was dizzy. He ought to go to the emergency room. But he was too inert, unable to gather his inner forces, and afraid to ask Seth to do anything so definite as going there with him. He was also afraid to leave him alone.

And . . . damnit, he was supposed to be getting back to Ruby. There was no time for this.

The hand, once bandaged, throbbed in desperate cadence with his pulse; his fingers didn't want to work. He tried to ignore all that, and followed Seth out to the kitchen. He'd taken the vodka out of the freezer and started to pour some into two glasses.

"I think you'd better finish sobering up, not head back in," he said, reaching for the bottle.

Seth shrugged and let him take it.

"You haven't picked up any of your messages, have you? Ruby came and you missed it."

A vein, blue beneath the skin, appeared jagging down from Seth's hairline to his left eyebrow. Jim saw it pulsing.

"Beautiful. You've done a beautiful job of things. Your sister's going to know, in a few hours, if she hasn't figured it out already, that you don't give a damn about her really."

"You don't fucking know anything about what Cassie is to me."

"Don't I? How d'you figure?" He was amazed to hear how calm he sounded, as the throbbing in his hand stepped up, the sting shooting up his arm. "How d'you figure that love means anything if you don't show up when showing up is what matters most? Didn't I show up for you out in Drinkwater, even after I knew how you'd lied to me? Because I felt a responsibility to you, even so. A responsibility I'd think you'd feel for Cassie. But no, turns out you're lying like a pig in slop while she was working her heart out for us."

Jim could see how hungover Seth was, every cell aching, his head as if impaled on a throbbing spike. Still, no matter how dismal your circumstances, you put your sorrows aside, without hesitation, when it came time to pull along with one of the handful of people you truly cared about. People who couldn't be relied on that far weren't people at all. "This isn't just about you and me. This isn't about that weird shit back in your hometown. This is you and your sister, the most basic connection you have! You've taken your last shreds of decency, and *pissed* them—"

"Shut up. *Shut up!*" Seth scrambled away from him, scarlet-faced, trembling with rage. "You don't know anything! I *couldn't*—!"

"Tell me, then! For chrissakes, tell me!" Jim roared, grabbed him by the shirtfront and shook him. "Enough of your lies—evasions—be straight with me for once or get out!"

Seth tore himself free. "I'll be getting out, don't worry. You wanna know what's disgusting, though? A man who's got a sob story he refuses to live down, who instead of keeping it decently to himself, *uses* it all his life to make himself a special case, to get special treatment. They call themselves *survivors*. People like that are everywhere, and they are foul."

"Seth—"

"Don't touch me! If that jerk Hecklin had minded his own business, you'd never have known any of this. I'd have taken it to my grave as *my* business and nobody else's! If I didn't get called back to that shithole—if I didn't have to find out about Cal Dunkett and my sister—if I didn't hear him tell me he'd tried, with *her*, to expiate—*I said*, don't touch me!"

Jim followed him to the front of the loft. Seth stood right up against the window, as if he wanted to fling himself through the glass to the street below. When Jim drew near, he whipped around. His boyish lovely face with the rubber-band mouth was transformed. Jim saw what Cassie had described that day at the botanical garden, and he'd not believed: the beleaguered kid whose wretched ugliness resulted from having no control whatsoever over any aspect of his life.

"*I* let you down? *I* let Cassie down? *I'm* a liar and a thief? What about them? Roy and Cal Dunkett and the others? They raped me! I was only fifteen years old. They tied me down and raped me!"

Suddenly Seth was a mile off and receding. Jim's heart seemed gone, too, and his lungs. He was a husk, his emptiness resounding with those words. Like a Jacob's Ladder tumbling with a harsh clatter, his understanding of Seth's mysteries fell out into a new pattern. One that connected every piece to every other. Seth to Roy to Cal to Cassie to . . . to Ruby. Shame welled up, like the blood from his bleeding hand.

"You wanted to know. So you know. And *I* know what you're going to say!"

"Oh, God, how can I say anything? That anybody should hurt you so. . . ." Jim edged nearer. "I hate it that anybody ever hurt you." He put a hand out, caressing not Seth's face, but his reflection in the window glass. "This doesn't have to come between us. Ruby isn't that man. She's brand-new, and she's ours. Seth, we can work through this."

"You don't fucking get it. There's no more 'we.' There's no more 'this.'" He spoke with his face pressed against the glass. "I didn't want you to know any of that. I just wanted to be someone you would *see*, so you would have me. I wanted you so much." The words came out, harsh and half-swallowed. "But *you* think, now I've let it out in this big crap made-for-TV catharsis scene, that everything's gonna be fine. You'll take me in your arms in a second, I'll cry and then you'll cry and I'll start to fucking *heal*. You're only as sick as your secrets, that's the mantra these days, isn't it? Everybody thinks that's the magic cure, *tell* your shame, and *poof!*—it goes away. Only guess what. It doesn't fucking go away when you tell it. It gets into the other person, the person you've told it to because you wanted no barriers between you, and then you find out it's there when he looks at you, and when he talks to you about anything at all it's there, under the words, between them, behind them. When he introduces you to other people, it's there, it's in the light of his eyes as he says your name, no matter how he *thinks* he's saying it. And in bed! It's never never never not there in bed. *Fuck!* I didn't want it in bed with *us!* The bed—the *life*—where I get to be a man who loves another man!" Seth shook his head hard, as if ridding himself of a swarm of gnats. "Now say you don't pity me! Say it!"

The sight of Jim, swaying uncertainly, looking so unhappy and guilt-ridden because his compassion, which he could never submerge for long, was made wrongheaded and rejected in advance, stirred Seth so that he had to turn away. Jim lacked the toughness to deal with this.

And he lacked the toughness now to deal with any more of Jim.

Seth started for the bedroom, Jim on his heels. In the closet he bypassed his new luggage and fished on the top shelf for the old duffel bag he'd come with. He shot the hangers, pulling out his old white Bombay suit, a couple pair of threadbare chinos. There wasn't much anymore remaining from the meager store of things he'd brought with him, but he was careful to grab only those.

Taking the wallet from his pocket, he removed the credit cards, and held them out to Jim, who stared at them blankly. "I . . . I'll leave these here," he said, and placed them on the nightstand. "I'm not going to touch any more of the money you gave me. It's not really mine. I'll write you a check for the whole amount now. There'll be tax shit about this, but you'll work that out later."

At the apartment door, Seth took his keys from the hook, then paused, and put them back. He wouldn't need the keys anymore.

Jim followed him silently with his eyes, unprotesting, bewildered.

Each step he descended was knee-high mud.

When the outside air touched his face, Seth realized, by the way the wind was cold on his cheeks, that he was crying. He wiped the tears with his sleeve.

With every step he took away from Jim now, he wanted to fall to his knees and howl.

Part Five

28

He tried smaller and smaller paper. Pages from the cheap sketchbook quartered, then halved again. Not the rapidograph—just a pencil. Not even a pencil—a ballpoint pen. These weren't really art supplies, they didn't count. Keep the stakes small. Made doodles, like the tiny drawings of amiable monsters he used to hide in Cassie's things when they were kids, to surprise and amuse her. Couldn't he just render a series of little heads on the little slips? He could evoke vast casts of characters out of the population of a subway car, out of his imagination. He didn't need to *do* anything with them, show them to anyone. Just get them onto the paper. Nice paper, good paper, friendly paper, with the sunlight on it, the torn edges soft and inviting; he loved paper, he always had. Because it received him so willingly, so unstintingly. Anything he wanted to give it, paper took.

Not anymore.

Tried something even more disposable—sketching directly onto pages out of the newspaper, just right on top of the columns of type, the Bloomie's advertisements. Nothing important, nothing lasting, so nothing to get worked up into a painful balk over. Right? Just an exercise, just practice. Work the muscle.

No.

The perfect circle. In his teens, he'd spend hours producing them. Feeling himself some undiscovered Zen master as he traced them out in the dirt by his mother's back door, in the margins of his school notebook, in the dust on the back of parked trucks, circles large or small, freehand circles that made him, for a moment, feel free.

No more.

The itching in hand and mind, to pick up the brush, the pen, the crayon, to expel energy and idea in fluid line, was still there. It was a torment now, not the mental horniness to spume and spill he'd had before. Desire seeping all through him like a stain of some dark thing spreading. When he had the pencil in his hand, it turned into some grubby stub. His supple hand was replaced with a sort of claw, disobedient, stupid. Facing the paper he could think only of the hundreds of things he'd burned to spite himself, his whole history as a maker of drawings, of paintings, as a fixer of moments in light and emotion, reduced to char. He could not imagine a life without them, he could not make more without them on hand. He could not redraw all those images, could not reimagine himself into the mind that made them with such concentrated bliss. Could not reimagine himself into the Seth who walked arm in arm with Cassie, the Seth who could bring anything of himself, however hard and hurt, to Hannah. The Seth who'd charmed Jim into loving him, because he already adored him with his whole heart.

29

He and Jim might as well have been in different cities. He'd dropped well down from Jim's orbit in the months after they parted, and never saw him or anyone he knew. He worked at the Long Island City atelier of a successful painter, a job he'd snagged with the help of one of his Cooper Union instructors. Commuting there from his shared apartment in Greenpoint, he didn't even pass through Manhattan. He stretched the painter's canvases, ran his errands, made his coffee, answered his phone and e-mail, did his scut work, at least ten hours a day, usually six days a week. Only got into Manhattan during business hours once in a while, usually to the painter's Fifty-seventh Street gallery.

He'd quit Cooper Union without finishing the program. His days with the painter were exhausting. At the beginning the painter had shown a polite interest in him, based on the praise of his professor, but when Seth had to admit that he'd destroyed all his work, the other man looked at him as if he'd confessed to butchering a pet, and never spoke of it again. He was self-absorbed, anyway, uninterested in nurturing young talent. Seth had to nurture *him*, through his constant on-again off-again affairs with a female former assistant, and a young man he'd encountered at an opening. The age disparities in the painter's cases weren't at all charming or romantic, not like his own with Jim. The painter was nothing like Jim, anyway. Seth was sure Jim would detest this guy; the way he lived with a cell phone clipped to his belt, a little headset constantly curled around one ear, the way he wolfed hard-boiled eggs (part of Seth's job was boiling them every other morning) and sandwiches, barely chewing as he talked and handled his papers and tools, the way he interrupted people when they spoke to him. He didn't so much paint his pictures as art direct them. Seth did a lot of that work, too, even as he felt, day by day, the deftness leave his hands.

He dreamed about his dead paintings now, and especially about the self-portrait with the pear, that earnest love offering, which was not dead, but lost to him. His dreams about the rape were less frequent, which he supposed was a good thing, but the painting dreams were just as shitty, if in a different way. He'd violated himself. Stage-managed, anyhow, the spectacular failure of his happiness.

Living again on coffee and lentils and greasy take-out, he never really slept well, and knew he'd lost ground on the looks front. But his life was on a fairly even keel now, after the four months it took to scrape himself together enough to find the job, the place to live. After leaving Jim, he'd floated around, sleeping on the floor of one art school acquaintance after another, too distraught and ashamed of himself even to tell Hannah where he was staying. He went to see her sometimes and ate the food she cooked for him, accepted the money she pressed into his hand. But he didn't take his checkbook and credit cards that Jim had left with her in a sealed envelope.

He'd begun to pay her back, and Jim, too; every two weeks when the painter paid him, he sent Jim a money order for twenty-five dollars, care of the advertising agency that still bore his name. This was all he could spare out of his hourly wage. He had no idea if Jim was cashing the money orders, but in a way it didn't matter; they were payments into his own pride, more than anything.

That convoluted pride felt like all he had left.

Drawings would not come to him in those months, but other insights did. Gradually, via the musings just before and after sleep, he crept back over it all, saw it differently. Jim's love. What *he'd* thought they were doing together, what he'd thought Seth was. Couldn't blame him for feeling betrayed, ill-used. He'd gone about everything all wrong . . . Jim was kinder through it all than most other men would be.

One day, without meaning to, he'd found himself on Bond Street. Looked up at the loft windows and found them blank. The piano, the plants, the shades, all gone.

Okay. Check. Got the message.

He didn't tell Hannah about that. Hannah would murmur to him, refilling his coffee cup, or leaning forward to caress his knee with her plump freckled hand, "You don't believe me right now because you are so unhappy but my God, Seth, most people are unhappy in their twenties, and if they aren't, it usually means they'll never again be happy later on. I know you've lost something you wanted very much, but . . . the painting will come back. And love will come back. There's so much time."

A slim pile of photos of Ruby at six months came to Hannah's hand from Cassie in Paris. He shuffled the snapshots, looking for what he'd been so sure of seeing, tortuous memory clinging to her like the demons to St. Anthony in that drawing by Dürer. But she was just a baby. A blue-eyed, round-cheeked baby and nothing else whatever.

He wasn't sure if he was relieved, or disappointed.

"There's still so much time," Hannah said, tucking the photos back in their envelope, an envelope addressed in his sister's looping handwriting. After reading all those books and spending all that time in New York just watching and waiting, Cassie was cleaning the apartments of American expatriates, and writing, as she enigmatically called it in a letter to Hannah, *a story.*

She'd written to him, too. An early note, bewildered, angry. Later two or three more forgiving missives. In the most recent, she said, *I hope someday we'll be able to explain everything to each other. Do you think? Eventually. Meanwhile, I love you.*

Cassie had time, plenty of it, and so, Seth conceded, did he. But time could be both hot and cold, fecund and thin, and nothing could convince him that his time was the same as Cassie's, or Hannah's or anybody's.

30

He hated museums on Sunday winter afternoons, but Sunday afternoons were all the time he allowed himself anymore to do anything but paint. That he could paint again—angrily, badly, the results sometimes looking so much like rotted meat that he'd gesso them over and start again—was a precarious thing. It might get snatched away anytime.

So he worked late at night—even tired from his job—and on Saturdays, squeezing other bits of life into Sunday afternoons.

Which was when the museums were best really only for people-watching—for overhearing inane remarks about cherished paintings by people who just *shouldn't bother even to look at pictures*, the fuckheads—and worst for actually seeing the collection. He threaded his way among the eddying crowds on the third floor of the Whitney, half a mind on the exhibit, musing on maybe getting out of there and doing a quick cruise in Central Park, see who might be around.

Near a doorway from one gallery into the next, Seth heard Jim say, "A mistake? No, I wouldn't go that far. The whole thing might've toughened my heart up, if not for Ruby. But now I see I was never going to stay heartbroken for long over—"

The voice receded, leaving him rigid, unbreathing. Seth forced himself to count to ten, then peeked into the next gallery.

There he was, moving toward the far side of the room, out of his earshot. Jim looking surreally, beautifully himself. Ruby, big and solid at nearly eight months, strapped to his chest. And the man Jim was talking with, the image of appropriateness: good, cultivated looks, an intelligent, open, Jewish face, forty, or close to it, anyway. And regarding Jim with the unmistakable mien of involvement. They were new together, still exchanging information, but the guy was clearly more than half-snagged. Well, Jim was one of those people you fell in love with at once.

Seth kept an eye on Jim and his companion as they moved toward the elevator. He slipped by the crowd to take the stairs, ran down two flights to the lobby, and then, on an impulse, down one more, to the basement. As he emerged from the stairwell, the elevator opened and the two men stepped off. They joined the short line for a table in the café; Seth hung back by the wall and watched their backs. Jim must have released Ruby from her Snugli, because she was blinking up over his shoulder, gazing around with bright interested eyes. Seth looked at her until she saw him. He smiled, and after a moment, the baby smiled, too; a wobbly wet smile that sent a silvery thread of drool down onto Jim's shirt.

Then Jim's new friend walked off toward the men's room. At the same time, the hostess came up and pointed Jim toward a table. The other guy would probably only be absent for a minute or two. Seth darted forward. The hostess tried to intercept him, but he murmured, "I'm with that gentleman—" and slipped past her.

Jim was seated with his back to him, still holding Ruby over his shoulder, fumbling around in his bag. He waited until Jim pulled out the small bottle of orange juice, then stepped around into his line of sight.

"Can I—may I look at my niece?"

Jim's mouth opened, and he moved as if he were going to spring up.

"I startled you. Sorry. It's just I wanted to catch you before—" *Before I could think twice about how dumb and heartbroken this is going to make me feel any second now.*

Jim tightened his hold on Ruby, drew her down and around to the side of his lap farthest from where Seth stood.

"This is unexpected. I didn't realize you were here. And you don't look the same," Jim said.

With the longer hair, dark brown now, and his reddish beard, acquaintances passed him on the street without knowing him. Hannah teased him about how every patch of hair on him was a totally different hue. He'd abandoned his eyeliner and his piercings, and taken to wearing dark, shapeless clothes that maybe hid the fact that he'd lost weight, didn't work out as often.

"I came to see the Reginald Marshes."

Jim nodded, then craned around to check for the reappearance of his friend.

"I just . . . I don't want to bother you, but there you were, and there was—" He said the name, *Ruby*, which had not passed his lips in many many months, and it seemed to burn his mouth. She had nothing to do with him, this baby, neither did this man; he'd thrust them away. "It's so weird all this time's gone by and I haven't even glimpsed you on the street, and so I couldn't leave without seeing my niece."

Jim recoiled at those words, *my niece*. He wasn't certain of it the first time, but Seth saw it clearly the second.

Jim's tweedy friend was approaching. "Just—before I go—for chris-sakes, you didn't mean all that bullshit you were spouting up there. You didn't *mean* it. You're just trying to impress him, let him think you're ready for—but—you didn't get over me so quick, did you? *Did you?*"

Jim drew his arms tighter around Ruby, and rose to face him, his face cool and contained. Seth knew that the friend was right behind him now, silently taking in the scene.

"I've had plenty of time to figure it out—that what I was so worried about—about Ruby—it was wrong. I mean, she's not Cal, she's got nothing to do with him. I see her now, and she's just—a little girl. Your little girl. Not that it matters anymore, but I get it now, my mistake."

He didn't know why he was trying to explain this, the sad epiphany he'd come to when Hannah showed him the snapshots. There was no time to talk about it sensibly, no time to make it sound anything but facile. Couldn't explain that he was unable to go to sleep at night—unable to do anything—without thinking of Jim and what he'd thrown away out of overwhelming shame and fear. Thrown away for nothing.

The friend squeezed past him. The Seth McKenna Mortification Moment was over.

But then the other man did an unexpected thing. "Y'know, I see that this is sort of an important meeting you're having here, so I think, um . . . I'm going to take my leave." He held his hand out for Jim to shake. "Call me tonight if . . . if you want."

Seth glanced after his retreating back. "Wow."

"Shit."

Seth turned back to Jim. "I'm sorry. But . . . that was kind of sensitive of him."

Jim sighed. "Seth, I'm not ready for this."

In his arms, Ruby began to fuss.

"She wants her drink," Seth said. An innocent curiosity came over him; he wanted to see Jim give her the bottle, wanted to watch her face for the ways she resembled Cassie.

Jim shot him a discouraging glance, but resumed his chair and gave Ruby her bottle. Seth hovered, taking it in greedily, although all of Jim's body language was unwelcoming.

"Is she good? Does she cry a lot?"

"She's a good girl," Jim allowed.

"Who helps you with her?"

"Clyde and Billy are there a lot. I've got a part-time nanny on weekdays."

"Oh. I thought you were so strong against hiring stran—" Seth stopped. He'd forgotten himself. Jim shot him a look that showed him, yes, he'd forgotten himself.

"Are you serious about that guy?"

"Please leave," Jim murmured.

"What?"

"I said—please leave. Either you leave, or I'm going to leave."

"I'm sorry, it's just I—"

"Please."

A few nights later, Seth's phone rang late, when he was in bed, eyes getting heavy over a book.

"It's Jim. I got your number from Hannah."

Seth waited.

"Are you there?"

"I'm here."

"You got me a little freaked-out in the museum on Sunday, appearing so suddenly like that. Were you following me around the galleries? That was creepy, Seth."

"No, I didn't know you were there, and then I heard you talking to the guy. Of course, when I recognized your voice, I listened. Especially since you were talking about me."

"Ah, yeah. So . . . ah . . . Hannah says you're working for a painter. How is that?"

"Axel is a charming individual, the way an eel in a bucket is a charming individual."

"Oh. And how's—"

"Don't ask me. Don't ask me about anything. I threw it all away. I threw my work away, I threw you and Ruby away—I threw my life away. And I blame nobody but myself."

There was a long pause. "Well, that's your case stated clearly."

"You didn't call to talk about me."

"Seth, I've been thinking . . . and I realize it's not fair to keep you from Ruby. Of course, she *is* your niece. So, if you want to see her . . . we can work something out."

"That's . . . that's kind of you."

"We moved. We're in the West Village now, so Ruby can be near the good playground and go to public school when the time comes."

"How nice for her."

"You can visit with us at the playground—you know, the one where Bleecker Street meets Hudson Street?"

"I'm not invited to your house?"

"Let's take this one step at a time. The playground. Next Sunday. Two o'clock. We'll be there, unless it's raining or too cold. You can show up if you like."

Come the day, it *was* cold. The wind whipped grit through the streets, stirred litter on the cobblestones. The playground was nearly deserted. A few older kids, bundled up to the nines, chased one another around. Hands dug hard into his coat pockets, Seth sidled around toward the gate. It was just two now, a nowhere hour for someone without anything to do. Jim wasn't there.

Then he heard his name called.

He looked around.

There he was, gesturing at him from the Bleecker Street side of the small park that backed up on the playground. Jim came no closer, just waited, his shoulders high against the wind that stirred the hem of his long overcoat. Slowly, Seth walked to him.

"It was too cold to bring Ruby out, but I didn't want to leave you out here."

Seth shrugged. "I figured. I wasn't going to wait."

The intense wind made his eyes tear. He blinked. The rims of Jim's ears were red.

"You can see her in the house. C'mon."

Seth followed, a pace behind. Not really surprised that it was to Clyde and Billy's Jim led him. Jim still didn't want him to know where he really lived.

In the kitchen, Billy was reading cookbooks spread out on the big table, Ruby in his lap. The fuzzy pink sweater she wore leapt into relief against his black one. Seth felt Billy's initial gaze as a searing brand of disgrace. But Billy only nodded, and said hello. Ruby waved and clamored, Jim lifted her into his arms, and Billy was gone up the stairs, hugging a couple of the large glossy books.

Jim turned to him. "Here she is. You should hold her."

And before Seth could think about it, he'd put the child in his arms. He expected her to squirm and kick immediately, but she only grabbed at his chin with both hands, chortling.

"Hey," Seth breathed.

"She likes beards, earrings, big noses, whatever she can get," Jim said. He was at the stove.

"Guess she'd have liked my nose ring."

"Yeah. I see you've given it up."

Holding her, he felt himself on the edge of this scene, on the edge of Jim, the house, life. Big sturdy child in his arms, but not connecting, not really present. Breath half-held. He wanted to say to Jim, *Send me away. Tell me this is it. First and last time.*

But he smiled for the red-cheeked baby, and she smiled back. "Hey, cookie." Her eyes were enormous, intense. She took him in with complete frankness, one hundred percent focus. She was solid, she was everything a baby is expected to be—a perfect cliché of a baby.

Slowly it occurred to Seth to be surprised at more than Ruby's friendliness. Jim wasn't hovering. Hadn't positioned himself between Seth and the nearest exit. He glanced around for him.

Jim lifted the lid off a large pot, peered inside. "I think she knows who you are."

Yeah? Who am I?

The pot released a rich scent of beef and bay leaf, adding another texture to the sensory richness piled up here. Jim stirred it, replaced the lid.

"I'm going to give Ruby her lunch now, and put her down for her nap."

Seth gave the girl back to him. Their hands touched in the transfer, and he wondered if Jim felt the same rush of heat and remorse and embarrassment. Except he couldn't possibly, because there could be no stronger feeling than his own, this minute, that he was trapped forever outside of everything.

Jim was quietly competent with her, firm, gentle, very, very fond. Watching him spoon pureed vegetables into the baby's mobile mouth, Seth knew that whatever occurred, they'd be fine, Jim and Ruby, more than fine, perfect together.

"She's really good."

"An angel," Jim agreed. "Everyone says so."

"So . . ."

"Seth. You remember where Billy keeps things. Set the table for lunch, all right? Soup plates."

Jim didn't look at him; he was zooming the spoon towards Ruby's face in a zigzag pattern, catching her off-guard before she could push it away.

Slowly he unfastened himself from the floor, moved toward

the big dresser where the plates lived. "Is Clyde here too, or—"

"Just set for two. Just us."

Seth froze with his hand on the cupboard knob. *Just us.* Did Jim hear himself, did he know what he'd just said? That magical word that was never to be used again, that he'd renounced by cutting out his own heart.

But Jim was unfastening the highchair tray, lifting her out.

"I'll be back in a few minutes." He started up the stairs, then paused, dipped down to see Seth below the kitchen ceiling. "Unless you'd like—? You can come watch me put her down."

He followed in silence, up three flights of stairs to a room in the back of the house, neatly fitted out with crib, changing table, rocking chair.

"They . . . they made a room for the baby? That was nice. I guess she's here a lot."

Jim pulled Ruby's pink sneakers off, drew her sweater up over her head to reveal a long-sleeved T-shirt underneath, also pink. Her hair fanned out, crackling against the collar of the sweater as he lifted it away. He took off the black corduroy pants, unsnapping the inseams to reveal a diaper he checked for wet, and laid her in the crib. Wound the musical mobile that hung above it, set the baby monitor. Last, he touched Ruby's cheek, smoothed the flying curls. Her eyelids fluttered; she was replete and nearly asleep already. Together they moved out onto the landing, and began to descend again.

"It's not that they made a room for her. We . . . this is where we live now. Ruby naps in her crib, but at night she sleeps with me."

"Oh. That's . . ."

"I'm buying the house from them. Clyde and Billy will be traveling a great deal come the spring, and they've bought a place in Key West. When they come to New York, though, they'll still stay here."

Jim paused on the second landing, faced him. It was nearly dark, the deep brown walls and carpet absorbing what light filtered down from the skylight above, the glass knob on each closed bedroom door faintly glowing. Seth backed up to the wall as Jim stepped closer.

"Seth . . ."

He turned his face away.

"Seth, what are you doing?"

"Huh? Not doing anything."

"That's what I mean. Why won't you keep what's yours? Why won't you concentrate on your own work? Hannah said—"

He shook his head. "Please don't—"

"And you're not looking after yourself. You're so thin now, you think I don't see it with those clothes you're wearing, but. . . ." He put a hand up to his face. Seth shied away.

"No, no," Jim murmured. "We don't have to be like that. I was so angry at you, Seth, and you . . . you were impetuous. But we should still be able to talk to each other. Look, look—come here." He dropped back, opening one of the glass-knobbed doors. Suddenly there was plenty of light; the large unmade bed that dominated the room faced nearly a whole wall of windows divided into smallish panes, looking down on the secret nineteenth-century garden in the block's interior, denuded now in winter. The sight of the unmade bed, the gray-striped sheets Seth knew so well, nearly felled him. Jim didn't seem to notice, he was drawing him around it, saying "Look here."

There, leaning against the wall, where it was most easily visible from the low bed, was the self-portrait with the pear. The corner was neatly mended, and it was framed now, in bands of blond wood as airy and light as the picture itself. The sight stunned him. He knew it still existed, that Jim must still have it, but he hadn't expected—

"Here, look," Jim was saying, hefting the picture by its edges. "You think there's nothing but darkness around you, but here in this picture—all this light—is what you really are."

Seth sank down on the edge of the bed. Didn't want to look at his beautiful picture, so vanishingly far from him. Jim held it with the same tenderness as he held Ruby. And it was all gone, everything he'd been and done and made, it was all gone.

"Seth, I don't enjoy seeing you this way."

He wrenched himself up. "Then I'll go. I shouldn't have—"

"I'm not asking you to go."

"But I should. I am."

Jim held the painting out. "Take this with you. I hate to part with it, but take it, let it inspire you. You should start again. You should use what's yours. Everything that's yours."

"No, keep it if you like it. It's what's left."

Jim set it down, and before Seth could dodge, caught him by the arms. The bed was at his back, the clean gray light of the tall windows made an umbra around Jim's dark curls. "I hate to part with *you*."

His mouth brushed the corner of Seth's before he pulled away. Jim let him go easily, as if nothing had happened. "Let me feed you at least. Come. I know you're hungry."

In the kitchen Jim filled him a big gold-rimmed soup plate, with the stew that had its own rim of gold in the shimmer of the rich broth at the edges of the dish. "Eat. Eat this up, and you'll have another bowl. Seth, what do you live on? I can't imagine . . ."

The stew smelled like heaven, steaming before him, but he only followed Jim with his eyes as he moved around the kitchen, slicing bread, pouring wine, bringing him things, butter, salt. He put the radio on, twirled the dial to find some Mozart. When he took his place opposite, Seth still hadn't touched the heavy silverware, his eyes fixed immovably on Jim.

"Eat," he said. "Honeyboy, eat."

Seth dropped his gaze then to his chapped hands, the nails ragged and stained with paint, protruding from the ragged sleeves of his gray sweater.

This couldn't be. That Jim should call him that again, that he should place food in front of him. This shouldn't be.

But he began to eat, because he knew if he didn't, tears would well out of his frozen face, and Jim would rise and come around the table and touch him again. He ate, unable to taste the beef, potatoes, and carrots cooked to the consistency of velvety pudding, the thick bread that Jim spread for him with butter, which balled in his parched mouth.

Jim refilled his dish. Said nothing, only watched him, tipping more wine into his glass.

He set down the spoon. "Thanks. This . . . this was good."

"Good."

"I guess I'd better go. It's getting late."

He couldn't imagine how he'd cross the kitchen floor, how he'd take the stairs. He was nearly undone by the sensory overload of all that whipped past his startled and defeated senses: Jim, Ruby, the painting, the unmade bed redolent of his lover, the stew, the wine, the pink roses with their delicate green leaves at the bottom of the china soup dishes. Too much.

Then Jim was there, slipping into the chair beside him.

"She liked you. Ruby did. As why should she not. She knows who you are." He paused. "And I do, too. I should have been more patient with you before. I jumped to the very worst conclusions, without pausing to think . . . that wasn't worthy of me. Of either of us. I'm sorry for that."

He could find nothing to say. Inside, the real Seth, or was it the false one, he didn't know—the one who was not impaled on shame like a moth on a pin—looked into Jim's familiar beloved face, yearned toward it, *knew* it for all that was home.

He skidded up, ran for the stairs. Jim caught him at the house door. "Seth. You'll come back."

"Don't—don't waste your—"

"You'll come see us again."

The baby's cry from upstairs cut him off. Seth felt at his back for the doorknob and escaped.

Jim phoned him on Wednesday and invited him to Sunday lunch. Seth declined. After the third Wednesday invitation, Seth drew a picture in watercolor of how he imagined Jim to look as he talked to him, leaning against the sideboard full of colorful crockery in that basement kitchen. He tried to imagine, as he made sloppy brush-strokes and hated the way he couldn't control his colors, that Jim was relieved by his refusals. He put a sly smile on Jim's face, and then tore the paper into soggy bits.

After that he stopped trying to paint and began to draw again. The drawings were clumsy, they weren't what he imagined; it was as if they were coming from some far-off place by way of primitive fac-simile, losing detail and meaning along the way. But he made more and more, and began to like them for their very gracelessness. They were like him; sad, awkward, trying to get on. Maybe improving, just a little bit.

He waited for Wednesday, and the phone rang again. This time he accepted.

"What did you do this week?" Jim asked him.

Seth dipped his head. "Painted my employer's pictures."

Jim didn't react to this. He was getting Ruby ready for her sleep again, as Seth hovered in the doorway. Already he was coming to un-derstand the implacability of the routine here. His soul-sickness must give way to the exigencies of baby's nap, of the lunch preparation.

Life didn't wait.

All around them, the old house sighed. Wind sang along the edges of the windows.

Jim led the way down. When he opened the one door on the dark landing, Seth again followed him into the bright room with the un-made bed, the room that smelled of Jim's own body, of cologne and some orange peel in a balled-up napkin on the nightstand.

They looked at the painting. The light in it shimmered in the vase water, in the curve of the bowl rim, in the eye whites and teeth of his own drowsy, knowing face. It was like visiting a sick darling who would not recover. But as he absorbed the painting's aura, Seth had the beginning of a feeling—in his fingertips, in his pulse—that there might be more where that came from. The well that was nothing but mud might bubble anew.

"Y'know," Jim said, "even when you think you're none of the things you were when you first came to me . . . even when you cannot conceive of yourself as being worthy of . . . of anything good. . . . I still . . . I can't imagine not . . ."

Seth was prepared to turn away from a kiss, as he'd done before. But Jim didn't kiss him. He dropped to his knees, yanked Seth's jeans open with a sharp motion that brooked no protest, and took his cock in his mouth.

Seth gasped, sinking onto the bed behind him, his body suffusing with brightness. Jim made a low sound of appreciation as he lengthened in his mouth. One of his big hands was wrapped now around the shaft, the other held his balls in a warm cocoon. He made everything wet, held Seth's cock in his mouth as he licked the underside, right behind the head, long deep maddening licks that made him flail, made him twist and speak words that came straight from his gut, bypassing his brain altogether. His jeans were pulled down just far enough to trap his legs, and this hint of restraint made what Jim was doing to him even more overwhelming. The sadness sloshed over him, threatened to swamp him altogether. "Oh, God—oh, God—stop—stop—"

Jim raised his head. "Do you really want me to stop?"

The sudden air on his drenched flesh was chill.

Jim's thumb passed lightly over the slick spot where his tongue had been, and Seth bucked. "Do you really mean to deny me this pleasure? To deny yourself?"

Seth shook his head. Threw it back, covered his face with his arms, groaned when Jim encompassed him again.

Too soon it was over, and Jim rested his forehead briefly on Seth's quivering thigh. Pushed the hem of his sweater up to expose the navel, kiss it. Then crawled up to splay beside him. Seth began to move, but he put a hand square on his chest and held him down.

"You don't have to do me. That's not what this was for."

He smoothed his hair, his big hands dry and gentle. "I missed your taste. The way you smell when you're excited. The feel of you in my mouth." His hand wandered down the expanse of charcoal sweater to the concave belly, the brush of hair, and cupped the spent cock. "Missed you."

Seth closed his eyes. Closed his empty hands into loose fists. Breathed.

"Seth—"

"I am sorry. I'm sorry. I'm so sorry. . . ." He tried to move, and couldn't.

"What happened to you is not what you are, Seth."

"Please don't."

"We don't have to have—what did you call it?—the big crap catharsis moment. We can just quietly pick up where we left off." Jim's breath stirred the hairs of his beard. "You can pick up where you left off. The painting, it's inside of you. What you made is gone, but there's more inside of you. Ruby is waiting for you. My love is there for you, it's never gone away. Come back to me."

He couldn't speak. Jim's hand was warm and heavy on him, his breath warm against his neck. Upstairs the baby slept, and on the nightstand a travel clock made a minute *click click*. He couldn't turn his gaze from the dove-gray ceiling. Jim seemed not at all anxious for his response, as if there could be no doubt of it, but just rested beside him, content to touch him. The smells in the room were so pleasant, the bed so large and accommodating. He had nothing like this in his life anymore, couldn't he just, for a few minutes, enjoy it, before . . . before. . . . His eyelids fluttered and closed.

A tinny wail awoke him. The baby monitor. Jim, lying close beside him, met his gaze with a smile. "You go get her. Change her diaper, bring her back down here."

"Wh—what?"

"All the stuff is laid out on the table in her room. Take off the soiled one, wipe her up, a little powder, put on a fresh one. You'll figure it out. I'll wait for you."

He sat up slowly. The cry intensified. He moved faster. Adjusted his clothes. Glanced back at Jim, who gave him a little finger wave.

Ruby was standing in her crib, fat fists gripping the bars. She shut up when she saw him.

"Yeah, I know," Seth murmured. "Who the fuck are you, and what've you done with my daddy?" He lifted her out. "C'mere, cookie. Gonna do this thing." He laid her on the changing table. She stared up at him, curious, unalarmed. Every part of her was connected to every other part with a neat wedge of fat. Even amid the stink of the diaper, she smelled sweet, her skin finely mottled like a peach. "We'll figure it out," he breathed, gaze riveted to her, hands feeling for what he needed. Aware of Jim in the room below, waiting.

He changed the diaper. It wasn't such a mystery. Ruby wasn't such a mystery either, except that she was, a compelling heart-tugging mystery that—as he lifted her legs in the air to clean her off, as he captured her wriggling hand grabbing again for his chin, as he fitted the tapes and made all snug while she kicked like a frog—he didn't want to miss another moment of.

He bore her crowing back into Jim's room, spilled her onto the bed, crawled on after. Jim captured her and lifted her aloft, tummy balanced on one large palm. They lay beneath her, heads together, while Ruby goggled down at them.

"She give you any trouble?"

"Nah. She was cool. She's good at getting her diaper changed by a guy with a beard."

"See?" Jim said. "She knows. She knows who you are. She knows all about us."

Part Six

31

Without pausing in his reading aloud, Jim reaches over and draws Phoebe's thumb down out of her mouth. This is a gesture he or Seth performs countless times a day. The thumb always finds its way back. *I hear the distant pounding of approaching orthodontist bills,* he thinks idly, most of himself still concentrated elsewhere. A little bit on the book he is reading, not for the first time, but mostly on the three faces in the circle of lamplight beside him. Intent, ruddy-cheeked, with the freshness of a group in a Sargent portrait. Seth, although he wears a beard and has let his hair grow in its natural gray, is still more like the babies, as they call them, than he is like Jim. After all, he's not yet thirty. The two sisters—Ruby with her cloud of light brown hair, Phoebe's darker, even curlier—lie huddled against him like two cubs, each defending with little squirms and pokes her territory against Daddy's chest, her claim to one of his encircling arms. Seth is, at least for the moment, Jim tries to assure himself, the favorite with them both, even though Phoebe was supposed to be *his,* as Ruby, so unexpectedly, has turned out to be Seth's.

Jim goes on reading, but it's more an excuse than anything else, to keep the light on, to go on feasting his eyes on them, his treasure. Phoebe's have closed; Ruby's lids flutter; she doesn't want to let go, but everything is against her: her cheek cradled on Daddy's smooth white T-shirted chest, the slow thump of his heart resounding in her own head, the warmth of the room and her flannel nightie, her sleepy sister's warmth right next to her. Seth is still listening, maybe, or else he's also thinking of other things, glancing absently from the tousled heads beneath his chin to the upside-down picture on the page of the book, and then at Jim, but not quite catching his eye.

So much is different since Seth came back to him.

They no longer sleep nude, and seldom, even now that the girls are six and nearly five, do they find themselves alone in their bed; it was Jim, during Cassie's first pregnancy, who had read the books about the family bed, but it was Seth who took the most comfort in Ruby's presence with them through the night. In the house on Perry Street the girls have a whole floor to themselves, but they still start most nights here between Daddy and Papa, where they have always been. Later they carry them, fast asleep, to their beds, but sometimes not. He feels closer to Seth, somehow, when the girls lie between them.

They also no longer kiss, not the way they did before Ruby came, kisses that melted into each other, one after the next, defined only by the pause to draw breath, to murmur, to groan. Kisses now are distinct, mark occasions: good nights, good-byes, good mornings. They are neatly placed on cheeks or foreheads or unmoistened lips, exchanged above the heads of two little girls who see everything and understand only some of it, but more, perhaps, than either man realizes.

For a time, long enough to make Jim fear that it was over forever, there was no sex. Seth turned away from seduction, until, after four or five attempts, Jim could no longer bear the silent rebuffs. They were the only point of outright discomfort between them. Seth was coming slowly back to himself, to his art; they could talk and laugh and be silent together, they had so much to do with the children, with the house. It seemed something he shouldn't push.

When Ruby was nearly a year old, they brought her to Paris, to see her mother, to show her that after their wobbly start as a trio, they were all right.

Cassie, who had changed so in that short time that Jim was continually surprised by her spicy, impish fearlessness, took it all in without being told anything: how Jim had stopped struggling with her brother over physical possession of the baby; how, in every way, he'd fallen just a step back, puzzled and reminding himself that, having gotten what he wanted, kept what he feared to lose, he was content. One evening, sitting up late over wine, she announced that she'd been trying to get her tubes tied, but couldn't find a doctor who would operate on such a young woman who'd only borne a single child. So she would, purely for love, because he'd launched her on her path, give Jim another baby first if he wanted one. They'd treated it, that night, as a pleasant fantasy, as if they'd proposed to all run off together to Tahiti. But when she brought it up again the following afternoon, outdoors in bright sun in front of the Musée D'Orsay, her seriousness was apparent. "We'll do the turkey baster thing, or"—her laugh was like something silvery and sleek—"you just come up to my room—not tonight, but the end of the week should be about right." She flirted with him, this brand-new confident expatriate Cassie, as she'd never dared to back in New York, the look she threw him like one of Seth's that he'd not seen since before Nebraska. It made him feel that things he'd never imagined were not only doable but were calling to him to be done.

She'd taken Ruby that evening—wrested her away, really, from Seth's nearly unbreakable grasp—so they could wander off together alone. It was then, standing on the Pont Neuf and looking down into the quivering light-spangled water, that Seth said, with an expression that made Jim feel he was winning a poker game by nefarious play, "I like the idea, but, of course, we'll do it through a doctor."

"Why of course?"

Seth looked at him then, his eyes wide, amused, suspicious.

Why of course? That was the night, the very first one, when Seth turned back to him, when they came together again with a passion that was equal parts anger and inquiry, clumsy and off-balance. An exchange of information in their hotel bed, none of it, on Jim's part, expected or easy to take. Seth, who had always loved above all else being borne down upon, in upon, the prolonged coring accompanied by trancey kisses, was no longer willing—seemingly unable—to give himself. Instead he took Jim hard, in positions where they could not look into each other's eyes.

It was like that ever since. Seth catching him outside the bathroom door in the middle of the night, bending him half-asleep over the stair rail, hot, impersonal, and apparently forgotten by morning. Frantic quarter hours in the laundry behind the kitchen while Billy played with the girls one flight up. Blind, blindsided quick ones, lightning strikes. Not that infrequent. Often more than once a week.

"Why," his therapist asked him, "don't you discuss your dissatisfaction with Seth? At some time when you're both feeling calm and receptive?"

It was the sensible question Jim would've asked, had he heard the problem from anyone else. "I can't think how to do it without it sounding like a rebuke. And isn't it pathetic, a middle-aged man nagging his young lover for something that's got to be freely given if it's going to be any good at all? It's not that he's forsaken me. His desire, when it's there, is there. He . . . he gives head like—"

"You believe this change has to do with your knowledge of what happened to him? That Seth can't cope with your knowing? Can't be sexual with you the way he used to be?"

"I'm sure it is. All his patterns have changed."

"And do you think he's getting sex elsewhere?"

Jim didn't like to think about the shameful episode of the private detective. Hadn't told the therapist, with whom he was always uncomfortably aware of his thinning dignity, nor Billy, whom he'd known would scold him for it. He'd almost told Clyde, but in the end restrained himself from fear he would show too much zest, recommend hiring someone else—Clyde always knew "someone better," whether it was a caterer, a haircutter, a masseur, a travel agent. And although he'd shrewdly started to collect Seth, right ahead of the surge he'd made from obscurity to prominence, he still, in his heart, thought him a bandit, and was willing to believe anything about him as long as it was bad.

The detective, after tailing him for fifteen straight days, reported nothing more than what Jim already knew. Which was that Seth's life was entirely about two things: his career, and his daughters. When he wasn't with the girls, between the time he dropped them off at nursery school in the morning and fetched them away, Seth was at his studio. No one visited him there. When he went to his dealer, or to Hannah, or the gym, there was nothing in the timing of his arrivals and departures to suggest anything other than the transparent reason for being where he was. Outside of their school hours, he took the babies with him nearly everywhere he could. "The only people Mr. McKenna is *seeing*," the detective said in his final report, "are the little girls."

Seth has no secrets, then, to explain his reserve. Jim has one. They saw a doctor in Paris, who took them through the artificial insemination procedure in the usual way. But on the last afternoon before they flew back to New York, when Seth was taking one last round of the Louvre with Ruby in tow, Jim had climbed the five flights of stairs to Cassie's tiny flat. There was no way of knowing which time was the one that "took," but even after five years Jim still thought often of those few hours, the rain sheeting the skylight above the bed, the surprise of Cassie's body, the invigorating force of her desire that got him past his misgivings and ignorance. From some previously unknown part of himself, a matching desire bloomed, all the hardier for being situational and temporary. He'd made love to her all afternoon beneath the rainy skylight, and she'd given him Phoebe.

Had he not done that, would he still look at Phoebe now the way he did, thinking *mine, she's mine?* Without those memories of her mother, it wouldn't be as real to him.

He reads the final words, saying "and that is the end," as he closes the book. The babies are both firmly asleep, but Seth dips his eyelids in acknowledgment.

"It's always a good story."

"Can't go wrong with Mr. Sendak," Jim agrees. "You sleepy, Skeezix?"

"Mmm."

He leaves them, his drowsy pack, to steal down to the kitchen. Pours a glass of wine and brings his briefcase to the table. There's always something in it to do. A year ago, when the teacher shortage was frequent front-page news, Jim signed on. Now he commutes to teach fourth grade in a crumbling school in East New York, spending most of the salary he's fortunate not to need on things the children cannot do without. The work exhausts him, and he's beginning to see that, much as he adores all children and books and making connections light up in young minds, he's not very good at this, doesn't have the temperament to really help children who are so different from how he remembers himself as a child. He'd wanted something to fill the time when Ruby and Phoebe are in school, and all the space they fill for Seth but not for him. It's difficult. He's too jealous of his beloveds; he wants always to be on the spot, even if that means, as tonight, sitting a little apart, on guard. He's let this happen, he tells himself, let Seth have Ruby, and then Phoebe, who must lay stubborn claim to everything her sister values, because Seth is the one with the larger need. He'd fill that need himself, if Seth would let him.

He marks spelling tests for an hour, eyes growing heavy.

Above his bent head, the stairs creak.

"What are you drinking?"

"The rest of the Chardonnay. Get yourself a glass, there's a bit left. Or—here, finish this. I've had enough."

Seth bends in over his shoulder to see what he's doing. He's done grading and now is engaged in sticking metallic stars on the papers. Green ones for top grades, red ones for most improved since last time.

"What are the blue ones for?"

"Blue ones mean—keep on attempting to spell." Jim sticks one on the end of Seth's nose.

"You're not gonna do this again next year, are you? I hate how tired it makes you." Seth threads his arms around Jim's neck, rests his face against Jim's. For a moment he just absorbs this, the touch, the thought.

"I have to do something."

"There's plenty with the babies."

"But there really isn't," Jim says calmly. "You've got that cornered. And those kids at school really need me."

"The babies miss you."

"They *miss* me?"

"*I* miss you." Seth's hand inches in past his waistband. Jim sighs and shifts, leans back in the chair. Seth's hand grasps and caresses and tugs. After a while they move toward the sofa under the windows. Seth grabs a dishtowel and the olive oil cruet off the table.

"Go slow, honeyboy," Jim murmurs. "This time, just slow. . . ."

Seth gives it to him this time almost as slow as he wishes, and afterward they lie spooned together on the saggy sofa, in the draft off the window glass. Outside, footsteps clatter on the slate sidewalk, and someone is singing. Jim thinks of their old room on Bond Street, the big plain square bed there where every morning Seth wanted him inside. Wonders, as he has over and over, how it can be that it is not the terrible thing itself but the knowledge of it between them that has taken those intimacies away from them both. And wonders why it has to bother him so much, when here they are together in every way, surely, that matters.

Jim speaks into the dim room, to Seth who is behind him and may or may not be awake.

"You know what I miss?"

Seth says, "I miss him, too."

Jim is surprised. "—*him?*"

"The Seth you miss. The boy in the painting." His hand moves from Jim's waist to his head, fingers working into the thick coils of his hair, smoothing them. "I know you want him. He was better than me. He made you happier than I can. Some mornings, right when I wake up, before I move or open my eyes, I *am* him. And I want to touch you and tell you, I want to give him to you before anything can happen. But just that is enough to make him lost again. He hunkers down inside so small I can't even feel him anymore."

Jim stays still, feeling those fingers in his hair, Seth's breath on the back of his neck, their legs tangled together. A car passes, and the refrigerator cycles. He knows he must assure Seth that he is mistaken, that he loves him and is satisfied with him and doesn't want him to think that way about himself.

In a moment. He'll speak in a moment. Meanwhile, that touch, that breath, he's there. Jim feels them, and waits. He doesn't want to scare him away.